AÍSEAL MÓR WAS BORN INTO A TRADITION OF IRISH STORYTELLING AND MUSIC. AS A CHILD HE LEARNED TO PLAY THE BRASS-STRUNG HARP CARRYING ON A LONG FAMILY TRADITION. HE SPENT SEVERAL YEARS COLLECTING STORIES, SONGS AND MUSIC OF THE CELTIC LANDS DURING MANY VISITS TO IRELAND, SCOTLAND AND BRITTANY. HE HAS A DEGREE IN PERFORMING ARTS FROM THE UNIVERSITY OF WESTERN SYDNEY AND HAS WORKED AS AN ACTOR, A TEACHER AND AS A MUSICIAN.

BOOK THREE OF
THE WANDERERS

THE
WATER OF
LIFE

CAISEAL MÓR

EARTHLIGHT

LONDON · SYDNEY · NEW YORK · TOKYO · SINGAPORE · TORONTO

www.earthlight.co.uk

You can visit Caiseal Mór's website at www.caiseal.net
or email him at harp@caiseal.net

First published in Great Britain by Earthlight, 2000
An imprint of Simon & Schuster UK Ltd
A Viacom Company

Simon & Schuster UK Ltd
Africa House
64–78 Kingsway
London WC2B 6AH

Simon & Schuster Australia
Sydney

A CIP catalogue record for this book is available
from the British Library

1 3 5 7 9 10 8 6 4 2

ISBN 0-671-03730-7

Printed and bound in the UK by
Omnia Books Ltd, Glasgow

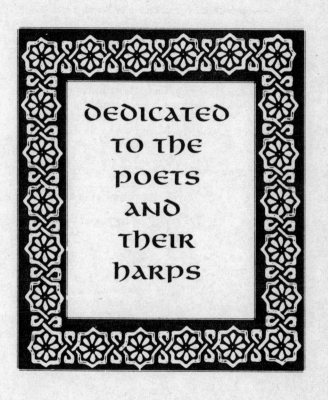

DEDICATED
TO THE
POETS
AND
THEIR
HARPS

ACKNOWLEDGEMENTS

he first name on my list of people who deserve heartfelt thanks is, of course, Selwa Anthony. Without her faith and vast experience, these stories would never have seen the light of day. Thank you, Selwa.

Julia Stiles edited all three manuscripts in this series and has always been a source of valuable, objective criticism. I am very grateful to her for the magnificent work she has done. Truly a Poet in her own right and possibly a little bit of a Druid as well.

Many friends helped me through this part of the tale of The Wanderers. Above all I would like to thank Traci and David Harding who inspired me with their positive thinking, understanding, countless cups of tea, herbal concoctions and relentless reassurances that all would be well. They were right.

I would also like to thank all at Random House for their help, support and patience, especially Linda Funnell who probably had to summon up more patience than most.

My gratitude to the many readers whose e-mail messages are a source of constant pleasure to me. To all those who kept asking when this novel would be finished—here it is at last.

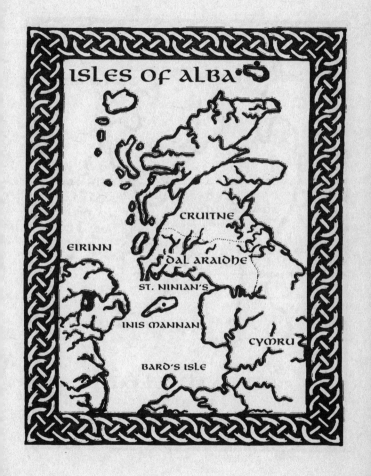

ISLES OF ALBA

CRUITNE

EIRINN

DAL ARAIDHE

ST. NINIAN'S

INIS MANNAN

CYMRU

BARD'S ISLE

TO
DUN BRETEANN

THE
GREAT FOREST

DUN RIGH

PENNISULA
OF
STRATH-CLÓTA

THE
SAXON
CAMP

TO
EIRINN

PENNISULA
OF THE
GAELS

ST. NINIAN'S

STRATH-CLÓTA
IN ALBA

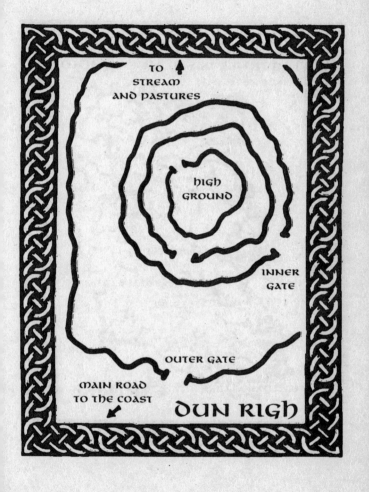

TO
STREAM
AND PASTURES

HIGH
GROUND

INNER
GATE

OUTER GATE

MAIN ROAD
TO THE COAST

DUN RIGH

HIBERNIA INSULAR REGNUM

DOBHARCÚ
SLANÉ
TEAMHAIR
RATHOWEN
BALLY CAHOR
CASHEL
ARDMÓR
BALLINSKELLIGS

EIRINN

PROLOGUE

tand on the high grassy hill of Uisneach on a fresh summer morning. Wander among the grey stone ruins that are smothered in soft dark mosses. Shield your eyes from the glare of the morning sun as you look out over the fields and forests towards the eastern kingdom of Laigin.

If the sky is clear you may well glimpse the distant ever-changing sea: a thin line of deep indigo lying like an embroidered edge on the bright verdant horizon. If you know where to look you may perhaps catch sight of the ancient hill fortress of Teamhair, home of the High-Kings of old and their Druid Councils, focal point of the five kingdoms and resting place of all the magnificent heroes of the legends.

Through seasons uncounted, through all the untold upheavals that have plagued Eirinn, Uisneach has stood a silent witness to the cycles of the world. Warriors and kings have made their names here. Poets and wizards have worked their magic in the deep dark blue of night. And among the ruins of this the first stronghold ever built on these shores, the ghosts of warriors long dead walk sentry in the night air as if there were still some secret here worth guarding.

Let me turn your mind now to day's end at that enchanted foothill. With the power of your imagination conjure up an image of the grassy fields surrounding the holy summit engulfed in the immense cold calm blueness of evening. At the horizon all colour fades to black, like spilled ink soaking into a page of bone-white parchment and swallowing the words that are scribbled upon it. Uncountable lights, tiny and insignificant if viewed alone, flicker on the surface of the immense carpet of darkness which is the sky.

It is as if some heavenly jeweller has deliberately scattered thousands of crystals across the firmament. The sparkling beads that are the stars seem to be waiting for an enterprising adventurer to pluck them out and bring them back to Earth to decorate the cover of a holy book or the jewelled sceptre of an all-powerful king.

There is one other object that sails through the heavens surpassing in its radiance even the delicate beauty of the stars. It is a wonder seen by all the folk who dwell on Earth. A pearl that changes night by night yet forever remains unchanged. The Queen of the Stars she is called by some. Empress of the Waters Beyond Our World others name her. She is a silver sphere set out for all to see on a bed of exotic silk.

The moon.

Pale white light falls on the fields of Eirinn, casting them in a mystical grey-green radiance, and in the glimmer of the moon's ivory lantern it is easy to believe that the doorways between the worlds remain forever open.

A slight breeze rises over the plain, enough to make one conscious that the air is slightly colder than warm skin. Other than that the land is almost perfectly still. In this serenity the tiniest movements of the night-dwelling creatures are easily detected, and those of the human kind impossible to ignore.

Gradually a low rhythmic sound creeps over the hills to disturb the stillness. Out of the east a solemn procession of twenty or so men and women dressed in long robes the colour of the night sky makes its way along the wide road to Uisneach. Flaming torches held high reflect orange against the pale skin of their holy faces, giving their complexions an unnatural ruddy glow. A steady chant flows from the robed group, at once cheerful and mourning, uplifting and incredibly sad.

Above the harmonic waves of sound a female voice begins delicately to trace the line of a melody. The words she intones are the lines of an ancient prayer for safe journey which has been known by my people for countless generations. This procession is a gathering of the holy Druid kind.

This prayer is not merely a plea for those who set sail over the sea or for those who wander foreign roads on the business of their master or king. This is a petition to the gods for all those who undertake the voyage of life, a supplication to the undying ones who watch over the travails of mortal souls.

There is a word for this long passage through the seasons that all the human kind must make; a word that also speaks of the great cycle of existence and the surety of its turning ever round and round again.

Imramma.

Voyage of discovery. Voyage of adventure. Voyage of the spirit within us all. Expedition of the inner self. This is the name my people give to the endless recurring dreamlike path that they and their ancestors have walked, and in this same way

3

the company of Druids now paces serenely towards the hill that will be the ceremonial ground.

From fields and hollows all around, more robed figures join the solemn march, adding their voices to the hum, filling the little valley with a droning call. Countless lights sputter into life as many more torches are lit. The chorus swells like an ocean wave about to break upon the rocks, but instead of reaching the expected crescendo, it fades, dying for a moment.

Then the holy ones take up the chant anew. The woman singer is joined first by one male then another who mirror her melody so perfectly that it is almost as if she and they are of one voice.

The procession sways gently as the Druids walk, giving the impression that they have all willingly surrendered their individuality to the larger purpose of the assembly. Somehow it seems that they have merged together as one creature that heaves its weight along the road towards the boundary stones marking the border of the ancient precinct of Uisneach.

Two stones guard either side of the road where the track begins to rise towards the summit. Here the procession halts. Two figures from among the many continue to march up through the midst of the throng. All the other Druids part before them to allow their passage. As the pair reach the front of the column all the torches are extinguished and the scene is veiled once again in darkness.

Anyone looking out over the fields at this moment will need to strain hard to observe the assembly of holy ones. Their robes give them the texture of night and among them all not one so much as stirs to scratch or twitch. The whole company is perfectly composed and hushed.

Only these two from among the many walk

forward past their comrades and into the dark, no lights to guide them. On and on the initiates trudge up the steep path, silent and tense with anticipation of the trial before them. This great knoll that marks the spiritual centre of Eirinn is the place where they will be confirmed into their vocation. At the mound of testing at Teamhair one moon earlier the ritual acknowledgement of their Druid rank was ceremonially enacted. Here the Wanderers will make another binding covenant; one which will set them apart from their brethren forever.

At the summit, among the ruins of a stone fortress, nine shadowy figures wait shrouded in the evening mist that commonly engulfs that place. These nine could easily be mistaken for a circle of carved granite stones. They are as motionless as the cold grey rock. Seven of them represent the inner council of the Druid kind: one for each of the arts of music, poetry, healing, law, building, spellcraft and divination. The other two figures are not of the Gael folk. They are not descended from the sons of Míl. They are of the bloodline of the Tuatha De Danaan who were in the land of Eirinn long before the earliest ancestors of the Gaels.

This is the time of moon-light, the three brightest days of the moon's passage. This is the time when the world is lit by her presence and she is at her most powerful. Just as the time of moon-dark is set aside for special observances that mark the three-day death of the silver orb, so a monthly ritual of rejoicing marks the occasion of her full bloom.

The two young initiates reach the top of the hill out of breath and sweating under their robes. They pull back the hoods of their cloaks to reveal their faces and shaven heads. The circle of nine elders opens to greet them, silently encouraging them to enter into their midst. Though the seven Gaelic

Druids uncover their heads, the Danaans keep their features shrouded, looking down at the ground as if they have not noticed the newcomers.

In the very centre of the circle a long flat stone lies on its side, propped up like a bench by two smaller rocks. Over the makeshift table has been draped a cloth of white upon which are arranged the implements of a ritual feast. The two newcomers make directly for this table and kneel before it without any prompting from their elders. As soon as the two are settled, the Danaans break ranks from the others.

One of these Otherworld folk walks swiftly and silently to one end of the table. His comrade takes up a position opposite. Then two of the Gaelic Druids stand to face the newcomers and the rest of the circle closes in.

On the table is a rich cloth of bright bleached white linen on which are laid plates of bread and a single cup. This chalice has been fashioned of silver and gold ornately decorated with spirals and strange animal motifs characteristic of Danaan metalwork. The Druid elders raise their staves to the heavens in a powerful unspoken invocation, then lower their rods of office to the ground. One of them nods almost imperceptibly to another. This nod passes around the circle as the Danaans lift thin wiry hands to remove the veils concealing their faces.

The initiates both shudder. Danaan hoods fall away to reveal two long pale faces that are almost the same shade as the light of the full moon. The features are ageless: youthful and bright but weighed down with the wisdom of old age. Immense age. Seasons uncountable.

One of the Danaans begins to speak and everyone present is moved by the sweet tone of his voice which reflects a compassion at once reassuring, resigned and immensely weary.

'We have come to celebrate the feast of life,' he states simply in a deep and soothing voice.

His companion raises the palms of her hands, keeping her elbows close to her side in the Druidic posture of prayer. Her eyes tell of the many sorrows she has seen and the many joys. They are grey glassy catlike spheres set in brilliant whites. Her face is unearthly, yet her expression is comforting and so like that of her companion that the two of them might be mistaken for brother and sister rather than husband and wife.

Jet-black strands of hair blow about her face as she speaks. 'This is the ancient rite of our people which we shared with the sons and daughters of Míl to cement our promise of peace.' The tones are strong, earthy and uplifting. 'For we of the Sidhe folk walk the same Druid path as your kind.'

Her comrade takes a slab of barley bread from the table and breaks it into two pieces with both of his hands. 'This is the Bread of Life,' he intones, 'of which all peoples who dwell upon the Earth must share if we are to live. Take it and eat of it and remember that there is nothing more sacred than the act of sharing bread with another living soul.' After he has handed the bread to the initiates, he reaches into the folds of his robe and retrieves a small pouch. His companion has brought forth a similar bag from her robe.

'We have come to share our bread with you,' the woman announces. 'You are about to partake of what our people know as the Bread of Life. Few among your kind have undertaken to share this with us.'

Together the Danaans empty the contents of their pouches onto the tablecloth. When they have finished, hundreds of tiny bright-red berries are scattered over the white linen. Each Danaan selects one of the rowan berries and reaches over to place it in the mouth of the nearest initiate.

'Receive now the gift of everlasting life given to us by our ancestors in the times of long ago,' they intone together.

The young Druids take the berries in their mouths and swallow them whole. Then each initiate takes a bite of the barley bread and chews slowly.

The male Danaan raises the gold and silver chalice into the air with both hands. He seems to be lost in deep and private contemplation, a concentration which is only broken after some moments. Finally he speaks. 'Drink now of the sacred water distilled from the berries of the holy Quicken Tree. This is the blood of the holy bough just as the berries represent its body.'

The Danaan Druid leans forward to place the cup at the lips of one of the initiates. Satisfied that the lad has taken a good draught of the brew, he passes the cup to his companion. She in turn places the vessel at the lips of the initiate who kneels by her. When the Danaan woman is sure that the dark-haired girl before her has taken more than a mouthful, she takes a sip of the cup herself then passes it back to her comrade.

The first Danaan quickly drains the contents of the chalice. In a simple gesture he turns the vessel upside down to show there is no liquid remaining. Then he places the cup back upright on the table.

'The company of the Wanderers accepts you, Sianan of the gentle eyes and Mawn of the shrouded heart. May the breeze be always at your back and may the sun go before you to light your way. May the seas carry your ship safely and may

8

the road yield to your tramping feet. We wish you easy passage on your long *Imramma.*'

The seven Druids move in close and help the two initiates to their feet. Then, leaving the Danaans standing at the table among the ruins of their long-abandoned hill fort, the elders lead the pair back down the hill of Uisneach towards the waiting throng of well-wishers. When the Gaels are gone, the Danaans melt back into the night, returning to the warmth of their own hearths and the company of their own kind.

At the foot of the hill torches are rekindled as the Wanderers approach. A great feast has been prepared in their honour at the edge of a nearby field. Suddenly, as though every star has become a flaming lamp, there are many lights to illuminate the way. The feast goes on until dawn and with the rising of the sun the great company disperses to the four corners of Eirinn, returning to their homes and clans once more. They all know only too well that there will be precious few times when they will meet again like this, for the world is changing swiftly and completely.

The two young Druids are taken from the ceremonial ground to join the great company of the King and Queen of Munster. They will with them soon leave Eirinn on a mission for the High-King, Leoghaire. Within another turning of the moon they will set foot in the land of Alba, in the kingdoms of the Dal Araidhan tribes.

The seasons turn and every seventh turning I go once more, as I did that night of my initiation, to the hill of Uisneach. There, in that most ancient place, I meet again with the Danaans and partake of their ritual. For even their wise craft cannot last forever without renewal. Every seven changes of the seasons I go to share the bread and the berries, to meet my lifelong friend who knelt that first night beside me among the ruined fortifications, and to sip the holy brew that the Danaans prepare for us.

The sacred water of life.

ONE

 wave of cold sea water washed over the seven sea travellers, chilling their bare feet. They immediately craned their necks in an effort to catch a glimpse of the approaching danger. For a terrible moment the ocean seemed to stand still as each one of them abandoned the steady rhythm of the oars, stunned by what they saw.

'Put your backs into it and pull hard!' the helmsman ordered, his cracking voice betraying the panic that was taking hold of him. 'Row for your lives or we'll all be killed!'

The wayfarers instantly responded to the call, straining at the oars and picking up the beat as though there had never been an interruption. With determination they tore their gaze from the fearful sight and concentrated on the task at hand. Every mouth was dry with fear, every mind filled with tales of other mariners who had suffered the same terrible fate that now presented itself to them.

The threat of being swamped by fierce seas was not what struck terror into the hearts of these voyagers. Even these waters between Eirinn and Britain held nothing as frightening as the menace that was bearing down upon them.

Out of the mists, no more than four bow shots away, sailed an enemy dreaded and cursed by all who plied the cold northern waters of the world. A dark brown shape resembling a huge raging

monster from out of the legends skewed across the
surface of the sea as it turned to give chase to the
little cow-hide curragh. But this giant was no
hungry creature of the deep seeking an easy meal.
Nor was it one of the dreadful floating ice mountains that could creep up on a boat in heavy fog
and smash it into a thousand pieces. This peril was
something far more dangerous than anything the
natural world could muster. And far more ruthless.

Saxons.

The sleek shallow-draughted warship cut swiftly
through the calm waters, smoothly bringing its
pointed bow around. In seconds the ship of death
was headed directly for the cow-hide vessel and
quickly gaining speed in the slight breeze. On
board the longship the raiders hauled on their oars
with such ferocity that the water all around their
vessel turned white.

With the increase in speed there could be little
doubt that the master of the Saxon warship meant
to ram the helpless curragh. Such a manoeuvre
would surely slice the leather craft in half, leaving
the travellers defenceless and at the mercy of the
savage raiders. A drummer on board the foreign
warship beat a rapid pulse for the warriors at their
oars. The low dull thudding of this instrument
travelled over the water, causing all the Gaels to
shake with fear at the terrible fate that awaited
them.

Every other sound was muffled in the thickening
mist. Even the lapping of the waters against the
leather hull of the curragh seemed far off and thin
compared to the incessant threatening beat coming
from the longship.

Their destiny sealed, a change came over the five
men and two women on board the curragh. One
by one the travellers let their resolve fade and

dropped their oars in resignation, so overcome by the awful presence of the Saxons that they seemed to abandon hope entirely.

Within moments the light had begun to fade as more mist rolled in and blocked out the otherwise bright morning sunlight. No-one would have blamed any of the Gaels then if they had believed that they had sailed into some shadowy dreamland or perhaps passed through a secret doorway into the Otherworld of the Sidhe folk.

The Saxon raiding ship picked up even more speed as it caught the current and changed course slightly. It took a few moments for the travellers to realise that the warship was no longer making directly for them; but when they did, they let their hopes rise that somehow they had not been seen in the gathering fog.

The enemy craft altered course again, turning further away from the curragh. On board the tiny leather boat the travellers prayed silently to their gods for deliverance. But seconds later a muffled cry in a strange language resounded across the water. Any hopes that the watchman on board the war galley had not spotted them faded.

'They're coming around to cut us off and then to board us,' cried the helmsman. 'They will easily catch us now. They have four times as many oars as we do and there is not the slightest wisp of a breeze for us to pick up on.'

'If we don't lift the pace of our rowing, they'll be close enough to shoot their arrows at us before we have a chance to get away,' one of the other seamen stuttered in desperation. 'We must pull harder at the oars. We must not give up.'

'Don't be a fool!' snapped a woman who sat in the bow. She caught up her long tangled brown hair and tied it back, out of her eyes. 'They will catch us no matter how much sweat we spend in rowing away from them. What is the use of wearing ourselves out at the oars? If we stop now and wait for them, we will at least still have enough energy to be able to put up a decent fight.'

Her companions had no opportunity to argue the point for just as she finished speaking the Saxon warriors let loose their first flight of arrows. The air was suddenly full of deadly iron-tipped shafts whistling in a high arc, ruthlessly cutting through the distance between the two vessels. Without a word, everyone in the curragh instinctively curled up where they sat, covering their heads with their arms and waiting tensely for the bolts to strike.

Seconds later the rain of death ceased as though it had been only a short sharp hailstorm. The Gaels rose cautiously to take stock of this first attack. Miraculously all the darts had landed in the sea or struck the leather sail, poking out of it like barbaric adornments. No-one made any effort to remove the bolts, preferring instead to be out of harm's way when the next volley of arrows came at them.

When the expected attack did not arrive, the woman with the long matted hair got up to check the position of the enemy ship. As she did so she wrapped her long blue woollen cloak tightly about her body. The garment offered her no protection from arrows but somehow made her feel much safer.

'They're still far enough away that their aim cannot be too accurate,' she observed, 'but the next flight could well claim casualties. We must take cover as best we can.'

The woman reached up to drag at the leather sail, pulling it down from the masthead with a jerk. One of the seamen got to his feet to help her, while another began pulling all the spare leather from the box under the covered bow where it was stored.

'What do you think you're doing to my boat?' the helmsman protested. 'I can't afford to waste valuable leather like that.'

The other travellers ignored him, quickly throwing the sail over the centre of the deck to make a tentlike covering. When the edges were secured there was just enough room underneath for everyone, and all save the helmsman slid through the opening to huddle together and wait for the next attack.

They did not have to wait long. Only seconds after they had all found themselves places, the next flight of arrows began its dreadful hail. Before the first bolt had landed, the helmsman had dived under the shelter to join the others, the sweat pouring off his face.

This time most of the arrows found their mark somewhere on the little vessel, puncturing the hide in many places. The iron tips penetrated the sail covering but not deeply enough to injure any of those sheltering underneath. When the rain of death ceased, all those aboard the curragh had escaped any serious injury, but a cry went up from the Saxon ship. A victory cry.

The woman in the blue cloak crept out from under the leather to see how close the enemy ship was and how their little boat had fared under the Saxon attack.

'What do you suggest we do now, Síla?' the helmsman yelled at her. 'Hide under the leather until they sail right up and take us as galley slaves?'

'If none of us is injured when they come upon us, then we have a chance of fighting them off and making a good escape,' Síla replied sharply.

'There's thirty of them and only seven of us!' the man gasped. 'Our ship is only twelve paces long and theirs is fifty at least. We have no weapons and no hope of beating them off in a clean fight.'

Síla was just about to say that she had no intention of fighting cleanly, when the next wave of arrows soared high into the air. The travellers scrambled for cover again. The Saxons were closing in fast and it was obvious that the helmsman was right to believe they intended to board them. Since the water was calm, it would not prove too difficult for the raiders to manoeuvre their ship close to the drifting leather boat. The master of the enemy vessel had already hauled in his sails in preparation, and his oarsmen were holding their wooden blades in the water to slow the ship down.

'They mean to take us as slaves,' the helmsman's mate cried.

'Let them come aboard to try and get us,' Síla retorted. Then she addressed the other voyagers, 'Do not raise a hand to resist them until they're standing in amongst the ropes. And whatever you do, don't strike unless you're sure your blow will count. Our only hope is to catch them unawares and hit them hard. Before they know what's happened we'll have cut them down to size a bit.'

'I've never known a Druid to be so stupid!' the helmsman shouted back in outrage. 'If we had made a run for it we might have stood a chance of escape. Now we're surely doomed to be overcome by the savages and spend our lives as galley slaves on a Saxon longboat.'

'Take up an oar and make ready to use it as a weapon,' Síla yelled back at him. 'And show some courage in the face of these foreigners. We're not slaves yet! All of you find something to strike back with.' With some hesitation they all moved to do as she said.

In the meantime the enemy boat had drawn close enough that its oars scraped the side of the curragh. A few of the Saxons were preparing to throw grappling hooks towards the defenceless boat. Since the sea was very calm, it was only a short while before one of the Saxons had caught a hook in the hide of the little craft. Then six of his comrades took hold of the line and together they began to haul the curragh alongside their own vessel.

While they were pulling it in, other hooks caught at the leather craft and dug into its toughened hull. One of the iron hooks snagged the floor, creating a small tear that began to seep water. The helmsman stood up and drew his knife, intending to cut the rope that attached to the grappling hook, but a Saxon arrow struck him in the back almost immediately. He fell forward onto the hook, his weight driving it deeper into the floor of the leather hull. Water began gushing into the boat and the deck was soon awash in ankle-deep brine.

Síla put her palms up to the others, urging them to stay where they were and not to rush to the helmsman's side. 'Let him lie. There is nothing you can do for him. Do not expose yourselves to the archers. Stay under cover.'

Síla believed that if the travellers bided their time, the Saxons' overconfidence would eventually get the better of them. With luck the foreigners might even try to board the little vessel without ensuring that no resistance would be offered.

The Saxons, however, had another deadly weapon in store for the travellers, one that Síla had not expected.

Fire.

By now there were five lines caught on the curragh and the master of the Saxon ship could plainly see that the Gaels were cowering in fear under their sail. Satisfied that all was going to plan, the war leader decided to have some sport with his victims. He climbed onto a raised portion of the deck and gave a shout to his men.

On the bow three archers lit the pitch-soaked tips of their arrows from an iron brazier that burned with a thick black smoke. As soon as the greasy fuel caught fire, the flaming darts were strung to bows and shot down at the curragh. The first three fire bolts struck the makeshift shelter. The flames caught quickly, and because the travellers did not immediately understand what had happened, the fire had spread across the sail before they realised they were in greater danger than they could have imagined.

When the smell of searing cow hide caught in the back of her throat, Síla quickly reassessed the situation and the new peril they faced. For a moment she regretted that they had not made an attempt at escape while they had the chance. But it was only for a fleeting moment. Deep down she knew that nothing could have saved the travellers once the Saxons had made up their minds to attack. By using fire in their assault it was obvious that these raiders were not just looking for slaves. They were also looking for some entertainment.

Two of the Gaels came out from under the cover to douse the blazing sail with buckets of sea water, but they only succeeded in making themselves easy targets for the archers. One of the sailors caught a fiery arrow in his upper leg and fell back into the shelter screaming. The flame was doused in the water at the bottom of the boat, but the shaft of the dart broke, pushing the tip deep into the man's flesh.

Síla decided that if they were to have any chance at all of survival she would have to take charge. She grabbed at the other sailor, holding his arm to stop him throwing water over the fire. 'Leave the flames! Let the leather burn. Pull our boat close to theirs and we'll set fire to them,' she yelled. 'Grab at their ropes!'

Without hesitation the sailor dropped the bucket and did as he was ordered. Meanwhile the others bravely emerged from the shelter to pluck the burning arrows out of the boat and toss them back at the enemy. The ropes that had been used to trap the curragh were now aflame and the fire climbed quickly towards the longboat.

It took the Saxons some time to realise what was going on, but when they did, Síla's clever strategy had a profound effect on them. The master of the Saxon raider watched in utter disbelief as the ropes spread the blaze towards his vessel. When it struck him that he could lose his ship to the fire, he bellowed out to the archers to stop shooting their flaming arrows. In fury he commanded a group of his men to climb into the curragh and quickly dispatch the troublesome Gaels. The war leader had abruptly tired of this game.

Síla did not understand the Saxon tongue but quickly surmised what had taken place when the archers suddenly had buckets of water in their hands and were dousing the sides of their own ship. Then four Saxon warriors clambered over the side of their vessel in preparation to board the curragh.

The first foreigner to leap into the cow-hide vessel landed so heavily that he put his large boot through the hull. He struggled to free himself, realising that he was virtually defenceless in this position. Before he could do so, one of the Gaelic seamen stepped up to him. For some reason the warrior must have thought that the sailor intended to help him, because the Saxon reached out to take the man's hand. Before he could clasp it, however, the Gael had drawn a long knife from under his brat-cloak. The sailor slashed at the Saxon's arm then grabbed him by the hair, drawing his head back to expose his throat. With all the Saxon warriors watching, the Gael ran the cold blade swiftly across the raider's neck, cutting deeply into his flesh. The blood spurted out of the wound as the Saxon grasped at his throat, trying desperately to stem the flow.

The foreigner hunched forward, shrieking in agony, and as he did so the sailor stabbed him in the back. The Saxon's arms dropped lifeless by his side, his leg still stuck fast in the leather hull. Almost immediately another Saxon warrior jumped down from the enemy ship. He was luckier than his comrade: he only slipped a little on the deck. As soon as he had gained his footing he made a grab at the sailor's arm.

The warrior missed his intended victim at the first attempt but struck the man with his fist and knocked him over. He raised his sword, intending to slash at the Gael, but the sailor managed to get up in time and grab the Saxon's wrist, preventing the blow from making contact. For a few tense moments the seaman held his enemy at bay, then one of the other Gaelic sailors struck the raider on the back of the head with a boathook. The Saxon's helm rolled off his head and his eyes widened before he fell over, dead. In moments his body had been rolled over the side to loll face down in the sea.

These two sudden successes gave the travellers some hope that they might be able to drive the enemy off. They stood up, defiant now, and waited eagerly for the next warrior foolish enough to jump into their boat. The master of the Saxon ship could see that throwing more fighting men at the crew of the curragh would waste many of his warriors' lives. The limited space on the curragh meant that only one or two raiders could board the craft at a time, so they would always be outnumbered.

His patience fast evaporating, the master came up with a much better way of dealing with his victims. He called to the warrior readying himself to jump onto the curragh and urged him to cut the remaining lines that bound the two vessels together. By now the sea was gushing into the little leather boat through two holes in the outer hull. It would not be long, the Saxon reasoned, before these bold Gaels drowned, drawn to the sea bottom by the weight of their own disabled boat. The Saxon master called all hands to the oars.

When Síla saw the Saxons cutting the lines and pushing the curragh away with their oars, she could not believe her luck. Not only had they beaten the Saxons off quickly and easily, but it seemed that the foreigners were going to retreat altogether. As soon as the lines had been severed she took one of the narrow oars and pushed at the side of the wooden longboat to separate the two vessels as quickly as possible. As the Saxon ship rowed away she and the others went about the desperate task of sealing the two holes in the bottom of the boat.

The biggest tear was at the spot where the Saxon warrior lay, his leg stuck fast. This proved almost impossible to clear because the dead man's armour made his body too heavy to lift. Finally, after many attempts in the confined space to remove the corpse, one of the sailors brought out a razor-sharp knife used for slicing at the leather sheets. Showing no emotion at this gruesome deed, he hacked away at the flesh and bone until it parted from the body, then pushed the severed leg out through the bottom of the curragh to clear the blockage. With the obstruction gone, two of the seamen were able to heave the dead body over the side without further trouble.

Pieces of the burned sail were cut to patch the gashes in the hull, and one of the sailors used twine made from strips of hide to stitch the patches into place. Two of the travellers used leather buckets to empty water from the boat while the others did what they could in the confined space to help.

In their rush to repair the boat the travellers paid little heed to the Saxon warship. It was only by chance that one of the sailors noticed the enemy had stopped rowing and was preparing to shoot more arrows in their direction.

By keeping his large craft within firing distance of the Gaels, the master was able to ensure that a steady stream of darts hampered the repairs. Every once in a while the archers shot a series of flaming arrows, most of which found a mark in the leather hull. Some burned fiercely for a time, only to be extinguished as soon as there was a lull in the attack, while others sputtered out on the water-logged hide.

The Saxons obviously thought this was great sport. Their laughter leapt across the water at the Gaels, chilling them to their core. Whenever an arrow took hold or one of the travellers made for cover, the Saxons called out insults or mockery in their own tongue. But their taunts were wasted on the Gaels for none of them understood their strange language.

Eventually, however, the Saxon war leader began to grow bored with this game. He was fairly certain there was no gold or other precious cargo to be had from these poor folk. They were not merchants. They were little more than fisherfolk, not even of value as oar slaves. The master climbed onto the bow of his vessel to peer at his victims for a moment and then gave the order to his oarsmen to row with all their strength towards the curragh.

When Síla realised that the rain of arrows had ceased, she looked out from where she was helping stitch the hull to see the bow of the enemy ship surging towards them at an alarming pace. The vessel cut through the water like a great sword cutting cleanly through a stand of wheat. Without any resistance the sea parted before the ship in a white foaming rush.

Panic took hold of the Gaels once more as they picked up their own oars. They were too slow, however, to make any difference to the outcome of this contest. The raiding ship picked up speed, and, after the master ordered the sails unfurled, the warship caught a slight breeze. Síla stopped rowing—there was nothing to do but prepare herself for the jolt of a collision. The Druid braced her feet hard against the floor of the curragh. The other woman was staring dumbfounded at the enemy ship, and all the other travellers grasped at the sides of the boat, their oars forgotten. There would be no escaping destruction this time.

The same wind that gave the Saxon ship a push brought with it a bank of mist which rolled over the enemy craft and overtook it so that in a very short time both the Gaels and the Saxons were engulfed in a thick soup of fog. Síla knew that they did not have much time before the enemy vessel hit, but even she was surprised when it slammed into the curragh's rear, dragging the little boat around and forcing its stern under the water. The sheer weight and momentum of the Saxon ship meant it pushed the light leather craft under the waves like a toy boat in a pond. The ghastly sound of wooden supports snapping and leather tearing was mingled with the hideous cheers of the Saxons and the rush of the sea.

Síla was rolled violently out of her seat. In an effort to steady herself she reached around to take hold of the side of the boat, but before she could do so properly, she felt herself lifted up as the curragh rolled completely over. Her hands slid over the wet leather hull as the boat capsized, and she had no chance of regaining hold of any part of the craft. In the next instant Síla was dumped down heavily into the cold water.

The Druid managed to keep her head above water after she was thrown clear of the curragh, but it was not long before she lost almost all hope of surviving the ordeal. Her eyes stung from the salt water and her ears were blocked so that she could not hear anything at all. Then she felt her body sinking under the waves even as she struggled to stay afloat. In the next instant the Druid was engulfed in the cold dark ocean, and although she flayed her arms about wildly, she could not raise her head out of the water.

The sea dragged Síla down into the depths as surely as if she had weights wrapped round her legs. She tried to breathe, but instead of taking in air she gagged on water that rushed into her mouth and nostrils, threatening to fill her lungs. She forced herself to expel the brine so that she would not choke on it, and blocked her nose with two fingers. Then she realised that it was her blue woollen Druid cloak that was making her so heavy. In the next instant she was desperately trying to worm her way out of it, abandoning her precious cloak brooch without a thought in the rush to pull the garment over her head.

When she was free of the cloak, she fought to swim to the surface, urgently seeking for air to fill her lungs. It was a long hard struggle up towards the light, and by the time her head broke the surface she had almost lost consciousness. Once above the waves Síla violently spewed out all the sea water in her body, taking deep gulps of air into her lungs as she did so.

Her soaked hair was spread over her face and blocked her vision, but her eyes stung so much that she could not open them anyway. The Druid coughed a little and tried to steady herself in the sea. Suddenly her hand touched a large piece of wood floating nearby. She grasped hold of it, leaning on the timber to test its ability to keep her afloat. When it passed the test, she hauled her body onto it and tried to settle her breathing so that she would not choke.

Síla cleared the blockage in her ears by rolling her head to one side and then the other so that the water drained out. When she could hear again she realised that the only sounds she could discern were muffled and distant. The Druid brushed the hair back from her face in an attempt to see what was going on around her, but the salt still stung her eyes and it was some moments before she dared open them fully.

When she finally managed to glance about her, all that she saw was fog and a few pieces of rope and leather floating nearby in the sea. The slab of wood that she was draped over had been the tiller. Still secured to its broad rudder this buoyant wreckage could easily support her weight in the water.

As for the raiders, they were gone. The warship had disappeared into the fog as swiftly as it had arrived. Their sport over, the Saxons had simply sailed on, not bothering to turn around to pick up their victims or even to see whether they had destroyed the curragh.

There was no sign of Síla's companions either. The Druid called out for a while, hoping to get some answer from at least one of her fellow travellers, but there was no reply, not the slightest sign that anyone else had lived through the ordeal. Eventually Síla had to accept that she was probably the only survivor of the vicious Saxon attack.

The Druid rolled over and lay on her back across the tiller, her arms outstretched to steady her and her eyes skyward. As the day wore on, the mist cleared to reveal a bright blue sky with only a few clouds. Síla forced herself to stop thinking as she breathed deeply. When the shock of the encounter had subsided a little, she began to appreciate the fact that by some miracle her life had been spared. In thanks to her gods she offered up a silent heartfelt prayer.

Then Síla began to focus her thoughts on making her way to dry land.

TWO

series of short sharp cries tore through the still night. Each shriek followed the last in quick succession, ending with a shrill call that sounded exactly like the wail of a wolf on the hunt. In the chapel of Saint Ninian's the aged and venerable Brother Kilian, disturbed from his prayers, reached instinctively for his gospel.

Without needing to open his eyes, he found the book on the floor in front of him and gripped its silver inlaid spine with strong wiry fingers. Then he slowly tucked the gospel up under his arm as he listened carefully for any further sounds. All the while he quietly mumbled the last words of the Pater Noster. When the prayer was ended he remained perfectly still.

Eventually the old monk was forced to shift his aging body in order to get comfortable. His flesh was cold from the draught that whistled under the door, so cold that he thought for a moment that winter had unexpectedly returned to the land of Strath-Clóta. His left leg had gone numb from kneeling too long upon the stone floor. As he began to rub warmth back into his limbs another inhuman cry, shrill and eerie, pierced the silence. The monk froze in terror as the shriek echoed against the walls of the small stone chapel, then faded.

Kilian held his breath as the minutes passed silently by. Nervous sweat from the old monk's brow rolled down the deep wrinkles of his face to slide off his chin and onto his homespun cloak. For a moment the world around the monastery of Saint Ninian's seemed calm and still and holy. Then, far off to the north, from among the hills where the Dal Araidhans dwelt, another howl rose on the breeze. Like a mighty avalanche of snow the shriek swept down the hillsides towards the sea, striking dread into the hearts of all who heard it. Kilian could not help but think of the cries of wolves, though he had never heard one and had only the tales of other monks by which to judge.

He knew well enough, however, that there had been no wolves in this part of Britain since the time of the Roman legions. These cries were the call of another race of hunter altogether. In many ways Kilian would have preferred to face an army of wolves than the foes he feared were even now bearing down on his settlement.

The monk steadied himself against the stone altar, taking a deep breath before rising creakily to his feet. A sense of dire urgency outweighed any fears he might have held for his own safety. It was his duty as senior monk to rally the community in readiness for an attack. His only worry was that he had stayed too long at prayer to save the lives of his comrades.

Kilian had barely got to his feet and crossed himself when he heard men arguing loudly outside the building. In the next instant the great oak door swung back violently against the stone wall of the chapel with a thud that shook the roof timbers. Suddenly the entire interior of the tiny church was alive with bright yellow torchlight and the sound of strange voices.

By the time the monk had turned to face the disturbance, three warriors had made their way through the rows of empty reading stools, knocking as many over as possible, and were standing menacingly close to him. They held their rush lights high in the air to get a better look at the old man.

As shocked as he was that the raiders had penetrated the monastery so quickly, Kilian took little immediate notice of the threatening Saxon raiders. He was much more concerned about their careless behaviour than any threat they might pose to his personal safety. Gasping, he scanned the dry thatched ceiling of the chapel, looking for smoke. A spark from any one of the torches could so easily take hold in the roof and then the whole church would surely catch fire. That would truly be a disaster.

He pleaded with the warriors not to raise their torches too high but that only served to make them frighten him further by deliberately pushing their rush lights up among the roof timbers. His heart beating wildly, Kilian shouted at them to stop, but the Saxons only laughed at him, pretending not to understand what was upsetting him.

Their mockery flustered the old monk so much that he did not notice the tallest of the foreigners lift his mailed fist above his head and bring it down to strike Kilian across the back of the skull. The monk teetered over, losing his balance and falling hard against the altar.

'Declan?' the warrior demanded in a rough accent. 'You Declan?'

The monk quickly regained his footing, summoning his pride so that he could stand before the warrior as if the blow had meant nothing to him. Abbot Declan always said that one must never show one's feelings to these savages. Kilian was

29

determined not to let them see how frightened and shaken he was by the unexpected attack.

'Declan is not here,' he stuttered. 'I am acting as abbot in his absence. What can I do for you?' It was well, he thought, that the abbot was away in Eirinn. Kilian had an uneasy feeling that these men had been sent to murder Declan.

The tall warrior growled from the back of his throat, raising his fist as if to strike again as he briefly explained the situation to his comrades. Anticipating another blow any second, the monk closed his eyes and leaned against the altar, praying silently to his God to give him strength.

This was the way of Christ, he told himself: do not raise a hand to your enemies; do not retaliate but instead forgive them their violent ways. The punch landed a second later and was even more shattering than the first, splitting the skin below Kilian's left eye so that blood began pouring out. The gospel that had been in the monk's left hand fell to the floor, its decorated silver back in full view of the raiders. The tall man laughed and immediately bent to pick up the prize.

Old Brother Kilian opened his eyes in time to see the foreigner about to grab his gospel. In his mind Declan's advice to turn the other cheek echoed like the bell that called the brothers to prayer each morning. The rule of his holy order to refrain from violence and to forgive all men was not forgotten. He even thought he heard the first abbot, Ninian, speaking of how the gentle of this world would one day inhabit all the Earth. Despite this, the monk could not bear the thought of one of those heathen savages defiling a holy book.

In an instant all the frustration of the last few months and the savage raids that had plagued the community boiled to the surface. Kilian could no longer stay calm in the face of such brutality. He could no longer pretend he was not angry. He had turned his cheek a dozen times since Declan had gone off to Eirinn, and had been beaten mercilessly every time. How could gentle folk come to inhabit the whole Earth if their lives were ruled by fear and brutality?

Kilian's rage took hold of him, pushing aside all he had ever believed about showing meekness in the face of enemy hostility and bestowing compassion and forgiveness on all wrongdoers. Without taking his eyes off his assailant, the monk smoothly drew from under his robes a long thin scribe's knife of the kind usually used for sharpening pens. He raised the tool above his head so rapidly and deftly that the foreigners were caught off guard.

In the blinking of an eye the narrow blade swept downwards, sinking deep into the tall warrior's exposed back at a point just behind the left shoulder blade. The knife was just long enough to pierce the man's heart and the foreigner fell forward onto the stone floor without another sound. Instinctively the warrior's companions leapt back out of range of the deadly weapon. As they did so they dropped their torches, plunging the chapel into darkness once more.

At that very moment Kilian slipped silently behind the altar, shaking from the shock of what he had done but knowing that he had very little chance of escape unless he acted quickly. Still gripping the blood-soaked scribe's knife in whitened knuckles, the monk reached up and grabbed the wooden cross that stood upon the altar stone. With a great effort he flung the cross as far as he could in the general direction of the door. It landed with a loud clatter against a bench at the back of the chapel. Less than a single breath later the two

Saxon warriors hurled themselves at the source of the noise, desperate that the monk should not escape them.

By the time they realised that they had been tricked, Kilian had slid open the stone panel at the rear of the altar, crawled into the gap and closed the tunnel entrance behind him. And he was not a moment too soon. At the very instant that he dropped the panel shut, three more Saxons entered the chapel with fresh rush lights. Kilian could hear the wild commotion as warriors ran this way and that, calling out to each other in their strange guttural Saxon tongue.

The old man took a deep breath, steadying his resolve and stilling his wildly beating heart. When the noise in the chapel had died down a little, he crept forward on all fours along the narrow passage away from the chapel and towards the abbot's private cell which lay just outside the walls of the monastery.

Kilian was not sure how quickly the time passed as he moved through the secret tunnel, but he was painfully aware of just how slowly he was moving. His legs and arms still shook from fear, and the aches in his joints prevented him from moving any faster. He could not be certain that the Saxons would not discover the secret entrance and he began to panic, thinking that they might well be waiting for him at the other end of the tunnel. By sheer effort of will he controlled his rising fear, reminding himself that only he and Declan were aware of the existence of this old tunnel.

A further two hundred paces the old monk crawled on his hands and knees until, with great relief, he found himself crossing onto the floor slates that marked the end of the passageway. Where the tunnel came up under the abbot's cell there was nearly enough height for a man to stand. A little stairway led to a loose stone which lay across a bench set into the wall of the beehive-shaped dwelling. Kilian climbed the four steps and put his ear to the stone.

His heart sank. Inside the hut he could distinctly hear savage Saxon voices raised in anger and the noise of heavy objects being thrown about. The old monk found himself sweating again and now there was a crushing pain in his chest.

'Why can't they leave us be?' Kilian wondered aloud and straightaway cursed his own stupidity at making a noise. But if the foreigners heard him they made no sign of it, so the old brother settled down to wait until they had finished their looting and had gone back to join their companions.

It was not a long wait. Declan, the abbot of the monastery, kept a small supply of wine in the cell out of reach of the younger monks. Apart from a few candles of purest beeswax there was nothing of any value in the abbot's hut, only clothes and a few roughly bound books. The savages found the Roman bottles and made short work of their contents before storming off, cursing loudly in their own tongue. Kilian waited a long while until he was sure they were gone.

When the brother was sure that no-one remained inside the hut, he carefully lifted the stone seat no more than the height of an ant so that he could detect if there was any light in the room. There was none, so he silently lifted the stone a little higher. All was still and dark.

Laboriously Kilian pushed the stone aside, and it landed with a loud thud on the packed earth floor of the cell. This sudden noise made the old monk's heart race again. He hauled himself up out of the tunnel and replaced the stone as best he could so that the Saxons would not discover the tunnel if they chanced to return. Then he made his way quickly out into the night.

The very instant that he was outside, Kilian strained his eyes in the direction of the walled monastery. Even with his poor sight he could make out the twisting orange shapes of flames rising from the thatched roof of one of the buildings. He was instantly overcome with guilt, convinced that his rash action in stabbing the foreigner would surely lead to the massacre of all the brothers at Saint Ninian's.

Kilian was thoroughly ashamed of himself for skulking off into safety when his companions remained behind to suffer for his misdeed. Hardening his resolve once more, the old man crossed himself, pleading silently for forgiveness of his sin. Then, determined to share in the suffering of his brethren, he made off up the path towards the monastery.

He had not gone ten paces, however, when he heard the sound of Saxon shouts nearby and his resolve melted away like thawed spring ice. He found a cow path that branched off from the main track and decided to follow it, skirting around the settlement at a safe distance.

The narrow track rose onto an area of steep ground that overlooked the monastery, and from here Kilian could see the full extent of the Saxon raid. At least three buildings were on fire within the walls of Ninian's, and a further four outside the walls were burning also. Kilian's eyesight was too poor for him to discern whether any monks had been harmed. All the nuns had long ago been moved to the comparative safety of the Gaelic fortress of Dun Righ.

Kilian could still hear many Saxon shouts and

somewhere near the fires one of the savages was singing a drunken song. To his relief the monk could not hear any moans or cries, nor any words or phrases in the Gaelic tongue.

'I pray, God, help them all as you helped me to escape,' he begged. 'It is a miracle that I am alive.'

Almost as if in answer, Kilian heard the neighing of restless horses close by. To begin with he thought that perhaps a lone stallion had strayed onto the far hillside to disturb the other animals that usually spent their nights under the trees near the spring. Then the monk heard the wild high-pitched shriek of a horse suffering great pain and a cold chill ran through his aching bones.

The old man's first instinct was to make off towards the spring, though he knew he would not be able to defend the horses against wild Saxon warriors. In the end his concern for the animals outweighed his fear of capture. He had already committed one act of cowardice this night. Kilian was determined not to commit another.

In his haste he forgot that he did not have a lighted lamp with him and he had not gone far along the ridge in the direction of the spring before he became disoriented in the dark. With a muttered curse at his own impatience and poor eyesight, the old brother turned around to try and get his bearings, but he could not recognise any landmarks. Frustrated, he reluctantly conceded that he had no alternative but to retrace his steps. He had only travelled a few short steps, however, when the cry of another horse reached his ears. He thought for a second that he recognised the call as that of the mare the monks used to pull the grain wagon.

The animal's shriek was frantic, as though she had been mortally wounded. When the call died away, Kilian stood still in his tracks, horrified. In the distance he could faintly discern the disturbed neighing of several other horses answering the mare's call, but he could not tell whether they were to the north or the east. The old monk realised that there was nothing more that he could do. Defeated, he sank to his knees in the grass and began to pray.

He did not know how long he stayed on his knees, but they were beginning to go numb again when Kilian heard laughter from the direction of the monastery. His eyes had by this time adjusted a little better to the dark and so he carefully made his way back to the top of the rise. From here he could just make out the ocean on one side to the south and on the other side the monastery nestled against the ridge out of the wind.

Most of the compound was engulfed in flames by now and, to his everlasting dismay, he found that he could hear the occasional Gaelic word among the fearful shouts. 'The Saxons have captured some of the brothers!' he exclaimed, grief stricken at this development. 'Please, God, I pray do not let them suffer.'

No sooner had he spoken those words than he heard the barking of many dogs not far behind him along the ridge and realised with sinking heart that the savages had let loose their hunting hounds to find him.

Eorl Aldor of the one-time Saxon royal house of Eikenskald lay on his back with his hands by his sides, looking up at the long white artery of stars that his people called the Trail of Spilt Milk. It was a warm night so he had made his sleeping place a little away from the fire. The flames quickly died down to coals, and in the diminishing light the stars stood out in stark contrast against the deep blue sky.

Aldor could clearly see that some of the stars flickered unceasingly, while others burned steady without any movement at all. He wondered as always what the reason could be for this. He knew that the gods had gifted mankind with sky lights so that sailors could find their way home. The eorl had memorised all their positions for they were a ceaseless fascination to him.

Behind his head and out of sight, one of the many sleeping warriors shifted restlessly. Without turning to find the source of the disturbance, Aldor slipped his long single-edged sword swiftly and silently out of its scabbard and laid it by his right leg.

Eorl Aldor had an uncanny gift. Whenever there was danger he was always the first to know. His men often joked that he could catch a whiff of treachery on the breeze in the same way that other men smelled the aroma of slowly roasting mutton. It was an instinct that had saved his life many times.

Aldor did not take his eyes off the stars as his fingers found the leather shield straps where they lay near his left thigh. A man coughed loudly in the night. Another cursed his noisy comrade. To anyone without the eorl's special sense for trouble these sounds would not have been remarkable. But Aldor was restless, certain that soon his leadership would be sorely tested. Apart from those few noises, however, there were no other hints that this night would be different to any other.

Since his war party had landed in Alba he had seen a good deal of fighting, mostly among his own men. The majority of the Dal Araidhan people were too weak to resist the raiders, and Gaelic warriors rarely seemed to have the stomach for real battle. They often ran away from a good fight rather than risk being beaten. As a result there had been very little action and some of his men had begun to soften, no longer having the opportunity to practise their war skills on a daily basis. Others had grown restless and openly defied his orders.

Aldor allowed his eyes to close. His muscular body relaxed. His breathing slowed. Eventually his gentle breaths turned to subdued snores as the rest of the camp grew silent for the night.

But Aldor was not asleep. His hand still lay around the leather-bound shaft handle of his sword in anticipation of the fight he hoped would come sooner rather than later. He was tired of waiting for the rebels to make their move. Perhaps, he thought, they haven't got the guts to strike at me.

The eorl was now nearly forty summers old, but there was not a hint of grey in his jet-black hair and beard, nor did he suffer from aching bones as his grandfather had done at that age. His only brother, Guthwine, had died valiantly in the service of King Dichu of Laigin when he was forty summers old. Their father, Onarr Eikenskald, had not lived much past forty either. He was slain by his trusted steward in his sleep. Guthwine at least had died honourably, fighting in Hibernia.

Aldor remembered how his father had grown fat, lazy and stupid, which had prompted his servants to murder him so they could distribute his treasure to their own folk. The eorl firmly believed that men such as his father, who allowed themselves to become indolent, deserved to die without honour. In many ways he considered such men to be dead already. To him they were no more than walking corpses, worse than the most miserable of slaves. It was left to the strong ones such as himself to take their lives and put them to some profitable use.

In a world without fighting, fear, womenfolk, strong drink, plunder and spilt blood, life to Aldor would not be worth living. It was these things that made him feel truly alive. They made his heart beat faster and stronger, instilling in him the courage to continue when other men might easily throw their hands up in despair. When the eorl departed this life it was his firm intention to do so with honour so that his entrance into the Wealhall, the feasting hall of heroes in the spirit realm of Asgard, would be guaranteed.

Aldor heard subdued voices nearby and the unmistakable sound of a sword being unsheathed from its scabbard. The eorl could feel his body begin to tense in anticipation. At last. This was what he had been waiting many months for. Ever since they had come to Alba his rival had been plotting for this moment, and now the traitor was finally going to make his move.

There was nothing so sweet to the eorl as the anticipation of a fight, the challenge to survive or be drowned in the blood lust of your enemy. Such situations as this were especially delightful for Aldor, for it was rare that he had foreknowledge of his enemy's intentions.

A few steps away Aldor heard a shuffle and a muffled whisper. In a flash the eorl had rolled away towards the fire and sprung to his feet, grabbing his shield and sword on the way up. Before he got his balance, though, the heavy blow of a battleaxe glanced off his metal-studded jerkin and sliced into the skin on his left shoulder. Aldor screamed, surprise mingling with enthusiasm. This was going to be a fight to remember.

'I am Aldor Eikenskald, Thegn and Eorl of the line of Vitr the Bloody!' he announced. 'What coward dares to suppose that he can strike me down in my sleep?'

Two of the three men who confronted the eorl looked frantically at each other. They had not expected the eorl to be waiting for them. The third man, however, was clearly not surprised at the eorl's readiness: he knew Aldor's reputation for being able to smell a fight brewing. This warrior was a much broader man than Aldor, though shorter, and he sported a dark brown beard knotted from neglect. In his unkempt hair were dozens of tiny silver trinkets, and his left eye was still bruised black from his latest raid on a farm to the south. His clothes were filthy and his breath stank of ale. He was no match for Aldor.

'I am Eothain Longbeard,' the dishevelled warrior boomed. 'I have come to announce the end of your eorlship and relieve you of your life.' Realising that half the camp had awoken to the disturbance and that he now had an audience, the man cried out again, 'I am Eothain, son of Aelfwine of the house of Eotenburg.'

Aldor noticed with amusement that the man was shaking, albeit almost imperceptibly. Was it possible that he was frightened? That was not like Eothain. Aldor decided that the traitorous fool had not been able to raise as much sympathy for his cause as he would have liked. After all, only two supporters stood beside him now; the rest of the camp was standing around to watch but had not made any open show of support for him.

The eorl began to relax again, seeing the odds were definitely in his favour. By custom Aldor was expected to answer Eothain's challenge with some derisive comments that would stir his opponent into launching another verbal attack. But the war leader waited until the crowd had settled before he hurled his first insult.

'When you mentioned your glorious ancestor, the one known as Aelfwine, did you mean the same Aelfwine who started life as a galley slave, rose to rule a family of thieving cowards and died at the hand of a woman? Is this the same house of Eotenburg who so wisely sided with the Britons when the Saxon uprising began because they sympathised with the poor unfortunate Cymru? Is this the same great family who was renowned in my father's time as goat breeders?'

Aldor paused a moment, gauging carefully the effect his sarcasm was having. 'Leave the real warriors to the sleep they've earned. Go home to your house of Eotenburg and curl up with the goats.'

Then the eorl took a risk. He allowed his eyes to stray away from his opponent and slowly turned around to address the crowd that had gathered among the trees behind him. 'Never trust a man who smells of livestock.' This comment raised a few sniggers. 'Except when he's guarding your women!' Aldor added and the crowd laughed heartily. Several men made bleating sounds and Eothain's face turned fiery red.

The eorl was so pleased with the way he was handling this rebellion that he almost underestimated his opponent. While Aldor was still taking in the praise of his audience, Eothain and his two henchmen made their move. The three stepped forward to attack but, just as they did so, six well-aimed arrows flew from out of the darkness. Both Eothain's companions fell dead not two paces from where they had been standing. The traitor himself stopped in his tracks, severely shaken by the deadly turn of events.

'You didn't really think, did you, Eothain goat-herd, that I would let you get away with your cowardly plan?'

Eothain searched the crowd for support, desperately pleading for the aid that so many had promised him.

'I knew about your scheme from the very start, son of Aelfwine the Oarsman. Planning my reply has kept me entertained when you were off raiding the south without my permission.' Aldor did not give the man a chance to make any excuses. 'Lay down your blade, coward. You will not get the opportunity to die with dignity and honour. At least your two friends fell in an open fight. They will surely go to the hall of heroes. I respect their valour, though their choice to die for their beliefs was somewhat misguided. But you,' Aldor spat, 'you do not deserve death. You will suffer slowly for your treachery. What kind of a man chooses to stab his lord in the back under the cover of darkness?'

Eothain breathed in sharply through his teeth. He knew the eorl well enough to understand what the war leader meant when he said that he would make him suffer for his treachery. 'I'll die as I choose!' the rebel screamed, raising his sword and lunging forward at the eorl. 'I am no coward.'

No-one in the gathering moved to stop him. They had strict instructions from Aldor not to strike at the man. The eorl stepped back nimbly to parry his opponent's blow, then he struck Eothain across the left shoulder with the heavy blunt edge of his single-bladed sword. The blow was immediately followed by a loud cracking sound as a bone in the traitor's shoulder splintered. Eothain fell forward in agony, dropping his sword in front of him as he broke his fall with his right arm. Aldor

42

turned his blade around in his hand and lay the sharp edge across the back of his opponent's neck as though he were preparing to sever the man's head.

'This is my sword,' the eorl hissed. 'This is Scaramsax. She has been my loyal friend since I first went raiding. She serves me well and in return I give her the blood of my enemies to drink.' Aldor looked up at the crowd of his warriors. 'Sometimes I am hard pressed to keep her satisfied with worthy victims, but I have never cut a coward with her bladed edge. I would not insult her with such an unsatisfying feast. Spineless scum like this one can only expect the blunt end of my sword and afterwards a life in chains.'

Then the eorl turned to Eothain. 'In recognition of your submission you will serve me from this day as a slave. Your family line is ended. No man will think twice about kicking you as he passes, and no woman will ever consider even talking to you again.'

Aldor put his booted foot flat on Eothain's back and pushed the beaten man down face first onto the ground. 'I am Eorl of Alba by right of conquest,' the eorl cried, raising his sword high above his head. 'Let every man in my domain know what becomes of those who dare to betray me.'

Síla had no way of knowing how long she had drifted in the open ocean. For a long while she simply lay back and let the current take her, wisely deciding to conserve her energy. Later, mostly to relieve the boredom, she started to swim but soon realised that without knowing in which direction the shore of Alba lay, she could easily be propelling herself further out to sea. So, tying herself to the tiller with a strand of singed rope, she lay on her back once again, her head resting on the highest part of the timbers, and tried to rest.

As night drew on, the wind rose a little and the ocean began to heave gently. Síla feared that a storm might be rising, but the breeze died again after sunset and the sea was calm once more. Nevertheless the Druid was very cold, colder than she could ever remember having been in all her life. Her legs and arms were growing numb and her breathing laboured. Every once in a while she made an attempt to swim, more to get her blood circulating and warm her body than with any hope of reaching land through the effort.

At dawn the surface of the sea was as still as one of the great lakes in the kingdom of Ulaid in northern Eirinn. A fog had rolled in during the night and where it broke the Druid glimpsed only more open ocean. Síla did not despair, however, for she knew that such thick fog only occurred where the sea met the coast, so she must be close to land.

The haze began to clear around midday, but still she could see no trace of land in any direction, nor any sign of any other debris from the boat, nor any other members of the crew. She was utterly alone and, despite the warming sunshine, her whole body remained bitterly cold.

The Druid had spoken to many sailors on her travels, for she had made the crossing between Eirinn and Alba ten or twelve times now. It was rare, she knew, for anyone to survive more than a day immersed in these waters, even at the height of summer, due to the ocean's cold bite.

Síla moved her legs in the water and realised that her toes were so numb that even the gentle prickling feeling that had plagued her during the night was gone. This put her into a panic and she frantically began to stretch her ankles and feet, believing that if she kept her body moving, the cold would not affect her so badly. But eventually she no longer had the energy to swim more than a few strokes at a time.

As the day wore slowly on, the Druid could sense her body weakening. By the time the sun was ready to set, she was very drowsy, finding it difficult to keep her mind focused on any thought for long. She drifted in and out of sleep, lulled by the gentle motion of the tide and the musical lapping of the water against the tiller. She woke once to hear a strange roar in the distance, but the sun had set while she had been asleep and she could see nothing in the dark.

Long afterwards Síla thought that she heard the sound of waves breaking on the shore. Somehow she roused herself enough to try to work out the direction from which the sound was coming. But her mind could not concentrate on the noise and was constantly distracted by the burning thirst in her throat and the overwhelming despair in her heart. She was too weak to swim and too exhausted to fight against her fate.

'I have passed on and it is the sound of waves crashing on the beaches of Tir Nan Og that I can hear,' she told herself and another voice replied to her in her mind: 'Come the morning you'll make your landfall. You will come home tomorrow. Do not fear.'

'I will be home tomorrow,' Síla repeated. A part of her was resigned to the inevitable, while another part, the practical healer, told her that she must not listen to voices in her head.

But the practical healer was incredibly tired. She

desperately needed rest and her words faded as Síla fell into a deep trancelike sleep. Once or twice that night the Druid woke as a wave washed over her or her mouth filled with sea water, but she could not rouse herself fully. The impenetrable night became an indecipherable mix of blurred images and unexplained noises, and the part of her that usually fought on against the odds finally gave up hope.

All of a sudden her body was rolled over violently and the Druid felt something hit her head hard. Her mouth was full of water and she coughed up salt; she could not find fresh air to breathe, only more sea water. Desperately clutching at the rope that bound her to the tiller, she managed to release her body, thinking that it had been the timber that had rolled over in the sea. When she was free she turned onto her back and took a deep breath. Then Síla lost consciousness again.

Bright sunshine was the next thing the healer was aware of. Then she realised that she was lying on her back on hard packed sand. Síla opened her eyes and had to shield them for a moment. The world glowed with a beautiful green luminescence and she felt very warm. When she tried to roll over onto her side, her body would not do as she asked and so she lay there on the sand for a long time, listening to the breakers crashing onto the beach.

'I am home,' she said aloud when she had the strength to realise what had happened. 'I have come home to the Land of the Ever Young.'

Síla closed her eyes, breathing in the sweet air and no longer caring that her throat was parched raw with thirst or that her body ached all over. Her eyes shut contentedly, the Druid lay soaking up the sun's rays, and for a long time she thought of doing nothing else. Eventually, however, her curiosity was aroused and she decided to try once again to get up.

With sheer force of will Síla garnered all her strength to the task. She pushed her left arm into the sand and rolled herself onto her right side, opening her eyes slightly as she did so. A large dark object was sitting in the middle of the sand not ten paces away from her. It took shape very slowly, reconciling itself through many forms as Síla's vision cleared. At first the healer thought it was a small tree that had fallen on its side and been washed up alongside her. She remembered the tiller that had kept her afloat and told herself that this is what the object must be.

Then her vision blurred again and the shapeless form melted into the image of a large stag with tangled antlers. No sooner had Síla recognised this shape than the stag transformed into the corpse of a mighty beached salmon at least five times larger than any fish she had ever seen. The salmon's scales glittered in the sunlight and then, without warning, the fish moved, twisting and smoothly stretching out. In a few moments the creature sat up on its tail and changed into a tall creature which Síla recognised as having the shape of a man.

The stranger stood up from where he had been crouching and strode over to her; when he reached her side he bent down to touch her forehead. Síla noticed immediately that his dark hair was shaved on the forehead in the Druid fashion. He pulled off his blue cloak to spread it over her and for a moment the healer thought she recognised him. She blinked to clear her vision and still saw the familiar face of her greatest friend.

Her heart filled with joy at finding him here for had she not parted from him to come on this

47

journey? What more could she wish but that they should be together forever in the Land of Youth?

'Gobann,' she whispered. 'How did you come to be here waiting for me in Tir Nan Og?'

The figure reached out tenderly to brush the hair away from her face. 'My name is Malchedoc and this is the land of the Strath-Clóta in the west of Alba. I do not know what has become of this Gobann you speak of, but you are safe now. Do not fear.'

Síla strained all her senses to try to discern if the fellow's face had changed form again but, try as she might, she could not keep her attention focused. Her eyelids closed against her will and the Druid healer lapsed once more into a deep sleep, succumbing at last to exhaustion.

THREE

he young boy's face was as white as the first snowfall, as pale with terror as if he had run into the Faerie hunt riding from the Otherworld to collect the souls of the unwary. Had he not been running for all he was worth, his family would probably have thought him gravely ill. It was his father who first noticed the lad as his short legs carried him at a frantic pace towards the little enclosure where they lived. He was yelling something at the top of his voice and shaking with fear.

The wind off the sea was blowing too strongly for the young fellow's words to reach the old man's ears. The boy tried to climb a steep bank near the main hut, but he was behaving so recklessly that he slipped his footing and rolled to the bottom again. Halfway up the bank a length of fishing net that had been hanging ready for mending caught on his breeches and wrapped around his legs, preventing him from climbing any further. In sheer panic the boy lay back against the side of the ditch and screamed with all the force of his lungs.

His father, mother and two brothers came running to see what had got into him, for he was usually a calm, reserved child. When they reached him he was slashing wildly at the precious net with his knife in a vain attempt to free himself.

'What do you think you're doing, cutting good

net?' the father yelled, genuinely shocked at the destruction of such a valuable item.

'What's got into you?' his mother echoed as his younger brothers sat down at her feet to better observe his erratic behaviour.

The lad looked up to see his family gathered around. He saw the anger in his father's face and the confusion in his mother's. 'Run!' he screeched. 'Saxons!'

Without a moment's hesitation his mother reached for the two youngest children, picking them up and running with all the speed she could muster to the storage pit. His father jumped over the bank and slid down into the ditch, drawing his own knife as he rolled towards his son. 'Calm yourself, Fergus!' he ordered.

'Their boats are down there in the bay!' the boy screamed as the last piece of net was removed from his legs.

'Go to the storage pit and help your mother. I am relying on you to protect her.' The boy raced off, skirting around the bank to where a pit was dug into the side of the mound. His father made for the path from which Fergus had come, hoping to catch a glimpse of the raiders, but he was already too late. A dozen wild looking men with battle fury in their eyes suddenly appeared at the top of the path, long-handled axes at the ready.

A few who had short bows stopped to let loose their arrows as soon as they spotted the helpless old man. Fergus did not see his father die. The old man's fruitless attempt at defending his family was ended before his wife had a chance to finish covering the pit entrance. Moments later the Saxons were swarming all around the little farmstead.

Fergus and his mother were about to cover their storage pit, the two youngest children inside, when they were suddenly confronted by four of the savage warriors. The foreigners slashed their swords through the air in threat as they slowly approached the woman, laughing all the while in deep ugly tones.

The fisherwoman understood what they had in store for her. She closed her eyes and threw her head back so that her neck stretched before them. And then she wailed. A high-pitched cry it was, like that of a wild animal cornered by the hunt. It chilled Fergus to the bone and he felt himself drawing back from his mother in terror. He had never heard her make such a sound before and it frightened him even more than the presence of the Saxons.

Though the cry had a devastating effect on the boy, it seemed to make no impression on the foreigners, except that they did not immediately come any closer to her. When his mother ceased her piercing wail, she stepped forward to stand between the warriors and her son and, from out of nowhere, an iron hoe appeared in her hands. In a swift and surprisingly forceful move she lifted the tool behind her and struck down at the nearest warrior, hitting him hard in the face so that he fell back with his cheek split open.

As the blow connected she turned to face her son. 'Run!' she screamed.

Fergus spun around and sprinted towards the woods, not thinking for a moment that he should stay to help protect the rest of his family, not considering that this might be one time when it would be acceptable to disobey his mother.

He bolted over the bare hill without looking back until he reached the edge of the woodland. There he stopped for just long enough to catch his breath. Then he heard foreign voices nearby and leapt into the dark safety of the wood where he thought he would easily be able to lose his pursuers. He ran on into the darkness of the forest, forgetting his father's many warnings to stay clear of the woods and unafraid for the moment of the terrible flesh-eating monsters that were said to dwell there.

When the trees closed in and he could no longer see a clear way ahead of him, he sat down amid the rotting leaves and the underbrush. Exhausted, he curled up to weep until, finally worn out by his ordeal, he slept.

And that was where the Saxons found him.

A beggar crouched low amid the mud and dung at the lower end of the hut where the horses of Dun Righ were stabled. His long matted hair trailed in the muck, but the cripple did not seem to care. He leaned heavily on his crutch, lowering himself closer to the floor. He placed one hand flat in the slime to support his weight. His arm sank up to the wrist in the strong smelling dung.

He strained his ears to hear every detail of the conversation taking place outside in the yard. Three warriors were arguing about a white mare that their chieftain intended to grant to a Druid poet as payment for a poem of hers.

'She's another upstart,' one said dismissively. 'I've seen poets like her come and go. He'll pay her well for a while and then she'll get tired of this place and head off to Dun Edin or Londinium or Dun Breteann. Remember Finacre? How long did he last?'

'Finacre had run out of young women to bed. That's why he left,' his comrade quipped. 'This one's got nowhere else to go. No-one else will have her. Gifted as she may be, there are those who say she's half Saxon.'

The beggar moved closer to the wall so as not to miss a single word. The conversation had suddenly become very interesting indeed.

'Don't talk rubbish!' a third warrior replied abruptly. 'I've never met a Saxon who knew anything about music or poetry. They don't have the gift.'

'I've only ever met a few of those savages myself,' the first warrior noted, 'but as I recall we had other matters to settle whenever we crossed paths, so we never quite got round to discussing the merits of one another's poetry.' The third warrior laughed, acknowledging that none of them really knew very much about the foreigners.

'I knew a Druid once who had been taken by the Saxons,' the second cut in, trying to keep a serious tone to the conversation. 'He told me that the thing they take pride in most of all is strength in battle. They are always fighting amongst themselves to prove how brave they are, even at the dinner table. This Druid told me that they commonly take their weapons into the hall, which of course results in many deaths. Music is only ever a distraction from the real business of boastful brawling.'

'Half Saxon or not, she's still not of our folk,' the first warrior said. 'Haven't we enough good poets among the people of this dun? Why does Cathal waste his time with her?'

'She has a way of getting what she wants,' the second warrior said, giving the first a wink.

'Maybe it is more than her Saxon blood that makes me nervous. Maybe she has designs on the chieftainship,' the first snapped. 'In any case Cathal

53

has made his decision and there's nothing we can do about it. I'm going down to the blacksmith to collect the harness. Do you want to come with me?'

The other two agreed and the three warriors strode off down the path on their errand.

The beggar waited a few moments and then carefully concealed his walking stick in the roof of the barn where no-one would find it. He took off his filthy rags and stowed them among the rafters, grabbing a bundle of clean clothes as he did so. Without a hint of the affliction for which he was recognised in the hill fort, he slipped nimbly out of the hut into the yard. There he quickly untied the loop of rope which secured the white mare, supposedly promised to the Druid, to a tree. After checking that he had not been observed, he set off at a fast pace towards a part of the wall where he could be fairly certain the sentries would not be overly vigilant.

The thief came to the place where a few dozen trees grew close together and offered cover for anyone attempting to breach the defences without being observed. He led the horse into the little wooded area, searching for the path as he stepped quietly through the underbrush. He was almost past the guards, who were seated around a stump engrossed in a game of Brandubh, when the white horse neighed.

But none of the warriors could be bothered to rise from his entertainment to find out what the trouble was. They didn't expect that anyone would dare try to enter the hill fort by this route, much less try to escape with the chieftain's white mare.

They went on with their game and almost immediately forgot the slight disturbance. The thief waited at the other side of the trees until he was sure that he had not been followed. Then he expertly mounted the mare's bare back and rode off over the rolling grassy hills towards the north-west.

A lone figure in a long dark-blue cloak, not unlike those worn by the Druid kind during their travels, stood at the summit of the steep hill, watching for any movement along the road. The cloak was wrapped tightly around the body, concealing all in its folds, giving no hint of whether the watcher was man or woman, rich or poor, young or old.

The afternoon had transformed into early evening and the birds were heading to their nests for the night and still the watcher remained on the hill, sometimes sitting, sometimes standing, always waiting, motionless.

When the Evening Star had just begun to show its flickering silver light, the stranger stood up abruptly, cupping his hands around his eyes to block out the glare of the dying sun on the western horizon. In the distance there was activity on the road. From the south a party of riders with wagons and warriors was making its way laboriously towards Dun Righ. Within moments the stranger was bolting headlong down the hill to the place where the road snaked around the lower slopes.

At the bottom of the hill the figure saw that there was still plenty of time before the riders arrived. The stranger checked the road in the direction of the hill fort and then stood in the middle of the path, arms folded, to wait once more.

Because the baggage train was moving no faster than the slowest wagon in the convoy, it was a long while before the leading riders rounded the corner within sight of the stranger. Even then the forward scouts did not notice the standing figure until they were almost upon the place where the watcher blocked their path. Straightaway a junior scout rode back to the column to summon his lord while the two veterans dismounted and kept a safe distance between them and the strange figure. In these dangerous times, when Saxon raiders could fall upon unsuspecting travellers without warning, it was wise to observe strict protocol, especially when it was close to dark.

The lengthening shadows did nothing to ease the suspicions of the two veterans, but the fact that the stranger made no move to approach was to them a sure sign of impending trouble.

It was a long while before the scout returned with three other riders, all of whom, by their dress, were wealthy warriors. The first was mounted on a pure white stallion and it was to him that the scouts saluted. The second rider wore a cloak of blue not unlike that of the stranger. This garment also concealed the identity of the wearer. The third rider wore a very long flowing cloak of scarlet.

The veterans made their report to their lord then remounted their horses to fall in behind him while the rest of the scouts came in to confirm that there were no other strangers in the vicinity.

The lord conferred with the two riders who had arrived with him and, when they had all agreed that this was probably not a trap, they rode forward to challenge the stranger. Ten archers on foot ran up behind them and kept close enough to deliver their arrows if it proved that their lord had misjudged the situation.

The three riders pulled up their mounts fifteen or so paces away from the cloaked figure and waited for a sign from the stranger.

There was none.

The warrior mounted on the white stallion impatiently turned his horse about in its tracks in an attempt to provoke some response. When he received none, he muttered under his breath in frustration and broke off from his companions to ride forward a few more paces.

'Who are you?' he demanded in the tone of one who is used to giving orders and having them obeyed without question.

'Who are you?' an old voice retorted half mocking, half stern.

'I am Murrough King of Munster travelling on the High-King's business,' came the quick reply.

'You are on the wrong side of the Hibernian Sea, Murrough, King of Munster. The business of the High-King of Eirinn is of little concern to my folk.' Then the figure broke into an indulgent old woman's laugh. 'Go home and take your warriors with you. We've seen enough war in these parts to last us a hundred generations.'

Murrough remembered the old Danaan woman who had haunted his wife for so long and it crossed his mind that this figure might be one of those creatures. Certainly her voice sounded very much like that of the hag known as the Cailleach whose dwelling was said to be in the Otherworld.

The king brushed the long strands of red hair away from his face as he pulled the travelling hood back over his head. 'Leoghaire of Eirinn has sent myself and my warriors to clear the Saxons out of Dal Araidhe. These men and women in my party mean your people no harm.'

'It's a strange wisdom that employs warriors in the effort to bring peace,' the figure responded sharply and derisively. 'And how do you think the Saxons will react when they see your brave little army? Will they simply throw up their hands and say, "Oh dear, here comes Murrough, the brave King of Munster. Don't you think it's time we went off home to the land of the Centi? I wouldn't want to have to tussle with him and his clansmen. Sorry for all the raiding and killing and robbing and rape. Hope we weren't too much bother. We'll be off now. Give our regards to Leoghaire." '

Suddenly the stranger's tone became extremely bitter. 'I don't mean to be too critical, but in case it hadn't crossed your mind, King Murrough, there are one or two problems which arise in implementing your grand plan.'

Murrough shifted uncomfortably in his saddle, disquieted that the stranger was speaking in so forthright a manner. The tribespeople of Dal Araidhe were renowned for their blunt behaviour. Often this was construed as insolence or arrogance by folk of the other Gaelic tribes, yet he could not be sure whether she was one of the Dal Araidhe or a troublesome Danaan come to play some mischief on him and his warriors.

Hot-headed Murrough would probably have leapt off his horse and come to blows with this creature had they been anywhere in the five kingdoms of Eirinn. But he was in Dal Araidhe now, where the High-King's name did not impress many people and the customs of the common folk were not as polite as those at the court of Teamhair.

'I have other duties as an emissary of Leoghaire of Eirinn,' the king informed the stranger. 'I have been sent to discover the extent of the Saxon incursions in this land and to see what may be done to prevent the spread of the savages elsewhere.' He did not mention the two young Druids in his company who had been given into his protection. That information was not for the ears of strangers.

'You mean,' the old woman's voice cackled, 'you are charged with ensuring that the Saxons are prevented from landing in Eirinn ... if that is at all possible. Let us be honest with one another. It is a long time since the High-King took a benevolent interest in the troubles and trials of the people of the Dal Araidhe.'

'We have had wars and strife enough of our own to contend with,' Murrough answered quickly. 'Ever since the failed rebellion of old King Dichu of Laigin ten winters ago, there has been constant conflict in the five kingdoms of Eirinn.'

'It is well,' the stranger said, 'that Dichu did not triumph in his ambition to seize Leoghaire's seat as High-King. For Dichu of the Laigin was a weak-willed man, easily led on by evil-minded advisors.'

'And the man who succeeded him as ruler of Laigin is not much better,' the king added. 'Enda Censelach is more dangerous than Dichu because he possesses a certain degree of wisdom.'

'Begrudging respect for a rival!' the stranger exclaimed. 'There is more to this tale than is heard in the first telling.'

Murrough bit his lip, realising he had disclosed too much already. He had no desire to discuss the High-King's other motive for sending him to Dal Araidhe, which was to prevent open conflict between himself and Censelach of Laigin. The King of Munster coughed and turned the conversation elsewhere.

'You have not told me your name or that of your tribespeople,' Murrough said haughtily, determined to get some information from the woman.

'You speak the truth.'

'What is your name?' Murrough insisted, clearly tiring of this game.

'Thank you for asking. I am called Ia of the Cruitne, Druid and judge. I am the youngest daughter of Ronan, chieftain of my folk.'

'Youngest daughter!' Murrough exclaimed, truly surprised that the voice he had just heard was that of a youthful woman. 'Druid tricks,' he muttered under his breath.

'Not so much a trick as a way of finding out who you were without letting you know too much about me,' the woman noted wryly as she briskly walked towards the king. 'It is common sense in these times. I hope you will forgive me.'

Murrough retreated to where the other two riders waited for him. As the woman approached she threw back her head covering to reveal long locks of golden hair twisted around in intricate patterns to keep the strands out of her eyes in the wind. When she finally raised her eyes to meet his, Murrough gasped at her beauty. He had expected to see an old hag before him but she was younger than any Druid he had ever met besides the Wanderers Sianan and Mawn.

'I am twenty summers on this earth,' Ia offered as if she had heard his thoughts, her bright blue eyes sparkling in the twilight. 'In Dal Araidhe and among the Cruitne people it is common for younger folk to take the Druid path.' Ia reached out gently to rub the flank of Murrough's horse. 'What a fine white war-mount you ride,' she commented, flashing her eyes teasingly at the king. 'Do you have a fine wife to match her, King Murrough?' she added boldly.

'He's a man well wed,' a woman's voice cut in tersely. The rider dressed in blue let her mount walk forward as she pulled back her own hood to reveal a mane of tousled red-brown hair. 'I am Caitlin Ni Uaine, Queen of Munster, Druid advisor to the High-King and wife to Murrough of the Eoghanacht.'

For a tense moment the two women sized each other up in the gathering darkness; then, unexpectedly, the younger Druid threw back her head and laughed in a high-pitched girlish voice.

'Welcome! Cathal of the Dal Araidhe sends me to guide you to Dun Righ of the old Kings. You are within five hundred paces of the stronghold. Soon you will be seated in the hall of the chieftain whom I serve.'

Ia turned around abruptly and walked off down the road with an air of confidence. She had gone twenty steps when she realised that the king and his companions were still sitting staring at her, their jaws slack with disbelief.

'Come along,' she called back. 'It would be a terrible shame if the Saxons caught you wandering so close to Dun Righ. They might think that you posed them some sort of threat, and then who knows what they might do?' Without another word, but obviously well pleased with herself, Ia turned around again to walk briskly on to Dun Righ.

Murrough stared after her for a few moments longer before he became aware that his wife was looking sternly at him. Coughing to cover his embarrassment, the king called a scout to his side and ordered the column to move on along the road towards their destination.

Then, avoiding the queen's gaze, he rode back down the column to check that all was well.

fOUR

hile Murrough and Caitlin dealt with Ia the Chief Druid of Dun Righ, two men at the rear of the convoy dismounted. Once they had tied their ponies securely to the back of a cart, the younger of the two went to get a bowl of water while the other, dressed in the black robes of a Christian monk, rummaged around in a sack that hung from his saddle. Eventually he found what he was looking for and pulled out a large piece of flat brown oat bread.

Quickly he made his way back to the last cart in the company. There, tied securely with a long rope to the back of the wagon, was a filthy individual dressed in tattered rags that had once been the black vestments of a priest. The poor dishevelled creature sat in the dirt in the middle of the road, bowed over with exhaustion, his hands chained together in front of him to ensure that he could not escape.

As the monk approached with his small loaf of bread the captive raised his head. The prisoner's face was covered by a leather mask which tied his jaw shut. He could breathe and see only through small holes in the mask cut for those purposes.

The monk, a somewhat smaller man than the captive, decided to wait until his companion had arrived with the water before he risked untying the prisoner. As always he found himself pitying the wretched fellow. He often wished that it was in his power to release the prisoner from this terrible punishment.

'I have the water, Declan,' the younger man called out as he approached. 'How is Seginus faring?'

'He is alive. He has survived remarkably well considering all that he has been through,' answered the monk.

The young man had thrown back his long cloak away from his arms to carry the large wooden bowl of water. He carefully set it down a few paces away from the prisoner. Once his hands were free, he unclasped his cloak completely, tossing it into the back of the cart.

'Shall I fetch one of the soldiers?' the younger man asked.

'No, Mawn, don't trouble them. I'll not be untying his hands, just slackening the restraints on his mouth so that he can take some refreshment.'

The one called Mawn shrugged his shoulders to indicate that he thought even this might be a little risky. He had never been able to understand how Declan could feel so much compassion for one who had committed such a vast array of vile crimes and who showed no sign of remorse for his evil doing. Mawn himself found it hard to look on the prisoner without loathing, for this prisoner, a Roman Christian priest, had been responsible for countless terrible crimes after the Battle of Rathowen. So many people had been affected by this man's actions that Mawn often felt his personal grievance with Seginus amounted to very little really. Yet he would never forget the first time he had heard the name Seginus Gallus.

'He has cut himself badly here on the leg,' Declan observed, 'probably as he was being dragged along by the cart. Go and fetch Isernus for me and tell him to bring a bottle of Origen's healing elixirs.'

Mawn nodded again but did not immediately move, unwilling to leave Declan alone in the company of this unpredictable priest. It was a few moments before the monk realised that his young friend was still waiting at his side. 'Go along now. I can look after myself. One doesn't become the abbot of a monastery like Saint Ninian's without knowing how to assert one's will at times. He will not harm me.'

'Be careful.'

'Don't be silly,' the abbot replied reassuringly. 'He dare not raise a hand against his spiritual protector and custodian. Besides which, my God is watching over me.'

'And I have a feeling that even your God would flinch at having to deal with that one unless he could be sure he was securely bound.' With that Mawn grabbed his cloak and went off in search of Isernus, the assistant abbot of Saint Ninian's and Declan's closest friend.

The abbot approached the prisoner carefully despite his declaration of confidence in the protective power of his God, and only when he was sure that Seginus was in a relatively calm state of mind did he reach out and touch him. The prisoner made no move and showed no objection, so Declan patiently began to staunch the flow of blood from the man's injured knee with a length of clean cloth.

Making sure Mawn was out of earshot, Declan stopped what he was doing and addressed the captive directly. 'You have only yourself to blame, my son. I pleaded with Caitlin to show mercy but you broke your bond one too many times and forfeited any trust that we had placed in you.' The prisoner appeared not to be listening, turning his head so he would not have to look Declan in the face. The monk poured some water from the bowl onto the cloth and then squeezed it out over the wound. Seginus threw his head back and flinched but made no other sign to the abbot.

'We will soon be coming to Dun Righ,' Declan went on, 'where we will rest before travelling on to Saint Ninian's. If you can give me your word that you will behave with the dignity of your rank as a priest of the Holy Mother Church, then I will see that you are released from your bonds and treated with more care.'

The captive still said nothing, behaving as if Declan's words meant nothing more to him than the buzzing of an insect.

'I must admit,' the abbot burst out, 'that I once regarded myself as a patient man, but of late I find that even I am beginning to become infuriated with your behaviour.'

The captive finally showed some recognition, turning his eyes to stare squarely at the monk. Behind the mask the man brimmed with a hatred that seemed ready to burst forth in a barrage of fury. Declan had the impression that it was only the leather head restraint that held his rage in check.

'You cannot go on like this forever, Seginus Gallus,' Declan sighed, going back to the task of bathing the wounded leg. 'One day you are going to have to face up to all that you have done and begin to make amends for your life. I only pray that you can do so before you go to meet the Lord your God in heaven.'

The prisoner's eyes suddenly opened wide in terror and it seemed to Declan that the mention of God's final judgment had been the cause of the unexpected reaction. The abbot took special note of this, glad in a strange way that there were still some things that frightened Seginus.

'Now I am going to take off your mask to feed you,' the abbot announced. 'If you want me to believe that you are going to behave in future, you must do your best to act in a civilised manner. I will need your help in the coming months if we are to complete the task that God has set for us in this land.'

With that Declan reached around behind the captive's neck to untie the restraints. In a few seconds he had unwrapped the flaps of leather and pulled the mask off. Seginus breathed out hard with relief as the leather was removed, and opened his mouth wide to stretch the muscles of his face. 'Thank God!' he cried. The abbot tossed the mask on the back of the wagon and fetched the bowl of water.

'Do not put that thing back on me,' Seginus pleaded, turning towards the abbot. 'I will gladly submit to being tied up to the back of this cart but I beg you to show me some mercy and leave my head unbound. It is maddening to wear that mask.'

Declan knelt down beside Seginus and put the water bowl to the man's lips. 'For the moment the matter is out of my hands. You will have to show Queen Caitlin that you are capable of some degree of remorse.'

'What more can I say to her? What more can I do?' Seginus spat, pushing the bowl away with his face. 'How can I convince her that I am genuinely repentant?'

'It will take more than words and promises, Seginus. Words are open to many interpretations and promises are easily forgotten or broken.'

'I have the desire to pray constantly to God for

forgiveness,' Seginus lied. 'Will you not grant me that opportunity? How can I pray with my jaw bound up like a corpse?'

'There is absolutely nothing I can do until we reach Saint Ninian's. Not until then will you come under my jurisdiction. For the moment you are Queen Caitlin's prisoner and you should thank the Lord she has allowed you to live at all after all you have done. The crimes that you committed would make a Scythian mercenary blush with shame, and your last attempt to escape custody was both fool-hardy and pointless. These people are not Christians, Seginus. They will not forgive your crimes just because you profess a degree of peni-tence. Only when you have served the sentence that is upon you and repaid your debt to them will they begin to believe that you are a changed man.'

'I am a priest of the Holy Roman Church!' Seginus spat. 'No king on earth has the right to sentence me to punishment.'

'In the land of Eirinn, Leoghaire is the overlord and he decided in consultation with Bishop Patri-cius, an ecclesiastical representative as you well know, that you would be left in my charge once we reach Saint Ninian's. When Caitlin hands you over to me I will be your captor, your judge and, if need be, your gaoler. I may not have had the advantage of your years as a warrior but I can be very tough on those who think they can manipu-late me. Serve out your penance like the humble servant of Christ that you are supposed to be and perhaps the Lord will grant you mercy. And make no mistake, Father Seginus, only God can grant you a mercy that will have any meaning.'

Seginus could see that he was getting nowhere with this avenue of pleading and so he did what he was best at in such situations: he changed tack.

'If you cannot save me the agony of the mask then at least let me ride in the wagon for the rest of the journey. The queen need never know that you granted me this one small request.'

Seeing the state of the man's wounded leg, Declan nearly weakened and let the priest have his wish; but then he realised that if he gave in to Seginus now, it would create a difficult precedent in the future.

'I will know that I broke my word to Caitlin and to Leoghaire,' Declan stated. 'And I will know that I have let Bishop Patricius down in his trust of me.'

'But I am so tired. My legs are more weary than I can tell from trying to keep up with that cart.'

'Count yourself lucky,' the abbot replied, trying to sound as if he were unmoved by the plea. 'Weariness of the legs is better than weariness of the spirit. Weariness of the legs lasts only for an hour or two, but weariness of the spirit lasts forever.'

'I know exactly what you mean when you talk of spiritual weariness, brother,' the priest sighed. 'It is a burden you do not bear alone.'

'You understand, do you?' Declan asked sceptically. 'Shut up and eat.' The abbot stuffed a piece of bread in Seginus' mouth to make certain he stayed quiet for a while. 'I won't be as easily fooled by you as others so obviously were. Remember, Father Seginus Gallus, I have seen you at your worst. Remember too that ten years ago you promised to kill me when I refused to fight on the side of that reprobate Palladius in his ill-fated rebellion against the High-King of Eirinn. I will never be able to rest while that threat hangs over me and I cannot be sure that you have truly repented your crimes.'

Just as Mawn returned with Isernus, Seginus

spat the chewed bread out at Declan so that the mess hit the abbot full in the face.

'What makes you want to waste your precious energy on one such as him?' Mawn exclaimed in disgust, offering a clean cloth from the cart. 'He'll never change.'

'Declan has a great gift, Mawn,' Isernus interjected. 'He has the God-given ability to love even the worst among us. He is a saint.' Isernus was speaking from personal experience.

'Be quiet please, brother,' Declan protested. 'I object to you speaking about me like that. I am nothing of the sort. I am just an ordinary brother of Christ who has been placed in extraordinary situations. That is God's design, not mine. If there is anything special about me, it is that God has smiled upon me and given me a difficult job to do.'

Seginus began to laugh as he watched the two men. 'A saint is he?' he chortled like a madman. 'Saint Declan of Ardmór. That is a great joke. Wait till I tell Linus about that.'

The abbot frowned. 'See what you've done! You've started him off babbling about his brother again.'

Isernus bowed his head in shame. In all the years that he and the abbot had worked together it had been rare for Declan ever to reprimand him. He was probably as disturbed by the prisoner's reference to Linus as if he were still alive as Isernus was.

The younger monk strode over to Seginus and looked down at him. 'Linus died ten years ago,' he reminded the priest. 'Don't you remember?'

Seginus stared back wild eyed at the monk. 'Oh yes,' he whispered, 'I remember well enough. And I know the man who killed him.'

Isernus was so shocked at this statement that he

almost dropped the beautiful green glass bottle he was holding in his right hand.

Declan looked at his assistant with compassion. 'Don't let him upset you, Isernus. He could not possibly know the whole story.'

'But I do,' Seginus sang. 'I know that it was you who murdered him, Brother Isernus. It was you. Linus told me.'

Suddenly Declan lurched forward and slapped the priest sharply with the back of his hand. 'Shut up, you filthy creature! Behave yourself or you'll be chained up again.'

Mawn stood shaking his head at what he saw. 'Why do you waste your precious time?' he asked again.

'Is this the bottle you wanted?' Isernus inquired in an attempt to change the subject. He took out the leather stopper and sniffed the liquid. The odour was very strong and Isernus recoiled from it slightly. 'I think this is the liquor that can be taken internally as well as rubbed into flesh wounds. I really can't be sure since I can't read the labels. They're written in Greek,' admitted the monk.

Mawn stepped forward and took the bottle from Isernus. He squinted a little as he looked at the paper that was stuck to the side of the glass. Then he read the words aloud in Greek, afterwards translating them into the Gaelic tongue. ' "Purified spirit of barley. No more than one cupful to be taken if the patient is weak. Do not administer to patients suffering stomach pain or impurity of the blood." '

'Where did a young Gaelic Druid learn to read Greek?' Declan exclaimed, truly surprised.

'Origen of Alexandria taught me. He and my teacher, Gobann, were great friends. Even though

Origen was a Christian he was respected among the wise as if he were a Druid of the highest orders.'

'Even Isernus here who is very learned cannot read the Greek letters and I do not understand them well enough to teach him. But you read as if it were your mother tongue. My monastery would certainly benefit from your knowledge. Would you come with us to Saint Ninian's and share your learning with us? I have a book of apocryphal gospel texts that I have been struggling with for years. Perhaps you could help me.' The abbot shook his head in wonder. 'I am still amazed you learned so easily.'

'I am trained to play the harp,' Mawn explained. 'I can listen to a tune once or twice and remember it forever. That skill helped me in my studies of the Greek language. Origen was overjoyed at how quickly I learned from him. As for the letters, they are similar to the Ogham.'

'The Ogham?' Declan queried, frowning as he pronounced the unfamiliar word. 'What is that?'

'Those are the Druid letters,' Mawn told him. 'We use them only very occasionally to help remind us of important points in a story or to mark boundary stones. They are also used in divination.'

Isernus crossed himself, not thinking that Mawn might have taken the action as an insult.

'And do you know the Latin language?' Declan pressed, getting excited.

'No, I do not,' Mawn admitted. 'Origen rarely used that tongue unless he was dealing with the Roman monks. I hope you will excuse me telling you but he considered Latin to be a vulgar language and he often said so. Among his own brothers he used his native Coptic speech or the Greek.'

71

'Greeks! They always think their ways are the best. Did he teach you any of his recipes?' Isernus cut in. He was also excited that some of the great scholar's knowledge may have been preserved.

'Sianan and I both learned from him how to make the healing liquors. It is a simple process really but very time consuming and it requires great patience.'

Both brothers could hardly contain their joy. 'Would you be able to explain to us the process?' Declan begged.

'I'll do more than that,' Mawn offered, 'I'll show you how to go about brewing the liquor when I come to Saint Ninian's to visit. If Gobann allows it, of course,' he added.

'I'll ask Gobann to release you to us as soon as you've fulfilled your duties at Dun Righ,' Declan promised. 'For now I would appreciate it if you could explain what is written on the labels of all the bottles so that Isernus can make a note of them in Latin. Origen passed away unexpectedly, as you know, or else I would have been able to find out from his own mouth what each liquor is used for.'

A scout on horseback rode by before Mawn could agree. The warrior was carrying the message that the column was on the move again and that they should prepare to continue their journey. Isernus passed the green bottle to Declan who forced some of the liquor down the throat of Seginus. The priest coughed as the fiery liquid hit his throat. Then Declan and Isernus placed the leather hood over the captive's face once again and tied the straps securely in place.

Not long afterwards the wagon that Seginus was tied to lurched forward and the man struggled to his feet just in time to stumble along after it.

72

Isernus made his way back to his wagon while Declan and Mawn fetched their mounts.

'Why do you waste your time with that creature?' Mawn asked when they were both seated on their ponies.

'He is a lost soul,' Declan explained. 'I hope I can help him to find the true path again. That is the job of an abbot: rescuing lost souls.'

The monk paused for a moment then plucked up the courage to ask a question that had been plaguing him for some time. 'I do not wish to intrude, Mawn, but it is apparent to me that you have never shown anything but the greatest contempt for Father Seginus. What reason could a young Druid such as yourself possibly have for holding the fellow in such disdain?'

Mawn looked sharply at Declan, realising that he could not conceal his bitterness when he spoke of the priest. 'On the field of Rathowen ten summers ago Seginus Gallus committed a crime which I will never be able to forget. I watched as his warriors stripped two trees bare and nailed Queen Caitlin's champion to one of them to bleed to death. On the other bough they hung my elder brother.'

Declan gasped in shock and dismay, suddenly lost for words. He realised that nothing he might say could possibly be of any comfort to Mawn. Seginus Gallus had committed the worst of all crimes, in the name of God and with the approval of Bishop Palladius. With a new-found understanding of the task ahead of him in repatriating Seginus into the Church, the abbot signed the Cross and turned his eyes to the road ahead.

In the semidarkness of early evening two warriors leaning on their long spears stood sentry halfway up a hill at the edge of a large wood near the hill fort of Dun Righ. They carried no rush lights, nor were they accompanied by any horses as was customary for warriors in the land of Alba. From deep within the woods, however, little slices of light occasionally escaped through the trees to betray the presence of someone trespassing in among the trees.

It was Sianan who noticed the sentries first, not long after Murrough's party forded the River Cree close to the fortress of Dun Righ. The men were at least two bow shots away from her, but Sianan's eyes were keener than most folk's and she was always on the lookout for unusual incidents to entertain her on long slow journeys. And this was certainly a strange occurrence worthy of investigation. These men had the appearance of warriors, even though they were clad in the flowing blue cloaks of the Druid orders, which ordinarily would have meant they would not be armed with spears.

Pleased with herself at finding an opportunity to leave the plodding of the convoy for a while, she spurred her pony on to catch up with her teacher's horse. As Sianan trotted forward she kept her eyes fixed on the spot where the sentries were standing and took note of how many times the lights flickered within the woods. Reaching Gobann's side, she found him rubbing the stubble where his forehead was shaved in the Druid fashion, deep in thought as he stared at the distant warriors. He was clearly as puzzled as she was by the presence of the blue-clad sentries.

'I noticed them as soon as we rounded that corner,' the poet said even before Sianan spoke. 'I sent a scout out to find out who they were. He rode close to the wood and then returned to report that they certainly are warriors even though they are wearing Druid cloaks.'

'That is a strange thing!' Sianan exclaimed.

'I agree. It is very unusual for Druids to be openly carrying weapons, but it is much rarer for warriors to be adorned in the blue of our order.'

'Are you not going to challenge them?' Sianan gasped, sensing that Gobann was content not to find out what was happening in the woods.

'We must remember that this is not our country,' the poet retorted. 'The Dal Araidhans may be Gaelic folk and many of them have clanspeople living in Eirinn, but their ways are not always the same as ours. If these Druids or warriors or who-ever they might be are engaged in some holy practice, it would be unwise and undiplomatic of us to interfere just to satisfy our curiosity.'

Sianan was not satisfied and she could see by the way that Gobann touched his freshly shaved chin with the tips of his fingers that he was not happy about what he had seen either. The beard that he had worn ever since Sianan had first met the poet had disappeared just before they left the shores of Eirinn. Gobann had told everyone that clean faces were the fashion in Alba.

'Surely the customs of our folk are not that different?' Sianan protested. 'If they are warriors they have no right to wear the blue of the poets or the green of the healers. What did they say when the scout hailed them?' she asked.

'The scout was wise enough not to say a single word to them. He approached them and they low-ered their lances at him to warn him off. It was right of him to ride away without causing an inci-dent. We have only been on these shores a few days. Let's not launch ourselves into a full-blown war just yet,' he laughed.

Sianan pulled the hood back around her face. Like Gobann she too had recently changed her outward appearance dramatically. Her once long locks of jet-black hair had been sacrificed when she had taken initiation as a Druid. With only a thin covering of short hair to keep her head warm, she felt the chill air much more acutely.

While she had been talking to Gobann the company had traversed a long straight section of road. Now they were about to turn a sharp bend that led in a steady rise to the outer defences of Dun Righ. Soon they would lose sight of the wood and its strange guards.

'Let me go and have a look,' Sianan blurted.

Gobann reacted immediately, reaching out to grab her reins. 'I will not! Do you know how dangerous it is for a rider to be alone in this country at night? Even if it were only a short distance I would not let you go. But those woods are too far for us to be able to send any help to you if you were to strike trouble. These people are Dal Araidhan,' he emphasised. 'That means they are the descendants of the Gaels who came here two generations ago from Eirinn to form the independent Kingdom of Dal Araidhe. But in two generations they have intermarried with the Britons of Strath-Clóta and the Britons have warrior and hunting cults that are sacred to them and of which we know nothing. They are to be respected!'

Sianan looked down, deeply disappointed. 'If we were in Eirinn I would be free to go where I please,' she began.

'This is not Eirinn,' Gobann insisted. 'This country is at war. There are Saxon raiding parties everywhere. I don't know how much you remem-

ber of the conflict between Dichu and Leoghaire
for you were quite young at the time, but even the
harsh brutality of that dispute was nothing compared to the brutality that exists here under the
Saxon threat. Dichu was a rebel and he sought to
take the High-Kingship from Leoghaire by violence, but he was not a savage foreigner. He was
a proud and skilled warrior, but he was not cruel,
for he knew the law.'

The Druid poet softened his tone a little then,
realising that he was perhaps being too harsh with
her. 'As soon as we are settled in at Dun Righ I
will find out what is going on, do not fear. The
chieftains of this land may not recognise the High-
Kings of Eirinn but their poets are still subject to
the Druid Council of the five kingdoms. Whatever
the ritual that is being played out in that wood, it
is open to the wider scrutiny of the Druid Council.
As a bearer of the Silver Branch it is my duty to
make enquiries. I promise you that we will have
an answer to this question in good time.'

Gobann released his grip on Sianan's reins,
remembering that she was no longer a novice
Druid. She and Mawn had been fully initiated as
Wanderers. In truth, he knew that he had no right
to hold her back if she still wanted to go, though
he was entitled to try and reason with her. Sianan
was wise enough to judge for herself and the poet
understood that he must allow her to do so.

'I am sorry, Gobann,' Sianan mumbled. 'I forgot
myself. Mawn and I have both been very appre-
hensive since we landed. This country has had an
unsettling effect on both of us. I will try to keep
control of myself.'

Gobann waited for Sianan to elaborate; when she
did not volunteer any further information, he did

77

not press her. The poet was well able to guess what it was that had upset her.

Throughout his life Gobann had experienced a recurring dream about a hill fort built beside a stream near a forest. In the dream a great calamity had come upon the people of the stronghold and many of them were killed. It was only when Gobann had first travelled to Dun Righ many years ago that he recognised that settlement as the hill fort from his dream. It was a revelation that had deeply dismayed him for in the dream Dun Righ was the place of his death.

Gobann noticed Sianan staring back towards the wood as they rounded the bend in the road. Perhaps, he thought, she had recognised the spot from her own dreams. If so, he could understand her curiosity. Best to take her mind away from it for the moment, he decided.

'Cathach your grandfather was much respected in this land,' he began, 'and his younger brother, Cathal, is chieftain of Dun Righ. You will be among your kinfolk tonight.'

'I did not know that Grandfather had a brother,' Sianan said, puzzled. 'Cathach never mentioned him.'

'They were brethren but they were not friends,' Gobann explained. 'Cathal was one of the warrior chieftains who rebelled against Leoghaire during the time of Dichu's revolt. The rebels wanted to appoint their own leaders and refused to acknowledge the authority of the High-King of Eirinn in this country. This placed the two brothers in opposite camps.'

The poet turned in his saddle to catch her attention for he wanted her to understand his next point well.

'Cathal and the other Dal Araidhans managed to

win their independence,' Gobann stated, 'only because Leoghaire was too busy dealing with Dichu and Palladius to do anything about them. They formed a joint kingdom with the Strath-Clóta Britons and elected their own king, Conaire. Such severe breaks with tradition always have lasting consequences. Many families in Eirinn were irrevocably split by the rebellion. Some chieftains in the five kingdoms still refuse to recognise the existence of their clanspeople in the Dal Araidhe. Change is always difficult to accept when tradition is strong.'

'Now it is Eirinn that is suffering great changes,' Sianan noted.

'Yes, and within a single generation Bishop Patricius and his new religion will begin to transform the five kingdoms completely. That is not necessarily a bad thing. All living creatures pass from one body to another at death, taking on new forms as it suits their needs and aspirations. Like a green worm that sleeps in its cocoon before changing into a bright blue butterfly, so the kingdoms of Eirinn are slumbering now. I will not be around to witness the rebirth, but you and Mawn will. It will be your task to teach the butterfly all about green worms so that it does not forget its origins.'

The poet glanced across at her again with a questioning expression. 'Tell me the history of Eirinn's people.'

'The tale of all the invasions?' Sianan asked, hoping that he might not be serious.

'Yes,' the poet replied quietly. 'The tale of the invasions.'

'In the days of long ago, before the Feni or the Desi set foot on the soil of Eirinn,' Sianan began, hoping to rush through this exercise as quickly as she could, 'other races tilled the soil of our homeland, other older peoples who have long since vanished from the world. To the hill of Teamhair the first invaders came, to the lands made fertile by the sweet flowing waters of the River Boann.'

She took a breath and then went on. 'Banba and the fifty women came first with three male captives; but they had not dwelt at Teamhair long before the harshness of the winter snows and driving rains of summer and the wrath of the goddess Dana, who called the land her own, drove them out. With nowhere else to go, they returned to their homelands in the east. Only Banba remained as a guest and a companion for Dana.'

Sianan paused for a second to recall the next part word for word. 'A long while later, after the Great Flood that drowned the Earth, Partholon and his people arrived from the lands far to the east where the snow never melts and the cold is unrelenting. They were not so easily discouraged in their desire to make Eirinn their own. They built great halls and houses out of stone and a fortress upon the hill of Uisneach, claiming that place as the spiritual centre of Eirinn. They ignored Dana and Banba and the other ancient gods, paying them no tribute or respect whatsoever. The Partholonians tore down the forests to construct their homes and cut open the mountains to raise their altars. Greedily they defaced the land for their own pleasure and in time the Old Ones were forced to take action. The gods summoned all their powers and sent a plague upon Partholon's folk which took the lives of every one of them. Their burial mound can still be seen from the heights of Teamhair.'

But then she came to a part of the tale that she loved to relate and so she slowed herself a little to do the story justice. As was the way with the great stories, even the storyteller was falling under a poetic enchantment.

'In the kingdom that was once known as Muinn the mountains are high and jagged and the pathways through them are rough and dangerous. To this land, which the tribes of the Feni call Munster, came the third great wave of invaders to beach their boats on the shores of Eirinn. Their chieftain was known as Balor of the Evil Eye and his tribes were the Fomor who came from the hot southern lands. They were a stunted people, ugly and deformed, masters of the dark arts of spell-making and adept at devising powerful and devastating weapons of war. The old gods did not stand against them, preferring to withdraw into the hills and secret places of Eirinn and live there in peace.'

She shot a glance at Gobann who had his eyes closed and was listening intently. Sianan knew that he did not mind that she was rushing through the story. This was just a test of her memory.

'When the gods retreated,' she went on, 'the Fomor spread across the land seeking out the Old Ones. Whenever they found them they challenged them to battle for, though they had won ownership of the land, they were a warlike people who were never happy unless they were fighting. The Fomor had not long been waging their wars when the next wave of invaders arrived in Eirinn drawn by rumours of the rich grasslands and abundant forests. These folk were led by a man called Nemed. They were a tall people with glowing eyes and a sweet lilting language, but they were no match for the Fomor.

'Balor devised a special weapon to deal with them. On the top of a tower situated on an island to the north, the Fomor built a giant iron eye that could look in any direction. When the Evil Eye lifted its lid, a beam of red light shone forth that could melt stone and turn rivers into steam. The light from this weapon was so bright that it blinded all who saw it. That is how the Fomor became known as the Children of the Dark for the victims of the iron eye were plunged into eternal darkness when their sight was ruined. Faced with such an awesome weapon, the Nemedians soon capitulated and became the slaves of the Fomor. Balor set the eye in the north because his powers of divination had told him that a folk known as the Fir-Bolg were preparing to invade Eirinn hot on the heels of the Nemedians. With a knowledge of spellcraft and the forces of nature, the Fir-Bolg proved worthy opponents to the Fomor. Through their magic the Fir-Bolg Druids brought down a mist that covered the Evil Eye, rendering it useless; and then, on the plains of MaghTuiread, the new invaders fought a great battle against the Fomor. After a hard day fighting, neither side had gained the upper hand and many lives had been lost, so a truce was called. For many centuries the two peoples lived in an uneasy peace until from the west came the mightiest of all the peoples ever to call Eirinn their home.'

Sianan came to the part of the story which dealt with the Faerie folk and once again she tried to slow her pace a little. Had she been telling this tale to an audience, she would have taken a lot more time about it.

'In ships of silver hung with sails of golden cloth came the Tuatha De Danaan. They were a race of bards, poets, blacksmiths and warriors who called themselves the Children of the Light. They carried with them four magic weapons: the Sword of Victory, the Spear of Light, the Cauldron of Plenty and the Stone of Destiny. And when the Fir-Bolg saw them coming, their Druids knew that these folk were unstoppable and so they laid their weapons aside, knowing that they could not defeat such a people.

But the Fomor, led on by the arrogance of their war leader Balor and ever willing to enter into conflict, rose to the challenge of a battle. They gathered all their warriors, both men and women, and every one of them was a crippled grotesque creature.'

Sianan stopped for a second and looked back over her shoulder at the hill where the strange Druid warriors had been standing. It was just a long enough pause to get Gobann's attention.

'MaghTuiread,' the poet prompted.

'At MaghTuiread once again,' Sianan went on, 'a battle was fought and, as when the Fir-Bolg had first come, there was a stalemate. In the battle King Nuadu of the Danaans lost his left hand and was thus no longer eligible for the kingship because of his physical imperfection. The Fomor urged the Fir-Bolg to join them to rid the land of this new invader once and for all. The Fir-Bolg king, Breas the Beautiful, led the assault on the fair-haired folk of the Danaans, thinking that without a king they would not stand long. But Lugh of the Long Hand now led the Danaan warriors and he was a bardic wizard who had enlisted the help of the old goddesses, Banba, Eriu and Fodhla. Lugh slew Balor and then he turned on Breas. The King of the Fir-Bolg surrendered and ended his days in captivity. Thus the Danaans, the Children of Light, put an end to the rule of the Children of the Dark and to the aspirations of the Fir-Bolg. Afterwards there was a long peace imposed by the Danaans.'

The next section of the story was considered by the Gaels to be the most important part of the tale of Eirinn.

'Many ages later my ancestors, the Feni, came to Eirinn. The five sons of Míl led the Gaelic expedition to Eirinn. The Danaans still had their magic arts but the Gaels had weapons made of iron, which was much stronger than the bronze of the Danaans. After a long and bloody war a truce was called between the people of the Danaan and the newest invaders. By mutual agreement the Gaels would take possession of all that was above the ground in Eirinn. The Danaans would take all that was below the ground. Thus Eirinn was split evenly between them. But this was to be no easy peace. At the end of the war only two of Míl's sons were left alive. The Feni argued between themselves as to which brother was entitled to the High-Kingship and in the end the Danaans were called in to mediate in the dispute. Their chief judge ruled that a giant black boar should be let loose from the east coast near Teamhair to roam until it reached the western shores of Eirinn.'

The poet nodded to show that he was happy with the recitation so far.

'The Danaans proposed that a great defensive dyke then be constructed,' Sianan continued, 'running between the place in the east from where the black pig set out to the point in the west where it touched the ocean. When the dyke was built, one brother would take everything to the north of the wall and the other would take everything to the south. The two brothers agreed that they would each have turns every summer as High-King for one full turning of the seasons. On the northern side of the black pig's dyke lived many of the Fir-Bolg folk who had chosen to accept the lordship of the Danaans and in turn the Gaels. It is said that the Cruitne tribes are descended from these Fir-Bolg. They intermarried with the Feni to create a new people who in time became known as the Desi. Ever since that time the Feni and the Desi have been rivals, both courting the support and help of the Danaans in their disputes.'

'And what became of the treaty between those two peoples?' Gobann asked sternly, indicating that she had forgotten to mention that part of the tale. 'The Feni and the Desi?'

'The agreement that passed the High-Kingship between the tribes of the north and those of the south,' Sianan recalled, 'was honoured down until the time of Niall of the Nine Hostages, a Desi king. Niall arrogantly refused to hand back the High-Kingship when the time came and backed up his claims by force. After his death the office of High-King was made open to any candidate who could prove descent from the sons of Míl, though it has been rare that the position has been filled by anyone who was not one of Niall's descendants.'

'What is each tribe known for?' the poet asked.

'The Feni came to be known as Druids of the highest order,' his student answered immediately, 'lawmakers, musicians, scholars, storytellers, genealogists and healers. The Desi were renowned as warriors, hunters, sailors, explorers, travellers and great chieftains. Whether it was the wisdom of the Danaans that fostered these different talents in each half of the kingdom, or simply good fortune, who can say? But each part of Eirinn relied on the other for the survival of the whole. This often fiery alliance lasted until not long before the first Roman Christians came. Then, in a great migration eastwards, many of the Desi departed Eirinn to create a new kingdom on the northwestern shores of Alba. They called their kingdom the Dal Araidhe and they have always been fiercely independent of the High-Kings at Teamhair, even though they were mostly born of the Desi.'

'And what of the latest news of Eirinn?' Gobann pressed. 'What will you be able to tell the people of Alba about our home?'

'I have heard tell,' Sianan began, 'that Bishop Patricius came to Uisneach and there he met an old Druid who related this tale of the Feni and the Desi to him. Patricius, it is said, berated the Desi for their warlike ways and praised the Feni for their knowledge. But the truth is never as simple as that. Many of the Feni were great warriors and many of the Desi became famous Druid teachers. And many of the Feni sailed to Alba and chose to live under the kingship of the Dal Araidhan chieftains.'

'You have studied well,' the poet acknowledged. 'And you have the gift of diplomacy.'

'Are we going to stay very long here in Dal Araidhe?' Sianan cut in, changing the subject before Gobann had a chance to ask any more questions of her.

'I will not leave these shores again in this life,' Gobann answered. 'It is near to the time when I have to move on, just as Cathach did. For most of us it is impossible to linger beyond our allotted span of seasons. You will stay here until it is safe to return to Eirinn. I do not know how long that will be,' he admitted.

Sianan bowed her head to acknowledge her teacher, not wishing for the moment to hear any more of the future. She knew only too well that she and Mawn would have to part from the poet one day, but she preferred to believe that it would be a long while before they went their separate ways.

Sianan noticed then that Gobann was looking towards the heavens, staring at the Evening Star. She knew that he was probably thinking of his soul friend, the Druid woman called Síla. It had been two months since she left Eirinn for Dal Araidhe with the intention of visiting her tribespeople. Soon they would both be seeing the healer again for a short while and Sianan was excited at the prospect of spending time with her other teacher.

Not wishing to disturb Gobann from his meditation, Sianan let her pony fall behind her teacher's mount and soon her mind began to drift back to what was taking place in the woods nearby. Soon after, just as the front of the column was approaching the outer defences of Dun Righ, Mawn caught up with her.

'Hello!' he called out, waking her out of her daydream. 'Sorry to disturb you but don't you think it's time you woke up?' Mawn joked. Then he noticed the frown on her face. 'What's the matter?'

'Nothing,' Sianan lied.

Mawn returned her frown and coughed to indicate that he didn't believe her.

'Well, nothing much,' she conceded, nearly telling him how frightened she was that Gobann was going to be leaving them soon. She wanted to say that she didn't know how they would manage alone without his guidance. But a voice of warning told her that this was not the time. She and Mawn would have to face the future together, without all their teachers. Their path had been decided for them when they were young. The best that they could do was to accept their mission with brave hearts.

'Did you see those Druids at the edge of the wood just back there?' she asked without any of the enthusiasm that she had felt earlier.

'Yes,' Mawn answered. 'What were they up to?'

'I have no idea,' Sianan answered.

'Then let's ride over there and take a look.'

Sianan turned to face her friend and then lowered her voice so that the poet would not hear what she said. 'Gobann warned me not to go off on my own in this country so close to dark, with the Saxons everywhere about.'

Mawn lowered his voice to match hers. 'I doubt there would be too many raiders who would dare come this close to one of the strongest forts south of Dun Breteann. Besides, you wouldn't be alone. I'd be with you.'

Sianan shook her head.

'Once we're inside that hill fort we're not going to have much time to ourselves,' Mawn pointed out. 'We will have to attend to all our duties and obligations. We will be called on to serve our teacher and bear his harp into the hall. As students of a poet of the Silver Branch we will be expected to share our learning with the novices and younger Druids and recite all the tales we have committed to memory.'

Mawn reached out to touch Sianan's hand and then added, 'Since our initiation it seems that there have been so many pressing matters needing to be dealt with that we have had time for little else but Druid work. This may be our last chance for a long time to have a little fun.'

Sianan smiled broadly at her friend. Despite her misgivings she found that she was still excited at the prospect of investigating what was going on at the edge of the wood. 'We'll have to be quick or Gobann will notice that we're missing,' she warned.

'He won't miss us,' Mawn laughed. 'He'll be too busy dealing with formal welcomings and other such business. If we ride quickly over there, have a look around, maybe greet the strangers politely without asking too many questions, then gallop straight back, no-one will even know that we've been away. My pony could do with a good gallop.'

'Whatever we do, we must not disturb the Dal

Araidhan Druids,' Sianan insisted, remembering the poet's caution about respect for the ways of these folk. 'We don't know their customs and we must not risk offending them.'

Sianan was struck with a sudden guilt at going off behind their teacher's back, and she was sure that Mawn had not considered the possible ramifications of their curiosity.

'You're not having second thoughts, are you?' Mawn teased, rolling his eyes to show his disappointment.

'No,' Sianan protested, not wishing to appear anxious or afraid. 'I really want to go with you. It's just—'

She did not get a chance to finish her sentence. 'Well, come on then,' Mawn urged, pulling his pony to a halt and turning around in the road. 'If we're going we'd better get a move on. We might not get another chance.'

Careful not to attract any attention to themselves, the two friends allowed their ponies to fall back to the rear of the wagons. When they were sure no-one was watching, they slipped off the side of the road and backtracked until they reached the bend from where Sianan had last glimpsed the warriors. There they halted and strained their eyes to see if the strangers were still near the woods.

For a long moment neither of them could make out any shapes at all in the distance. 'They've gone,' Mawn finally grunted, obviously let down. 'We've missed them.'

'What's that there?' Sianan cut in, pointing to a sliver of light that seemed to emanate from the very heart of the wood.

Mawn saw the light too, though it showed for only the briefest moment. 'Let's go!' he cried as he gave his pony a kick. Sianan's mount followed after dutifully and the two made their way across the fields towards the lower slopes of the hill.

In the short time since they had left the column, the sun had set completely and the land had grown dark. Clouds blocked out the moon, and the black shape of the wood loomed ahead of them looking like an ancient giant sleeping peacefully on his side.

All the birds had stilled their calls for the evening except for two owls who hooted to each other from just within the wood. The Wanderers rode on until they reached a patch of higher ground that had been levelled out. Here the open grasslands ended and the forest stood like a stone wall, dark and impenetrable. This was the spot where they had seen the warriors dressed as Druids standing guard.

Looking back in the direction from which they had come, they could see all of the downs to the south and east, and further inland the outline of sharply rising hills set starkly against the subdued light of the moon. Slightly to the east of the forest the flames of many torches could clearly be discerned. Not much further on there was a hill covered in spots of yellow light.

'That must be Dun Righ,' Sianan piped up.

At that very moment there was a rustling of underbrush just inside the wood.

'Who's there?' she challenged, trying to sound as though she had not been startled.

There was no answer, only some further movement nearby.

'Let's go back to the column,' Sianan whispered to her friend. 'We're in danger here.'

Before Mawn could answer, a large figure stepped into the moonlight from between the trees. The sudden appearance of a stranger in the dark startled the ponies. Both animals turned their heads away from the noise, neighing in fright.

'That hill you are looking at is known as Dun Righ of the Kings,' boomed a deep, heavily accented voice. 'But this forest is my country and you are trespassing upon it.'

Mawn shot a guilty glance at his friend, finally realising that they may have placed their mission in peril by being so inquisitive. Sianan immediately regretted not taking her teacher's advice. What had they thought they were doing riding across the fields unarmed and at night?

'Who are you?' the stranger demanded. It was obvious by the way he talked that he had not spoken Gaelic in a long while, for though his grammar was correct, he was slow and careful in phrasing his words.

'Stand back!' Mawn yelled, trying to sound threatening. 'I have a drawn sword here and I will use it if you come too close.'

The stranger gave a deep throaty laugh. 'You are not armed. I can see that plainly.' With that he took several steps towards Mawn's pony, reaching out for the reins as he did so.

'Ride Sianan!' Mawn cried. 'Ride to Dun Righ and get help. I'll hold him here as long as I can.'

Sianan managed to turn her pony around, ready to make an escape, but the animal had been frightened by Mawn's raised voice and it took her longer than she would have liked to control him. While she was concentrating on her mount the stranger swiftly caught hold of the bridle of Mawn's pony. His mount panicked at being grasped by unfamiliar hands and raised itself up to kick at the stranger with its forelegs.

But the attacker's hands held tight to the bit. The animal could not raise itself up enough to kick. All it could do was cry out in fear and try to pull away. With a great tug the pony lowered its head and slipped out of the stranger's grip. The man managed to hold onto the reins, however, and so the pony tried to twist its body and kick at the assailant with its hind legs.

As the pony struggled, Mawn's foot slipped out of the stirrup. He attempted to find the foothold again but only succeeded in sliding sideways in the saddle and falling heavily onto the grass. He groaned loudly, winded by the tumble.

Sianan had not got more than a few steps away when she heard Mawn cry out as he hit the ground. With sinking heart she saw his pony break free and bolt off in the direction of the road. No matter what the danger, she could not leave Mawn now. As the stranger was bending over her friend she rode up to the assailant and leapt from her saddle onto his broad back.

'Leave him alone, you Saxon savage!' she screamed.

The stranger did not seem too concerned at her attack. He simply reached over his shoulder, laid a big hand on her arm, and pulled her over his head as if he were removing an old rain-soaked cloak. She fell forward, tumbling head over heels onto her back to find herself looking back at the dark threatening shape of her attacker.

As she lay trying to catch her breath, the stranger drew a steel blade from a scabbard at his side. The polished surface reflected the moonlight as he levelled it at her face. It was a short broadsword unlike any that Sianan had ever seen.

'Lie still or it will be worse for you,' the man ordered. Then he turned his attention to Mawn. 'Are you hurt? Can you walk?' he asked, seemingly genuinely concerned.

92

Sianan was still shocked by the turn of events, so it took her a few seconds to realise that her pony had run off to find Mawn's. If they escaped this predicament, they would have to find their way to Dun Righ on foot.

'Stand up!' the stranger snapped, trying to keep his voice low. 'And help your friend to his feet. He hasn't broken anything. He'll be able to walk.'

Sianan rolled over towards Mawn, careful to move very slowly so as not to provoke their captor in any way. When she was certain that her friend truly was not badly injured, she helped him up.

'Who are you?' Sianan ventured once they were both standing, Mawn leaning against her. She could see that the stranger wore a dark blue Druid cloak and his forehead was shaved in the style of a poet of the holy orders.

'Never you mind who I am for now, my dear,' the stranger answered in what sounded like a mocking tone. 'Let's get under the cover of the woods. There are folk abroad this evening who would surely do me harm if they had the chance.'

He motioned with his sword for Sianan and Mawn to move towards the trees. There, concealed by branches at the edge of the wood, was a path that led into the forest.

'And mind you don't try to get away from me,' he warned. 'I will not hesitate to strike you down if you make a move to do so.'

Sianan cursed her curiosity and her lack of restraint, but she had no choice save to do as the stranger ordered. With Mawn still leaning on her arm, she stepped into the wood. In a few moments they were enveloped in utter darkness and she was unable to tell in which direction the narrow path lay.

Behind her she heard the sound of stone striking

metal and out of the corner of her eye she saw a few sparks fly. Then suddenly the stranger had a torch in his hand and was holding it above his head. Now Sianan and Mawn could make out the track as it wove in amongst the trees. They could also clearly see the man's face.

This was no Saxon. Around his neck he wore an old-style silver torc capped in two dragons' heads, one at each end of its crescent. He wore a very long thick moustache and long wild brown hair tied at the back to keep it out of his face. He wore riding breeches and a white tunic under his cloak.

'You are a Druid!' Mawn exclaimed.

'Get a move on!' their captor ordered. 'This is no time for introductions. Believe me, if we are caught, I will not be the only one to regret it. You will suffer for it too.'

'We are Druids also,' Sianan insisted. 'You have no right to—'

'Shut up!' the man snarled.

Realising that there was very little they could do for the moment, the two friends supported each other as they trudged deeper and deeper into the forest. Before long they passed into a part of the wood where there was no light at all, not even moonlight, other than the stranger's flaming torch. They were so completely cut off from the world outside that to Sianan the glow of the rush light became as bright as the sun.

The track widened a little and the trees seemed to fall back before the light as if they feared what it might reveal. Then, as the path began to climb a steep rise, another light appeared before them, flickering between the trees. There was someone standing waiting for them at the top of the hill.

Another forty paces revealed a boy of no more than twelve summers standing at a fork in the path with a rush light in his hand. The stranger moved close to Mawn and stuck the point of his blade in the young Druid's back.

'Go no further,' he commanded.

Sianan and Mawn stopped dead in their tracks while the stranger passed between them to go to the boy.

'And do not think to try and escape,' he added, turning back to them. 'You would not get a hundred paces before you would be utterly lost in the dark.' Then he greeted the lad who waited patiently ahead of them. 'Fergus, is everything well?'

The boy approached the older man, lowering his voice so that Mawn and Sianan could not hear what was being said. The two strangers spoke for a long while. The Druid, their captor, was clearly very upset about something the lad was telling him. Finally the man turned around and stormed back towards his two prisoners.

'You will not make a sound. Do you understand? If you do, you will be putting us all in danger for we cannot be certain who or what is abroad in the woods this night.' The stranger was abrupt and derisive in his tone. Both Wanderers were taken aback at this breach of politeness but it was Mawn who decided that he had had enough of being ordered around. If this man was a poet, as it seemed he must be, then he had no right to treat them in this way. 'Who do you think you are?' he asked indignantly. 'We are Druids. By ancient custom you have no right to treat us as your prisoners. You are committing a grave offence in behaving this way to us, even if this is your forest.'

'We have a long way to go yet before we are safe in my wife's house,' the stranger answered coldly. 'Hold your tongue and you may live long enough to see one or two other ancient customs dispensed with this night. Your people may wear the blue of the learned orders but that does not make either of you Druids in my estimation. Dress a goat in fine clothes and it's still a goat.'

With that the boy called Fergus lifted his light and led the way down a fork in the path that wound off to the left. Mawn and Sianan saw that the stranger had levelled his blade at them once more and so, without any more argument, they followed the lad, passing carefully by their captor as they did so.

FIVE

he first sight that Declan had of the hill fort of Dun Righ was the many fires that burned around the perimeter of the inner enclosure. He had travelled to this stronghold many times since taking over the monastery at Saint Ninian's, but he had never seen such a large number of hearth fires burning within the walls.

The leading horses of the column would have been a hundred or so paces from the outer rim of defences when the abbot noticed that the fields to either side of the road were swarming with the noiseless forms of warriors grimly escorting the party into the Dun under the cover of darkness.

A shiver ran down his spine as he recalled the first time he had encountered fierce Gaelic warriors. In many ways it had been a situation similar to this one. Ten years had gone by since he had first landed in Eirinn as a member of Bishop Palladius' doomed mission to convert the island people to Christianity. The tribespeople of the hill fort of Ardmór had escorted the missionaries in much the same manner as Murrough's party was being shadowed now.

At that time the abbot had been a young monk with no experience whatsoever of the Gaels. The manner of dress, especially the fierce looking paint with which they adorned themselves for battle had struck him as savage. They also had a disturbing ability to appear out of nowhere. He would never forget the awe they had inspired in him as the bishop's party had approached Ardmór.

But the hill fort of Ardmór was a much smaller settlement than the fortress of Dun Righ. Here there were seemingly hundreds of armed men travelling alongside the wagons, where there had been no more than fifty at Ardmór. And there was a different air to this welcome than that which he had experienced ten years ago. In the short time that Declan had been away in Eirinn, the situation with the Saxons must have deteriorated greatly. Only that could explain the armed escort, the many hearth fires and the palpable tension in the air.

The abbot decided to ride up to the front of the column to find Murrough and Caitlin. Declan had good standing with Cathal, the local chieftain, and he thought his presence might aid the King and Queen of Munster. As he rode forward he passed the small company of Imperial foot soldiers that had accompanied Patricius to Eirinn when he was ordained by the Pope to replace Palladius as bishop of the five kingdoms. These men, he thought, were probably the first Roman soldiers to march on British soil in two and a half centuries.

Bishop Patricius had agreed to send the company to Dal Araidhe so as not to risk offending Leoghaire, the High-King of Eirinn, with their presence in his kingdom. Patricius was a much abler diplomat than his predecessor had been. The Saxon threat to Saint Ninian's proved to be the perfect excuse to send these battle-hardened veterans to a place over the sea where they could not be seen as a threat to the sovereignty of Eirinn's kings.

Murrough and Caitlin's troops were mostly spearmen but also included twenty specially trained archers who marched ahead of the Romans.

After passing them Declan came upon the mounted troops of Munster, of which a small contingent were of nobles, most of whom were veteran warriors. There was also a number of men and women who had joined the expedition in exchange for grants of cattle and shared rights in grazing land when they returned home. These were mostly warriors who had seen service in Leoghaire's armies guarding the coasts of Eirinn from foreign raiders.

At last, having pushed his way through the ranks, Declan reached a small entourage of personal guards who constantly shadowed the royal couple. Recognised as a friend, the abbot was allowed to pass and approach the king and queen, who were engaged in a discussion with Tatheus the Roman centurion. So engrossed were the three of them in their conference that Declan only managed to get their attention just as the royal party reached a point in the road where a great stone wall had been newly erected. This marked the place where the inner defences of Dun Righ began.

Waiting at the breach in the wall was the chieftain of the hill fort, Cathal who called himself Mac Croneen, meaning in the Gaelic language, 'the son of Croneen'. Sianan's grandfather, Cathach, had also used that epithet. The warrior chief recognised Declan immediately; however, protocol demanded that he address the royal party first, so Cathal only nodded in the abbot's direction.

Declan noticed a golden-haired young woman dressed in a dark blue Druid cloak escorting the chieftain out to where Murrough, Caitlin, Tatheus and the abbot had halted their horses. He had never seen this woman before and wondered who she might be.

At that moment Gobann, dressed in a long flowing cloak of Raven feathers, rode his pony up to stand beside Declan's. This beautiful black garb marked Gobann as a Druid of the Silver Branch, a select group of poets who were recognised as among the finest in their own lands. All the main representatives of both parties were now assembled and the formalities could begin.

Without the ritual invitation to enter the dun, not even the High-King with all his armies would have dared to ride beyond the breach for fear of insulting his host. The five visitors dismounted as Cathal approached and waited for the customary challenges to be delivered.

'Who rides in armed force through the land of the Strath-Clóta without seeking leave of Cathal Chieftain of Dun Righ and King of the Southern Dal Araidhe?' the warrior leader bellowed.

Declan raised his eyebrows when Cathal referred to himself as King of the Southern Dal Araidhe. Certainly many things had changed since the abbot had set out for Eirinn. Cathal had not called himself king then.

The woman in the Druid cloak spoke next. 'This lord is known as Murrough of the Eoghanacht, emissary of Leoghaire of Teamhair. He is King of Munster. He has brought his army to offer them in aid to the Strath-Clóta in their struggle against the savages.'

Murrough shifted his feet awkwardly, feeling the same discomfort as he had when he first met this Druid woman. The king realised that he had not made everything about his rank and position clear to her. It was not he who was in command of this expedition. At the risk of breaking with protocol he cut in, relieved that Caitlin had not done so first.

'It is true that I am an emissary of Leoghaire,' the king stated, 'but this army is not under my jurisdiction. My wife and queen, Caitlin Ni Uaine, was given the office of command by our High-King. It is for her to offer the warriors in service as she will.'

Cathal put a hand to his shaven chin and stroked his grey moustache, his mouth dropping a little in surprise. The chieftain looked to his Druid counsellor; she shrugged her shoulders. After a moment's hesitation he spoke.

'Welcome, Caitlin. You are likely the first woman to lead warriors on the soil of this land for at least two generations. Since my people came here in the times of my great-grandfather, only men have taken on the role of war leader. In this we follow the custom of the Britons, who in turn took their tradition from the Romans. In these days only the wild Picti elect women to rule them in battle.'

'And the Gaels of Eirinn,' Caitlin corrected quickly, her stern manner making it clear that she was an able adversary. 'Perhaps a woman's presence will bring a perspective to the campaign that will gain your people the victory you have all been wishing for,' she added.

The comment was well meant but Murrough detected an edge to his wife's voice that indicated she was not impressed with anyone she had met so far in this country. Once again the king cut in before Caitlin had the opportunity to say anything more.

'This is the poet, Gobann of the Silver Branch, my own advisor and a Druid of great renown in the lands of Eirinn.'

Gobann stepped forward and bowed to Cathal who returned the gesture with a flourish to show his great respect. Then the poet stepped back behind Murrough.

'This warrior who stands at Caitlin's side is called Tatheus,' the king went on, continuing the

101

introductions. 'He is a centurion of the Imperial Roman Army and he brings with him twenty veteran legionnaires.'

Cathal's eyes widened in wonder, then he laughed; but he stopped suddenly when he recognised the style of armour and clothes the soldier wore and realised that this was no joke. 'The Romans were driven out of this land by the naked screaming Picti when Cormac Mac Airt was High-King of Eirinn. And ever since that time the kings of the Britons have been trying to persuade the Romans to send troops here to quell the revolt of the Saxon mercenaries. It is a wonder to me that they have finally sent soldiers to aid us, even if there are only twenty of you.'

'I was originally commissioned to escort Bishop Patricius Sucatus on his journey to Eirinn,' Tatheus piped up as if he were reporting to one of his superiors in Rome. 'When that duty was discharged, the bishop placed my soldiers at the disposal of Queen Caitlin to aid her as she saw fit until we are recalled to Ravenna by the Pope.'

'Romans,' muttered Cathal incredulously, 'commanded by a woman! If I told the Council of British Kings about this, they would laugh at me and call me mad. Such a thing was never seen in all the old empire from Gallacia in the east to Iberia in the west. I am nevertheless overjoyed at your arrival. You have come not a day too soon.'

Cathal turned to Ia the Druid woman and issued his orders loud enough that as many people as possible would hear what he said. This chieftain was a man who prized his reputation for hospitality above all else.

'See to the comfort of the folk of Eirinn and house them within the ramparts close to the main buildings. Give the Druids among them the best sleeping places and the warriors the best cuts of meat. I will walk the defences before we eat.' Then he remembered that he had seen Declan earlier and added, 'The Abbot of Saint Ninian's will share the high table with the royal party and will be treated as befits his rank: as a learned Druid.'

With that Cathal walked straight up to Murrough and Caitlin and, lowering his voice so that only they could hear, said, 'Forgive me for not leading you straight to the table. There has been some unsettling news of a large Saxon force massing on the west coast. A rider came to the dun in the late afternoon with word that raiders have been scouring the countryside for food. The more established Saxons have their own reliable supplies and do not generally need to raid too far afield. We fear that these raiders may be the vanguard of a new force. My scouts have not confirmed any of the reports as yet, but I fear the worst and will take no chances. I have roused the people of the Strath-Clóta to arms.'

'We must talk urgently then,' Caitlin urged.

'Let us walk the ramparts together now. There is much to be said,' Cathal agreed. 'Leoghaire sent a messenger two moons ago to let me know that you would be coming, but I was expecting you to arrive much sooner.'

'There were many things for us to see to before we left Eirinn. The High-King was married not three weeks ago and we remained to witness the event. Leoghaire was wed in the Christian rite and he was not sure what the people would make of that. The presence of the four lesser kings meant that the tongues did not wag quite so much as they might have,' the king explained.

'Leoghaire a Christian?' Cathal exclaimed, unbelieving. 'That I should live to see such a thing!'

103

'Bishop Patricius is an aggressive exponent of his religion,' Murrough went on, 'and the new High-Queen is one of his strongest supporters. We were forced to delay our departure until we were sure that this new bishop would not prove to be another Palladius.'

'Palladius!' the chieftain spat. 'That is a name I wish I had never heard. That man has been spreading lies and rebellion in the Strath-Clóta for nearly ten summers. I wish I could find a way to rid myself of him. You may wonder why the Gaels of Alba do not care very much for the High-Kings of Eirinn, but remember that whenever Leoghaire banishes a wrongdoer, a boat sails to the land of the Strath-Clóta and unloads a criminal. When Eirinn is plagued with trouble, Dal Araidhe is sure to suffer also in time.'

'I am surprised that Palladius has not learned his lesson,' Caitlin declared, 'but don't worry too much about him. I have a commission from Patricius to seek him out and arrest him on the charge of oath-breaking. So I may be able to do your kingdom a service in ridding this land of his evil. For now there are many more pressing problems for us to resolve.'

'You are right,' Cathal agreed. 'Let us walk.' The chieftain took the queen by the arm and led her towards the ramparts, Murrough and Tatheus following. Declan stood watching after them, amazed to have heard them speak so of Patricius in front of him. It was then that he understood that he really had gained the trust of many of the Gaels, so much so that they often forgot he was not one of them.

Aldor's plan to use the treacherous actions of Eothain to reignite the waning support of his men succeeded brilliantly. It was a shame, the eorl admitted to himself, that the cost had to be three good warriors. Eothain was a man capable of bringing out the best in those raiders under his command, even if he often attacked the Gaels without the eorl's approval and was often insubordinate.

During one unsanctioned raid at the beginning of the last spring, Eothain had gone too far. At the monastery of Saint Ninian's the rebellious warrior had seized almost everything the brothers possessed. Testing his lord, the traitor had hanged one young monk of the community while the eorl sat in his hall totally unaware of the situation. Since then there had been many such attacks, all without the eorl's blessing.

It was not that Aldor was squeamish about raiding. On the contrary, he rarely shied away from a good fight, but he was only too aware that unless his men were more selective in their foraging, every bit of farming land would be stripped bare in a few seasons and they would all starve. There was a delicate balance that had to be maintained if the very country they were slowly conquering was not to fall victim to famine. How could the monks continue to supply them with food and ale if they were too weak from hunger to bring in their harvest?

The eorl also had to consider the fact that he did not have a large army at his disposal. If the Gaels were subjected to too much brutal raiding, they would surely rise up to attack their new overlords. Aldor was a brave man but not so foolish that he let his confidence get the better of him. He knew that the few warriors at his disposal would not be able to withstand a coordinated resistance by the Gaels while they were in alliance with the Strath-Clóta kings. Until more Saxon raiders arrived from the treaty lands, the eorl's first priority would have to be to establish a secure stronghold for the future expansion of his kingdom.

When Eothain and some of the other men had begun raiding indiscriminately, the delicate balance of the situation in Strath-Clóta had been disrupted to the point of crisis. Aldor had berated them constantly for their lack of restraint, but they accused him of being reluctant to fight. They could not see that he was only being cautious about the consequences of their actions or that their impatience for victory could ruin all their hopes for a new Saxon kingdom. Then Eothain had begun to stand up to Aldor in the war moot where the warriors met to discuss the progress of their invasion.

It was then that the eorl had come to the conclusion that the only way he could be sure Eothain would be no threat to his leadership would be if the rebel were discredited and removed from a position of influence over the other men. Nevertheless Aldor had bided his time through the summer, waiting patiently for the best opportunity of ridding himself of his rival.

As it happened, the answer to his problem had come from a somewhat surprising quarter. When the autumn rains had begun they brought with them a visitor from the southeast Angle country of Centiland. His name was Tyrbrand and he was a rare thing among his people. He was a holy man.

Tyrbrand had not reported directly to Aldor when he reached the peninsula of Strath-Clóta as most of the mercenaries did on arrival. Instead he had spent a moon cycle among the Gaels of

Cathal's people, disguised as a crippled mute beggar. This ruse had enabled him to find out a great deal of information about the people of Strath-Clóta and the defences at the stronghold at Dun Righ. So successful was his initial visit to the Gaelic hill fort that he would often return there afterwards to obtain snippets of information, disappearing for days at a time but always making a memorable entrance whenever he returned to the camp.

However, the most remarkable thing about Tyrbrand was not that he walked fearlessly into the midst of the enemy fortress, but that he had the air of one who has seen things not meant for mortals. He was possessed of that mysterious force the Angles and the Saxon folk called Weird.

Like all of his kind, Tyrbrand's main claim as a holy man stemmed from a visit he had supposedly received from a god; in this case the God of War, Tyr, who had come to him three times during his life cloaked in the guise of a giant Raven. On the occasion of the god's last visit the deity had apparently told Tyrbrand that he must seek out Aldor, brother of Guthwine, and aid him in his fight to win the lands of the Strath-Clóta for the Saxons. So the holy man took a name which meant 'the flaming torch of Tyr' in the tongue of his folk, and he set off in search of Aldor.

Of course, when Tyrbrand had first presented himself to the eorl, Aldor had been certain that the fellow was mad, for he dressed entirely in foul-smelling rags and spoke in a most erratic manner. His hair and beard were dark brown but streaked with clay and lime and full of parasites, which the holy man had an unnerving habit of picking out to chew on whenever he was involved in a serious discussion. Tyrbrand also carried a massive archaic wide-bladed war axe wherever he went, parting with it only when he set off on one of his visits to the Gaels.

Whatever Aldor's initial misgivings about Tyrbrand, he had not been able to help but notice that his warriors showed a great deal of respect for the new addition to their company. Such was the man's gift at storytelling that before long it was rumoured he possessed the power to raise the dead and heal the wounded. A few believed that he was in fact the god Tyr in disguise, come to help establish a northern Saxon kingdom. Whoever he really was, he had given Aldor's eorldom new life and the war leader wasted no time in turning the holy man's talents to his advantage.

Eothain had made the mistake of trying to recruit Tyrbrand to his cause. That was the blunder that had cost the traitor his freedom, for the holy man was utterly convinced that he had been sent to serve Aldor and Aldor alone. In this belief he was fanatical and unswerving, and the other warriors listened to his advice.

Now that Eothain had been dealt with, the eorl decided it was time to build his forces for a final assault on Dun Righ, hoping in this way to rid himself of all Gaelic resistance on the peninsula. This action would give the entire southwest of Strath-Clóta over to Saxon farms and homes. The problem of where he would get enough troops from for this campaign was solved almost immediately and in a very strange manner.

The day after Eothain's defeat five longboats full of Anglish raiders from Centiland came ashore half a day's walk from Aldor's camp. Their leaders told Aldor of how they had been led to this spot on the coast by a huge Raven that had called to them constantly from the morning they set out in search of new lands, until the moment their longships beached. The great bird had then disappeared as if it had never existed. So the raiders sent out scouts to find out more about this land, and within a short time the newcomers had stumbled on Aldor's camp and the eorl struck up an alliance with their leaders. Since he knew the lay of the land and had experience of the local tribes his advice was heeded. But it took some clever posturing of one war chief against another before he was elected as overall commander of the combined raiding force. As none of the Angles could trust each other, Aldor was the only possible candidate for the position.

The eorl could not help but marvel at his luck. One day his men were plotting against him out of boredom and arrogance; the next he was in command of four hundred or more willing warriors. He was beginning to believe that it was more than just luck that had delivered the reinforcements into his camp and that he probably had more to thank Tyrbrand for than he was openly willing to admit. On that last point Aldor was absolutely right. The holy man had brought all his influence to bear on the Angles, even calling on kin ties to achieve the result he wanted.

Aldor summoned Tyrbrand as soon as he heard that the fellow had returned from the Anglish camp, hoping to seek his advice and to inform the holy man of his own plans.

Tyrbrand took four days to answer the summons and Aldor was beginning to lose patience waiting for him, but the fellow turned up unexpectedly at the eorl's tent and, as was his custom, sat down on the grass floor waiting for Aldor to speak. Trying to disregard the fact that the holy man had all but ignored his summons, the eorl offered him a cup of ale.

'I do not drink,' Tyrbrand protested, recoiling from the cup as if it were full of poison.

Aldor placed the cup on the table and sat down in his chair, determined not to be annoyed by this fellow's strange habits and insulting ways. 'What does a holy man drink?' he inquired.

'The purest mountain water,' Tyrbrand answered. 'Though once I took a sip of the brew made from honey that the Gaels drink. But I will not touch ale. It rots the mind.' He tapped a finger lightly to his forehead.

Aldor drained his own cup and then reached for the jug to refill it, ignoring the holy man's warning of its ill-effects. 'I hope you don't mind if I indulge myself?'

'I have brought you a gift,' Tyrbrand announced as if it didn't make any difference to him what the eorl did. 'I stole it from under the very noses of the warriors of the Strath-Clóta. It was the property of the chieftain of Dun Righ, promised to one of his Druid women, and now it is yours.'

The eorl sat up suddenly. 'Where is it, this gift?'

'It is tied up outside your tent waiting for you to receive it.'

Aldor got up from his seat straightaway. Delighted, he strode across the tent to pull back the flap. As he drew the oilskin door cover aside, his eyes fell on a beautiful white mare not very tall but stocky and obviously more than strong enough to bear a warrior in full battle gear.

'You never cease to impress me, Tyrbrand,' the eorl said approvingly. 'She will come in very handy when I lead the attack on the Strath-Clóta.'

The holy man frowned deeply. 'What did you say?'

'The assault on Dun Righ will begin in a day's time at sunrise,' Aldor casually informed him.

'With the number of warriors at our disposal it should not be difficult to overrun the hill fort.'

Tyrbrand lay back on the ground slowly, his hands behind his head. As soon as he was comfortable he began to chuckle loudly. Aldor let the tent flap fall back again and turned to face the holy man, furious at his lack of respect.

'Do your scouts tell you nothing?' Tyrbrand asked between mirthful giggles.

'What are you talking about?' Aldor spat, striding back to his chair.

The holy man sat up on the grass, suddenly deadly serious. 'Were you not informed about the Gaelic reinforcements that arrived on the coast yesterday?'

'I was not!' the eorl bellowed.

'That is because you have not sent your warriors abroad to scout the countryside, have you?' Tyrbrand laughed like an old man who knows all the tricks and loves to observe others less experienced than himself fall for them. 'Your brave raiders sit around the fire all day drinking. What little energy they have they squander gambling for possession of the few Gaelic women they've captured.'

'How do you know about these reinforcements?' Aldor demanded.

'I have seen them. I have seen many things.'

'Why did you not inform me as soon as you became aware of them?'

'Gathering information that will lead to victory is your responsibility. You are the war leader. I am just a madman who believes that he sees visions,' Tyrbrand noted with a sarcastic twist in his tone. 'When you are ready to talk with the gods, I will sit down and plan your battles for you.'

111

'I will send out riders immediately,' Aldor grunted, draining his cup again.

'You will need many more warriors than you have at present if you are going to stand any chance of breaching the defences at Dun Righ. Some of your men have been careless in their raiding and this has put the Gaels on edge. They are expecting a fight. Many of them have been so completely stripped of their dignity that they are eager to face you. They have strengthened the defences of the hill fort and brought in every willing warrior in the Strath-Clóta. Even their women are taking up arms.'

'Women are no match for Saxon swords,' the eorl laughed uneasily, filling his cup from the jug as he did so.

'You don't know much about these people, do you?' the holy man snorted, showing the whites of his eyes as he did so. 'Have you learned nothing about their customs in the whole time you've been fighting them?'

Aldor looked into Tyrbrand's eyes and saw there mirth mingled with pain, reflecting the wild visions he had witnessed. In that moment the eorl had no doubt that this holy man was one of those afflicted individuals who walked the narrow border separating sanity from raving madness.

'It is the women of the Gaels who train their men in the art of war, Aldor,' Tyrbrand explained.'To the north of here lies an island called Scathach's Rock. Scathach is the name of one of the many Gaelic war goddesses. I have travelled to that place and I have seen with my own eyes what happens to those of their warriors who fail to pass the tests presented to them by their gods. The lucky ones are sent to be galley slaves who drive the great ones about in their travels. The unlucky ones become the servants of Scathach, doomed to walk the earth as mindless slaves or sent to serve the wishes of the more powerful deities. Make no mistake, the gods of the Gaelic folk are very powerful.'

'But they are no match for Tyr, I'll wager,' Aldor grinned enthusiastically.

'Are you mad?' the holy man exclaimed. 'You and I cannot count on the good graces of our gods. We have to earn their support. We are just part of a great game that the mighty ones play among themselves. Sometimes our gods gain the victory; sometimes the gods of other peoples are triumphant. It is our duty to strengthen our gods for the fight as we would our own bodies and minds.'

'How do we do that?' Aldor asked, unsure if he understood what was being suggested.

'We must offer them sacrifices as our ancestors used to do before our people became soft and squeamish and no longer thought it necessary to venerate our benefactors.'

Tyrbrand stood up and raised his hands to the sky in silent prayer while Aldor sat back watching in awe. The eorl noticed that the fellow's arms were scarred as if he had been wounded by sword cuts on countless occasions. Both of his hands were missing their smallest finger, but whether he had lost them in battle or in some unknown ritual, Aldor could not tell. Abruptly Tyrbrand's strange and sudden meditation ended and he pointed a long bony index finger at the eorl.

'We must even court the Christian god, welcoming him into our camp before the Gaels have an opportunity to win him over for themselves. I have seen the power of that god at work. With him on our side we would surely be victorious.'

'I know nothing about these matters.' Aldor felt out of his depth and wished that he had not had quite so much to drink. 'But I will do all within my power to ensure victory so that these new lands can be ready for our people to settle in earnest within a year.'

Tyrbrand smiled, showing his yellowed teeth. 'Your power alone can never be enough to ensure your success.'

'Then I will seek the blessings of the gods.'

'Excellent,' the holy man purred. 'You must always listen to my advice in these matters for I have spoken with the God of War and with his son, Seaxneat, friend of the Saxons and the God of Laws. It was he who sent those Angles to us to make sure we can defend our camp until the winter.'

Aldor was certain now that this fellow was not in control of his senses. It was madness to talk of gods visiting like so many friends who come and go from your hall at will. It was not that the eorl did not believe in the deities of his people. It was just that he had no personal experience of them. Perhaps, he thought, it would not hurt his cause if he took such matters more seriously.

'What sort of a god is Seaxneat? How do I seek his blessings?' Aldor inquired.

'Seaxneat is a god revered most of all by the Angles who live in the lands once occupied by the Centi peoples,' the holy man explained. 'Seaxneat gave the Angles that land after he chased the Briton tribes out. So powerful was his presence that the British Centi left everything of value behind them in the rush to escape his wrath. Now he is offering the same service to you because many of your warriors are Angles who come from the land of the Centi. Of course, there are certain conditions which have to be met if you wish him to support this campaign and further your cause.'

'What conditions?' Aldor snapped, beginning to suspect that perhaps all this talk about gods had merely been a thin disguise covering the holy man's greed for riches.

'Seaxneat asks for very little.'

'What amounts to very little for a god can add up to a fortune for a mortal,' Aldor noted cynically, his suspicion that Tyrbrand was attempting to get his hands on a large share of the spoils of this war more or less confirmed.

'It was Seaxneat who taught our people all our laws and stories. Seaxneat gifted our ancestors with the secret of using horses for work and war. He also bestowed upon them their skill at the single-bladed sword such as the one you carry at your side. The Angles of Centiland call that kind of weapon a seax, in honour of their benefactor. Your people may be cousins to the Angles but it is obvious that you do not share the blood of their tribes. You Saxons have forgotten that your folk take the very name of your people from him.'

'Few holy men have ever come raiding with my Saxons. Warriors soon lose touch with the things of the spirit and the old tales,' the eorl argued. 'We have not forgotten the ways of the gods, it is just that we do not have that many visits from them.'

'Believe me, from this day forth Seaxneat will not be far away from you. He will watch over you and guard you and help you to destroy your enemies.'

'You still have not told me what he asks in return for these favours.'

'Seaxneat resides in the spirit land of Wealhall,' Tyrbrand continued, seating himself down again and crossing his legs, speaking as if he were addressing a child, 'where the slain souls of brave warriors spend their days in merriment without ceasing, fighting without injury and feasting without the need to forage.'

Aldor could understand the great reputation this fellow had earned as a storyteller.

'The God of Laws has a white horse,' the holy man went on, 'a stallion who is his best friend. None but the mighty Seaxneat may ride upon him. The glorious dead who inhabit that realm also each have a pure white steed of their own, but every day more and more warrior spirits arrive to take up their seats in the Wealhall. Now there are not enough mounts for all the souls in the heroic company for it has been many generations since the folk of the Saxons or the Angles or the Franks offered a worthy sacrifice to the gods. Seaxneat demands that you send him more white horses so that all the heroes may ride pure spirit mounts. If you fulfil this request, the God of Laws will assure you a swift and complete victory.'

Aldor's eyes widened and he felt his guts tremble with apprehension. He realised suddenly that the mare tied up outside was not meant to be the sort of gift he would be able to cherish for very long. Even to a warrior who was used to ugly battlefield carnage the idea of the ritual killing of a fine mount was a barbaric one.

The eorl had heard ancient stories of how the first Saxons sacrificed horses to the gods, but that had been done in the times of long long ago. In these days a horse could mean the difference between victory and defeat to a warrior in the field. No war leader in his right mind would waste such a valuable resource in a pointless sacrifice.

Tyrbrand saw the expression on Aldor's face change but he pressed on. 'It will be your task to supply suitable horses from among the herds of the conquered Gaels. It will be my duty to slaughter them in the manner of our ancestors.'

Aldor poured the last drops of ale from his jug and pressed the cup to his lips, savouring the bitter taste of the brew. Then, without taking his eyes off the floor, he made his answer in a low voice. 'I revere the things that I can see and touch and hold. I have not met with this god Seaxneat of whom you speak. I have only your word that he has spoken thus. But I know that horses are too precious to waste indiscriminately in the pursuit of some holy folly.'

The eorl looked up at Tyrbrand. 'If your Seaxneat wishes me to send him a gift of slaughtered horses, let him come and speak to me in my own hall and ask me in his own words. If he wants me to follow him and venerate him, let him come here now. What sort of god would send a madman such as you as his messenger?' Aldor spat.

'Have you never wondered what it was that brought me to madness?' Tyrbrand chuckled. 'Have you forgotten so soon that it was Seaxneat who saved your life and prevented Eothain from taking the eorlship? And remember, although you may not have had any previous experience of the gods, many among your warriors have. They listened carefully to me when I told them Seaxneat and Tyr would be angered if they supported Eothain. They heard my advice when I told them you were their rightful lord and would lead them to a glorious victory. The wise ones among your warriors know better than to question the gods. You owe a debt of gratitude to Seaxneat for his indulgence. And though it pains you to admit it, you owe a debt to me.'

'I owe you a debt,' Aldor agreed, slurring his words slightly as the ale began to take effect. He did not allow any of his frustration to show as he awaited the reply.

'Then you must wait until I give the signal before you attack the stronghold of Dun Righ. You must slowly build your forces until nothing is more certain than victory. You must not make any moves before the first winter snow has fallen.'

The eorl clenched his fist, determined not to allow this man to manipulate him. The strong drink no longer made him feel light-headed. Now it fed a rising rage. Aldor looked down at the ground again so that when he spoke Tyrbrand would not see the anger in his eyes. 'I will not take orders from one such as you. If Seaxneat does not come to me himself to warn me of danger, then I will be leading an attack on the hill of Dun Righ within a day. Go and tell your God of Laws that and see what he has to say to it.'

Tyrbrand did not wait to hear any more. He stood up swiftly and moved to the entrance of the tent.

The eorl thought that the fellow was retreating from him like a coward and could no longer conceal his contempt. He raised his eyes to Tyrbrand's and snarled at him, 'Believe these words, holy fool—if Seaxneat proves to be unavailable before tomorrow evening, you would be well advised to find yourself safe passage out of this land. I do not like being manipulated by one of lower birth than myself.'

'Are you sure that is what you want?' Tyrbrand asked with just a hint of threat in his voice.

'I am certain,' Aldor spat.

'So be it. May Seaxneat have pity on you.'

Having experienced the treacherous behaviour of Seginus on more than one occasion, Caitlin wisely decided to take no chances with the priest once the company was within the walls of Dun Righ.

Before she went to walk the ramparts with Cathal, the queen ordered that the penitent be placed in the same chains that had secured him during the sea voyage from Eirinn. He would not be allowed to enter any of the houses in the hill fort but would remain in the wagon in which he had slept since they had arrived in Strath-Clóta. She stressed to the guards that he was to be watched constantly.

Father Seginus Gallus did not struggle when the guards clamped the iron chains about his limbs. He was happy to give everyone the impression that there was no more fight left in him. He stared off into the distance, his eyes glazed over, while the warriors secured him. However, the priest found that as he let his vision blur he could perceive shadowy forms moving about him. Seginus was certain that these grey shades, which he had often glimpsed on other occasions, were evidence that the ghost of his brother Linus was hovering in the background, watching events as they unfolded.

The eerie spectre was less frightening to the priest these days than it had been when he first experienced it. During his time as a prisoner of the Bishop of Nantes he had become quite used to his brother's visits. Indeed the appearance of the ghostly shape was sometimes a welcome respite from the pain of his penance.

As soon as he had been secured Seginus was placed in the back of a wagon and a sentry posted beside him to ensure that he remained alone. But the guard knew there wasn't much chance of his captive being rescued—the priest certainly did not have any sympathisers—so after a while he wandered off to get himself some food and chat with his friends.

Seginus heard the guard stroll off but thought that he had just gone to relieve himself. A long time passed and the man still did not return. Curious as to the warrior's whereabouts, the priest rolled over to look out of the back of the wagon. The guard was certainly gone, but Seginus immediately sensed another presence nearby.

'Are you there, Linus?' he mumbled through the tight restraint of the leather mask.

'I am always here, brother,' came the whispered reply. 'I will never leave you until I am avenged.'

There had been a time when those words would have held nothing but terror for Seginus. Now he found that he was greatly comforted by the spirit of his murdered brother for he was the only one who cared something for what he was suffering. The priest looked out into the night. By the edge of the road he could just make out a shimmering grey figure. The spirit hovered closer so Seginus could more clearly see him. This was not the evil looking spectre that had confronted him in the dungeon at Nantes.

Seginus had been carrying despatches to the Pope when he was captured and thrown in prison by the corrupt and self-serving Bishop of Nantes. Whilst in a cell reserved for the condemned, the ghost of his dead brother Linus appeared to Seginus for the first time.

His brother's spirit had promised to help Seginus escape from the bishop if he would in turn promise to seek out and kill the man who had murdered him. The chill returned to Seginus' flesh as he remembered that first hideous apparition. And then he recalled how swiftly he was delivered from that dungeon once he agreed to the ghost's demands.

Since that time Linus had rarely appeared to him in such a horrifying form as he had in the dungeon of Nantes. When his brother came to him now he had the form of a bright young man with clear eyes and a mischievous expression, which was how Seginus preferred to think of him.

'Is it really you, Linus?' Seginus mumbled.

'Save your strength, brother. No harm will come to you while I am here. You are safe now. Soon you will be released from the Hibernians and given into the care of that fool Declan. In time you must earn his trust and then, when he least expects it, we will strike and take our revenge on them for all the wrongs they have done us. Take care to ingratiate yourself to the good abbot for the day will soon come when my murderer is no more and I am avenged. Then I will be free and you will be able to plan your revenge on all those who have set their hands against you.'

'Declan, Caitlin, Murrough, Patricius and even Tatheus,' Seginus murmured.

'All of them,' the spirit agreed. 'But take care. Be patient. Earn their trust.'

'Yes,' the priest nodded, closing his eyes to savour the thought of retribution.

'I have a gift for you,' the ghost hissed gently. 'Open your eyes.'

The priest peered through the slits in his mask. Linus was holding a beautiful white horse by a golden bit attached to reins of bright silver. Across the chest of the magnificent steed were harness straps of fine red leather inlaid with gold. On the creature's back was a costly high-backed saddle trimmed with black velvet. Their father had been granted such a horse from the Roman Senate for his services to the Empire. Seginus had once longed for such honours himself. Now, however, the prize seemed shallow.

'She will be yours one day, I promise,' Linus sighed. 'If you keep your word to me. If you kill the one who murdered me.' Then horse and spirit faded swiftly from view as if they were no more than smoke dispersing in the wind.

Seginus lay his head down to rest, though he did not close his eyes for a long while. In fact, that night he did not sleep at all. Instead he spent the dark hours planning reprisals for all that he had suffered since he had been captured by the Hibernians. He had a special fate for each person who had wronged him. Caitlin, Queen of Munster and her husband, Murrough, had been the ruin of his former master Palladius, one-time Bishop of Eirinn. They were also Seginus' gaolers, for the queen blamed him for the death of her first lover, Fintan. But these two were at the bottom of his list of priorities, inconsequential in the greater scheme of things.

Then there was Declan, the Abbot of Saint Ninian's monastery, which was also known as Candida Casa, the Pure White House. Declan had worked with the heathens against Palladius, but Declan did not have the excuse of being born an ignorant Hibernian. He had been amongst those monks who first landed with Palladius' mission to Eirinn, and had turned traitor. The abbot had denounced Seginus and schemed against him, but in truth he was worthy only of contempt, hardly of any importance to Seginus.

It was the man whom Declan had protected from punishment that Seginus concentrated his hatred on. The man who must suffer even if the others were never brought to account. The man who had murdered his brother and then settled down to a monastic life without ever having to adequately answer for his crimes. That man would pay a high price.

That man was Isernus.

Sianan and Mawn were absolutely correct in thinking that their teacher would be too distracted to notice their absence. Gobann was so busy with formal welcomings and the business of receiving greetings from his fellow Druids that he did not have time to think of the whereabouts of his students.

When the poet finally had a moment to himself, the warriors returned from walking the perimeter of the walls and he found that he was in demand again. Both Caitlin and Cathal wanted his advice on the battle strategies they were developing and his evaluation of the overall situation.

In between all of these duties he found a little precious time to make inquiries about Síla, who had left Teamhair two moons earlier. When she departed she had promised to meet Gobann at Dun Righ, but there was no sign of her and no-one at the hill fort had received any word from her.

The poet had so many pressing demands on him that when a warrior came to report that Mawn and Sianan's ponies had been found wandering near the outer wall, he lost his temper with the man and ordered him to find them immediately.

Gobann told himself he would have to reprimand his students severely for not stabling their mounts properly. It never crossed his mind for a moment that they might be anywhere but safe within the ramparts of Dun Righ. When the man had gone, Gobann pushed the matter out of his mind and concentrated once again on his many duties.

It was not until the whole company was seated at the chieftain's welcoming feast later that evening that the poet noticed his students were not present. His first reaction was annoyance at them both for being so disrespectful to their host. It was unthinkable that they should not be present for the opening of the feast. However, the poet was wise enough to realise that he was utterly exhausted and probably overreacting. Deep down he knew that his two students would not intentionally ignore their duties. So he sent out one of the younger Druids of Dun Righ to find out what might have kept Mawn and Sianan from the welcoming meal.

Cathal had finished his eloquent greeting speech and cow horns filled with mead were being passed around when the young Druid returned to make his solemn report. He had searched the hill fort from the lower reaches of the defences to the top of the ramparts and had not been able to find any trace of the two students.

'I know this stronghold well,' he added gravely. 'If they are within the walls of Dun Righ, then they have the gifts of the Danaan folk for I could not see them.'

This information left Gobann feeling very uneasy. He had been so caught up with fulfilling his other duties that his main task of seeing to the safety of the Wanderers had been sorely neglected. Without wasting another second he rose from his seat and made his way to where Tatheus was bent over a large flat wooden plate, chewing heartily on a generous cut of roast pork. The poet quickly explained the situation and urged the Roman

124

centurion to do what he could to locate Mawn and Sianan.

'I must remain here,' Gobann explained. 'It would not be seemly for a poet of the Silver Branch to walk out in the middle of a feast.'

From his seat beside Cathal, Murrough caught sight of the Druid and the soldier whispering to each other. Then he watched with interest as Tatheus pushed his plate aside to stand and leave the hall. The king caught Gobann's eye, silently summoning him to the high table. The poet acknowledged Murrough and made his way around behind the tables to where the king was seated. Careful not to say anything in front of the chieftain that might cause unnecessary panic, Gobann explained that Mawn and Sianan had not arrived for dinner, but quickly added that there was nothing to worry about. He addressed the chieftain of Dun Righ when he made his apologies. 'Please excuse me for sending Tatheus off to look for them. They have much to learn about showing respect for their hosts.'

Cathal was not at all offended by their absence, nor in the least concerned about their whereabouts. But then he knew nothing about the true purpose of their presence in Alba. Indeed it had been agreed that no-one outside the small circle of Murrough, Caitlin, Gobann and Síla would be told the truth about the Wanderers' mission or their importance to the plans of the Druid Council.

The poet decided to remain near the high table until Tatheus returned, so in the meantime he busied himself by helping to serve Cathal and the others. It was not uncommon for a Druid to wait on a chieftain or a ruler, but Gobann was one of the poets of the Silver Branch. He was one of the elite who rarely indulged in such gestures and so

125

his actions could be considered as a great mark of respect to the chieftain of the dun.

Cathal's tribespeople could not help but notice that a high ranking and renowned poet was honouring their chieftain. In so doing, the Druid was also honouring them. Cathal pretended not to notice the gesture, acting as if this were an every-day occurrence, but he smiled discreetly at the poet to show that he was immensely grateful to Gobann for bestowing such a high status on him in front of his clan.

It was a long while before Tatheus returned to the hall. Gobann noted as soon as the centurion appeared at the door that he was alone and clearly distressed. The centurion made his way towards Gobann and whispered that he had not located the students; then, at the poet's insistence, he repeated his news to Murrough and Caitlin, striving not to speak too loudly so that only those at the high table would have any indication that something was wrong.

Caitlin, disciplined in the Druid ways herself, listened dispassionately to the report, showing no outward sign that the tidings held any significance for her. Murrough, however, frowned deeply and turned in his seat to address the poet. At that point Gobann placed a hand on the king's shoulder to silence him and Caitlin astutely picked up her cue.

'It seems that your students have forgotten their manners,' the queen proclaimed so that all could hear. 'Do they not know that they are shaming us by failing to appear at the welcoming feast?'

Gobann was thrown off guard a little by her severe tone, but he quickly realised that Caitlin had found a perfect way of making their absence gen-erally known. If someone in the hall had any information about the Wanderers that they had not yet shared, they might do so now.

'It is unlike them to be so inconsiderate,' the poet agreed.

'Yes,' Murrough chimed in, understanding what was expected of him. 'Perhaps they have found more interesting company than the royal party.' The King of Munster turned to Cathal and addressed him directly. 'Have you any idea where the two young Druids might have got to?'

The chieftain looked up from his food, certain that this had become more than a private matter between Gobann and his students. He sensed correctly that his guests were asking him to lend his aid to help locate the students.

'If they came through the breach with the rest of your party, then they are safe. If they are within the hill fort, we will find them. Put your mind at rest. They have not committed any breach of hospitality in our eyes. The tribespeople of the Dal Araidhe are not as easily offended by the behaviour of the young as are our cousins in the land of Eirinn.'

Cathal summoned Teighe, his old steward, and sent him out to search the stronghold with the other servants. With that done he begged his guests to finish their meal in good humour.

The feast was nearly ended and most of the guests had gone to dance outside by the fires when Teighe returned with his assessment of the situation. By that time only Gobann, Murrough, Caitlin and Tatheus remained with Cathal and his nobles in the hall.

'One of the watchmen who was on duty at the parapets when you arrived reported that he saw two riders leave your column before the company had passed through the breach,' the steward announced solemnly. 'It is possible that they did not enter the encampment of Dun Righ at all. I am afraid for their safety if they are still outside the walls and without their horses at night. Wild Saxon bands wander the hills after dark.'

At that moment a clear picture flashed into Gobann's mind of the warriors in Druid robes he and Sianan had seen from the road. The poet had a terrible feeling that the young Druid's curiosity had got the better of her judgment. Sianan must have convinced Mawn to go with her to the edge of the woods to find out what was going on. There was no other explanation.

'We must send a search party out as soon as the warriors can be roused from their beds,' Gobann urged. 'I have a sense that some great danger has befallen them.'

Cathal coughed loudly as if he had swallowed some mead too quickly and it had caught in his windpipe. 'The barricades are not lifted after dark,' he stated coldly when he had cleared his throat. 'It is simply too dangerous to allow our defences to be compromised. We will search for them after the change of watch at first light.'

'In the meantime their lives may be in peril!' the poet exclaimed, forgetting himself in his concern.

Cathal was surprised at the tone of Gobann's voice and wondered whether there was some story here that he was not being told. For a moment he considered granting the Druid his request and allowing the barricades to be raised. After all, the poet had paid him a great honour. But Cathal had been elected chieftain because his people were confident that his first priority would always be the security of their community. That meant the safety of individuals sometimes had to take second place

128

to the greater good of the clan. He knew he had very little choice of action in this matter.

'If they are smart, they will stay well hidden through the night,' Cathal stuttered almost apologetically. 'If they have already been captured, then there's nothing we can do about it save hope they will not be harmed. Either way they will learn a hard but valuable lesson about the many dangers of travelling in the land of Alba, especially on the peninsula of Strath-Clóta.'

'Surely we could gather some of our own warriors to the search if none of the Dal Araidhans are willing to venture beyond the walls before light?' Gobann countered. It did not cross his mind until he had spoken that Cathal might be deeply insulted by the insinuation that his people were cowardly.

'You are naturally distraught by the disappearance of your students and so we forgive you your hasty words,' Caitlin cut in, acutely aware that guests should never offer any offence to their host, however slight. 'I think we would be wise to take the advice of the chieftain and wait the few hours until morning. Our warriors do not know the land and it would be inviting disaster to send them out at night with Saxon raiders abroad. Calm yourself, brother Druid. All will be well. Let us gather again at dawn to begin the search.'

'The best thing we can do now is to rest,' Murrough affirmed. 'At first light we will trust to our host that the students are found. We place their lives in your hands, Cathal.'

'Go to your rest,' the chieftain replied, relieved that good sense had prevailed and even more impressed with Queen Caitlin's leadership. 'In the morning we will do our best to find them. Believe me, if there were any chance of locating them at this hour, we would be out searching right now. But it is better that we wait.'

Gobann breathed in, taking a deep draught of air. He was very tired and almost at his wits' end. Naturally he understood that Murrough and Caitlin had been very wise to play down his concern. The poet resolved that if Mawn and Sianan were found safe he would never allow such a situation to arise again.

Murrough and Caitlin said their goodnights to the chieftain, closely followed by Gobann and Tatheus. Then the four left Cathal in his hall among his own kinsmen to plan the morning search. Tatheus went off to make sure his legionnaires were ready to rise at dawn, while Caitlin and Murrough took Gobann into their own quarters.

The three of them sat in the guesthouse wide awake but silent through most of the night. None of them was willing or able to sleep. Gobann sat for a long while by the hearth fire, prodding it occasionally with an iron rod. Later he moved to sit by the door in case some word of the Wanderers' fate should arrive during the night.

Though he fought off sleep, the poet finally succumbed to exhaustion and slumped forward in his chair, snoring quietly. His dreams were full of visions of Síla and Mawn and Sianan and Cathach. Visions of the past mingled with visions of the future and with sights of things that had never been nor ever would be. His imagination created people and places that he neither recognised nor understood.

At one point he thought he had woken up and was sitting in front of a monstrous creature with fish scales and webbed toes and greenish clammy skin but with an unmistakable feminine air about her. The monster reached out to touch the poet on the knee, and when he looked into her eyes they were full of compassion and wisdom. Had he not met her in the land of visions, he would have been terribly frightened by her appearance. But he felt that she offered no threat to him. Besides, the poet recognised that so many people judged things by their outward appearances—that was why he had cut off his beard: so he would not be out of place among the Dal Araidhan Druids—and he was determined not to do so himself.

When Tatheus came to rouse them at dawn Gobann was dozing, but Murrough and Caitlin were dressed and ready to ride. The king and queen were heavy hearted, fearing that some mishap had claimed Mawn and Sianan, but Gobann woke refreshed and much calmer than he had been the night before.

The poet did not say much to the others. He unwrapped his harp and took her out into the morning to play a welcome for the sun. Gobann had come to the conclusion that whatever else happened he must be more mindful of those whom he loved and cared for on this Earth. If he had not neglected Mawn and Sianan, perhaps they would not have ridden off without his knowledge. The poet was also aware that since Síla had left two months earlier he had gradually lost contact with her spirit; he had drifted away from her in a way that had never happened before. This upset him a great deal for he realised that it was possible that she had travelled beyond the realms of this world into the domain of the spirit.

Gobann could not believe that his friend and lover could have left the world without saying farewell. It would have been so unlike her to do such a thing. And it was strange too that he had not been given any answers in his dreams as to what had become of her or Mawn and Sianan. Resolving that the search for his students would also be a search for Síla, he packed up the harp and carried her to the Druid hall for safe keeping.

When the warriors of Munster and the Roman legionnaires were assembled, Murrough chose ten horsemen from his personal guard. Cathal suggested that the king head more or less northwards towards the foothills. From there, he told them, it would be best to sweep around in a great loop back towards Dun Righ. Murrough was glad of the opportunity to range over such a large area. Even if he found no sign of the Wanderers it would be a chance to discover whether any Saxons had recently ventured further inland.

Caitlin decided to take ten riders, including the poet and a Dal Araidhan guide, to the forest where the warriors dressed in Druid cloaks had first been noticed. Cathal was as perplexed as the poet by the presence of the strange guards at the wood.

'None of my people was abroad before your arrival, other than a few scouts and the guardsmen who escorted your party into the hill fort,' the chieftain asserted as Gobann was readying his mount. 'No Druid from this dun would be foolish enough to wander the hillsides at dusk. It would be courting death or capture. Warriors among my people do not dress in the blue.'

Gobann ignored the inference that his students had not been very wise, though he shared the opinion himself. He was impatient to begin the search—every minute spent discussing what might have happened was a minute wasted.

Caitlin sat high on a warhorse waiting for Gobann to catch up with her. When he had finally mounted his pony she marshalled the party through the breach in the inner wall which had

132

been opened once again to enable all the riders to leave Dun Righ. In the meantime Cathal and a large contingent of his men also assembled outside the walls.

It was the chieftain's intention to ride towards the Saxon encampment on the southwest of the peninsula to see what he could learn from the locals in that area. The only safe way to approach the enemy camp was in force, although Cathal knew that even superior numbers would not ensure that the foreigners would not attack.

Three other scouting groups comprised of warriors of the Dal Araidhe and Roman soldiers were ready to go out on foot to scour the fields all around the hill fort for any clues that may have been left by the two Druids.

Before the groups parted company outside the walls, Cathal gave last-minute instructions to Caitlin and Murrough, mindful that the safety of guests was in the main his responsibility. 'If you find anything significant, send up a thick white smoke to signal the other groups. On that sign we will each send a messenger for word of what has been discovered. And do not give chase to the Saxons if you see them. They have a habit of laying elaborate ambushes for the unwary.'

Then, almost before the chieftain had finished speaking, and while all the other parties were still getting into a marching order, Murrough's team pounded off along the northern road, their horses galloping away as if they had some inkling of the importance of their mission. As Caitlin watched them go she could not help but recall the way she and her husband had both galloped together over the great southern road all those seasons ago in their effort to save the Quicken Tree.

'May the goddess Brigid grant us more success

on this quest,' she whispered to herself as she touched the little black silk bag that hung around her neck. 'And bring Murrough back to me soon.'

Caitlin had a strong sense that Murrough was riding into some danger unrelated to the perils Mawn and Sianan might be facing. She felt a sudden desire to ride after him to warn him, but the leader inside her refused to be distracted from her duty and the queen pushed all such thoughts from her mind. She knew too well how a feeling of foreboding, if left unchecked, could grow until it took on a life of its own.

Calming herself, the queen watched after her husband until his company had disappeared from view. Then, putting her mind to the task at hand, she busied herself organising her own team of searchers, making sure that they were riding in a tight formation that could be easily defended.

Perhaps if Caitlin *had* galloped after Murrough when the compulsion came upon her, she might have seen the lone rider who leapt up onto the road and joined the king's party as they passed the last guardpost of Dun Righ. Perhaps if she had called out to him, he and his warriors would have been more watchful for strangers on the road. But as it turned out, Murrough's company was so intent on riding directly to the hills with all speed that no-one noticed the mysterious rider tagging along.

Gobann had borrowed a war-pony from Cathal's stables since the mounts brought over from Eirinn were not well adapted to the hills and grassy slopes of Alba. It was a strong little animal with broad shoulders and a long white mane which contrasted sharply to its grey coat. As the poet rode alongside Caitlin he became more and more convinced that Mawn and Sianan had simply gone off to satisfy their own curiosity and perhaps met with an accident. In the back of his mind, however, a nagging doubt remained that their disappearance might have something to do with their mission as Wanderers.

When Cathach the High-Druid had been alive, he had warned Gobann time and again not to allow a situation such as this to eventuate. The old man's words came back to the poet and for a moment Gobann was certain that Cathach was present, looking down on him with scorn. It would not be surprising, the poet thought, if the old man's spirit were as concerned for the Wanderers' safety as everyone else.

In Gobann's mind a clear picture formed of the last time he had seen Cathach the Druid. The old man had been dressed in his long blue cloak with the hood wrapped up around his head to keep out the night air. The image would not leave the poet's mind and Gobann realised then that he was experiencing a very intense and immediate memory similar to the visions he had when the Faidh took hold of him.

It was almost as if Cathach were there beside him as he rode along. Gobann even thought he could hear the old man calling out to him. This worried the poet even more for he knew that if his students were safe, Cathach would not bother to visit him in the spirit form.

Abruptly the message grew more intense and insistent and Gobann was forced to rein in his pony as the vision clouded his awareness of the world around him. Caitlin immediately noticed that he had come to a standstill and she ordered the party to halt a short distance away.

'Ride! Ride like the wind.' Cathach's voice cried out to Gobann, and the poet could almost see the expression on his old teacher's face as he called out the words. 'The Wanderers are in grave danger. You must ride straight to the centre of the wood if you are to have any chance of saving them.'

In the next instant Gobann kicked his pony hard in the ribs to spur it on and repeated his old friend's words. In less time than it takes to draw a deep breath he was off over the fields, heading for the edge of the wood. Caitlin called out to him to wait, but perhaps she too had sensed Cathach's ghostly entreaty, for it was only a matter of moments before she and her company were galloping off after the poet as fast as their mounts could carry them.

As they approached the wood Caitlin saw Gobann pull his horse up to a halt and dismount, slipping gracefully out of the saddle. Caitlin was a very skilled rider—she had been surrounded by horses all her life—but for the briefest of moments she felt herself shift in the saddle so that she thought she might lose her balance. The sensation passed almost immediately, but the uneasiness it had caused was still with her when the poet called out that he had found a path into the wood.

'There is no room for horses to enter here,' Gobann yelled excitedly. 'We must dismount and take to the forest on foot.'

'Is there any way around?' Caitlin demanded of the Dal Araidhan guide.

'The wood is bounded by water on two sides,' the man replied. 'There is no way to ride right around it.'

'I am certain that they are in the centre of the forest. We do not have time to sit here discussing alternatives. We must hurry!' the poet asserted. 'Cathach has visited me to tell me to make haste.'

Caitlin did not doubt for a second that the old

High-Druid was present or that the two missing Wanderers were in the middle of the woods as Gobann said. She had rarely seen her poet friend as agitated as he was now. Without any further discussion she gave the order to dismount.

The queen swung herself off her mount, but as she did so the saddle girths broke. Leaning forward, she tried for a second to regain her balance, but before she knew what had happened she was lying flat on her back in the grass underneath her horse. No sooner had she landed than the heavy reinforced saddle fell on top of her, making her gasp in shock and pain.

Gobann reached her side in a moment. By the expression on the queen's face this fall had not been a simple unfortunate accident. Some sort of message, perhaps not unlike the one he had received from Cathach, had been imparted to her as she fell.

The poet's unspoken question was answered a moment later. 'Sianan was here last night, lying on her back on the grass,' Caitlin announced. 'She was thrown here by her attacker.' The queen frowned deeply.

'Tell me what else you saw,' Gobann pressed. 'No matter how strange it may seem to you, for we must have more clues as to where they are.'

'She was not hurt by the attack, but Mawn was slightly injured. I saw a white horse in a golden bit led towards a large open field. The one holding the steed was dressed all in white and carried an unusual and archaic sword.'

'Yes?' the poet prodded urgently. 'What else did you see?'

Caitlin's eyes widened in sudden terror. 'It is the old Cailleach!' she shrieked. 'She has come to take Mawn and Sianan.'

Gobann grabbed the queen by the shoulders. 'Are you sure it is the same old woman who haunted you for so many seasons?' He recalled the dream he had experienced last night. That strange fish creature he had seen had comforted him even though her outward appearance was monstrous. His question went unanswered for the queen was shaking and sobbing.

'I see blood!' Caitlin screamed. 'Blood spattering the white gown and soaking into the ground!'

The poet held her close, rocking her gently back and forth as he might a frightened child until she had stopped sobbing. The warriors stood back at a discreet distance, muttering amongst themselves. It was well known that Caitlin had been followed by a Sidhe-Dubh, one of the dark Faeries, for many seasons. The strange creature was said to have been responsible for the deaths of her unborn babies. That was why Caitlin had left her two surviving children behind in Eirinn under the High-King's protection. Caitlin could not be sure that they would be safe if they accompanied her.

Abruptly the queen stopped crying and settled her breathing. She wiped the tears from her face and sat up as if she had just awoken from a nightmare but had realised that it was, after all, only a dream. The poet saw her change and noted it well for he had a great deal of experience of the Faidh. That other sight often came unbidden and departed just as swiftly, leaving the afflicted person dazed and confused.

'It is gone now,' she announced. 'The vision is gone. What does it mean?'

'I understand the first part. Sianan and Mawn were attacked here last night. We are surely on the right track. But as for the second part of your vision, I have no idea what it could mean,' Gobann admitted. 'Are you feeling fit enough to come with us into the woods?'

'Yes, of course I am,' Caitlin insisted. 'I've walked away from worse falls than that.'

The poet remembered how the queen, though badly wounded at the Battle of Rathowen, had insisted on being allowed to ride with Murrough on his mission to save the Quicken Tree. Gobann knew she could be very stubborn once she had made up her mind about something. How else could she have survived the long draining fight that she had waged with the Cailleach?

'Very well then,' the poet said. 'We must get moving immediately.'

Caitlin got straight to her feet, behaving as though nothing had happened to her. She drew her sword from its sheath in her saddle which lay on the grass, and stuck the blade through her broad brown belt. 'Let us go then,' she agreed.

Gobann took his walking staff from where he had stowed it behind his saddle and, grasping it firmly in his hand, strode off along the narrow path into the heavily wooded forest. The poet had not gone twenty paces when the sunlight began to fade. Soon he could not see even a few paces ahead of him. Cursing his unfamiliarity with the land, he finally had to admit to himself that they would need torches to find their way through this forest. To send a rider back to Dun Righ for rush lights would waste precious time but they had no choice.

The queen chose her best horseman and ordered him to ride off with Cathal's guide to fetch as many rush lights as they could carry between them. The pair were gone for what seemed like an eternity. Gobann paced up and down along the edge of the wood while he waited, searching for clues in the long grass and feeling utterly helpless. Caitlin could hear him mumbling endlessly to himself under his breath.

The queen decided to rest while she had the chance. She had a feeling that she would need every bit of energy and determination that she could muster if they were going to find their way to the centre of this dark wood. As she sat on the soft ground looking out over the fields below the rise, she remembered the Cailleach, the old Danaan woman who had haunted her since the Battle of Rathowen and had only been driven off with the help of Síla, the Druid healer.

'I felt certain that the old hag must have been killed,' Caitlin said aloud. 'I was so sure that Síla had defeated the Cailleach.' Then the queen remembered that the Druid healer had left Teamhair for Dal Araidhe long before they had. She should have been waiting at Dun Righ for them when they arrived. With concern Caitlin called out to Gobann, 'Have you heard from Síla?'

The poet was startled from his thoughts and shook his head tersely, frowning all the while. Caitlin understood now that he was as worried about his lover as he was about the Wanderers, and she found it suddenly easy to forgive him for his outbursts at Cathal and his uncharacteristic behaviour at the feast.

Wishing that the rider would arrive back soon, Caitlin scanned the fields again. All around as far as she could see there was no movement on the road or in the countryside, save for one great white hare which almost bounded right up to them before it realised its mistake. The unusual animal was half the height of a man and obviously capable of putting up a fight if need be. It nevertheless turned away, leaving its feast of woodland berries until another day when there were no strangers about. The hare was no supernatural being—Caitlin had seen it clearly enough to understand that—but such white animals were very rare and their presence often indicated that Danaans dwelt nearby.

The queen lay back on the grass and thought about her children, wondering how they were faring in the household of the High-King and his Christian wife. Caitlin did not care that they would most likely be taught the Christian ways in preference to customs of the Druid kind. She was not even worried that her children's children might have very little knowledge of any of the old traditions that she took for granted. What did concern her was that, should any harm come to Mawn and Sianan, the great plan of the Druid Council to preserve the ancient customs within the framework of the new religion would be placed in dire jeopardy. Without the Wanderers it was almost certain that all the Druid laws, stories, music, healing arts and lore would be lost.

Without the Old Wisdom to balance the fanaticism of the Christians, Caitlin's children and grandchildren would surely forget the ways of the Gaels. She realised that if future generations knew nothing of their origins, they would soon cease to be Gaels at all. They would be merely another conquered people like the Latin-speaking Gauls.

'If a people neglect their past,' Caitlin said to herself, repeating the words of the great Druid teacher Lorgan Sorn, 'they also place their future in peril.'

The queen sat up and drew her cloak around her tightly, but the woollen warmth of the garment did not stop her shivering as she understood how right Lorgan had been.

SIX

awn woke to find that his legs were very cold. His cloak had slid off him in the night, exposing them to the cold air. As he moved closer to the fire to warm them he sneezed and Sianan began to stir at the sound. It was still dark where they had camped in the woods, but high above in the treetops there were little sparkles of light that looked at first like stars. He sat back, his feet near the fire, and stared at them.

'Don't look too closely, young Druid; they don't take kindly to strangers in their forest.'

Mawn spun around to face his captor but could not see him for the stranger had placed himself just beyond the reach of the firelight.

'What are they?'

'They are creatures of the forest. Spirit creatures who spend all their energy caring for this place.'

'Who are you?' Mawn asked. 'And why won't you tell us why you have taken us captive?'

There was no response other than a muffled cough in the dark. Then the lad they had seen last evening walked through the underbrush at the edge of the tiny clearing and entered the lighted circle. He carried a few pieces of firewood and an iron pot full of water. He lay the wood in the centre of the flames and nestled the pot in among the coals to boil. On the other side of the fire Sianan slowly sat up, spreading her cloak out to straighten it. Then she quickly wrapped the warm wool around her again.

'It is so cold in this forest!' she exclaimed, rubbing her hands together under the cloak.

'You will get used to it,' the lad remarked.

'I hope we will not be here long enough,' Sianan quickly replied.

'I cannot let you leave now that you know where I live or the paths that lead to the forest's heart,' came their captor's mocking voice from out of the dark.

'The King and Queen of Munster will come looking for us. Then you may regret abducting us.'

'Since when do kings and queens go searching in the woods for young untried Druids?' The man stepped into the light and Sianan saw in his face a quality that reminded her of something very ancient, like an old oak tree. 'What brought you poking around so near to my home, unwelcome and unannounced?'

'We rode off from our column,' Mawn began, 'drawn by the beauty of this wood.'

The stranger laughed gruffly, not believing Mawn's lie for a moment. 'A long distance out of your way to take in the charm of an old forest. Are there no trees in Eirinn?'

'We did not mean to offend you,' Sianan cut in. 'We just wanted to look on this forest.'

'I hope you do not have the impression that I was born a fool or that I just walked in from the cow pasture,' the stranger snarled. 'Where are your companions?'

'They are within the fortress of Dun Righ by now.'

'Who is the chieftain there in these days?'

'Cathal Mac Croneen of the Dal Araidhe,' Sianan

answered, a little surprised that this man could live so close to the hill fort and yet not know the chieftain's name.

'I do not know of any Cathal,' the stranger admitted. 'But that is not a Cymru name so he must be one of the Gaels who have come to take this land away from the Britons.'

'He is a Gael,' Mawn confirmed. 'He is of the tribes of the Dal Araidhe.'

'I do not have anything to do with those folk; they are not my kin and I do not trust them. What brought you and your people from Eirinn to my country? Is there not enough land for all the Gaels on that island? Have your people taken to raiding like the wild Pretani?'

'Our company have come to reinforce the Dal Araidhans against the Saxon raiders who are harrying the whole coast of the Airer Gael,' Mawn explained.

'What land is that you speak of?'

'This land,' Mawn stuttered in surprise. 'This land and the country as far north as Dun Edin have been known for a generation as the Airer Gael—the coastline of the Gaels. This southern land is the home of the Strath-Clóta but the tribes of Dal Araidhe share this country with the Britons.'

The stranger spat, 'You Gaels came to defend the Strath-Clóta against the Saxons? The Gaels and the Cymru in an alliance? I do not believe it.'

Fergus moved closer to the fire to see to the boiling water, and Sianan noticed that his hood covered his face almost completely. The boy sat down and leaned forward to take in the warmth of the flames. As he did so his hood fell forward to partially reveal the features of his face. Sianan could just make out that the boy's hair had been burned away and the flesh was still weeping from the scorching of the skin. Such was her shock at this sight that she gasped in horror.

Straightaway Fergus covered his face with his hands and retreated to the edge of the light.

'It was Saxons did that to him,' the man explained. 'They murdered his family, burned down his home and destroyed everything that those poor fisherfolk owned. He came to the forest to seek sanctuary but even here he was not safe from the savages. When the Saxons caught him near the edge of the woods, they tied him up and shoved his head into the flames of their fire. Then, when they had finished their sport, they left him for dead. I found him before the life had left his body. I nursed him until he was well enough to look after himself. He has been with me since and very likely he will never leave this place. You are not the first woman to recoil in terror at seeing the handiwork of the Saxons. Even my wife cannot look on him without distaste.'

Mawn looked towards Fergus, moved by what he had heard. 'I too lost my family to a Saxon raid,' he said gently.

'But I see the savages left your body unmarred,' the stranger barked. 'You survived well.' The man stood up and drew his short broadsword. 'Now you are going to tell me what you were doing at the edge of my wood with so many warriors. And if you do not speak, I will do to you what the Saxons failed to do.'

'We were alone,' Sianan said. 'We saw two warriors from the road. That is why we rode up to the forest.'

'There were at least thirty men armed with spears roaming around the edges of the woods before I captured you. Tell me what you were doing there.'

'We had nothing to do with those warriors,' Mawn protested. 'We did not see the thirty men of whom you speak.'

'Stand up!' the stranger bellowed, drawing his sword again. 'I won't listen to any more of your lies. We will see how long you can keep up these stories when you are confronted with the evidence.'

'What are you talking about? Where are you taking us?' Mawn asked.

'While you slept last night I travelled to the other edge of the woods. There, amongst the ghastly work of your fellow Gaels, I chaired a meeting of all the woodland creatures to decide your fate. If you have the stomach to deny knowledge of this atrocity when you are faced with evidence of the crime, then perhaps I may begin to believe that you know nothing of it. Now, get to your feet. I would prefer to deal with you before any of your warriors have the opportunity to attempt a rescue.'

Mawn and Sianan had no choice but to comply. Fergus led the way through the wood again, a lighted torch held in front of him. Behind them at a distance the stranger followed with a rush light in one hand and his sword gripped firmly in the other.

They walked a long way and the forest floor became more and more soaked the further they trudged. Sianan's stomach was rumbling from hunger and she realised that it was probably around midday, when the air suddenly became much colder and damper. Still they marched and at one point Mawn stopped to listen carefully to a sound in the distance. Sianan also halted, wondering what had caught her friend's attention. Then she heard it. Where there had been perfect silence there was now a low thundering noise, constant and deep.

Sianan had noticed many things as they trudged along the track. To either side of the path was an enormous variety of plants and mosses. At the foot of every tree grew mushrooms in a range of colours and sizes, some bright yellows and oranges, others in varying shades of brilliant purple. The only species that she recognised, however, was the tall red fungus with white spots on its crown. These, she remembered, were used by healers to treat pain in the aged or to ease the final suffering of the dying.

Though she had studied herbs and knew as much as one could learn about the medicines that were native to Eirinn, she knew relatively little about the herbs available in this land. She wished she had the time to stop and study all these unfamiliar plants. There was so much to learn here. It was a great pity that their captor was so convinced that they had committed some crime. Sianan would have liked to learn some of the herb lore of this country.

As they progressed, the distant thunder grew in intensity until it was impossible to ignore. Mawn strained his eyes to see what lay ahead and caught sight of a bright greenish light that poured down through the trees, lighting the path ahead. Within thirty paces the strange light had become so bright that neither Mawn nor Sianan could see anything to either side of it. Ahead of them Fergus extinguished his torch and beckoned them on.

The whole area was filled with sunlight where a great hole had been cut in the canopy of the trees. The light descended deep into the wood, taking on the eerie green of the leaves and boughs and mosses. After so long in the dark Mawn found that his eyes were stinging from the brightness and he had to shield them. The thunder was almost deafening now. Sianan had to yell at the top of her voice for Mawn to hear what she said. 'What is this place?' she called.

'I have no idea,' he bellowed back, but had to shrug his shoulders to be understood.

The stranger came up behind them, pushing them along the track until they came to where Fergus was waiting. A few paces beyond him there was a steep cliff and the track fell away as if it had subsided. Mawn walked up to the very edge and then saw what it was that was making such a noise.

Below him there was a huge pool of black water set amidst dark grey-green moss-covered rocks. The small lough was fed by a massive flow of water which tumbled over a high cliff to Mawn's left. The Wanderers gaped awe-struck at what they saw. The waterfall was taller than any tree in this forest and as wide as four tree trunks.

The rocks looked as though the water had gouged out great holes in them with its force. There were caves set into the cliffs all around, and the pool itself was littered with long-dead tree trunks. The banks near the bottom were clogged with leaves and twigs and other debris from the forest. Sianan realised that she recognised most of the varieties of trees that grew around the top of the cliff: she had studied them all in her training.

Ahead of her, on the opposite side of the lough, grew a great oak. On either side of that grew what looked like a formidable white thorn and a spreading holly. Further along there stood a yew tree older than any she had ever seen. Within the circle there grew one of each of the thirteen great tree tribes; birch and alder touched limbs with ash and blackthorn, and so on around the perimeter.

In the centre stood a tree that was obviously older than any of the others. To Sianan it was almost as if all the other trees had come to pay court to this immense and intimidating hazel tree. She had never in her life seen such a massive living creature. She had heard stories of large animals that dwelt in the oceans; she had even seen their bones washed up on the beach. But this was not an animal; this was a creature of the plant kingdom.

The hazel tree was constantly bathed in the spray that flew up as the waterfall dashed on the rocks below. Although it was already past midsummer, there were nuts still ripening all over the tree and not a single leaf or branch was dead. The wind blew down from above, shaking the limbs of all the boughs and the hazel tree also shivered violently. Suddenly a large number of the hazelnuts were released by the breeze and scattered in a wide circle in the pool.

Mawn watched them as they fell, still unable to believe the great beauty of what he beheld. As the nuts struck the water some floated, while others sank almost immediately. Mawn found that his eyes were drawn to the surface of the water as if the hazelnuts had one more surprise in store for him.

In the next second Sianan felt her friend gripping at the sleeve of her tunic and pointing down towards the black pool. He was screaming at her, but the waterfall thundered on and she could not hear a word that he said. In frustration she followed the direction of his finger.

At first all she saw was a little splash which she thought might have been a fish jumping out of the water to catch an insect flying by. Then she saw that indeed there were fish in the pool.

Salmon. Hundreds and hundreds of salmon.

Straightaway she recalled the ancient tale of the Danaans and their pool of knowledge where grew the hazel tree from which the nuts of learning were harvested. In those waters, the legends said, lived the clan of the Salmon of Wisdom who feasted exclusively on those hazelnuts. If a mortal ate of the nuts they could expect no benefit at all. But if they caught and ate one of the salmon clan who inhabited that place, then great wisdom was imparted to them.

Finn Mac Cumhal of the Fianna who lived in the time of Cormac Mac Airt was said to have discovered that pool on one of his many travels. Finn caught a salmon for himself, but before he could cook it he was challenged by Aengus Og, one of the Danaan princes. Aengus informed the hero that only those who were given permission by him could eat of these sacred fish. Since the warrior had not asked anyone's permission before he threw his line into the pool, the Danaan forbade him to eat it. Instead Aengus ordered Finn to boil the fish for the Danaan's supper.

The story went that as the hero of the Fianna was cooking the salmon in an iron pot the water boiled over onto the fire. In his attempt to take the lid off to cool the liquid, Finn's thumb was splashed with the hot soup stock. The flesh scalded and the warrior stuck the thumb in his mouth to ease the pain. Thus Finn Mac Cumhal tasted the sacred salmon and was granted his famous wisdom. It was said that whenever he needed inspiration ever after, Finn would simply suck on his thumb. Indeed since that time, whenever a Druid judge had a difficult problem to solve, it was said that he was going off to chew the thumb, meaning that he had to give the matter careful consideration and bring all his wisdom to bear upon it.

Sianan was stirred from her thoughts by another movement in the water. This was obviously a much larger creature than a salmon and she thought at first it might be someone swimming in the black lough. By the time she had focused properly, the disturbance had faded to a ripple, revealing only that some large animal had moved through the water.

This puzzled Sianan so she waited for the creature to surface again. A long while passed. She decided that it could not have been a land-dwelling creature that had caused the rippling or it would have surely suffocated by now. Yet the animal was too large to be a fish; at least any fish that Sianan knew.

Mawn had also seen the ripples and he too waited patiently for the animal to return to the surface. But it still had not reappeared when the stranger began prodding them in the back with his sword, urging them to follow the path around to the left to where the stream tumbled over the cliff. They were just about to move off when the creature surfaced.

Sianan thought she made out the shape of a human form that had been layered in moss and weeds. However, if it had the look of a human, this creature moved like a creature of the oceans, rolling its body around in the water before diving down into the depths once more. Sianan could feel her jaw drop and then the stranger was prodding her in the back with his sword again and she had to move on.

The path passed under an outcrop of rock leading to a short tunnel which was lit through a narrow shaft in its ceiling. The two young Druids walked another forty steps before coming to a wide cave illuminated by many torches. The noise of the waterfall sounded very distant here. Sianan decided that it must be some trick of the caves that dampened the thunderous noise.

There were tables and chairs and bedding laid out but obviously not made much use of in a long while. In one corner of the room Mawn noticed a pile of armour similar to that worn by the Roman troops under the command of Tatheus.

'This is my winter home,' the stranger announced. 'We will stop to eat now for it is already late afternoon. Rest well tonight; tomorrow we move on.'

He disappeared through a cleft in the rock, leaving the boy to watch over the prisoners with a drawn shortsword. Fergus was careful to keep his face well covered, though he kept a constant watch on his captives.

When the stranger had gone, Mawn wasted no time in addressing his young guard. 'Did you see that creature in the pool?'

The boy nodded almost imperceptibly under the hood.

'What manner of animal was it?'

Fergus stood up, walking to the other side of the cave to check that his master was nowhere about. 'That was the Glastig. She is my master's wife. And she is a monster of the deep who feasts on human flesh.'

Mawn looked at Sianan in amazement and then asked the question that had been vexing both of them. 'And who is your master? What is his name?'

The boy did not have a chance to answer for the stranger came back into the room at that instant.

'I am called Malchedoc the Wanderer,' he announced. 'This is my wife's house and she is of the

Danaan folk, so you are under their protection, but do not think that they will defend you if you are foolish enough to stray outside this cave tonight. My wife has quite an appetite, especially for Gaels. Tomorrow you will appear before the high council of the forest dwellers. Fergus will bring some food to you soon and then you will rest.'

Mawn opened his mouth to speak but Sianan grabbed at his shoulder, digging her fingernails into his flesh. Mawn heeded her warning and held back from mentioning that he and Sianan were also known as Wanderers. He opened his mouth to ask Malchedoc how he got his name instead but the stranger had already gone.

SEVEN

he two riders who had been sent back to Dun Righ eventually returned with two dozen rush lights. Caitlin and Gobann were waiting anxiously for them at the edge of the woods. As soon as they dismounted, Gobann produced a spark from the flints in his tinderbox and before long all the torches were aflame and the company had set off into the depths of the wood.

Every second man in the single file carried a light, and the spare rushes were distributed among all the warriors. There was no way of telling how long they would be within the forest and in need of man-made light, so the riders had brought many more rushes than they could burn in half a day.

Once they had ventured a good way into the unearthly darkness, the party came across evidence that several people had trudged this track recently. Four sets of footprints led along the path which wound its way around the trees and ever deeper into the forest.

'I cannot be sure that this is the same path that Mawn and Sianan have taken,' Gobann admitted to the queen, trying to relax himself so that he could listen to what his instincts were telling him.

'How many paths have we to choose from?' she quipped.

Gobann did not answer. He only looked along the track, perplexed. 'Very well, we will go on until

we are sure whether or not it is Mawn and Sianan
we are following. I know they were brought into
this wood against their will and that if we perse-
vere we will find them.' But Gobann was afraid
that his usual ability to read signs and portents was
failing him.

By midmorning the search party had reached the
fork in the path where Mawn, Sianan and their
captor had met with Fergus the night before. The
leading guards, acting as scouts, reported that all
footprints in this area had been deliberately oblit-
erated. Caitlin ordered a thorough search for thirty
or forty paces along each fork, but it was impossible to tell whether the party of four had taken the
left or right track.

Not wishing to split her force into two, Caitlin
had to make a decision as to which way to go.
Gobann was unable to satisfy himself that his students were anywhere nearby and would not
commit himself to either path.

'Whoever has covered the tracks knows what he
is doing,' he observed. 'I doubt that the best tracker
in Eirinn would be able to tell if anyone has passed
this way.'

Caitlin had to agree. 'He has done his job well,
which tells me that he did not want to chance being
followed. This makes it more likely that if Sianan
and Mawn are among this group of four travellers,
then they are unwilling in their journey. Whatever
we do we must make haste.'

'It is also possible that the party split at this
crossroads, two travellers going to the left and two
to the right,' the poet offered.

Caitlin considered that possibility for a short
while, then with resignation made her decision.
'We will all follow the right-hand track. I know that
we are taking the risk of following the wrong path,

but we have no alternative save to make a choice and hope for the best.' Without another moment's hesitation she strode ahead hastily, a torch held above her and the search party following.

Wherever the track was straight for any distance, the scouts had to run to keep a faster pace than Caitlin. Everyone moved with greater urgency now, but neither the queen nor any of her warriors had any way of knowing that Sianan and Mawn had in fact been forced down the other fork in the path.

Gobann judged that it was about midday when they stopped to rest by a swift flowing stream that cut across the path. It was still very dark for the tree covering had not thinned at all and they had not come upon a single clearing. The poet seated himself on a stone by the stream and removed his boots so that he could dangle his feet in the cool water.

Gobann had expected that it would be quite cold in the forest because the sunshine could not penetrate the canopy of leaves, but the air was surprisingly warm. As he bathed his feet he decided that this must be because there was no breeze at all and the trees all grew so close together.

The poet had just splashed his face in preparation to rise when he noticed on the opposite bank a tree that he could not immediately identify. It was unusual for Gobann to come across any plant he did not recognise. He had spent many seasons studying the secret lore of the trees and was conversant with all the many varieties that made Eirinn and Alba their home, even those that the Romans had brought with them to Britain.

Cautiously he crossed the stream to take a closer look, wading through the cool waters with his boots tucked under his arm. He went up to the unfamiliar bough and placed his hand flat against the bark. One thing was immediately obvious to him: this tree was immeasurably old. Still unable to put a name to the tree's clan, Gobann called out to Caitlin to come and see what she made of it. She was just as surprised as the poet to discover such an ancient bough, but it stirred a memory in her almost as soon as she saw it.

'It reminds me of the Quicken Tree,' she said as she laid the flat of her hand against the thin bark. 'I get a strange feeling from it, almost as if the tree is observing us and passing judgment in some way.'

Gobann looked up at the tree's canopy to see if he could recognise the foliage or some of the fruit, but the poor light of the torches did not permit him to see much. 'If I didn't know better, I would say that this is a white thorn tree. An impossibly large one, I'll grant you, but a white thorn nevertheless.'

The poet bent down to pick up some of the fallen leaves that lay about the trunk. As he held them up both he and Caitlin let their mouths drop open in astonishment. 'I swear it is a white thorn tree,' Gobann stammered and then he craned his neck to look up to where its branches blended with those of all the other trees.

At that moment one of the guards came to report that he had found footprints in the track ahead. This time there were six separate sets of prints leading along the path in the same direction that they were travelling. Caitlin did not waste another second in calling the warriors to assemble. Gobann, however, stood by the massive tree trunk a little while longer. White thorn, he knew, was the tree that the Danaans held especially sacred.

In the land of Eirinn it was forbidden to cut a white thorn on pain of banishment. But the High-

King's punishment was nothing compared to the vengeance of the Sidhe folk. They had a reputation for brutality when it came to penalising those who had desecrated their holy trees.

As a boy the poet had been told the story of a chieftain called Turnan who lived in the north of Eirinn. Turnan had ordered the cutting of an old white thorn to make way for the construction of a defensive wall. On the day that the tree was to be cut, an old woman came to the chieftain and warned him not to injure the white thorn.

She told Turnan that if the tree was cut the Danaans would seek a fine for the murder of one of their kin. Such fines were known as eric payments and were commonly levied against murderers. The chieftain had never heard of an eric fine levied against a cut tree and he certainly wasn't afraid of the old woman. None of his warriors, however, would lift an axe to cut the tree. In the end Turnan chopped the white thorn down himself and made a fine chair out of its timber. Before the passing of a moon the chieftain had disappeared without a trace.

In his absence the people were beset with a famine, all their cattle withered and died, and no children were born to them for three summers. Whichever man or woman sat in the chieftain's chair fashioned out of the white thorn's timber took ill within a short while and died. In time no-one would dare accept the chieftainship out of fear of the consequences. Eventually the entire tribe moved on over the sea to Dal Araidhe in the great exodus of the northern folk. There at last they were said to have rediscovered the prosperity they had known before their greedy chieftain had offended the Danaans.

As for Turnan, Gobann had heard that the man

was returned to his dun after all the rest of his people had gone over the sea. Turnan lived in the deserted settlement, maddened by his ordeal at the hands of the Danaans and, it was said, mindful ever after of all living things.

Gobann touched the bark of the trunk once more in a silent farewell. Then he pulled his boots on and raced off to catch up with the rest of the party, who by this time had advanced quite a distance along the path. After that the poet took a lot more notice of the trees and shrubs that grew beside the track, and before long he discerned a definite pattern in their arrangement.

On either side of the path a pair of birch trees, symbolic of the new year to anyone who knew the Druid ways, intertwined their branches with two rowan trees, which gave their name to the second month of the season cycle. Two alders were next in line. To one who was learned in the ways of the moon cycles, their arrangement clearly represented the third month. Then came two willows for the fourth month of the cycle, and so on down the rows of trees until the thirteenth month which was represented by two elder trees. Then the cycle repeated itself, starting once more with the birches.

It was obvious that this was no chance arrangement. These trees must have been deliberately placed in this order many generations ago to symbolise the passing of the seasons.

After a while Gobann realised something else. All of these trees were very ancient, but the further one walked along the track, the younger the trees became. The poet understood then that someone had planted one pair of trees of each variety to mark every phase of the moon, going back perhaps to long before the times of the Roman lordship of Britain.

Gobann knew that seeds will not sprout in the colder seasons and so it was obvious to him that the Danaans had lent their skill to the arrangement of this forest. Only the ancient ones had the necessary knowledge to create such a marvel as this avenue of the seasons.

Later he was struck by the idea that as the members of the company passed each bough on the track they were journeying not simply along a woodland track, but also through the seasons as symbolised by the arrangement of the trees. But most exciting of all they were, even now, headed inexorably towards the spot where the last two trees must have been planted to represent the present phase of the moon. After that there would be a place where no trees grew at all. That place would represent the unrealised future.

In terms of the Druidic philosophy this configuration was a perfect illustration of the changing cycles of the world. How Cathach would have admired the ambitious gardeners responsible for this wonder. The poet could almost hear his old teacher repeating the liturgy that he loved so well.

'At every moment new life springs forth,' Gobann said under his breath, 'and every living thing is linked to every other being in an intricate pattern that repeats itself forever and will still do so long after the chieftains and kings of our time are turned to dust and forgotten. As the leaves and dead branches of the forest enrich the soil that lies at the base of each tree, so too do all living things enrich those with whom they share the Earth.'

Gobann stopped in his tracks for a moment and took a deep breath. Then he recalled a verse that dealt with this subject.

*'Every acorn that pushes its new green leafy stem
into the sunlight
Knows that one day it will be as all its ancestors
are and does not fear the future.
Only the human kind forget
That there is a secret force in the world
That guides us on our path.
Even the bee who leaves his hive and sets out for
fields unknown
Finds his way home again at the end and trusts
in the watching eyes
Of the spirit kind, our guardians.
The seasons pass and with them all things change,
And because they change all things remain the
same.
World without end. World without end.'*

Murrough and his team of horsemen galloped over
the ground that rose steadily towards the northern
hills. They pressed on without stopping until their
mounts, needing water and rest, began to show the
strain of the hard ride. Murrough knew that if he
did not give the horses some rest soon, they would
not be able to keep up the pace. He also understood that if they came across any Saxons, his
warriors would need all the speed their horses
could give them if they were to escape. He was not
willing to engage in any fighting. That was not the
purpose of this expedition.

On a hillside far above Dun Righ the king
noticed a brook that tumbled noisily over jagged
rocks down towards the River Cree. In a place
where the water slowed somewhat he decided to
call the company to a halt, and there his troops

dismounted. He set sentries to watch so that the company would not be ambushed while their mounts rested, then he grabbed his saddlebags and led his horse to the brook for a well-earned drink.

While his men shared their rations Murrough chose a quiet spot to do some thinking and to decide in which direction he should aim the search. It was about time they swung around in an arch to carry their hunt back down towards Dun Righ. The king knew they had little chance of finding Mawn and Sianan. This mission was in truth more of an opportunity for him to make some detailed maps of the area and to discover whether any of the Saxons had been abroad in the north.

Murrough took out a piece of charcoal from his saddlebag and rubbed it into his hand to see that it was of a good enough quality to make a drawing. On the grass near the edge of the pool he laid out a smoothed sheet of goatskin that had been cleaned of all hairs and carefully dried. He examined the skin closely. When he was satisfied that the sheet was in good condition, Murrough sat down on the grass to note all that he had seen so far. First of all he sketched in the hills and the stream and the approximate position of Dun Righ. Then he tried to make the signs for different trees in the Ogham script, as Caitlin had taught him, to indicate the position of the forest. But Murrough was not as confident with letters as he was with sketching and soon abandoned the script for a drawn representation of the River Cree, which he could see sparkling in the distance like a silvery snake.

After a while Murrough finished his map and laid it aside. It was obvious to him that the Saxons, who had few horses, would probably not bother raiding in these hills unless they fell on hard times. Even so, the number of settlements up here had obviously dwindled since the coming of the foreigners. The dozens of empty dwellings they had passed attested to this. It seemed that the folk from this peninsula preferred to live close to Cathal's stronghold rather than risk living this far out in the wilds.

There was nothing to be seen in these hills, he decided, and then he began to question why the chieftain had suggested he ride up here at all. The king tried to remember if Cathal had mentioned whether the Saxons had ever launched an assault on Dun Righ itself. In all the briefings on the defences that Cathal had given them, Murrough could not recall any mention of a Saxon attack ever having taken place. The king shrugged off his confusion and resolved to bring the matter up when he returned to the stronghold.

All about him was lush countryside and it seemed a pity to Murrough that so much good cattle land up here was lying empty because of the fear of raiders. Raiders who probably would never venture here anyway.

Stirred from his thoughts by a movement a few paces away, Murrough realised that one of his warriors was standing nearby, probably waiting for the order to move on. The man had his cloak wrapped about him so that it covered his face, and his arms were folded firmly in front of him.

'Assemble the men,' Murrough ordered. 'We'll move on back towards the dun as soon as everyone is mounted.'

As he began to roll up his map Murrough noticed out of the corner of his eye that the man had not moved to do his bidding.

'Did you hear me? Gather the warriors,' he repeated.

The horseman still did not make a move.

'What is your name?' the king demanded, surprised that one of his men would dare be so impudent as to ignore him.

The warrior coughed a little and then slowly drew back the hood that concealed his face. From underneath the riding cloak a mass of yellow-gold hair tumbled over the warrior's shoulder. 'Didn't you recognise me?' a soft voice chided. 'It is me, Ia the Druid.'

Murrough was dumbfounded. 'When did you catch up with us?' he sputtered. 'Why didn't my sentries announce your arrival?'

'I have been travelling with you since you left the hill fort,' she laughed. 'Don't tell me you didn't notice.'

'I have had my mind on other things,' Murrough admitted, nervously tying the leather cord that held his goatskin map in a tight roll.

'It is very strange, isn't it, that such lovely country lies virtually uninhabited?' she commented, striking at the heart of what the king had been thinking.

Murrough almost dropped his map in shock at her words. This Druid must have the skill of hearing the thoughts of others, he told himself. She had listened to his mind when they had first met and it was obvious that she had done so just now as well. He resolved that he would have to exercise some discipline over his wits in her presence.

'You have nothing to fear from me,' Ia exclaimed. 'I will not betray your suspicions.'

Murrough had never experienced a Druid with such skills before. How could he guard his thoughts from her when he had no idea how to defend himself from her intrusions?

'What suspicions are you talking about?' he asked, pretending to be unsure of what she meant.

'You must have asked yourself whether Cathal might have reached an agreement with the Saxons to leave certain areas in these hills unsettled.'

'That thought did not cross my mind.'

'He and his clan do quite well out of the business of housing the hill people's cattle, feeding the starving mountain folk and most of all protecting them from the threat of raiders.'

'What are you saying?' Murrough gasped. 'That a chieftain would seek to profit from the misfortunes of his own folk?'

'No. Not from the troubles of his own folk. He profits from the misfortunes of his neighbours, the people of the peninsula of Strath-Clóta, the Cymru.'

'But Cathal refers to *his* clanspeople as being of the Strath-Clóta.'

'Cathal is a Gael of the Dal Araidhe. The king of this peninsula is a Briton, a Cymru as they call themselves in their own language. The Cymru king demands the allegiance of all the Gaels in his kingdom. The Dal Araidhans were only allowed to remain here because of their solemn promise to help defend the Strath-Clóta against further invasion. In the north, in the lands of the Airer Gael, the Dal Araidhan kings have ensured that all the Britons have been slowly pushed out of the country or bred into the rest of the population.'

'Cathal referred to himself as King of the Southern Dal Araidhe,' Murrough remembered aloud as he moved to stand up.

'Cathal has become very powerful with the influx of many Gaelic warriors from the lands of his kinsmen in the north. The Council of the British Kings does not dare challenge his ambition lest he be given the perfect excuse to begin a campaign against them. Cathal has a large force at his disposal and would think nothing of turning his warriors against the Cymru of the south. The Britons will cast a blinded eye on his claim to kingship until the moment he attempts to exercise his false authority. For now the threat of the Saxons is a much more pressing problem to them.'

Murrough brushed the dirt from his riding breeches. 'And what of the Cruitne people? Where do their allegiances stand in all of this?'

'They have been slowly forced to migrate to the far northern lands,' Ia sighed bitterly. 'To the rugged mountains. The British kings used the Cruitne warriors as a first line of defence when the Saxons invaded. Most of their best were slaughtered needlessly in wasteful engagements. Without their warriors to protect them, the Cruitne strongholds lay open to Saxon attack.'

Ia brushed her forehead with her gloved hand. 'Cathal was charged with defending the Cruitne peoples in his territory,' she went on, 'but he was deliberately incompetent in protecting them from the Saxons. I have heard that his own warriors were involved in a raid on the settlement of Cú-Ainé in which more than a hundred of my kinfolk died.'

'Your kinfolk?' the king exclaimed. 'I thought you said your father's name was Ronan? That's not a Cruitne name. It's Gaelic.'

'Ronan was his name, Ronan Mac Breac who was descended of Queen Ethne of the Niallgallach.'

'So your ancestor was Niall of the Nine Hostages?' Murrough asked.

Ia nodded. 'Ethne married into the Cruitne people on the condition that all their folk trace their lineage from the female line. Thus, though I was born of the clans of the Cruitne, my bloodline is of the Gaels. But Cathal's folk consider us to be Cruitne and therefore worthless.'

'Since when has there been enmity between the Gael and the Cruitne?'

'Since Cathal realised that he could rule the whole peninsula of Strath-Clóta alone if he set one tribe against another. He started that by stirring up a fight between the Cruitne and the Cymru. There has been enmity ever since. Cathal has slowly been ridding the land of those he considers unfit to share its bounty with his folk. And the coming of the Saxons has given him an excuse to employ more and more warriors to his own ends.'

'But you are his advisor!' Murrough spluttered. 'If all this is true, how can you serve such a man?'

'I have no choice in the matter. I am no more than a hostage. In return for a promise of safe passage to the north for my surviving clanspeople and peace with those who choose to remain among the clans of Dun Righ, I offered myself to Cathal in servitude as an advisor. He sees the arrangement as confirmation of his conquest of the Cruitne lands in Strath-Clóta.'

Murrough could not help but sympathise with Ia's plight. She was forced to serve the very man who had been responsible for the destruction or dispersion of her clan, and if she did not do so diligently, Cathal could so easily take it out on those of her folk who remained in Strath-Clóta. 'Where is your father now?' he asked.

'He is in Dun Breteann under the protection of the Cymru. He managed to stay out of the fights that raged between our peoples, but he is very old now and has lost his senses. His life is ended. It was more than he could bear to see his people treated so cruelly. It broke his spirit.'

'And your mother?'

'She returned to her own folk when I was very young. I do not remember her. The Cruitne would not have her as wife to their chieftain after the first of the foreigners brought war to our land.'

Murrough frowned. 'I don't understand.'

'My mother was called Egfrith. She was a Saxon.'

Murrough could not prevent himself from gasping at Ia's admission. Before he had been elected King of Munster he had been unfortunate enough to experience the brutality of the Saxons. In the time of the false bishop Palladius, Murrough and Caitlin had been sent to protect the Quicken Tree from a band of foreigners who had been in the employ of the rebel, King Dichu of Laigin. Murrough and his party had been ambushed by the Saxon savages not far from their destination.

Even after the passing of many seasons the king could still picture the way the Saxons had revelled in their surprise attack, slaughtering any who offered resistance. He could still hear their wild battle cries and the sound of their strange guttural speech. And he would never forget his fight with the Saxon who had taken Caitlin as his hostage. To Murrough all these foreigners were filthy, barbaric, savage and fierce. He looked at Ia and he could not imagine that she had the blood of that wild folk running in her veins.

'My mother was different from the other Saxons,' the Druid stated, once again indicating that she had overheard Murrough's thoughts. 'She was a Druid among her people. That is why I was chosen for this path. She was a keeper of their traditions and songs. They called her the Warder of the Lore.'

'I have heard that even the Saxons have holy orders, though I would be surprised if they were anything like our own Druids,' the king said.

'Even the wild Saxons have holy men and

women. Though they are not forbidden from taking up weapons in wartime.'

'That is a very disturbing skill that you have,' Murrough noted, changing the subject.

'If you mean the gift of hearing thoughts,' Ia laughed, 'my mother passed it on to me. No-one at Dun Righ knows of it. I am usually very careful whom I reveal my talents to.'

'You were not very careful with me,' the king remarked as he tucked his map under his arm.

Ia came close to him and reached out to touch his hand. 'But you, King Murrough, are very different from most people,' she said smiling. 'Very different indeed.'

The king smiled awkwardly, clearly uncomfortable that the Druid was standing so close to him.

'You could help my people and myself return to the land which we once called home,' she said in a gentle voice. 'You could help us to be rid of Cathal.'

Caitlin and her party had been walking many hours in the dark woods when she finally called them to a halt and summoned Gobann to ask his advice.

'Each man has burned through three rush lights,' she told him. 'Judging by that, it must be well after sundown now.'

'We should let the men rest and eat a good meal,' the poet suggested. 'We can set off again at dawn.'

'In this perpetual darkness, how will we know when dawn has come?'

With the palm of his hand Gobann rubbed the top of his forehead where the hair had been shaved away in the Druid tonsure. Caitlin was familiar with this gesture. It usually indicated that the poet was deep in thought.

'We will have to find some other measure of time than the passing of moon and sun,' he explained. 'Set each of the watchmen to guard for as long as it takes for two rushes to burn through. Three changes of watch should take us through the night and ensure that the men are well enough rested to march hard tomorrow.'

'I wish we did not have to tarry in this forest tonight,' Caitlin whispered in reply. 'I cannot help but feel that this place is the home of some very dangerous predator.' She turned her head as if she had heard a noise in the underbrush. 'There is certainly a presence here that I am sure would prefer we did not stay.'

Gobann saw her turn her head sharply again. 'Have you seen them too?' he asked.

'If you mean have I seen movements in among the trees that I cannot explain,' she began, 'yes, I have. Are they some sort of inquisitive woodland creature?'

'There are many things under the canopy of these trees that you or I have never seen before. I have not had an opportunity to get a good look at these creatures,' the poet admitted. 'By the time I look in the direction of the movement, whatever caused it has vanished.'

'Like the Cailleach used to do when she was stalking me,' Caitlin murmured half to herself.

Gobann hissed loudly, calling her to silence. 'Do not mention her name in this place. Doubtless the hag has many kinfolk and I would not dare to wager that this place is not home to some of them.'

'Do you think there are Faerie folk in this place?'

'This wood has all the hallmarks of one of their

favoured dwelling places,' Gobann answered. 'We can only hope that these Danaans are of a friendly persuasion and not of the Sidhe-Dubh tribes. If they are related to the Children of Light, we have nothing to fear.'

Caitlin shivered for, though there was no breeze, the air had become suddenly cold. 'I'll set the men to gathering timber for a fire,' she said.

'Tell them they are not to cut any living wood but only to collect dead timber. We cannot risk the wrath of the forest dwellers. And the fire is to be built in the middle of the path so that no living thing will chance being burned by flying sparks.'

Caitlin nodded in agreement and strode off to make the arrangements.

'And be careful not to make too many flames,' Gobann added as an afterthought. 'We must do as little damage as possible while we are here.'

It did not take long for the warriors to collect enough fallen timber to last the night. When that was done, they all brought out their rations and the various cooking utensils that soldiers on campaign and far away from home always carry with them. Then the company began to prepare a meal.

Caitlin and Gobann sat together at one side of the fire, chewing on some of the dried herbs and oatcakes that the poet was famous for bearing about his person at all times. The warriors passed around meats and roast fowl left over from the feast at Dun Righ.

The sweet brown bread that they had acquired at the hill fort was plentiful, and one of the men had a small cask of Briton-style barley ale that he had carried all day over his shoulder. His comrades had laughed at him for struggling to bear such a burden, but they were all glad he had done so now for it helped make the meagre meal much more satisfying.

Gobann had picked a dozen small wild onions at the stream earlier in the day and he sat roasting them in the coals while the warriors settled down for the night. This was the first night in many seasons that the poet did not have his harp by his side. He had not expected that they would be gone all day, let alone overnight, otherwise he might not have left her at the stronghold in the care of the other Druids.

Even though he was without a harp, however, he was well aware that the warriors expected a tale from him. A story would help them take their minds off the day's long march and the prospect of another tomorrow. When everyone had finished eating and the Cymru ale was finished, Gobann brought out a flask of his own and passed it to Caitlin.

As the queen twisted the cork out of the neck the poet told them a story about the little leather bottle. 'It was made for me many seasons ago by a blacksmith called Midhna.'

'A champion at the Brandubh he was,' one of the older warriors chimed in. 'And a master of iron-work and mead brewing.'

'All of those things he was,' Gobann agreed. 'And no man or woman who tastes the drink in that flask will disagree about his brewing skills.'

Caitlin took a sip from the bottle and hummed in appreciation as the sweet warming liquid flowed down her throat and into her stomach.

'Pass it round,' Gobann insisted and the queen handed it to the man who sat beside her. 'I have heard it said that Midhna learned his arts from the Danaans, but then I have heard folk say that about every gifted craftsman in Eirinn,' the poet joked.

172

'Midhna was a great man who did not live long enough to see the war between Dichu the King of Laigin and the High-King come to an end.'

'Slain by the Saxons he was,' another warrior confirmed. 'All his kinfolk too.'

Caitlin shot a glance at Gobann. They both knew that one of Midhna's kin had survived. Mawn was the youngest son of the blacksmith.

The poet pretended not to notice Caitlin and went straight on with his story. 'Midhna's grandfather, of course, was Cianan of the Sweet Melody, and so it is not surprising that the blacksmith had a great talent at whatever he turned his hand to.'

A chorus of agreeing 'oohs' came from the assembled warriors. Now that the poet had established that the tale was going to focus on Midhna's grandfather, the sentries tried to get as close to the fire as they could without compromising their duties, for Gobann's talent as a storyteller was famous.

'Cianan the Wanderer he was called also,' the poet informed them, aware that they all knew this tale very well. 'Cianan of the River Crossing.'

Some of the men stared into the fire, some into the blackness of the tree cover above them. Caitlin lost herself in the bright orange embers of the fire.

'The first name he got because he was the greatest harper in the living memory of the Gaels. Even his laments were sweet enough to calm the sadness of the grieving. So he was nicknamed Sweet Melody. The second name he got because he travelled so far in his life. As to how he got the third name, you will learn that from my story.'

The poet paused to take a breath and allow his audience to take in all that he had said. 'In his waning years Cianan was supposed to have travelled to this land. Near to where the fortress of Dun

Righ now stands he met an old chieftain who complained to him about an evil Danaan woman who had set a terrible price on the peace of the land. Every Samhain the monster demanded the sacrifice of one of the old chieftain's tribe. If she did not get her tribute, the terrible creature would embark on a rampage, destroying crops and cattle, and in the end many folk would invariably suffer. The chieftain thought it was better to lose one of his folk each winter than many in famine the next spring, so he always paid the terrible ransom.'

Gobann had every ear in the company and, though their eyes were focused on the things of this world, their minds went where the poet led them.

'The monster was known to those who feared her as the Glastig and she was said to dwell in a pool in the centre of a dark forest, much like this wood in which we are sitting now. After much persuading, Cianan agreed to use his harp to put a charm on the creature, forcing her to make amends for her terrible ways.'

One of the sentries coughed in the darkness and everyone jumped a little. Then, as if the flames would keep them safe from all harm, those listening by the fire drew themselves closer to the light.

'It was a long journey that Cianan took into the forest and a day and a night before he heard a rumour of the Glastig's whereabouts. Eventually, however, he found himself standing at the edge of a waterfall that ended its tumbling in a vast black pool. There he discovered a seat cut into the rock, and once he had made himself comfortable, he began to play his harp.'

It was now that Gobann missed his own instrument for at this part of the tale he loved to mimic the music of Cianan, thus adding an extra depth to the story for his listeners.

'He played the sleep music, and when he had strummed at that for a while, he began the strains of the sorrow music,' the poet went on. 'And then last of all Cianan of the Sweet Melody struck up the music of war and love. He had not long been playing one soulful air when the surface of the pool began to bubble and boil as if it were a cauldron full of water placed upon a fire.'

Gobann pointed at the flames of the campfire but his audience did not notice him. They were all lost in their own visions of that fateful meeting in the forest of long ago. The warriors only stirred to take the bottle of mead from their neighbour as it was passed around.

'Up out of the pool, bathed in foaming bubbles, came a creature dressed in black shades that befit the depths of ponds. The monster rose out of the water to sit upon the bank near Cianan. She listened to his tunes and swayed to the gentle music that came from his harp. So moved was the Glastig by the wondrous sounds that she softly began to sob; the moment that the harper heard the noise of her crying, he knew that his spell had worked. Cianan put the harp down from his knee to look upon the monster that had so frightened a great chieftain and all his people.'

The mead bottle reached Gobann at this moment and he stopped his tale long enough to take a quick mouthful. Then he passed the precious liquid on to Caitlin.

'But beware the workings of spells and enchantments for every one of them has a price, and some demand higher than you or I may be ready to pay. Beware what charm you use to ensnare a lover for the power contained in such clever tricks has the nasty habit of turning back upon the one who made the spell. And so it was with Cianan, or so I believe, for when he looked upon the face of the Glastig he did not see what other men saw. The harper did not see a hideous flesh-eating creature. Cianan of the Sweet Melody saw the most beautiful woman he had ever laid eyes on and he instantly fell in love with her.'

The poet's audience gasped collectively, although they all knew very well what had happened to Cianan because they had all heard this story many times when they were children. No-one told this tale like Gobann, however, even without his harp to add ornament to the telling.

'And the Glastig,' the poet continued, 'of course she fell under the enchantment of Cianan's harp as we all fall to the spell that our lovers wield upon us. And there at the edge of the pool, I am told, they made a pact. She promised that she would cease her attacks on the people of Strath-Clóta, and he vowed to stay by the pond to play for her every day for the rest of her life. And foolish Cianan agreed without thinking of the consequences. For if he had thought on the future and on the nature of the Glastig, he would have realised that she was of the Danaan folk who live on from age to age as unchanging as the mountains, untouched by time as is the ocean.'

Caitlín thought of Mawn and Sianan and she finally began to understand what it meant for them to have been chosen as Wanderers. She had heard Cathach when he was alive refer to them as gifted with the water of everlasting life, but only now did she realise that Gobann in fact considered their state to be an affliction.

'So they say the Glastig got the better of the deal. For though she had to give up her vicious ways, she gained a companion who would be with her for the eternity she had yet to live upon the Earth. Cianan was burdened with the curse of immortality.'

Once more the poet paused to let his audience ponder the moral of the story.

'Cianan of the Sweet Melody was spotted occasionally after that day, walking the shores of Strath-Clóta, combing the beaches looking for anything washed up from Eirinn. Sometimes he was seen ranging across the wild mountains, stopping now and then to help those who were lost or to give gifts of food to the hungry.'

Gobann picked up a stick and poked it at the glowing coals. 'I met him once,' he revealed, and everyone present looked up in surprise. It was not that they did not believe him, only that the old stories rarely had sequels in the present time and the poet had never revealed this information to anyone here.

'I encountered him a long time ago when I was young and travelling in the north of this country. I had just fallen in love with a native of this land and so I could sympathise with his predicament on that count. If it had not been for my calling, I would have stayed with Síla and followed her on her journeys among the Cruitne folk.'

The poet realised that he had begun to stray from his tale. 'Cianan was not an unhappy man when I spoke to him,' he continued. 'He had always been very wise, and that wisdom had been tempered with resignation. It was he who taught me that it was best to walk the Druid path only as far as the end of my days and not to wish to inhabit one body for longer than is comfortable.'

Caitlin looked at Gobann carefully. Suddenly she

was beginning to understand much about him that had been a mystery to her in times past.

'The lesson we all have to learn from Cianan is that we each have talents that we choose to employ for whatever purpose we set our minds to. It is a rare person who, being desirous of something, whether it be a beautiful golden torc or of helping someone in need, considers the consequences of their actions through to the very end. The few among us who can manage that are generally those elected as our kings and queens and chieftains.'

The mead bottle came round again and Gobann took it gratefully. 'I would dearly like to meet the Glastig,' he added. 'There were those who talked of her as the most disgusting creature on the face of the Earth, yet Cianan thought her the most beauteous. Is that not always the way? Only a goose could find a gander attractive.'

His audience smiled, satisfied with the story, and a few rolled over where they sat to settle in to sleep. Caitlin pulled her riding cloak over her shoulders and lay down beside the fire where she could stare into the embers. She wondered why Gobann had chosen to tell that particular story. Was it Cianan or the Glastig that had been following them all day? She was about to ask, but the poet anticipated her question.

'The watch will be changing soon,' Gobann noted. 'It is time we all took our rest.' With that he stretched himself out a little away from the fire and wrapped his own blue cloak around him for the night. Caitlin took the hint that this was not the time to talk of such things and she remained quiet.

Gobann closed his eyes. For the first time in many months he was feeling the weight of his tasks. The woods were so peaceful that he found he was slipping quickly into that semiconscious state before sleep when the waking world can warp and change to meld with the world of dreams. On a few occasions his body jolted as it began to relax, but soon the exhaustion had gripped him body and soul and he started to slip into a deep sleep.

The poet was usually much more careful about falling asleep after such rigorous exercise and after having gone without proper rest for so many days. He knew from experience that telling tales at such times often drained the last resistance he had to the Faidh—the future-sight.

The watch changed while Gobann was still half awake but not entirely aware of his surroundings. As the warriors who had sat the first sentry duty passed him by in the firelight their shadows fell on his face and he dimly perceived their movement, though his eyes were shut.

In his mind the power of the dream world took over, transforming the shadowy figures into dancers who kicked up their heels in a wild jig that circled the fire. The poet found himself longing to join in the revelry, but his Druid training told him to sit back and observe and not to take any part for the moment. The dancers, however, had certainly noticed him. Suddenly he found himself standing in their midst, though a part of him knew that his body was still asleep by the fire.

A second later Gobann jolted in his sleep and sat bolt upright, wide awake and alone by the fire. For a moment he was very confused, then he remembered that he was in a wood where the sun rarely shone.

'Caitlin,' he mumbled, trying to work out what had become of the company that he had just been telling a tale to. 'Caitlin, where are you?'

He noticed that the fire had not died down, so the warriors could not have gone far, and he resolved to stay awake and wait for their return. It was not long before he began to see shapes moving around near where the firelight faded into the darkness. Were these creatures the same ones that Caitlin and he had noticed playing a game of hide-and-seek with them all day? He could not be sure.

Perhaps, the poet thought, he was actually asleep and all this was a confused dream. He tried to stand up but his legs felt incredibly heavy and his arms simply would not budge from his sides. Gobann was completely paralysed.

There were voices behind him speaking in the Cymru tongue; though he could not understand what was being said, he could hear that they were raised in a dispute of some kind. Suddenly he felt hands touching him and he was lifted up onto his feet. Gobann had no sooner stretched his cramped legs than he felt himself rising higher to float just above the ground. In a flash he was spiralling upwards into the night, crashing into the treetop branches as he rose.

This was so unexpected that Gobann could not stifle a loud cry. Within seconds, however, he had cleared the branches and gained control of his fear. Then he tried to settle his nerves enough so that he could take in this whole experience.

Past the point of doubting that this was a dream, Gobann looked about him. He understood that he was no longer restrained by the mundane world and that he had taken spirit form. When he was very young, Gobann had learned that it didn't really matter whether information was imparted in dreams or visions or in the waking world. What mattered was that he should always take careful note of all that happened to him, remembering as much detail as possible.

As Gobann felt himself rising higher and higher above the trees his vision became blurred then blacked out completely. All that he was conscious of was his own steady, if strained, breathing. The slow intake of air rang in his ears, making a rattling noise. A startling thought struck him: perhaps he was dying. In his life he had witnessed many peaceful deaths; indeed it was one of his duties to play the harp for folk as they departed this world. He had heard the death-rattle breath a hundred times.

No sooner had the thought of death entered his head, however, than his eyesight cleared and he found himself looking out into a night sky filled with stars and lit by the fullness of the pearly moon. Down below him was spread the canopy of the forest, seemingly as impenetrable from above as it was from below. Although it was night Gobann could see in incredible detail every leaf on every tree and hear them all rustling against one another in the wind.

The poet stretched his spirit body, enjoying the new-found freedom, taking in the clean air that was free to circulate beyond the confines of the stifling woods. He flexed his arms out to their fullest extent and instinctively pushed downwards, taking note of the strange sensation as the air was forced between his fingers.

He discovered that the feeling of the wind on his hands was extremely satisfying. So he raised his arms again to repeat the action. This time he noted that every hair on his arms and hands felt as if it were cupping the air and trapping it. If he could push down hard enough, he thought, it would not be difficult to keep himself aloft. His arms felt like wings.

When that thought struck him, Gobann glanced

to his left and, in bewilderment at what he saw, immediately stopped flapping his arms. Astonished, the poet dragged his hand towards his face in a growing state of fright. What he saw made him want to call out in alarm, but the only sound he managed to make was a rough squawking gargle that came from the back of his throat.

Where there should have been hairs on his arms, Gobann could see only large black oily feathers. 'My Druid cloak,' he struggled to say aloud. But these feathers were not stitched into any fabric. These feathers grew out of his arms. These feathers were alive.

He did not have time to question what had happened for in the next second he was falling to Earth, tumbling head over tail. Instinctively he stretched out his wings and in a second he was in full flight, soaring over the forest canopy, searching the branches and the far distance as if he had been a hunter all his life.

His fears were abruptly banished. Not caring whether this were a dream or a vision, he sucked in the air that blew around his face. This transformation was a dream come true for the poet. Ever since his initiation into the Silver Branch Gobann had prayed for just such an opportunity to present itself one more time in his life. Now his prayers were finally being answered.

'Raven!' he shrieked joyously at the top of his lungs. 'I am a Raven!'

EIGHT

sernus, assistant to Declan the Abbot of Saint Ninian's, walked along the walls of Dun Righ as night was falling, silently praying and repeating his rosary. Occasionally he stopped to greet the sentries who were stationed at regular intervals along the defences, but for the most part he avoided the company of his fellow human beings wherever possible.

For as long as he could remember, this had been the way Isernus preferred to live, serving humanity in his own way but as divorced from the day to day strife of temporal life as he could be. His world was the world of the Holy Spirit, where God in His Majesty looked down on the Earth and instantly knew every sin that had been committed there and each transgression against the faith.

Isernus had never shown much interest in the great debate over the true nature of God or whether or not Christ had been of the flesh or of the spirit. He had never cared to delve into the errors of the heretics or the recently popular cult of Christ's Mother. None of these matters concerned him. If he had views on any of these subjects he never mentioned them to anyone, not even to Declan, his trusted confessor and soulfriend. All Isernus cared about was that he had a daily opportunity to serve God and so to make some recompense for his sins.

The monk walked on around the walls until he found a spot between two sentries where he was fairly sure he would not be disturbed. He sat himself down on the earthen embankment with his legs dangling over the edge. Once settled he closed his eyes and clasped his hands in front of him in the distinctly Roman attitude of prayer.

Not until the air had become quite cool as darkness fell did the monk stir from his meditations. Not wishing to catch a chill, Isernus pulled up his hood to cover his head, then he tucked his hands into the deep sleeves of his robe and clasped them together again to continue his supplications.

When he had finished his customary prayers, he opened his eyes to look out across the countryside. From the surrounding fields mounted scouts were riding in with their reports, the last of the day. Men and women were coming into the hill fort with wagons and horses loaded with their possessions. Though the barrier at the breach should have been closed at dusk, the people were still passing through in ones and twos.

'They are preparing for a siege,' the monk realised, speaking aloud to himself, confident that no-one would hear him. 'They are bringing in all the folk from the countryside around about and laying in supplies.'

It was obvious that the Gaels expected trouble, but what puzzled Isernus was that no-one had mentioned anything to Declan nor, to his knowledge, to any of the company that had arrived from Eirinn. There had been some general talk of preparations for war, but such activity as this was more than simple precaution. Cathal, he decided, must have a very good reason for bringing the farmers in for protection.

With all the torches in the dark and the hill fort

fully mobilised, Isernus could not help but recall that night all those years ago when he, Declan, Bishop Palladius and the other monks had been led into Ardmór. That had only been a few days after they had landed on Eirinn's shore for the first time.

Abruptly the monk's thoughts turned to the landing of that missionary party during a severe sea squall. Isernus knew that he would never be able to forget the terror he had felt when their boat had been overturned in the raging surf. The taste of the salt sea was still strong in his mouth even after all these years. The monk had swallowed so much water that day that he thought he would surely drown. But he did not drown when he was thrown from the boat. Linus had pulled him from the water. Linus had been his best friend in the world, perhaps the only real friend he had ever known aside from Declan. It was Linus, the half-brother of Seginus Gallus, who had saved his life. As Isernus had been tumbled under the waves during the storm a hand had reached out to grab him. The monk could still recall that he had known immediately whose hand it was, even though he could not see the man's face.

Linus, strong and reckless, had dragged him from the water; but it was Seginus who had carried him up onto the beach and dumped him unceremoniously in the grass. Seginus had always hated Isernus. From the moment the monk had become friends with Linus at the monastery of Saint Eli, Seginus had done all in his power to keep them apart.

'If only he had succeeded,' the monk whispered to himself. 'If only I had listened to what the others said about Linus.'

Isernus struggled in vain to hold back his tears.

'I should not have trusted him,' he sobbed. 'I should have scorned his company.'

Despite his words Isernus knew in his heart that Linus had been a young man who could have charmed anyone he set his sights on. Many were those at the monastery who said that Linus had a touch of evil about him. But to his close friends he was never anything but kind and caring. How could Isernus have scorned the company of one who seemed so innocent even though he was so despised by his elders?

Suddenly Isernus became aware that two sentries, walking their appointed patrol, had climbed the rampart and were approaching the monk.

'Good evening, brother,' the senior of the two warriors called.

'Good evening, my son,' Isernus replied.

'It looks like you are keeping our watch for us up here. It's hardly worth us passing by.'

'I was just admiring the view,' Isernus replied, making sure that his face was well concealed. He did not want these men seeing that he was so upset.

The warrior came up close to the monk and slapped his hand across the brother's shoulder. 'You let us know if you see any of those murdering Saxons about,' the man commanded in a mock serious tone. 'Don't you try and sort them out alone, mind you. You leave them for us lads to look after.'

The other warrior was trying hard not to laugh, covering his mouth with his hand to stifle his amusement.

Isernus immediately understood that he was being made fun of. Some of the Gaels, especially the warriors, made a sport of mocking the Christians. The monk put it down to a lack of respect due to the reputation that Palladius had earned for himself.

'I wouldn't dream of it,' Isernus spoke up. 'I am a holy brother. It would be against my calling to raise a hand to any man, Saxon or Gael.'

'You'll be in a bit of trouble when they storm the walls then, won't you,' the first warrior quipped. This was too much for his younger companion and he broke down laughing as the two men sauntered off to continue their duty.

Isernus could hear the younger man talking as the two warriors reached the bottom of the hill. 'Are all the Christian monks like that one?'

'Aye, lad, many of them are forbidden the company of women,' the older man said. 'It isn't a life that any man would take to willingly, unless of course he didn't care for the company of women in the first place,' he added before the warriors passed beyond Isernus' hearing.

The monk looked down at his hands which lay palm uppermost in his lap. His stomach churned with hatred and his face flushed. Ever since the missionaries had landed at Ardmór nearly ten years before, Isernus had struggled to conceal the crime he had committed on his first night on the shores of Eirinn. No matter how many penances he ascribed to himself, no matter how hard he worked at his redemption, the guilt always found a way to resurface and torture him.

'Linus had evil intent,' he whispered as if he was giving evidence before a tribunal of church elders. 'He lured me to the beach for his own gratification. I had no way of knowing what he had in mind.'

His hands clasped tightly together now, knuckles whitening with the wringing of his fingers.

'I knew that Declan thought that I could have put Linus off, though he never said it to my face.

"You could have reported it to Palladius," he said. I should never have expected the abbot to understand. I'm sure that he still believes deep down that I encouraged Linus. I know that Declan still thinks of me as a coward, a weakling who gave in to unnatural desires.'

Isernus looked up at the stars in the black sky, no longer struggling to hold back the tears.

'I had no choice but to strike back. He threatened me. I didn't mean to hit him. He was my friend,' he cried. 'I don't even remember the knife being in my hand.' The monk was sobbing uncontrollably. He pulled the cowl further over his head, burying his face in the woollen hood.

'Christ, in your mercy, forgive me,' he appealed. 'Forgive me my wretched sins. Forgive me for my disgusting cowardice and my feeble attempt at self-control. God of mercy, God of love, forgive me for not fighting against the feelings I had for Linus. Forgive me.'

Isernus curled up on the edge of the wall and cried until the pain had eased. A long while later he realised that Declan would miss him, so he dried his eyes and quietened himself in readiness to return to their shared billet.

He arrived at the little roundhouse Cathal had provided for the duration of their stay and was surprised to find that the abbot was not sitting by the hearth. Isernus immediately thought that Declan must have gone out searching for him. He made his way down to the nearest house, which was occupied by several local Druids. He poked his head through the door to see if his abbot was inside and received a terrible shock at what he saw inside.

On a bench in one corner lay the old monk Brother Kilian whom Declan had left in charge of the monastery while he and Isernus travelled to Eirinn. The old man's cheeks were horribly bruised and his arms looked as if some wild creature had tried to tear the skin off them. Declan was sitting on a stool near the monk and three Druids were standing nearby. The air was thick with incense.

The abbot turned around and noticed Isernus standing at the door. Declan stood up and strode towards his assistant with his arms outstretched. 'Brother! Thank God you are safe. I was so worried about you.'

'I was walking and praying,' Isernus explained. 'What has happened to Kilian?'

'A Saxon war party caught the monastery unawares,' Declan whispered almost inaudibly, the shock of the news setting in. 'A number of the brethren are dead. Conran, Fidach, Bran, Euan for certain and possibly three more. Kilian managed to escape from the raiders, though their dogs had him cornered at one time and he had to beat them off with a branch.'

Declan took Isernus by the sleeve, leading him out into the night where Kilian would not hear what was being said. 'He is very badly wounded,' the abbot admitted sombrely. As the older monk wiped his brow Isernus could plainly see that Declan was overcome with grief, though he masked it well. 'The Druid physicians do not expect him to live to see the sunrise. He has lost a lot of blood and he is utterly distraught at the destruction of Saint Ninian's.'

'Destruction?' Isernus repeated in horror, hardly able to take in what he was being told. 'The Candida Casa has been ruined?'

'It would seem that Ninian's White House has been burned to the ground, yes. If we are to take Kilian at his word. Though I must admit that he

189

was quite confused when he was brought in. A patrol of horsemen found him wandering along the main road to Dun Righ this morning—how he got that far I'll never know. They had to move him slowly for fear of his injuries.'

Declan dragged Isernus further away from the Druid house. 'We must return immediately,' the abbot informed his assistant. 'That raid last year left only one of our number dead. This is a different matter. We must show Aldor that we are not afraid of death.'

'There are hordes of Saxons waiting in ambush to kill us,' Isernus gasped.

'Yes, I know. Even if all the barbarian armies of the east were assembled together to surround the monastery, it would still be our duty to return straightaway.'

Isernus stared at his abbot in wide-eyed disbelief, remembering the young monk who had been hanged almost a year before. 'We might as well ride right into their camp and give ourselves up,' he railed. 'Did you miss us when you visited the monastery last? Well here we are, now is your opportunity to murder us also.'

Whether it was the shock of seeing Kilian so badly wounded or surprise that Isernus could speak to him in such a way, Declan raised the palm of his hand and slapped the younger man hard across the cheek. The jarring blow caught Isernus unprepared and he staggered back, unable to speak, his hand nursing the spot where the slap had landed.

The abbot immediately regretted his rash reaction but he could not believe that Isernus had been so disrespectful to him. 'What is the matter with you?' he demanded. 'A brave man lies in there dying because he had the conviction of his faith to stand up to those vile foreigners. How dare you speak that way to me? I am your superior and I have decided that it is of the utmost importance that we return to Candida Casa as soon as possible. You will follow orders and remember your place.' The abbot calmed himself a little and then said, 'I am sorry for striking you. I didn't mean to hurt you.'

Isernus stood without moving a muscle, the indignity of his situation clearly showing in his expression.

'Are you not going to apologise?' the abbot asked.

There was no reply.

'Very well then,' Declan replied coldly, 'you will remain here safe in the stronghold of Dun Righ. I will take the nuns with me to rebuild Saint Ninian's.'

With that the abbot stormed off towards the roundhouse, leaving Isernus still clutching his stinging cheek. However, Declan began to regret his unseemly show of temper long before he made it back to the hearth fire. He knew that Isernus was probably right. It was stupidity to want to return to the monastery unguarded, for Cathal could not spare any of his troops to escort them in the current crisis.

'You are a proud and foolish man, Declan,' the abbot rebuked himself. 'Yet what would happen if every monastery that was threatened with destruction was simply abandoned to the heathens? What would become of the Church? What would become of the followers of Christ who depend on the clergy for their spiritual guidance? What would become of the faith?'

Declan threw himself onto his bed and lay with his hands behind his head. 'If I had stood up to

Palladius a lot sooner, there would never have been a war between the High-King of Eirinn and the King of Laigin. If I have learned anything from that experience it is that I must do as my heart bids me. And now my heart bids me to return to Saint Ninian's to minister to my flock.'

At that moment Declan became aware that Isernus was standing at the open doorway listening to him as he addressed the empty room.

'I will go with you, master abbot,' the monk stated. 'I will make all the arrangements myself. It would be best that we wait for the troops under Tatheus to return, but we could set out tomorrow morning if you think we can make the journey without their help.'

Declan was silent for a moment, glad that Isernus had changed his mind. 'I think we can wait until Tatheus can escort us. I am sure they will be back tonight.'

'Then, if you will excuse me,' Isernus said, 'I will go to begin the preparations.'

'Good night, brother,' Declan offered sincerely.

'Good night, father abbot,' Isernus replied and then, as he was about to leave, he said, 'I am sorry, father abbot. Please forgive me.'

'It is an easy matter to grant forgiveness, my son, when it is petitioned with such humility.'

Isernus had not long gone when a messenger came to Declan with the news that Kilian had succumbed to his injuries. Declan did not respond to the news, except to thank the messenger politely. Then he went outside again to arrange for Kilian's burial, his heart wearier than he could ever express.

Murrough and his company began their sweep back towards Dun Righ in the early afternoon. The ten warriors accompanying him spread out in a long line which stretched for hundreds of paces as they headed back down the hills. In this manner they were sure to search as much ground as possible.

Ia rode beside the king with the next guardsman thirty paces on either side, just out of earshot. And Murrough was very glad of that. This Druid was unpredictable and he did not want any rumours that might stain his character circulating among his warriors.

But Ia said very little during the whole afternoon, until just after they had passed another deserted settlement about an hour before dusk. At the sight of this latest group of empty farms she dismounted to examine the hearth of a roundhouse.

'The coals are still hot,' she declared. 'And the rushes are still fresh on the floor. These people fled only yesterday or last night.'

'We are only a short way from the dun,' Murrough observed. 'Why would they have left their homes unless they had been threatened by some immediate danger?'

Ia bent down close to the ground near the doorway and brushed the soil there with the palm of her hand. 'The farmers have carefully covered the passage to their underground store. They must have thought the Saxons were about.'

'We have not come across one Saxon all day. Do you think the savages have been here?'

'No,' Ia replied confidently. 'Not yet. Most likely these folk heard a rumour and rushed into the hill fort for safety.'

'Let us ride on,' Murrough urged. 'We are not

far from Dun Righ now and I am anxious to return there before dark. All we have seen since this morning are the abandoned homes of poor farming folk. There has been no indication that the enemy has travelled high into the hills. Not even a discarded blade or a deliberately burned house. Yet all the people are gone. There is something wrong with all this.'

'Cathal is spreading fear of the savages to strengthen his own hold on the country. The farmers and fisherfolk rely on him for their protection and they would gladly give him a share of their produce to ensure their safety.'

'That is a very Saxon way of looking at things, Ia,' the king exclaimed. 'Surely Cathal would face the anger of his own clan assembly if he engaged in such a selfish tactic.'

'The assembly was suspended last winter,' the Druid answered coldly.

'Suspended? If there is no assembly, who elects the chieftain?'

'There was no election this season. Cathal turned the counsellors away because of the foreign threat. He has convened a council of war that now has authority over everything from the supply of grain to the flow of water through the stronghold. His chief steward holds office still, but only because he is an old man who would not dare to question Cathal's actions.'

'If this were true, surely Caitlin and I would have become aware of it immediately,' Murrough scoffed. 'It is very difficult to believe that he would not have informed us of such an unusual situation. You have to admit that this would be a very unlikely course of action for any chieftain to follow. In a time of war, when there is so little stability and the common people are apt to be highly critical of leaders who flout the law, a chieftain treads softly.'

'He is not very happy about your presence here,' Ia stated. 'It has thrown his plans into disarray for now he has a king and queen who owe him no allegiance living in his hill fort. And with you is an independent Druid, a poet of the Silver Branch no less. You and your retinue have created quite a problem for Cathal.'

'I don't understand,' Murrough said, shaking his head.

'I believe that Cathal has been in close contact with the Saxon commander for some time. I have been watching very carefully all that has happened since last winter and I am convinced that the chieftain has made some sort of pact with the enemy. He does not believe that he needs your warriors because, due to his secret truce, there is no real threat for the time being. At the same time he is taking advantage of your arrival to make the most of the people's fears of attack.'

'He must know that the day will come when he will have to face election again. Surely he doesn't believe that he can go on becoming more and more powerful without someone raising an objection. The Druid Assembly will surely raise its voice in objection to this behaviour. In any case, you have no solid proof for your assertion, only rumour, hearsay and intuition.'

'I am surprised that you speak so of a Druid's intuition. Are you not married to one?' she snapped. 'Cathal has appointed me as his chief Druid advisor, secure in the knowledge that I will not dare gainsay any action that he takes. If I were to criticise him publicly, the survivors of my people would die at his hands. The chieftain of Dun Righ is a clever man. Cathal has made sure that everyone knows of my Saxon heritage so that it will be easy for him to discredit me should the need arise.'

'If the chieftain has made this pact with the foreigners, then he is not serving the interests of his people and can be therefore impeached by the Druid Assembly as an unjust ruler,' Murrough countered. 'If these charges are true, he has forfeited his rights under the laws that govern leaders, and you have a duty to stand up and demand that he make account for his actions.'

'But who will join me to speak out against him? The people who live inside the dun feel safe and are making a little gold out of the misfortunes of the country folk. The country folk dare not speak out for fear of being cast out to face the savages alone. The Druid Assembly still has not recognised my appointment as chief counsellor. Its members will not speak out until the prosperity that has come to Dun Righ as a result of Cathal's policies has begun to wane.'

'Then the Druid Assembly is just as much at fault here as Cathal,' Murrough noted. 'It should have moved against him when he suspended the clan assembly.'

'I am an outsider here,' Ia admitted. 'I am certain that a great deal of information has been deliberately kept from me. The Druid Assembly informs me of its decisions long after they have been made.'

'I cannot imagine a council of learned Druids behaving in such a way,' the king exclaimed.

'You are in Dal Araidhe now. The traditions valued in Eirinn have no bearing on matters in these lands.'

Ia brushed the dirt over the entrance to the storage pit, making sure that it was once again well concealed. Then she stood up to address

Murrough. 'I have an intuition that the Saxons are very cleverly using Cathal's selfishness to their own advantage.'

'The Saxons!' the king spluttered in disbelief. 'The Saxons are using Cathal?' Murrough was finding this story more and more fanciful at each turn.

'There are nowhere near enough of the foreigners to attempt a successful attack on Dun Righ right now,' Ia explained. 'I think that by agreeing a truce with Cathal they are buying time to build their forces while maintaining a presence on the peninsula. New troops arrive each day from the Centi lands. Aldor, their war leader, is a shrewd man. If he feigns peace and alliance while his army is weak, he can spring a trap when his enemy least expects an attack. With superior forces and surprise on his side, he will easily defeat the Gaels.'

Murrough glanced across at Ia, trying to decide whether he believed her wild story. 'I will watch what happens in the next few days,' the king finally promised. 'I will note every word that Cathal speaks and when I have listened well and spoken to Queen Caitlin about this matter, I will send for you. But even if we can confirm your story, I doubt that there is much Caitlin and I can do to change the course of events. We were sent here to help drive out the Saxons, not interfere in the lives of the Dal Araidhans.'

'I am powerless in this situation, lord,' Ia said, bowing her head, 'but you and your queen may be able to help deliver the people of Dun Righ from this tyrant. I am sure there is a way.'

She had no sooner spoken than one of the warriors further down the line called out that he had spotted half a dozen men on foot some distance to the east and nearer to the road to Dun Righ.

'It will be getting dark soon,' Murrough stated.

'We will see who these men are and then ride back to the hill fort with all speed.' He stood up in his stirrups and gave a hand signal which meant swing to the east in formation. The message passed on down the line.

The warriors immediately fanned out to form a wide crescent shape which converged slowly around the foot of a low hill. Within a short while Murrough and Ia had caught sight of a group of men who had by this time lit a fire and was seated around it.

'They must be Saxons,' Ia declared. 'None of the Gaelic folk would dare to announce their presence to the enemy with the smoke of an open fire.'

Murrough nodded, remembering that Cathal had advised them to light a fire as a signal to the other parties. The king asked himself if a trap had been laid but quickly dismissed the thought.

Once the king had appraised the situation he gave another silent signal for his men to converge on their quarry. Quickly and quietly the warriors encircled the men, taking care not to give away their position with any undue noise. The six men were so involved in their conversation that they did not notice the mounted Gaelic warriors until it was too late. In the end it was a warrior's horse that gave their presence away, neighing loudly as it stood waiting in the thicket.

At that sound all six men jumped to their feet, drawing their swords and axes as one. Four reached for their small round shields but all were standing in a tight fighting formation near their fire within moments.

'Throw down your weapons!' Murrough called out, aware that he probably would not be understood.

None of the men made a sound, so the king

motioned for his warriors to draw the circle closer around the group. They were certainly Saxons by the colour of their clothing. The foreigners generally wore brown undyed clothing, and their leather belts were rarely tanned to black as was the leather of the Gaelic peoples. And only Saxons carried such large axes, meant for war rather than just cutting timber.

One of the foreigners stepped forward when he had sized up the odds and bellowed something unintelligible at the Gaels. His tone was obviously defiant and very likely insulting.

Ia shifted in her saddle. 'They mean to fight,' she cried out.

'They have no hope of escape at these odds,' Murrough assured her. 'The fellow in charge must be able to see that.'

The Saxon who had stepped forward laid the blade of his axe in the dirt behind him. Then, never for a moment taking his eyes off the king, he walked slowly towards Murrough, dragging the weapon along the ground as he did so. The axe left a narrow trail on the ground where the blade cut the earth.

'Watch him,' Murrough ordered to his men. 'If he is wise, he will lay that weapon at my feet; but if he is like most Saxons, we should expect some trouble.'

The man stopped only a couple of paces from the king's horse. He stood there dour-faced, looking up at Murrough. Then unexpectedly the Saxon broke into a broad almost friendly smile. The king found himself returning the grin and for the briefest moment felt a strange kinship with this savage. Up until then he had never thought of the Saxons as being anything like his own folk. He was surprised that one of them seemed to be showing a sign of friendship.

The king could plainly see many scars on the fellow's upper body, the result of a lifetime of war no doubt. His dark brown hair was tied in a bundle on top of his head and knotted in such a way as to cushion a helm if necessary. His arms were covered in shiny black tattoos of strange beasts. How different, Murrough thought, were the blue tattoos of the Cruitne which usually only consisted of intricate designs.

The man kept smiling as he began to speak, loud enough so that his own men could understand him, though Murrough could make no sense of the foreign language. The Saxon lifted the great war axe before him as if to hand it to Murrough and then stood waiting for the king to come closer to receive it.

As Murrough's horse stepped forward the Saxon loosened his grip on the bladed end of the weapon and slid his left hand down the handle to meet with his right in a pose that would enable him to strike easily at the king. Murrough saw this but was so amazed by the foreigner's smile and the tone of his voice that for a brief moment he did not suspect that there might be any immediate danger.

In that moment the Saxons acted, and they did so with such swiftness that the king had no opportunity to respond. First, the Saxon leader said something in his own tongue which caused his warriors to brace their weapons in readiness; then the foreigner lifted his great axe in a wide arc behind him. By the time Murrough realised what was happening, it was already too late. The weapon was ready to be hurled at him and he had no chance of getting clear of it or of deflecting its devastating force.

Then the king caught a glimpse of a silver flash of steel that spun through the air very close to him, tumbling end over end towards the Saxon leader. In less time than it took for Murrough to gasp in shock, the spinning object had found its mark and hit the Saxon in the middle of the chest. Blood spurted out from a deep wound as the foreigner let his axe fall to the ground. In agony the Saxon clutched at the small blade now hopelessly lodged in his upper body. All the while the stranger kept staring at the king, a hint of the smile still playing over his face.

It took Murrough a few seconds to understand that it had been Ia who had thrown the blade. The Saxon's knees buckled under him as the king turned to thank her with a glance, and by the time he turned back the foreigner was lying face down on the ground in a spreading pool of his own blood.

In the seconds after the Saxon was struck down, Murrough's warriors surrounded the five remaining foreigners. The raiders offered no resistance when they saw that their leader was mortally wounded and the horsemen quickly disarmed them without a fight. The prisoners were each tied by their wrists to the saddle of a horse.

'We must get back to Dun Righ,' the king declared, still shaken by the incident. 'It is far too dangerous for us to be abroad after dark.' His second-in-command formed the men into a defensive line for the march, and once the scouts had located the road, the company headed directly for it. Murrough knew that if they made it to the road to Dun Righ, it would not be long before they reached the outer defences of the hill fort and safety.

The king led the column with Ia at his side and three other warriors with drawn swords close by in case of any surprise attack. Although Murrough managed to calm himself before too long, aware that his behaviour would affect the morale of his men, his face showed that he had suffered a great shock. He was pale and he said very little to any of his men, allowing instead his second-in-command to give orders to the troops.

After they had found their way to the road and the horsemen had been able to spread out a little more, Ia brought her horse closer to the king. Murrough sensed her presence, though he did not at first look directly at her.

'How did you know what the Saxon intended to do?' he asked her.

'My mother was of their people,' Ia reminded him. 'I understand their speech.'

The king turned his head sharply towards her to look her in the eye, but she avoided his gaze. 'Why did you not warn me earlier?' he hissed.

'I was frightened,' she answered. 'Please do not tell anyone what I have said to you about Cathal and the Saxons. It would put the lives of all my people and myself in danger.' She paused for a moment and then added, 'No-one at Dun Righ knows of my talents nor that I understand the Saxon language. I would prefer to keep those things private for the moment.'

'Very well, but I will tell Queen Caitlin and my Druid counsellor everything that you have told me as soon as I meet with them this evening. I share everything with Caitlin, and Gobann is my trusted advisor. You need not fear that we will betray your secret until we can confirm or refute all the details of your story.'

'Your wife and your Druid will not return this night,' Ia stammered. 'They are even now camped deep within the dark forest that is the home of the monster, the Glastig. Perhaps tomorrow they will find their way out.'

Murrough did not say anything more, preferring to hope that Ia was not as good at seeing the future as she was at hearing the thoughts of others.

Gobann soared above the forest for a long while, just as he had done during the time of his great initiation at Teàmhair ten seasons before. On this occasion, however, he did not feel compelled to travel towards any particular destination, nor was he propelled helplessly along by any spirit wind. Now the poet felt that he was being encouraged to go wherever he would.

Below, Gobann could see the forest treetops. Ahead he discerned the far-off mountains and the white water of the streams in the distant hills. His sharpened senses missed nothing that took place below him.

The poet was enjoying his flight, savouring the experience of being in the form of a bird once again, when underneath him, to the northeast, he suddenly caught sight of an unusual movement on the edge of the forest. Gobann concentrated all his attention on the disturbance for something about it fascinated him. With his accentuated Raven sight the poet could plainly see five men dressed in Druid robes attending to horses that were secured to the low branches of an oak tree.

Gobann swooped down in the direction of the men, forgetting that he had very little experience of flight. It was as if he had always been a Raven. It was as if this were his true nature. He tucked his legs up close to his body as he soared earthward, wings fully extended, revelling in the exhilaration of this freedom.

As he approached the edge of the woods where the Druids were untying their horses, some instinct warned him that he should be very cautious from this point on. There was something strange in the air; a scent, a sensation that alerted him to danger.

Gobann's senses were suddenly overwhelmed by the proximity of these five men. All around the area where these Druids stood there was an odour; strong, sweet and tempting. The poet was so drawn by the scent that he could not help but seek out its source. Nevertheless he had a nagging sense that if he did not take the utmost care, his life would be under threat.

The faster and louder his heart beat in his tiny Raven breast, the more Gobann tried to tell himself that these were Druids. They were his own kind. No harm could possibly come to him from them. Yet every time the sweet aroma drifted in his direction it startled him so much that he had to catch his breath. He was fascinated by the smell and drawn to it against his will. The poet resolved to take the path of extreme caution rather than to listen entirely to his new-found animal instincts.

In a graceful dive Gobann glided down closer to the Druids, taking care not to flap his wings too much lest the noise attract their attention. He was still a distance away from them when two things became apparent. Firstly, the men all spoke a harsh language that the poet did not immediately recognise; secondly, the alluring scent that Gobann had picked up emanated from one of these men.

The poet decided that it would be worth getting closer to unravel the mystery. The thought crossed his mind that these men might be from the lands of northwestern Gaul since he did not understand their speech. The people of the Bask land had a language the poet had always considered rough and strange. Though what five Bask Druids would be doing at the edge of a wood in North Britain was beyond him.

With very little effort Gobann brought himself down to land on the ground about forty paces from where the men were making ready to saddle their horses. Once he was standing amid the rotting leaves he began to walk slowly and quietly towards the men, his body heaving in an ungainly manner from side to side as he moved. Once a Raven was standing on the ground, the poet realised, it shed all its airborne grace.

Gobann was very close to the strangers when he finally recognised their language, and in that moment he also understood what the enticing smell was. The man closest to him turned suddenly, saw a jet-black carrion bird before him and called out several words in the Saxon tongue. The poet did not understand much of the language but he had heard it spoken on enough occasions to remember what the words sounded like.

This confused Gobann greatly. These men all wore the blue Druid robes of Gaelic fashion, but underneath they wore mail armour and weapons. Two of them carried long spears with elegant leaf-shaped points. They were masquerading as Gaels; but to what purpose the poet could not discern.

The Saxon approached Gobann slowly and quietly, holding out something to the poet in an

effort to enticе him closer. The foreigner could
almost have reached out and touched Gobann
when the poet saw the source of the scent. The
stranger's arms were covered up to the elbows in
a dark red sticky substance that dripped from his
fingers.

Blood.

Gobann shrieked in surprise when he understood what he was being offered. Without looking
back he took off frantically along a path that led
back into the forest. His wings beat down hard
against the air as he flew on and on, his heart
racing in shock. When he came to a clearing he
decided to rest for a short while and catch his
breath. In the low branches of a tree he crouched,
confident that if the Saxons had decided to follow
him, they would be a long while on foot.

Still reeling from the sight of the Saxon covered
in fresh blood, Gobann stretched his wings and
shook himself. Clearly his Raven body enclosed a
still very human spirit. Calming himself, the poet
scanned the clearing to check that there were no
other Saxons about and noticed a large white shape
lying in the middle of the grassy clearing.

Gobann could smell the scent of death much
stronger here. Now he understood how the Saxon
had managed to get so much blood all over him.
A murder had taken place.

One part of the poet, the carrion part, longed to
take a closer look at the corpse for the aroma of
freshly spilled blood was more enticing than ever.
But the part of him that still had human fears and
thoughts made a quick decision not to tarry in this
place. To do so would certainly risk capture. His
wings spread out like a great fan and Gobann leapt
out of the branches and flew further along the path.
He was sure that if he kept following this track,

sooner or later he would find his way back to the camp where Caitlin and her troops were sleeping.

Gobann followed the twisting winding path a long way before he caught a glimpse of a light through the thick trees. Instinctively he knew that this was the place where his body lay caught in the net of a strange dream while his spirit wandered in the form of a Raven.

Within moments the poet rounded a bend in the path and then, as abruptly as it had begun, the adventure ended. Gobann's vision unexpectedly blurred as he heard voices muttering in Gaelic. His wings were suddenly far too heavy for him to lift and his energy was swiftly draining away. Unable to fight these afflictions, he flew on as best he could, until one of his wings clipped a branch, throwing him off balance. Frantically he struggled to regain his bearings as he fell through the air. Gobann spread his wings once more and then with a loud thump hit the ground to roll in the dust in the middle of the path.

The poet struggled for a few moments more to move his limbs before he noticed a man standing very close and staring at him in fear. Gobann tried to speak, hoping to reassure the warrior that he had nothing to fear from him. But the only sound that the poet could make was a feeble shrieking cry which caused the warrior to retreat swiftly back to the safety of the fire.

Gobann brought all his will to bear in an attempt to raise his Raven body on its long spindly legs, but he fell over almost straightaway, exhausted by the effort. Before he had a chance to try again, his vision blurred for the last time and the poet was plunged into utter blackness. Gobann listened as his own breathing became laboured but there was nothing he could do. His spirit was returning to the body of the Druid harper. He lay his beak down on the dirt and let the breath escape from his lungs, and then he knew no more.

Cathal ordered the war council to convene in his hall as soon as all the search parties, save one, were safely back from their mission. Murrough ignored the summons. He left the handover of the Saxon prisoners in the hands of one of his senior officers and took some bread and water to the walls. There he sat at the breach to wait for the return of Caitlin and Gobann, taking the opportunity to be alone with his thoughts for a while.

But the night dragged on and still there was no sign of his wife and her party. With a heavy heart Murrough began to believe that Ia's assertion must be correct. If the group was camped somewhere deep within the forest, the king could only hope that the monster known as the Glastig would not pose any threat to them.

It was quite late when Murrough finally decided to go to Cathal's hall. Despite his concern for his wife, he understood how important it was that he not miss any of the reports that had come in for the day. He knew from speaking to the guards at the wall that no-one had seen Mawn and Sianan. But he had not heard if any sign of them had been found or what news there was of the Saxon preparations for war. He appointed one of his warriors to remain on duty so that he would know immediately if Caitlin and Gobann returned.

By the time Murrough entered Cathal's hall it was already near to midnight. Some members of the war council were already sitting apart from the main gathering, discussing tasks that had been allotted to them. Others had left to go to their rest, while three elder men were sitting at a table near the door, eating and drinking. Cathal was seated on a Roman style chair near the large hearth fire in the middle of the hall. Ia stood behind him.

Murrough went straight up to his host and bowed before him as was polite. But as the king raised his eyes he saw Cathal was holding out a cup of mead to him. Murrough cast a worried glance at Ia. By tradition only one of equal rank or higher was supposed to make an offer of drink to a king such as Murrough. For the King of Munster to accept the gesture would imply that he acknowledged Cathal's self-appointed status as King of the Southern Dal Araidhe.

Ia rolled her eyes towards the ceiling to indicate that her chieftain obviously thought very well of himself, enough at least to ignore established protocol and place Murrough in a difficult position.

The King of Munster coughed uncomfortably. Acceptance of the cup could create a dangerous precedent, lending credibility to Cathal's claims of kingship. In the end Murrough decided that a short-term insult would be less harmful than a long-term compliment that would be open to interpretation. He decided to decline the offer as graciously as possible.

'I will not take drink while the whereabouts of my wife is uncertain. Please excuse me,' Murrough apologised.

Cathal narrowed his eyes. His face contorted into a forced smile. 'I understand your concern, King Murrough. I am sure that Caitlin and her warriors will return by morning. She is a very resourceful woman.' The chieftain gestured towards a chair on his right. 'Come and sit and I will tell you all that we have learned today.'

Murrough took his place, relieved that Cathal had decided not to show offence at his refusal of the cup. He threw his cloak back away from his shoulders as he sat down, and Ia took hold of the hood, easing the garment away from the king before he had a chance to protest. She smiled at him as she folded the cloak over her arm. 'Allow me to take care of this for you, King Murrough.'

Murrough nodded impatiently, sensing that there was a lot more going on here than met the eye. He also had the feeling that as an outsider he had very little hope of unravelling the many strands of meaning that his hosts were weaving into their speeches and actions. He did not have the same ability to read hidden meanings as Caitlin and Gobann did.

'We believe that your queen may have discovered the whereabouts of the two young Druids,' Cathal announced. 'She sent a rider back to Dun Righ for torches as soon as she reached the edge of the dark wood not far away from here.'

'Why would Caitlin have needed torches on a bright day such as this?' the king exclaimed, genuinely confused.

'Forgive me, I almost forgot that you do not know much about our country. Within that forest hardly any light penetrates for the trees grow so close together. Rush lights are a necessity under such conditions. My people will not usually venture into that place, so it was lucky in many ways that it was Caitlin and Gobann who volunteered to search in that direction.'

'Why don't your folk like to enter the wood?' Murrough asked.

'They have a silly fear of hauntings, and there is

a story about a monster that the Cymru tell. That is more than enough to ensure that the trees will not fall to the woodsman's axe for a few generations yet. I am sure Caitlin and Gobann are safe. They must have come across the tracks of your missing Druids and decided, for whatever reason, to stay the night in the forest. There has been no sign of them leaving again and I know of only one entrance on this side. The only other track through the wood comes out near Dun Breteann.'

'So they have found Mawn and Sianan,' the king said with relief.

'I would think so by now,' Cathal soothed. 'But we have more pressing worries than two young and irresponsible Druids. It seems that the Saxons have massed not far away and may be preparing to attack the hill fort at this very moment. I will brief you on the situation and then I would be honoured if you would give us your insights, King Murrough.'

'I would be happy to aid you in your defence in any way that I can.'

'The first thing you could do is to speak to Declan of Saint Ninian's. His assistant, Isernus, tells me that they have decided to return to the monastery in the morning and, now Tatheus and his men have reported in, it is likely that the Christians will be taking all the Roman soldiers with them.'

'Bishop Patricius sent the Romans with us for the express purpose of aiding in the defence of Declan's monastery,' Murrough answered quickly but politely, perceiving correctly that Cathal wanted the Romans to help defend Dun Righ. 'They are not under my command,' the king went on. 'Caitlin has control over the expedition. She might be able to persuade the abbot or Tatheus not to leave the safety of the stronghold, but the queen is not present and this matter, I am afraid, is beyond my jurisdiction.'

'This is madness!' Cathal blurted. 'We need every able-bodied warrior here to lend their hands in the defence of the dun. Once this fortress is secure we can look to the damage that has been done at Saint Ninian's.'

'Damage?' Murrough queried. 'What damage?'

'The Saxons fell on the monastery three nights ago. One of the old brothers escaped and he claims that most of the buildings were torched. Sadly, I have just moments ago heard the old monk died of his injuries. Declan will perform the funeral rites before dawn as is their custom. The abbot is very distressed by his brother's death.'

'In that case it is probably of the utmost importance to Declan that he return. I will talk to Tatheus but I think I know what his answer will be. He is a man who holds great respect for the orders he is given.'

'They will not get two hundred paces from the gates of the fort before the savages attack them and cut them to pieces!' the chieftain argued.

'I am afraid that the decision still is not mine to make. I am sorry that I cannot be of assistance.'

Cathal ground his teeth together in an effort to control his tongue and hide his frustration, but Murrough could see that the man was fuming at the loss of the Roman soldiers.

'Naturally my warriors will remain here,' the king assured his host. 'It would take a highly organised force to storm your walls and drive you out of the dun. I have never heard of a Saxon band that was anything more than a rabble, no matter how many troops they had gathered together. Their warriors are reckless and determined but generally undisciplined and rarely any match for Gaelic warriors. I was witness to their efforts at the Battle of Rathowen and so I speak with some authority. As soon as their leaders are killed or wounded they lose their will to fight.'

'From the prisoners that you brought in we learned that there are upwards of four hundred of the foreigners massing near the road,' Cathal groaned. 'Four hundred! I pray that you are correct in your estimation of the Saxons, King Murrough, for though we have equal numbers to them and our walls are strong, I have a feeling that not everything will go well for us tomorrow.'

'Tomorrow?' Murrough repeated. 'Did the prisoners tell you that they plan to attack tomorrow?'

'They did not. I have a feeling,' Cathal spluttered. 'That's all. A feeling.'

The king glanced up at Ia, who was staring back at him, eyebrows raised. 'Is it not time that we walked the defences?' she suggested.

The chieftain looked over his shoulder at her, frowning. 'You are right,' he agreed. Then he faced Murrough again. 'You are welcome to come along and see the defence that I have in store for Aldor and his marauders.'

'Yes,' Murrough replied. 'I think that would be a very good idea.'

NINE

short while after sunrise Malchedoc shook Mawn and Sianan awake. Fergus brought two bowls of thick oat porridge for them, which they gratefully accepted.

'You may be criminals but no-one, not even a murderer, faults my hospitality,' the stranger declared. 'Now, get yourselves fed and we'll be on our way.'

When they had finished their meal, Malchedoc led them to a corner of the cave where a large grey fur hung from the ceiling. By the entrance was a small shoulder bag of woven of reeds used for gathering herbs. Sianan thought of her teacher, Síla—she rarely went anywhere without such a herb bag. The stranger pulled back the animal skin to reveal an entrance through which he gestured for them to pass. Once they had entered the tunnel their captor took a torch from an iron support on the wall to light their way.

Fergus made as if to follow, but Malchedoc spun around and warned him off. 'Stay here, lad,' he said firmly. 'Tell my wife that we have gone to the assembly of the Tree folk.'

The boy's eyes widened and he nodded. It seemed to Sianan that Fergus was relieved not to have to accompany them on this part of the journey. In a flash he had pushed the fur aside and disappeared back through the entrance into the main part of the cave. Malchedoc laughed a little to himself then grunted at Mawn and Sianan to indicate that they should walk ahead of him.

The passage was only about forty paces long but the floor was very uneven. Water dripped from many parts of the ceiling, soaking the stones beneath their feet and making the path dangerously slippery. Making slow progress, Mawn held Sianan's arm to steady them both so they would not lose their footing. Ahead of them the passage turned sharply to the right and sunlight streamed through a narrow gap in the rocks above. As they got nearer to the bend they could hear the roar of the waterfall again.

Around the corner the floor was dry and even. The sunlight entering the passage was warm and inviting after the dank tunnel. Nevertheless Sianan felt a chill run through her body. To her this whole journey was reminiscent of the initiation she and Mawn had undergone in order to be admitted to the Druid path. This passage was not unlike the one which led into the mound of testings where they had been confined during the great ritual of initiation.

It had become apparent to her from the very moment they had been led into the dark Otherworldly forest that there was something highly unusual about Malchedoc. At times he seemed to be nothing more than a grumpy old man who enjoyed bullying his captives. However, there were rare occasions when Sianan perceived a quality about him that was very familiar, as though she had known him all her life. All the extraordinary sights they had seen along the way had only compounded the sensation she had that she was revisiting this place after a long absence though she could not recall whether she had met Malchedoc

215

while in spirit form. Everything they encountered in this place had an air of the great initiation ritual about it. Even their emergence once more into the sunlight could have been a part of some obscure and ancient Druid ceremony.

Malchedoc had an unearthly air about him, yet there were many aspects of him that were quite unremarkable. His hair was cut close across his forehead in the Druid fashion, though it was obvious that he had not had the opportunity to shave it in a good while. His beard was neatly combed and he bore the long, carefully rounded fingernails on his left hand that marked him as a harper. Then she remembered the Faerie Kings who had welcomed them into his hall while they were spirit travelling. Malchedoc was much like him, she thought. His demeanour and careful ways marked him as a learned and gentle man, despite his wielding a sword to threaten his prisoners.

Why then, she asked herself, did he feel it necessary to treat Mawn and herself as if they were some sort of criminals? Did he consider that they might pose some danger to him? What could someone like him have to fear from two such as they? And why had he not formally recognised Mawn and herself as fellow Druids?

All these questions buzzed through Sianan's mind. But in the end she could only bring herself to ask Malchedoc one. 'Where are you taking us?' she piped up, as they reached the foot of a rough-hewn rocky staircase that led up into the light.

'I am taking you to see the handiwork of your kindred,' their captor boomed. Any gentleness Sianan had been crediting him with was now well hidden beneath an angry exterior. With a thrust of the sword Malchedoc motioned for them to climb the stairway.

At the top of the ten stairs an overgrown path, obviously little used, led back into the woods. The track lay alongside the stream that poured over the cliffs. Malchedoc's cave seemed to be situated in a natural hollow underneath the waterfall, and the passage they had just passed through lay directly under the stream.

'We have not far to go,' the stranger informed them. Abruptly he strode off ahead of them, apparently expecting them to follow. Mawn shrugged his shoulders at Sianan as if to say, 'What else can we do but follow?'

The path led directly into the forest, though this part of the woods was not as dark as the area on the other side of the stream. Before long they had left the noise of the waterfall far behind. They both noticed that the air was stifling and fetid as if no breeze had passed through for generations. The soil was as dry as if no rain had fallen in weeks and the trees were all grotesquely gnarled and twisted. Most disturbing of all, however, was the sense that some malicious presence was eyeing them both intently as they walked. At times Sianan was almost certain that a feeling of great hatred was emanating from the trees all around them.

Mawn was so certain someone was observing them that he began turning his gaze sharply from the left to the right, hoping to catch a glimpse of the watcher. To Sianan the feeling of foreboding intensified with every step that they took. She grasped her friend's hand tightly to reassure herself that they were safe.

Ahead of them to the left of the path stood an old oak tree wider and taller than any Mawn or Sianan had ever seen in Eirinn. All the feelings of hatred and anger that flowed from the forest were concentrated in the spot where this bough grew, as if it were the centre of a mighty storm. They passed by quickly, not wishing to provoke the tree further by their presence.

They were no more than ten paces away from the venerable oak when one of its high branches thundered down from high above. The thick limb crashed through the lower foliage of the surrounding trees to fall across the path where they had been walking only seconds before. The impact shattered the branch into splintering fragments, turning up a cloud of dust and leaves.

Malchedoc stopped in his tracks, then raced back to the source of the disturbance. When he realised what had happened, he raised his torch above his head to survey the situation. The dust took some time to settle; when it had, he turned to face the oak tree. 'They have not been judged yet!' he protested. 'Control your outrage unless you would prefer to deal with me.' Then, without looking back at his captives, he strode off along the track once more.

Within another hundred paces a clearing came into view where the trees had been planted with much more space between them and the ground was much drier. But those hundred steps were the most frightening Mawn had ever walked in his life. All along the way the forest called out at them in one voice as the boughs and branches yawed and creaked. Masses of leaves rustled in the surrounding undergrowth with a sound like some mighty beast spitting its venom.

Sianan forced herself to stare into the forest, determined not to let the trees know that they had frightened her. On a few of the older tree trunks she thought she could see ancient faces etched into the bark, their eyes burning with a fierce malevolence. Confronted with such hatred, it was not long before she gave up any idea of hiding her fears.

The edge of the clearing was just ahead, and Mawn and Sianan found themselves holding each other very close. The air was as still as death itself and as hot as the inside of a sweat house. They soon drew near to a place where the trees grew in a large circle around a well-tended lawn. As they stepped onto the soft grass all the noise of the forest abruptly ceased, as if by order of some chieftain of the trees.

To their dismay the two young Druids noticed that there were hundreds of birds of every kind congregated in the branches of the woods all around the clearing. Ravens, eagles, seagulls and robins all sat side by side, watching silently with a thousand eyes. Owls, pigeons, doves and crows, every one of them as quiet as the Earth itself, full of malice, as still and cold as ice. Interspersed among the birds were countless woodland creatures; hares, rabbits, mice, badgers, otters, dogs and deer.

Malchedoc waited within a ring of ancient weather worn stones which marked the inner circle of this holy ground. He still held his torch high above him, and in the light Sianan guessed that the whole lawn was no more than seventy paces across, although it seemed much larger because of the sunlight which was not hidden here by the dense encroaching forest. She could clearly see that the stones in the circle were carved with the spirals and dots of the Old Ones. Once more she was sharply reminded of her own initiation into the Druid path.

In the centre of the open ground, standing out in the dim filtering sunlight, a single tall stone stretched up into the sky like the lifeless trunk of a mighty oak. Upon the very top of this stone sat a giant black Raven larger than any that either

Mawn or Sianan had ever seen before. Mawn was awe-struck by the bird for it sat so still upon its perch that it might have been carved out of the standing stone.

Malchedoc turned his rush light upside down and pushed it into the ground to extinguish the flame. Then he silently ushered his prisoners towards the central pillar. They were within several paces of the stone when Mawn caught the terrible sweet stench of fresh blood in his nostrils. He had not eaten flesh for many seasons and found the smell so unbearable that he had to cover his mouth and nose to stop himself from gagging. Only then did he notice an enormous body the size of three men lying at the other side of the clearing.

The corpse had been covered by heavy cloaks and the cloth had soaked up a great amount of blood. It was immediately obvious to both of the Druids that they were looking at the scene of a disturbingly violent murder.

Sianan opened her mouth to speak, but before she could say anything, the Raven on top of the stone screeched loudly. All eyes instantly turned to the great black bird on the perch of solid stone. When the Raven was certain she had everyone's attention, she opened her mighty wings and swooped down to the ground to stand within easy striking distance of Mawn and Sianan.

Malchedoc bowed his head to the bird, placing his hand upon his breast in a gesture of respect. Then he addressed the Raven in a language Mawn could not understand, though the young Druid recognised some of the words as belonging to the Cymru tongue. Sianan, who was very good with languages, identified the dialect straightaway as that of the Strath-Clóta peoples, though she herself could not speak the language. Nevertheless she was able to catch the general tone of what was being said.

'He is welcoming the Raven, as a queen of her folk, to judge some solemn matter,' Sianan whispered to Mawn.

'Pray be silent!' Malchedoc snapped as he turned to face them. 'The matter to be adjudged is a very serious one. You and your people are implicated. I warn you not to try the patience of the forest dwellers any further or else you will certainly find yourself at the receiving end of their wrath.'

Sianan bowed her head, shamed by the strange man's words, but her gaze did not linger on the ground for long. A strange croaking voice called the assembly to order in broken but intelligible Gaelic. Sianan looked up and eventually realised that it was the Raven who had spoken. The young Druid was stunned. She had heard many stories of these magical beasts. She had even known of one or two birds that had been specially taught to repeat phrases in Gaelic, but this was her first direct experience of a creature that could communicate directly with humans.

Sianan was so fascinated that she could only stare in wonder at the bird, half as tall as a man and with an eerie intelligence reflected in its eyes. It was as if somehow the old bird already knew the outcome of this bizarre trial.

'These ones?' the creature asked the general assembly. 'Killers?'

'It was the work of their kind,' Malchedoc answered. 'Without doubt it was Gaelic Druids who murdered our friend.'

'These ones, Druids?' the Raven queried in a disbelieving tone.

'We are Druids,' Mawn answered before

Malchedoc had the chance to reply for him. 'From Eirinn of the Five Kingdoms.'

'You, killers?' the bird pressed.

'We are not murderers,' Sianan interjected. 'We came to the edge of the forest to investigate a group of blue-cloaked men who seemed to be engaged in some holy duties. We assumed they were Druids. When we arrived at the spot where we had seen the strangers, this man Malchedoc launched an unprovoked attack on us. Since then we have been kept as prisoners, contrary to the laws of hospitality and without respect for our rank.'

The Raven stared steadily at Sianan, forcing her to gaze back into the two dark pools of the bird's eyes. For a moment the young Druid thought she could see flames reflected in the depths of the creature's black globes. Then she caught sight of another movement deep within, as if the Raven's eyes had a life of their own, independent of the great hunting bird. Abruptly the creature broke the connection and left Sianan feeling as though the Raven had reached into her very soul.

'These two, not killers,' the creature croaked.

'They are of the people of Dun Righ,' Malchedoc insisted, his voice rising in anger and frustration. 'Their people have encroached upon us for three generations and now they are bringing their ways into the heart of our forest! How much more do we have to take of this? Do we have to wait until there are only a handful of us left before we strike back at them for what they have done?'

'We have not long come from Eirinn,' Mawn interjected. 'You cannot hold us responsible for the deeds of the Dal Araidhans who have dwelt here for three generations.'

'All your people are the same,' Malchedoc spat. 'You take what you want from our land with no

222

regard for the feelings of my people. The forest has been steadily cut back for your defensive works. The river has been soiled by the many who wash in it. The air is full of smoke from your hearths. The land is hunted bare by your warriors. Your roads cut through the glens where only the deer once walked. And now your folk are venturing into the heart of our woodland to murder the forest dwellers.'

'These two, not killers,' the Raven repeated firmly but quietly.

Malchedoc clenched his fists, shaking with rage. He stepped towards the corpse and grabbed at the cloaks that covered it. As he made ready to remove the covers from the body Sianan closed her eyes, not wishing to see the bloody mess. Mawn, however, could not help but watch, mesmerised by what was to be revealed.

When she heard her companion gasp, Sianan was tempted to open her eyes. But still she could not bring herself to look and instead cast her gaze on Malchedoc who stood grasping the bloody cloaks. When the stranger noticed Sianan watching him, he tugged at the covers.

The wrapping came away from the whole body then, and a great head flopped out onto the ground. The eyes of the corpse were still wide open and for a brief second Sianan could only look at them in the same way as she had at the Raven's eyes. So entranced was she by the creature's dead gaze that it was a long while before she realised she was looking at the body of a beautiful white horse.

Several days before his planned attack, Aldor had sent his scouts to search the countryside and gather information about the strength of defenders within the Gaelic stronghold. The party of warriors that Murrough and his men captured had been among those scouts. Had their report reached the eorl he might have realised that his assault was expected, for they had got closer to Dun Righ than any of the other scouts and had seen some of the activity as the people of the hill fort prepared their defences.

Other Saxons followed each search party that went out from Dun Righ to look for Sianan and Mawn. The eorl never learned the purpose of the Gaels, search though; he could only assume that the Dal Araidhan warriors were riding out to scout his own position. Obviously Cathal was planning a major offensive and Aldor surmised that it would not be long before the Gaels launched an attack of their own. This heightened the need to strike first, before the Gaels were properly prepared.

A small group of the eorl's men had walked around the forest as far as they could after they had observed Caitlin and her warriors marching into the wood. None among the Saxons was brave enough, however, to enter the forest for more than a few hundred steps. When the foreigners had found no other entrance or exit from the woods, they returned to the Saxon camp none the wiser as to the reason for the strange expedition. Their leader told the eorl that the forest was a haunted place full of demons. The warrior had heard that even the Gaels usually refused to enter under the canopy of the trees for fear of a monstrous being known as the Glastig.

Despite the fact that he had heard many stories of ancient Saxon heroes who had faced such beasts,

Aldor openly scoffed when his scouts talked of a flesh-eating dragonlike being. Deep down, though, he knew that only a very powerful force could strike such fear into the hearts of his hardened warriors.

Was it possible, he thought to himself, that the Gaels were travelling far and wide to gather their gods for the fight against him, as Tyrbrand had said they would? Could Cathal be hoping to enlist this creature, this Glastig, into the war? The thought plagued him as he continued the preparations for his attack. What if Tyrbrand was right to advise caution? What if this proved to be the wrong time to storm the defences of Dun Righ?

That night the eorl was unable to rest. He spent hours theorising about the outcome of the approaching battle. Aldor had only been half serious when he told the holy man that the god Seaxneat would have to visit him in person to warn him off the assault. But no gods came calling at Aldor's tent as he lay awake in his bed. Every time he heard a noise outside he jumped up to see what it was. He began to wonder whether Seaxneat really had the power that Tyrbrand attributed to him. What if the God of Laws refused to help him? Should he order the sacrifice of the white horse the holy man had brought him?

Aldor was so plagued with doubts that he began to believe his battle strategy would fail. In the middle of the night he found himself overcome by anxiety and he decided to ride out to the hill fort to check the defences of Dun Righ once more.

Under the cover of darkness the eorl came to within a stone's throw of the enemy walls, but he did not take the time to speak to any of his troops stationed on the way. Convinced that all was well here, he stayed with his forward scouts for only a short while before turning around to ride back to camp.

On the way back the eorl realised that he was travelling alone but for a single guardsman to escort him. Suddenly he was very shocked at his own foolishness. This, he knew, was not how a successful war leader behaved. So distracted had he become that he was dangerously neglectful of his own safety. This, Aldor rebuked himself, had to stop. If he was to have any hope of victory in the morning, he would have to discipline his thoughts and concentrate on the challenge ahead.

By the time he had got back to the camp the eorl had shrugged off any doubts that had plagued him. He had decided that he would win the field in the morning with or without the help of the gods.

'They never stood by me before in any other conflict or made their presence known,' he said aloud once he was back in his tent. He drank a long draught of ale as he sat down to relax. 'Why should I believe that the gods would suddenly take an interest in me now after all these years? Every battle that I have fought was won by my wits and skill alone. I don't need any spirit beings to help me.'

By the time Tyrbrand came to ask Aldor to reconsider the attack, the eorl had convinced himself that he was invincible as long as he did not falter in his strategy.

'Have you considered all that I had to say to you?' Tyrbrand inquired.

Aldor allowed a smile to play across his face, but it was a smile full of contempt and hostility. 'I have decided that the assault will take place at dawn,' the eorl announced.

'I have spent weeks sowing subtle discord among the Gaels, inquiring into their habits and observing their customs,' Tyrbrand said softly, trying to reason with his lord. 'I and a few of your loyal warriors have risked our lives in performing our sacrifices close to the enemy fortifications and in the guise of the Dal Araidhans' own holy folk so that, should we be observed, suspicion will fall upon those who have the most influence in their society. I have even made personal contact with the chieftain of the stronghold, though he had no idea that I was anything more than a blind beggar without any clanspeople to support him in his infirmity.'

Aldor coughed dismissively, obviously unimpressed. 'And that is supposed to help our warriors win the stronghold when the time comes? I do not think so.'

'I have spent long days enlisting the aid of the creatures of the forest; most importantly, the Ravens.'

'What are you talking about?' the eorl spat. 'Are the birds going to join my war band now?'

'They are the strong spirits of this land,' the holy man warned. 'Do not speak ill of them for they are powerful. The Gaels also venerate the Ravens, though not as the servants of Tyr, but some of the tribes of the black birds have long-standing grievances with the Dal Araidhans and might be persuaded to side with us.'

'Are you mad?' Aldor cried. 'I do not care about carrion birds. What possible help could they be to me?'

'You must be patient,' Tyrbrand warned, ignoring the eorl's question. 'The time is not yet right for an attack. If we wait until the winter we will catch the enemy unawares.'

'Winter!' the eorl shouted in disbelief. 'You have my leave to do so but the rest of my warriors will

227

be taking the field tomorrow. If you have the stomach to join the attack, your strong arm would be welcome.'

'Many men will die,' Tyrbrand predicted dourly. The holy man was obviously surprised at the eorl's decision.

'If you do not leave me alone this minute, you will be the first to perish,' came Aldor's ferocious reply.

Tyrbrand bowed lowly and withdrew; there was no sense in trying to make his lord see reason. The eorl had made a terrible mistake, but Tyrbrand told himself that sometimes a fool can only learn by being punished for his foolishness. Seaxneat the God of War would be forced to bring Aldor to obedience by the hardest method.

'When the sun rises I will wake you,' Tyrbrand offered as he retreated through the tent flap.

'If you are not careful it may be *me* who wakes *you* with the blade of my sword at your throat,' the eorl spat.

But the holy man was already gone, leaving Aldor to curse his own foolishness at allowing the fellow to frighten him and to influence so many of his raiders. For a while Tyrbrand's fantastic tales of the gods had so distracted him from the task at hand that the eorl had endangered his own life. With that understanding, Aldor became all the more determined not to allow the holy man to ruin his plans.

The eorl spent what remained of the night trying to recall the lie of the land around Dun Righ. He drew maps in the dirt of the defences he had just visited and went over every possible counter-attack Cathal might throw at him. By the time he had eventually worked out a way of effectively breaching the ramparts, it was time to don his armour and leave for the battlefield.

Aldor should have been exhausted to the point of collapse but he found instead that he no longer felt the slightest weariness. The eorl was beginning to fill with that special kind of elation that always came to him in battle. This, he knew, was the secret of his fearlessness in a fight. When Aldor was overtaken with battle fury, he was unstoppable and invincible. When the fury took him it was as if he was walking outside his body, observing the fighting as it took place around him. This gift had often helped him to fend off unexpected blows. It had also been the basis of his remarkable reputation for devastating tactics in the heat of the moment.

The eorl had mounted his new white horse in full battle gear by the time Tyrbrand appeared dressed in his own rather simple leather armour. As was the custom of such folk, the holy man wore a bright red wool cap pulled down over his ears. This marked him for all to see, for none of the Saxons usually wore this colour. Over his shoulder Tyrbrand carried the heavy broad axe that he was renowned for.

'I thought you were advising *against* a fight,' Aldor stated, obviously confused when he saw the holy man. 'Why are you making ready for battle?'

'The gods have told me that I am to serve you faithfully,' Tyrbrand answered calmly. 'Since you are resolved to go into battle against their advice, I think that the best service I could do for you today would be to remove your body from the field. To do that I will need to be dressed to defend it against the bloodthirsty Gaels. I have heard that they behead their enemies in war and hang the dried skulls over their hearths as trophies.'

Aldor could barely contain his rage. 'Your gods

229

obviously did not mention to you that your insolence could cost you your life,' he snapped, truly
hating the man now. 'When you speak to the gods
next time, tell them that I do not tolerate insults
from the likes of you, Tyrbrand. Give the spirits
my regards but inform them that I will be along to
the feast at Wealhall when I am good and ready. I
do no man's bidding and I will not do the bidding
of any god, no matter how powerful he may claim
to be.'

Tyrbrand dropped his axe to the ground and
held his walking staff in front of him. Then he cast
his eyes downward to ward off the eorl's rash
words.

The war leader was so enraged by this that he
drew his sword with the intention of striking
Tyrbrand down while the man was defenceless.
Before he could do so, the holy man lifted his head
and swung the staff up at the eorl's horse. The
animal screamed in fright and Aldor was almost
thrown from his mount.

'That animal was meant to be a sacrifice to the
great god Seaxneat,' Tyrbrand hissed. 'And you
have the arrogance to ride it to the battlefield. Be
careful, Eorl Aldor, lest the gods change their
minds about letting you die with honour today. Do
not anger them or you may find that your wounds
are not quite bad enough that you die by them.
Seaxneat will not let you enter the Wealhall if you
insult him.'

Aldor sheathed his sword without a word then
spurred his horse to ride to the head of the column.
The foot soldiers were assembled and waiting to
set out on the short march to Dun Righ. Out of
deference to his lord, Tyrbrand fell back to the rear
of the column.

The Saxon raiders marched quickly to the hill

fort and took up positions as dawn approached. The army settled into the cover of a hill some five hundred paces from the breach that the Gaels used as the main entrance and exit to the stronghold. Perhaps it was because so few of them had ever ventured this close to the dun that the warriors managed to remain silent, dulling even the rattle of their war gear.

This was not the Saxon way of conducting a fight. Even though the raiders were known for their skill at ambush, they still preferred to challenge their enemy head-on, intimidating them with cries and songs and the beating of their weapons against their shields. The Gaels rarely gave them the opportunity for such display, however, often launching their attacks as soon as the Saxons arrived on the field. Aldor had decided that a surprise would offer their best opportunity to scale the ramparts of Dun Righ.

The walls were not very high, but all along the defences were spearmen and archers who could concentrate their attention on any one spot at short notice. The only place where the defences were weak was at the breach where there was not much room for the Gaels to manoeuvre their troops. The eorl reckoned that if he could get fifty men through the gate and behind the Dal Araidhan archers, the enemy would not be able to hold the wall for very long. Then it would be a simple matter of driving the Gaels back to the inner wall.

Though the gate to the inner stronghold would likely be open to allow the Gaels to retreat, Aldor expected heavy casualties once his warriors had breached the outer defences. The Dal Araidhans would very likely throw everything they had at his troops in order to drive them back, and if the Saxons and Angles faltered they would be swept away like driftwood in the surf. Nevertheless the eorl was certain that if he could encourage his troops to keep up a steady determined attack, the inner wall would surely fall to their assault.

Aldor looked down the lines of men who crouched behind the hill. He had split his forces into three waves that would attack one after the other. This way even if the Gaels managed to inflict heavy casualties on the first line, the second would be able to attack another part of the defences. The effect would be to spread the Dal Araidhan archers so thinly that they would be virtually ineffectual.

Each of the eorl's raiders was dressed in a long mail tunic made up of hundreds of small loops of iron which interlocked to dull the blow of a sword or axe. If the impact was heavy, however, the iron rings could severely bruise the flesh they were supposed to protect. The mail suit could not stop an iron-tipped arrow either, which would simply slip between the tiny gaps and force the rings apart.

Under the rings most of the Saxons wore a leather jerkin which prevented the iron links rubbing directly against their bodies and cushioned any blows. At his side each man carried his favourite weapon. These ranged from sharp polished single-bladed swords to long-handled axes to clubs and spears that had slender jagged points. Of the four hundred and fifty men that mustered that morning, nearly a hundred were raiders who specialised in the use of the short Saxon hunting bow as well as the axe or sword.

The archers all wore thick undyed woollen caps which would not restrict their vision. Most of the other troops wore conical iron helms over leather caps to protect their heads in a close fight. The helms generally had a narrow piece of hammered iron attached to the front which extended down from the forehead to cover the wearer's nose and mouth. Their shields were of rough-hewn timber held together by iron casings, of which almost all had begun to rust in the damp climate of North Britain. Only a few of the warriors carried anything more valuable than their armour and weapons.

One or two of Aldor's Saxons owned long brass horns which they blew when charging into battle or whenever the eorl considered it desirable to taunt an enemy. These beautiful instruments were usually of Briton or Gaelic make, having been captured in raids or stolen from the corpses of their enemies. None among the Saxons could get more than a single note from the instruments, though they had all heard the Gaelic trumpeters play very elaborate tunes on them.

Only fifteen of the eorl's warriors possessed horses and all these were underfed and overworked. These horsemen were some of the richer among his raiders. Few of the mounts sported saddles or bridles because they had been stolen from farm dwellers who could not afford such luxuries. Their owners made do as best they could with what they had, but Saxons rarely rode into battle anyway. Horses were considered excellent for transporting soldiers to the site of a conflict, saving the warriors the exertion of carrying all their armour and weapons before a battle. But no-one in Aldor's company would have considered riding into the fray. Their overlord would have seen that as an act of cowardice.

As always Aldor himself would lead this charge on foot and with a drawn sword. His banner of a black carrion Raven soaring on a bright blue field would be carried at his side by one of the younger men of the company. The standard was a rallying point for the men in time of confusion or rout, and it clearly declared that he was still alive and in control of proceedings.

Most of the ordinary warriors in his army this day were Angles, easily distinguished by their preference for wearing blue coloured cloth. Blue was a sacred colour to these folk. They believed it helped their chances of being admitted to the afterlife of Wealhall if they were wearing blue at the moment of death.

Their armour was sparse, generally only consisting of a rusty iron helm to protect the head, and a large round shield fashioned from oak planks and bound with leather. Many of the Angles carried long spears with leaf-shaped blades, not for throwing but for stabbing at the enemy at close quarters.

Only a few wore any body armour for it was expensive in the Centi lands. There were two types of armour: mail consisting of hundreds of interlinked iron circles, invariably rusty and browned with the weather, and leather armour. The leather protection was good for stopping a spear point or a sword thrust, but not much use against iron-tipped arrows or axes. What they lacked in weapons and equipment, however, the Angles made up for in ferocity.

The Saxons, a far more practical folk than the Angles, had no particular preference for the colour of their battle clothes. They tended to wear anything that was available, the warmer and heavier the better.

Some of the eorl's own men had taken to sporting plaid woven garments of Gaelic origin because they were so easily obtained and lasted for many seasons. This gave the Saxons a strange hybrid look: not quite Saxon and not quite Gael.

The sun lit the land in a grey half-light coloured

by the mist as Aldor walked along the lines of men, giving words of encouragement and promising good shares of the spoils to all, but he had not managed entirely to shake off the sense of unease he had experienced the night before. The eorl noted that his men seemed confident enough and that cheered him immensely. Aldor had a reputation for winning every fight he took on. He had never been defeated in any engagement. He tried to tell himself that all would be well.

The night sky paled as the sun made ready to rise above the horizon. Aldor took one last look at the lines of warriors and was just about ready to give the order to advance when a scout ran up to him with a report.

'The guards on the parapets are changing!' he gasped.

'They're early. They usually don't change until well after dawn,' the eorl hissed, knowing that the success of the whole attack relied on his men getting to the breach before the fresh troops of the new watch had a chance to take up their positions at the outer ramparts. Aldor had counted on being able to bottle them up within the inner defences while his warriors dealt with the tired troops of the night watch.

'Shall we still attack?' the scout asked.

Aldor looked up and down the line as if an answer to this problem lay concealed somewhere among the waiting raiders. The scout's report had passed as swiftly as the wind along the ranks. This was not an army fighting to protect their homes and families. These were raiders who lived for easy plunder; they did not like to take risks.

If he faltered now, Aldor could be sure that the Angles would begin to desert the field, unwilling to throw in their lot with him. If they walked off, his own men would surely follow, and more than a battle would be lost then; his position as war leader would be under threat.

Yet what else was he to do but turn around and go home? The guards on the walls would be fresh after a good night's sleep. Most of his army had not rested since yesterday. His men still had to cross five hundred paces of open ground in their armour before they reached their objective. Most would be tired before they even had a chance to land a blow. The Gaels, however, would not have to make a move at all until their enemies were well within bow shot.

The eorl looked down the rows of warriors again, peering towards the road. At the very extremity of the line a warrior in a red woollen cap stood leaning on a staff. Tyrbrand. All of a sudden the eorl knew in his own mind how the Gaels had been warned of the attack in time to change their guards. Only Tyrbrand knew exactly what had been planned, and of all his warriors only the holy man had spent any time among the Gaels.

The eorl reasoned that Tyrbrand must have stacked the odds against the Saxon warrior in the hope that Aldor would back down from the fight. There was no other way that the Gaels could have known to change their sentries just at that time. Aldor decided that for all his talk of loyalty, the holy man was a traitor.

This realisation enraged Aldor. He drew his sword and strode down towards Tyrbrand. He had not walked more than ten paces, however, before a brilliant idea came to him and all other concerns melted quickly away.

The road.

The road to the dun was well sheltered by trees. If his warriors followed the road, they would not be seen until it was too late for the Gaels to do anything. Instead of covering five hundred steps exposed to enemy arrows, it was a mere forty paces between the last trees and the outer wall. And if Tyrbrand had somehow informed them of his plan, then the Gaels would not be expecting an attack from that direction.

Aldor turned to give a command to the man beside him and the orders were passed down to all the other warriors in each direction. A few men put their shields over their shoulders, shook their heads and walked away from the fight, but they were only a handful. With relief the eorl realised that he had the support of most of the men.

Confident that he had outwitted Tyrbrand, Aldor turned to face the holy man, again intending to berate the fellow for his treachery. What he saw when he looked in Tyrbrand's direction made the eorl's jaw drop. Beside the holy man there stood a warrior in full black mail armour with a brilliant white steed at his side.

The strange warrior looked directly at Aldor then mounted his warhorse and galloped out into the field. Once out in front of the eorl's troops the stranger turned his mount around before the army and raised his mighty battleaxe in challenge. He swung the heavy weapon around his head as if it were no more than a toy. Then the stranger spurred his horse directly towards Aldor, picking up speed by the second.

The warrior's face was completely concealed by the nosepiece of his helm and a leather hood which poked out from under the headgear, so the eorl had no idea who he was. Just when Aldor thought the man was going to ride him down, the stranger brought his warhorse to a halt not four steps away from the war leader.

Aldor asked himself if this could possibly be the god called Seaxneat come to order him home to the Wealhall or to warn him off the battle. Or could this be one of the other old gods summoned by Tyrbrand to threaten him? The eorl made no move, defiantly standing his ground for all his uncertainty, and eventually the black rider dropped the axe to his side. Then the warrior turned his steed around and rode towards the hill fort at a slow trot. In a few moments more he had passed over the crest of the hill and disappeared from Aldor's view.

The eorl was determined not to let his men see the profound shock that he felt. He raised his sword in the air and pointed it towards the road. The warriors began to move off quietly as they had been ordered. As they passed by, the eorl realised with a cold shiver that no-one except perhaps himself and Tyrbrand had witnessed the strange apparition. This above all else convinced him that Seaxneat had come to make his displeasure known. Aldor sensed then that the attack was doomed but he could not reverse his decision. He was too proud to admit that Tyrbrand had been right. The eorl preferred to die in battle than have his men think of him as weak-willed.

TEN

hile Aldor's army was gathering behind the hill Declan the Abbot of Saint Ninian's was making final preparations to depart for his own community in the far south of Strath-Clóta. In the hours preceding sunrise he had seen to the last burial rites of Brother Kilian, saying a mass in the open air as his old friend Origen of Alexandria would have done, then offering up prayers for the old monk's soul. That done he had added another personal supplication begging that Christ guide him as abbot and protect him on his journey back to Saint Ninian's.

The cows had been milling around him when he finished. Cathal would not spare any other ground for Kilian's grave and so the monk had been buried in the cow pasture on the side of a hill. Nothing marked the last resting place of his body save a simple cross of wood tied together with strips of leather.

With his farewells said, Declan had returned to the house where he and Isernus had been staying as guests. There he packed all his valuables: his portable altar, his handwritten gospels, his vestments that had been a gift from Patricius Sucatus and, last of all, the silver gilt cross that High-King Leoghaire had presented to the monastery.

Satisfied that all was ready, Declan knelt down again to pray while he waited for a summons from

Isernus who was seeing to the carts. The abbot, however, found it very difficult to concentrate on his devotions.

He reckoned to himself that if the roads were good and the party not unduly delayed, the trip would take a full day to complete at a moderate walk. Declan knew only too well that it would be courting disaster to be travelling in the south after sunset.

The escort of Roman soldiers was organised by Tatheus into a defensive marching line that would be spread out alongside the two wagons. The Roman centurion appointed Birinus, an able veteran of the Frankish wars, to head the team of four scouts who would travel ahead of the main party.

Despite the thorough preparations, Declan knew he would not feel safe until all of his party were well within the walls of the monastery. Kilian's report of the Saxon attack on Saint Ninian's had disturbed him greatly. He had thought that Aldor was finished with them for the time being at least. But Kilian had told him, before he died, of at least five raids that had taken place since Declan had gone away to Eirinn.

What disturbed the abbot even more was that, according to Kilian, several pleas for help had been sent to Cathal but all had been ignored. Declan could not help thinking that if Cathal had kept his promise to help protect the monks, the Saxons might never have bothered raiding the monastery at all.

When the sun rose red against the light clouds in the east, Declan took it as a sure indication that it would very likely rain later in the day. All the soldiers were assembled and Tatheus had given his final instructions to Birinus. Murrough and Cathal appeared together near the breach and then waited at the guardpost with a large group of their warriors.

Cathal had sent a warning to Declan that he would give the order to begin sealing the breach in the defensive wall as soon as the abbot and his men had passed through with their wagons. He also mentioned that they should be as swift as possible in leaving the hill fort so that if the Saxons intended to spring a trap, as the chieftain suspected, the breach would not be open when they did so. Declan realised that Cathal had no intention of offering support to him and his party if they were attacked. As chieftain his main concern was the safety of Dun Righ.

When Murrough rode down to say his farewells, the abbot was still going around both wagons making sure that all was in order for the journey. The rest of the hill fort inhabitants were just beginning to stir from their sleep. On tracks that led around the dun people were making their way down to the wells to get water and gathering turf and timber from communal stacks for their breakfast fires. A few hearth fires were already sending up little billows of smoke as flames took to new kindling. The warriors on the ramparts were leaving their positions as fresh troops who had rested through the night gradually arrived to replace them.

The change of watch was uncoordinated and disorderly, Tatheus thought, but then none of the warriors were professional soldiers like the centurion and his legionnaires. Only a few of the Gaels had ever seen service in foreign armies, and those few were glad not to have a centurion yelling at them to get to their positions.

The abbot noticed with interest that those warriors who had sat sentry through the dark hours did not go straight to their homes but began gathering near where the walls of the inner defences began. He was a little confused by this unusual behaviour because the off-duty watch usually went directly to their breakfast. He shrugged it off as Cathal ensuring that there were enough warriors ready in case the Saxons did attack. The abbot tried not to think about the nervous upset that had taken hold of his stomach but he could not help feeling that something unexpected was about to happen.

For all that, he was determined to leave, whether the Saxons were waiting in ambush or not. His own safety was not a consideration. Declan was responsible for the community of Saint Ninian's. He did not want it said that the Saxons had successfully destroyed one of the first monastic settlements in Britain while he was abbot. And he knew that the savages would not expect him to return so soon after their attack. This would give him a chance to rebuild and raise a good solid wall around the monastery.

He was distracted from his thoughts by Tatheus who interrupted to report that both the wagons were ready to depart and a runner had been sent to Cathal's warriors at the barricade to let them know it was time to clear a path for the party. Declan quickly blessed his little convoy, and the wagons lurched forward along the dirt track out of the dun.

It was a slow steep journey downhill towards the great wooden fence that temporarily closed the breach in the outer wall. Both drivers leaned heavily on wooden staves that acted as brakes, rubbing against the wheels to slow the carts down. Declan had loaded as many provisions on each wagon as possible and as a result both of them were very heavy. This meant that if the drivers did not take great care, the carts could pick up too much speed down the steep incline and run over the ponies.

Even at that slow pace, however, the breach was not clear by the time they reached it, and the wagons ground to a halt within the outer wall. Declan could see that the work was not far advanced and that they would probably be delayed here quite a while yet. He began to notice the nervous unrest in his stomach again and wished sincerely that the journey was already over. The abbot whispered a prayer, begging his God that there would be no further delays.

As he was crossing himself to end the prayer Declan noticed Murrough approaching with Tatheus. Behind them were two soldiers who held Seginus firmly between them. The priest was still bound and gagged. As soon as the two warriors put Seginus down beside Declan, the abbot looked Murrough in the eye sternly. 'Don't you think he's had enough?'

'That is no longer my concern,' the king explained. 'You are his gaoler now. I would advise you to keep a close guard on him at all times. If I know this creature he'll be back to his treacherous ways the moment his tongue is free to wag.'

Declan turned to one of the guards. 'Untie him,' he ordered in a firm but gentle tone.

The soldier hesitated for a few moments, unsure whether the abbot had the authority to give such an instruction. Murrough said nothing, turning away as if he had not heard the abbot's words.

Declan breathed out loudly in exasperation. 'He is mine now,' he pointed out.

Realising that Declan was not going to be swayed, Murrough pointed to one of the soldiers and gave the order to release the priest.

The soldier took out a knife to cut the ropes

which tightly bound the prisoner's wrists, while his companion began to unravel the chains that were wrapped around the man's legs. By the time they had removed all the restraints, the barricades were cleared and only the leather mask remained to show that Seginus was under sentence for his crimes. Declan took his own little knife and cut the straps on the mask, letting it fall to the ground.

Seginus blinked as he faced the sunrise, then he spoke quietly in a real effort to show his gratitude. 'Thank you, brother, for your mercy.'

'I am placing a lot of trust in you, Seginus Gallus,' Declan warned him.

'I will wear the chains on my legs as Patricius ordered me to do,' the priest answered to everyone's surprise. 'When I have proved myself worthy then you can decide to release me from that penance.'

'I have no wish to see you suffer any more, brother,' the abbot answered, suspecting that Seginus had some other motive for this request.

The priest gritted his teeth with determination. 'Do as I say. Please. I am determined to pay for my crimes and show you my contrition.' Seginus closed his eyes and looked towards the sky so that if anyone suspected he might be lying, they would not see it reflected in his face. It was better to appear remorseful for the time being; later, when the opportunity arose, then he would strike. Earn their trust, he told himself. Earn their trust.

The abbot weighed up all his options. It might be better, he reluctantly admitted to himself, to ensure that Seginus was properly restrained. Anything could happen on the road and he knew he would regret it if the man escaped into the wilds to join up with the Saxons or to find his old master Palladius. Nevertheless Declan could not bring

244

himself to chain the man in the same manner as he had been bound for the journey from Eirinn.

'For the moment one of your wrists will be bound to the rear of the wagon by a rope, but when we arrive at the monastery you will be released. After that I will have to trust that your conscience prevents you from attempting to escape.'

'He knows too well what would become of him if he managed to get away from those who wish to see him justly punished,' Murrough added. 'It would be all the excuse Caitlin and her warriors needed to hunt him down.'

Declan helped Seginus onto the back of the second wagon where he was secured, and then the abbot took his seat at the reins of the leading cart. He was by now very anxious to get moving—they had wasted too much time with all this talk. The abbot said hasty farewells to Cathal and Murrough, reminding the king that when the danger had passed, Mawn and Sianan should be sent to him, as they had expressed an interest in seeing the monastery.

'If they are found, I will send them to you as soon as the Saxon threat has been properly dealt with, and Strath-Clóta is free of the cloud of their raids,' Murrough promised.

Isernus was seated beside the driver of the second cart and as it passed through the breach the younger monk called out his farewells to Murrough. 'Do not fear, Lord Murrough, Caitlin will find Mawn and Sianan if anyone can,' he called out. 'You must come and visit us when this war is finished.'

Declan breathed a sigh of relief when they were past the walls and on the road. He did not look back at first, though he could hear the warriors sealing the breach behind them. Carefully the abbot

checked the position of the sun and swiftly reckoned that they had already squandered much
valuable daylight with the various delays.

'Can we travel a little faster, driver?' he said to
the man at the reins.

The driver grunted that he might be able to push
the ponies on for the first part of the day as long
as the weather stayed cool and there was no rain.
The abbot thanked him and then took out his
daybook to make a note to that effect. As he was
scratching his words with a stick of charcoal Declan
heard the raised voices of many warriors at the
wall behind him. But he was determined not to be
distracted from his book and to finish what he had
to write.

As soon as he had completed his notes, Declan
turned back to see what the commotion was all
about. It was then that he noticed twenty or so men
rushing out through the breach in the outer wall,
making directly for his convoy with their weapons
at the ready.

'Lord, do not let this be another delay,' the abbot
breathed with exasperation.

The words had barely passed his lips when he
heard another series of shouts, this time from the
wooded area that fronted the hill fort and sheltered
the road from the view of the sentries. Declan spun
round in time to see a large number of warriors
standing in a long line and blocking the road
ahead.

These warriors had their weapons drawn and
were thumping them in a slow rhythmic fashion
against the front of their shields. Every so often
they would let out a low humming grunt that
startled the abbot. He had never heard or seen
anything like this in his life. Just as the driver
brought the wagon to a halt the warriors ahead of

them ceased their noise and broke into a charge. Because the morning sun dazzled his vision and he could not see whether these warriors were Gaels or Saxons, it was not immediately apparent to Declan what was happening.

Such was the abbot's confusion that the warriors had almost converged upon the two wagons before he was certain that these men were foreign raiders. At first guess he reckoned there to be a hundred or more of the savage Saxons charging directly at him with their axes and swords raised in war fury. Then he noticed many more of them coming in from the right and left of the road where they had been waiting in ambush.

Declan froze with fright. He and his party were trapped. The driver of the cart had already gone running back to the safety of the ramparts, but Declan had still not moved from his seat. With a jolt he realised that if he did not jump from the cart, he would be in great danger.

As the first of Murrough's men made it to the front wagon the abbot landed on the ground. One of the Gaelic warriors grabbed him by the sleeve and dragged him back to the second wagon where Isernus was already being bundled off by two more of Murrough's men. The younger monk was struggling with the warriors, refusing to abandon the supplies that were bound for Saint Ninian's. In the end the two men were forced to half carry and half run with him towards the breach in the wall.

Declan spun around to take another look at the enemy and noticed that Tatheus and his men had formed a wall of shields, their spears lowered at the foreigners. Moments later a large group of the Saxons ran straight into the tight formation and many were impaled on the fine Spanish steel of the

Roman lances. Still Tatheus and his men stood firm, the foreigners making little impact on them.

Declan understood that, despite the discipline of his soldiers, Tatheus would not be able to hold out for long once the Saxons managed to surround them. It would only be a matter of time before the Romans were overwhelmed by the sheer numbers of the enemy and butchered. The Gaelic warrior who had been dragging the abbot back towards the walls abruptly let go of him at this point and Declan realised that Murrough's men were preparing to make a stand in defence of the Romans.

A dozen Saxons managed to push past the Roman formation, and within minutes the fight had become so confused that Declan couldn't be sure in exactly which direction he should run to find safety. There were warriors everywhere and he was glad that he was not one of them for he could not tell who was friend and who was foe. Out of the corner of his eye the abbot caught a glimpse of Isernus in the middle of the fight, but then the warriors packed together in a great swarming melee. In this situation none of the combatants had room to swing their weapons. They resorted to pushing against each other in an attempt to shove their enemies back to their own lines.

At this point the abbot slipped over on the road and rolled into the ditch at the side. By the time he had regained his feet, the great pack of opposing warriors had broken apart again and the Gaels were falling back to the hill fort. Before he knew what was happening, the abbot was running back towards Dun Righ, his heart pounding loudly in his ears and all thoughts of the provisions for the monastery taking second place to that of his own survival.

As he scuffled along in his old sandals a man dressed in mail armour pushed past him in a great rush, knocking the abbot aside as he forced his way towards the walls. Declan realised to his horror that the man was a Saxon. However, the raider travelled only a few more steps before he was struck down by a flight of arrows that came from behind the ramparts.

Clearly Cathal had planned his defence well: no-one was going to get past the outer defences of the hill fort without the chieftain's leave. The Saxons had picked a bad time to launch their attack with all the best warriors of Munster on the ramparts and the new sentries fresh from a good night's sleep.

A rain of arrow bolts flew high into the air from the Gaelic lines and Declan made a dive towards the ground to cover his head in fear of being hit. As he lay there many warriors passed him by, making for Dun Righ, but it was a while before he realised that they were all Saxons. Another wave of arrows burst forth from the ramparts just as Declan decided to get up again. He had no choice but to curl up in a ball on the ground and hope that he was not hit.

The deadly forest of missiles did not seem to deter the Saxons, however. They continued to rush forward to where three ranks of Murrough's men stood in front of the breach blocking their path. Somehow Tatheus and a dozen of his men had made it back to Murrough and had joined his troops in their attempt to drive the foreigners back.

In a great clash of arms the Gaelic warriors brought their weapons to bear against their enemy, but their efforts did not slow the foreigners' advance. The Saxons were clearly not interested in the carts or their contents. They were not interested in these few Gaels and Romans who stood in their way. All they wanted was to get within the walls of the stronghold as quickly as possible.

Once more both sides pushed at each other in a press of warriors. Again neither side had the advantage of being able to get a clear strike at its foe. Only the archers, Saxon and Gael, managed to make any impact, dropping their arrows with deadly accuracy on the helpless foot soldiers.

Declan was relieved to find that the Saxons had ignored him in their advance, so that now he was actually behind their main line. But then it struck him that if he wanted to get back to safety he would have to get past the enemy first. He made up his mind to try going around the place where the fighting seemed fiercest, but within a few paces he had stumbled forward over the corpse of the foreigner who had pushed past him earlier.

The abbot fell hard in the dirt, opening his eyes to find himself staring directly at the warrior's bloodied head. In horror he forced his gaze away from the seeping wound and onto the foreigner's hair. It was a sandy yellow colour and braided together like a fine rope. 'I wonder if that would make strong bindings,' he said to himself, disoriented and in shock.

In that instant the abbot thought of the rope which had tied Seginus to the cart, and he let out a cry of anguish. In a flash Declan was on his feet again and frantically trying to get his bearings. For a little while he could not even see the carts.

'Calm down, brother abbot,' he told himself. 'God will watch over you if you only trust in him.'

Declan could plainly see many more Saxons charging towards the hill fort, and then he noticed the second cart behind him. The abbot was not as frightened of the foreigners as he was of what might happen if Seginus escaped, so he hesitated, taking his time to decide in which direction it would be safest to run. Then, skirting around the road in the ditch, Declan made off as fast as his legs would carry him towards the second wagon of his convoy. He had not quite reached the cart, however, when he clearly heard the voice of Seginus calling out something to the savages in their own tongue.

As soon as the carts had passed through the outer defences of Dun Righ, Seginus Gallus sensed that freedom was not far away. Something warned him to keep his wits about him. The priest searched the sides of the road, hoping to find some clue as to what was going on. Like Declan he noticed that the night watch at the hill fort did not return to their homes but remained mustered behind the inner ramparts.

This puzzled him until he realised that there was only one possible explanation. Cathal must be certain that an attack was about to be launched. So intent was Seginus on trying to seek out the places where the Saxons might be concealed that at first he did not notice the figure that had settled itself beside him. It was not until he turned his attention to the front of the wagon that the priest saw the ghostly apparition curled up in a corner beside a sack of oats.

The shock of the appearance made Seginus call out in alarm, but neither the driver of the wagon nor Isernus acknowledged him.

'Shh. He is sitting in front, brother,' the spirit whispered. 'The one who murdered me is so close that I could reach out and touch him from here.' The figure held up a thin bony hand and squeezed his fingers around an imaginary neck as if he were strangling his victim.

Isernus must have sensed something for he stood up in his place and peered over the top of the supplies to check that the priest was still well secured. Seginus did not even look at the monk. He only stared into the distance as if there was no-one blocking his view.

'Don't worry, my dear brother, he cannot hear or see me. Isernus does not even suspect my presence.' Sure enough the monk resumed his seat again as soon as he was sure the priest had not escaped.

'What is happening?' Seginus demanded. 'Something is afoot. What have you done? Tell me!'

'Not so loud, brother,' the ghost answered, a smile broadening across his grey face. 'He cannot hear me but he can still listen to what you have to say.'

'Tell me what is going on,' Seginus repeated in a hushed tone.

'This is your chance for freedom, my brother,' the spirit hissed. 'I have arranged a rescue for you and the opportunity for you to finish the job I have long requested of you.'

'What rescue? What are you talking about?'

'Saxons,' came the ghostly reply. 'Just ahead are four hundred and fifty of the wildest foreign raiders north of the fortress of Eboracum. They will create a little diversion while you escape.'

'Escape?' Seginus muttered, confused. 'But, Linus, you told me to work at earning Declan's trust. How will I do that by attempting to escape?'

'It has all been arranged,' the spirit explained impatiently. 'Just do as I say and you will be presented with an opportunity to punish Isernus once and for all.'

'I will do as you say,' the priest answered meekly. 'Just tell me what I must do.'

'As soon as the Saxons launch their assault, you must work at cutting the cords that bind you to this cart. You will have to move quickly or you will be caught up in the fight, and then I cannot guarantee that you will live to see the sunset today. Once you are free, get yourself away from the main fight. I will lead you on from there.'

'Very well,' Seginus agreed. 'It is time to avenge your death, isn't it?'

'It is time,' the ghost confirmed.

'And will I ever see you again after this day?' Seginus asked, strangely saddened to be finally cutting the bond between them both.

'For your sake I hope we never meet again. I still have a while to spend atoning for my sins and enjoying the suffering of my dear friend Isernus. You would not want to visit the places where those torments take place.'

'What will happen to him?'

'Isernus will be mine,' the spirit cried, his face distorting with wicked glee. 'Mine! He and I are bound together forever.'

Seginus was about to ask what his brother meant by 'bound together forever' when the ghost stood up suddenly and stared at the road ahead.

'They are moving!' the creature declared. 'Farewell, brother. May we never meet again.' Then the spirit reached out a hand to Isernus. From where he sat Seginus could not clearly see what his brother was doing, but it seemed to him that Linus was touching the monk tenderly on the back of the head.

'I will see you, Isernus, very soon,' Linus promised, and then his form faded away from view and

Seginus was left alone. In that instant a great weight lifted from the priest and he knew that he would not really miss Linus at all.

Remembering his brother's advice to work the rope free as quickly as possible, the priest reached silently across the cart to where a large bolt protruded from the side of the wagon. He ran the rope over this piece of metal and gradually the strands began to unwind and sever.

At the same time Seginus heard shouts from the ramparts and he realised that the Gaels must have spotted the approaching Saxons. In a few seconds he had broken the rope that bound him to the wagon and started working at the piece that held his wrists together.

The next thing Seginus knew was that the wagon was surrounded by Gaelic warriors who were dragging the occupants from their places. The priest rolled over to hide himself behind the sacks of grain, hoping that he would not be noticed. After a short while he realised that the Gaels had indeed passed him by, and then he stood up to look out for the Saxons.

What he saw took his breath away. Everything that his brother had said was true. There were hundreds of foreigners rushing forward to the attack. These fierce looking raiders were all laughing with the joy of battle and the prospect of pillage. In excitement Seginus called out to them.

'I am here! Help me!' he cried before he realised that they would not understand him. It had been a year or more since he had spoken with any of these people and then it had been to Franks, who spoke a different dialect of the Germanic tongue to these warriors. He had to try and remember Guthwine and Hannarr, the two Saxons he had served with in Hibernia.

When he thought he knew what to say, he called out again in what approximated the Saxon tongue, appealing for help from any of the raiders who would hear. To his utter surprise one of the warriors stopped and levelled a blade at him. Seginus repeated his plea for help and held out his wrists. In a moment the warrior had sliced the bonds apart and then dashed off again to take part in the fight.

Seginus jumped down from the wagon as soon as his hands were free and there he caught sight of Declan running towards him through the crowd. In a desperate attempt to escape, Seginus skirted around the front of the wagon and under the ponies which were still harnessed to the cart. He rolled away just out of reach of the abbot and then ran off to find a safe place to sit out the rest of the fight.

As the priest was running along the ditch at the side of the road he noticed that King Murrough and his warriors were making a stand just outside the breach. It was obvious that the king's guards were hopelessly outnumbered and that they would very likely be driven back inside the fort. Seginus squatted down behind the lip of the ditch until he was sure that he had not been seen, then he lay flat on his stomach to watch the rest of the battle.

Not long afterwards Seginus sensed the presence of someone behind him. He rolled over quickly but there was no-one there. Then he heard the voice of his brother's ghost. 'Don't just lie there skulking,' Linus sneered impatiently. 'Get to your feet and find the murderer Isernus. You must reach him before it is too late.'

Seginus sprang to his feet but realised immediately that he had no idea in which direction he should go. There were hundreds of people all around the rampart breach. Perhaps it would be best to check the carts first. Even from where he stood, however, it was obvious that there was no-one alive anywhere near the wagons. Not only that but the priest had a hunch that Isernus was somewhere in the thick of the fighting. He scanned the area where the main fight was taking place.

Saxons and Gaels were battering at each other with their swords and axes. Most of the spearmen had withdrawn, their weapons virtually useless at such close quarters. But the archers on both sides were letting loose hundreds of shafts that fell among the struggling warriors of both sides and took a deadly toll.

Then, unexpectedly, a man dressed in the dark brown robes of a monk staggered out from among the melee and fell onto his back close to the grassy edge of the road a hundred paces away from where Seginus was standing. He had three arrows stuck very close together into his chest and he clutched at them desperately.

Without a moment's hesitation the priest gathered up his tattered garments and ran headlong towards where Isernus lay, heedless of the constant stream of falling arrows. Seginus dodged around the corpses which littered the road and passed by many wounded men who called to him for water in the Saxon language, but the priest paid no attention. He was only interested in the monk. The murderer.

Seginus was desperate to reach Isernus before the monk breathed his last. It was clear even from here that the wounds were fatal. Another wave of arrows fell. Seginus ducked down, covering his head as he ran; not that it would have made very much difference if one of the bolts had struck him. The priest looked up after the storm of arrows had subsided and saw that Isernus had been struck once more, in the throat just above the collarbone.

During his service in the legions Seginus had seen many such wounds. He knew only too well that such an injury caused the victim to choke to death or suffocate within minutes. Now he was all the more desperate to reach Isernus before the monk slipped into unconsciousness; that is, if he had not already done so. The priest skidded the last few steps along the grass and came to rest at the monk's head.

Isernus opened his eyes in that very instant. To Seginus' relief he was still conscious. Here was the man who had killed his brother in cold blood and thereby set into motion all the disastrous events that followed after. Everything that had befallen Seginus in the years since he had first arrived in Hibernia with Palladius had happened because of the sins of this man.

'I could kill you now,' Seginus grunted, 'and no-one would ever know that I had done it or how much you suffered.'

Isernus struggled to lift his head and with great effort he spoke one word, 'Yes.'

Seginus was shocked. He had expected the monk to put up some sort of a fight, to refuse to succumb to mortality. That was only natural. Seginus had never known anyone to go willingly to their death. Suddenly he felt cheated. He grabbed the man by the shoulders and screamed at him. 'You will not die yet! I will not let you. I want you to suffer.'

The dying monk looked back into the eyes of the priest and whispered something unintelligible. Seginus bent down to put his ear close to the man's mouth.

'Absolve me,' Isernus begged. 'Forgive me.'

'No!' bellowed Seginus. 'I will not do that for

you. Who was there for my brother when he breathed his last? Who heard his confession and blessed him as his soul fled into eternal damnation?'

Isernus twisted his mouth in the effort to answer. Finally he managed to get enough air in his lungs to speak. 'I absolved him,' the monk gasped. 'I wanted to send him on his way but he would not accept the sacrament.'

Seginus stared at the monk in disbelief. He refused to accept this. Isernus was trying to trick him into giving him the last rite so that the sin of his brother's murder would be wiped away forever. The monk shook his head and then his eyes rolled back in their sockets and his skin began to turn blue.

All around them the Saxons were walking away from the ramparts as if they had gone out for a stroll in the countryside. Everything had suddenly taken on a dreamlike quality. The priest sensed the ghostly presence of Linus nearby. He knew straightaway that his brother had come to gloat over the suffering of Isernus. Seginus turned to look behind him and drew his breath in horror for there stood the hideous monster that had first come to him in the prison of Nantes. He was shocked, for Linus had not taken on this foul form for a long time. The face was pale and waxy and the lips were contorted in a strange expression that seemed at one moment to be full of joy and at the next to be an intense burning agony.

Suddenly the misshapen form of his brother, twisted with hate and the desire for vengeance, moved close to Seginus and stooped over the body of Isernus. The priest could hear the apparition laughing in a low guttural wheeze that mocked the pain of the monk who lay dying on the ground.

'At last you know what it is like,' the ghost hissed, pressing forward to hover less than a finger's length from the face of Isernus. 'At last you understand what it is to have your life slowly drained away from you, drop by drop, breath by breath.' Linus reached out a skeletal hand and clasped his fingers around his victim's throat, slowly stifling his breath. The priest could see that the dying monk was labouring hard to draw air into his lungs.

In that instant Seginus understood that the spirit of his brother was pure evil. Perhaps because Linus' attention was focused elsewhere, the priest was suddenly free of the strange spell that had afflicted him for so long and driven him to do whatever the ghost bade him. Seginus watched the scene before him and, instead of revelling in his brother's revenge, found that he was utterly disgusted.

'That is enough!' he cried, moving to drag the ghoulish fingers away from the throat of the choking monk. He could do nothing, however, for the ghost's fingers had no substance even though they seemed steadily to be drawing the life out of Isernus. 'Stop!' Seginus bellowed.

Linus released his grip and, in a hissing voice filled with derision, turned to face his brother. 'How dare you interfere with my sport? You who could not make a success out of even the most mundane profession.' The spirit reached out and plucked contemptuously at the priest's robe and then laughed harshly. 'Leave me. I am finished with you.'

Those words struck deep and hard at Seginus. Ever since he had first encountered his brother's spirit he had done all he could to help him towards this goal. Now he realised that it had all been for nothing more than the perverse enjoyment that this creature was having in seeing another soul suffer. He knew that he was of no value to this demon save as an instrument for evil. Seginus could hardly bear the pain of this realisation and he wondered that he had not understood it earlier. He reached into his robes and drew out his cross, holding it before him like a warrior holds a shield when the arrows are falling.

'Leave this place, servant of Satan,' he began, but Linus only laughed louder. 'Leave this brother in Christ to breathe his last in peace or I will call on God to intervene.'

'Please do!' Linus snapped. 'Will your God hear you? Does he care about one who has broken so many of his commandments? You and I share more than a common father. We are very alike indeed, dear Seginus. You are as evil as I am, perhaps even more so. You are not worthy of God's love. God does not come and go at the bidding of one such as you.'

The priest did not wait another moment. 'I call on the Archangel Michael and all the saints in Heaven,' he intoned. 'I call on the blessed Virgin and her Son, the Christ, to intervene and banish this monster from Earth forever.' Seginus closed his eyes and concentrated all his thoughts on this one objective, to drive the evil spirit of Linus off and save Isernus some of his pain.

But nothing happened. And when after a few more moments there was still no answer from heaven, Linus began to laugh in his customary mocking manner. He laughed until the gurgling fluid in his throat erupted as foul smelling spittle, showering the priest and making him recoil in disgust.

Then abruptly the laughter stopped. Seginus

opened his eyes hesitantly, half afraid of what he would see. The ghost of his brother was still stooped over Isernus but the expression on his face had changed completely. Linus was no longer jubilant. He was frightened. The spirit turned to face his brother and Seginus could now plainly see that the ghost had been struck by some unspeakable terror. Linus reached out a thin bony hand to the priest, but before he could touch Seginus the creature began to melt away like mist in the morning sunshine. In a few more moments, without another sound or cry, the spirit was gone, leaving only the memory of his contorted features burned into the priest's mind.

Seginus forced himself to steady his laboured breathing as he tucked the cross back inside his robe. Then he turned his attention back to Isernus and found that he could not help but still feel that the monk deserved to suffer for the murder of Linus. He could not banish the thought of revenge from his mind entirely for it had become as much a part of him as his name. In a flash of inspiration Seginus realised that if Isernus lived he would suffer for the rest of his life from these wounds.

'I will take you back to Dun Righ. You are not going to get off so lightly, you murdering bastard!' he yelled.

But Isernus just smiled up at the priest and with the last of his strength lifted his hand to make the sign of the Cross in front of Seginus. Then the breath ebbed out of him and his eyes glazed over.

The priest leaned over the body of the man that had been for so long the focus of his hate, who had represented to him all that was wrong with the world. As he looked into the eyes of Isernus he knew that the monk had told the truth. Isernus had absolved his brother. He had given Linus the last blessings, even though he had been responsible for his death.

Seginus looked up and knew also that his brother's spirit would never return. It had fled to the realms of hell or wherever it was due to serve its penance. He was certain now that Linus would never haunt him again. He was free.

The corpse lay on its back. Seginus adjusted the head so that the chin rested once again on the chest, and he closed the eyelids to give Isernus an attitude of peace. Then, leaning in close as if the monk could still hear, Seginus whispered a few last words. But he was not addressing Isernus; he was speaking to Linus.

'Thou art avenged, brother,' he said in Latin. 'Thou art avenged and absolved.'

eleven

eclan could not speak a single word of the heathenish Saxon tongue so could only guess what Seginus might be saying when he called out to the enemy. He quickly decided, however, that the priest could only be appealing for help to escape, and at that instant Declan made up his mind to stop him, no matter what the cost.

The abbot shoved his way fearlessly through the oncoming enemy warriors, but Seginus had already untied his bindings and jumped down from the cart. The abbot thought he understood what Seginus intended to do and so he cut around behind some of the foreigners in an attempt to catch up with him.

Gaelic arrows were falling all around. The abbot dodged miraculously between the flying bolts but did not manage to get close enough to Seginus to grab at him or drag him to a halt. At one stage Declan let fly a punch at the priest but he missed Seginus completely. Instead Declan's fist connected with the body of a nearby Saxon and he heard a crack as his knuckles crunched into the foreigner's armour.

It was then that Declan lost sight of the priest as he tried to soothe his injured hand; by the time he had regained his wits, Seginus was gone. The abbot cursed his own foolishness. He had little hope of finding the man again in the heaving crowd.

Declan was caught up in the throng of enemy soldiers, and though they did not seem to care very much about him, he knew he was in great danger if any of them should decide to turn on him.

With the intention of running back towards the carts Declan made his way through the warriors. It was his hope to reach a place where he could shelter until the fight moved on or the Saxons were driven back. Declan had only gone a few steps, however, when all the luck that had followed him so far ran out.

An arrow soaring down from the Gaelic battlements struck the abbot hard in the left shoulder. As much out of shock as pain Declan gave a howl as the shaft hit him. The force of the arrow striking him pushed his body forward and jolted his head back. Declan lurched and fell to the ground between two dead Saxons. He lay there for a few seconds in bewilderment for he had not expected such a blow. The first thought that came to him when he regained his senses was that an axe-man had hit him in the neck from behind.

When Declan reached around to touch his sore shoulder he realised that it was an arrow tip not an axe that had cut deep and hard into his flesh. With this realisation the pain intensified and the abbot turned over to lie on his stomach. He gasped in agony as the iron tip scraped against bone, and then he understood that he had to remain as still as possible.

But when Declan had recovered a little he could not resist clutching at the shaft with his right hand in an attempt to dislodge it. The hooked head of the bolt was firmly lodged and he nearly fainted from the intense pain as he touched the wooden shaft. It would not move without causing him great distress from its tearing barbs.

The abbot was now in a grave position. He knew that it would be nothing short of a godsend if he escaped from this battle with his life, yet he resolved to try nevertheless. Somehow he managed to get to his knees without jarring his shoulder too much. In the desperate hope of catching the attention of a Gaelic warrior, he lifted his right arm in the air. There seemed to be only a sea of Saxons all around him. He could not even tell from where he was whether the defences had been overrun by the enemy or not.

Everywhere he looked there were foreigners charging about madly, screaming and yelling and laughing with battle lust. Declan could not remember any situation in his life that had been nearly so chaotic or frightening or desperate as this. He was only grateful that the Saxons seemed so intent on making their way into the hill fort that they completely ignored him.

By this time the abbot's robe was drenched in blood and he was beginning to feel light-headed from the great loss of the precious fluid. In one last desperate effort he called out to the battlements, but this only attracted the attention of several nearby Saxons who turned around to see what all the fuss was about.

One of them, a tall man with jet-black hair flowing from beneath his battle helmet, strode towards Declan with a great single-bladed sword raised at the abbot's head. Declan recognised him almost immediately. The abbot had gone many times to the Saxon camp to plead for mercy on behalf of his flock.

'Aldor!' he called out. 'Eorl Aldor, I have been wounded. Help me.'

The eorl stopped dead in his tracks to laugh. 'Help you?' he asked in thickly accented Gaelic.

'You are of no importance to me. I have a greater prize in my sights.'

The eorl pointed with his sword to the stronghold then stormed off, making for the middle of his mob of warriors.

'I am a man of God!' Declan screamed. Too late he remembered that Aldor's folk worshipped other gods.

Even more of the Saxons swarmed in from all around like a plague of locusts from the Old Testament. The Gaels were being forced steadily back by the sheer numbers of their enemy, and it was apparent that the foreigners were only moments away from gaining control of the breach.

As best he could Declan sized up the situation and decided to do the only thing he could think of that might help win the day. He clasped his hands in front of him in the Roman fashion, careful not to aggravate his wound, and offered up a prayer for the deliverance of the people of the Strath-Clóta.

The abbot was not sure whether God heard his plea among all the din of battle, nor indeed if anyone noticed him at all. All he knew was that in the few seconds after he began to beg for the intervention of Christ and the Saints, his fortunes and those of the defenders of Dun Righ changed completely.

Declan heard an anguished shout from near the ramparts, followed by a short period of eerie silence as if every warrior on the whole battlefield had paused to take a breath at the same time. This distracted the monk from his devotion long enough for him to comprehend that Aldor had suddenly stopped in his tracks and was no longer pushing forward. The Saxon war leader was frozen, seemingly in fear of something, though the abbot had no idea what it could be. Then Aldor's knees buckled slightly and he began to turn around to face Declan.

It was not until the warlord was looking directly at the abbot, his mouth wide open, that Declan understood what had happened. Two arrows had lodged deep in the eorl's body; one striking him in the chest after it had pierced through his mail, the other sticking out from a gap in the armour under his right arm.

The abbot could see straightaway that the second arrow could not have come from the direction of the hill fort. The angle of protrusion indicated that it must have been loosed from behind the eorl by one of his own men.

Declan raised his right hand and, without considering for a moment that the man before him was a heathen, slowly made the sign of the Cross. The eorl's eyes widened in recognition of the sign and his fear seemed to intensify. Then he slumped forward onto his knees not twenty steps away from Declan.

The abbot would have tried to get closer but he did not get the chance. A warrior in a long brown cape and a red wool cap, a huge battleaxe in his hands, approached the eorl. Abruptly he shoved Aldor to the ground with a brutal kick which knocked the breath out of the eorl. The strange warrior stood then behind Aldor and laughed, not loudly but just enough that Declan could hear the sniggers.

The abbot watched horrified as the strange man bent over to pick up a horn that had hung about Aldor's waist. He put it to his lips and blew three times. All the Saxons instantly ceased their fighting and, after a short period of confusion, began to walk quickly back towards the spot where Declan lay. This sudden silent retreat struck even greater fear into the abbot than the initial shock of the original assault. The savages were turning around to attack him, or so he thought in his confused state.

Declan saw their leering faces as they passed by like figures from a child's nightmare, and he waited, certain that he was about to be struck down and killed. One or two looked as if they would certainly kick him as they passed, but the expected blows never came.

Instead the abbot felt his head spinning and his vision begin to blur. He did his best to remain upright to face the raiders and show that he was not afraid of them, but his body was no longer up to the task. He searched in his robes for the small gospel that he always carried and this last act sapped what little strength he had left. No sooner had he opened the book than he fell face first into the dust.

Some time later Declan awoke to feel hands groping at him from above. In a desperate attempt to fend off the attackers he grunted loudly, kicking his legs about as best he could to keep them at bay.

'Stay your hand, Brother Declan,' a familiar voice urgently called to him in the Gaelic language. 'It is I, Murrough. I have come to bring you safely back to Dun Righ. If you struggle with my warriors your wound will be worse for it.'

The abbot opened his eyes and immediately the world began to spin violently as if he had been twirling around in a Gaelic jig all night. He could just make out Murrough's features a short distance away and the blurred shapes of several warriors who were trying to help him to his feet, but the spinning was now so terrible that he had to shut his eyes once more. But this only made his giddiness worse, so that he was soon retching from the sensation. The nausea reminded him of his first experience in a high sea when he had set out as a member of the mission of Palladius. How Seginus had laughed at his seasickness on the voyage from Gaul to Eirinn.

'Seginus!' Declan called out. 'Where is he?'

'I am here, brother abbot,' the priest answered in a soothing and subdued voice, though Declan still could not see him. 'I am doing the work of a priest.'

Declan struggled to focus and eventually he discerned the figure of the priest kneeling over a body dressed in dark brown robes. This jerked Declan back to full consciousness for among the whole party that had set out for Saint Ninian's only he and Isernus had been dressed in monk's attire.

The abbot could see that the corpse was lying face up on the road. Four arrows protruded from the upper torso and another was lodged in the thigh. The dead man's skin was as white as chalk and his mouth was awash in blood, so that at first Declan hardly recognised him. He could hear Seginus talking to the man, so for a moment the abbot thought that perhaps Isernus was alive after all. Then he heard the words that the priest was muttering.

'*Benedicámus Dómino. Deo grátias. Requiéscant in pace. Amen.*' Seginus crossed himself, signed the Cross over the body and muttered a few more words in his own Gaulish tongue that Declan could make no sense of.

By this time the abbot was being carried past the body of his assistant towards the dun. His bearers were already near the breach before Declan managed to gather his wits enough to react to what he had seen.

'Isernus!' he cried, the anguish of the disaster engulfing him. The vision of his good friend lying dead on the road was too much for the abbot to bear. Declan struggled against the warriors who carried him, but the effort drained the very last of his energy and he lapsed into a deep numb state. The bearers felt Declan relax and Murrough was relieved that he was not fighting them, for his wound seemed very serious.

But the abbot had not slipped into unconsciousness. The figure of Father Seginus Gallus performing the rites of the dead for Isernus remained in his mind as he was being taken to the house of healing. There, as the warriors laid him down on a bed, he awoke and a strange sensation came over him. He did not know if it was just his imagination but he was certain that he heard the voice of his old friend Origen of Alexandria lecturing him, as he had so often before he died, on the Eastern philosophy of cycles.

Origen had pointed out that this was a belief his people held in common with the Gaels. The old man had stated many times that the basis of Christ's teaching was that everything on Earth and in heaven moved in great ever-turning circles.

Declan heard his friend as if he were standing in the room beside him. So strong was the feeling that the abbot was afraid to open his eyes in case he saw Origen standing before him.

'We are all bound to the cycles of the cosmos, though we may resent their motion and deny their hold over us,' the voice said softly. Declan remembered that Origen had stressed to him that to deny the movement of the cycles was to deny the Earth itself. For had not God created everything in cycles?

'For every single thing there is a season,' the

gentle voice whispered. 'A time for planting; a time for reaping. A time for joy and a time for sorrow. A time to embrace your fellow creatures and a time to be alone.'

When he heard those words the abbot relaxed, suddenly sure in his own mind that Seginus had come to the completion of a circle, just as Isernus had. Their two circles had crossed and were now spinning off in different directions once more. Declan lay back and closed his eyes, breathing deeply and peacefully.

TWELVE

alchedoc broke the silence in the clearing after he had covered the slain white horse once again. 'This was no act of senseless violence perpetrated by a people who hold little respect for other living things. This murder has all the hallmarks of a ritual slaughter done to honour some god or demon or other such being.'

'Mawn and I are both initiated Druids,' Sianan protested, appalled that she could be accused of such a crime. 'Such acts are as abhorrent to the Gaelic folk as they are to your people.'

'Yet it was blue-robed Druids of the Gael who did this deed!' Malchedoc barked. 'They have been observed skulking around the edges of the woods for weeks now. Explain that to this assembly.'

'You wear the blue cloak,' Mawn pointed out. 'You have the shaved forehead of a poet. You know that such sacrifices are not practised within our tradition. Do you really believe that your brother and sister Druids could be responsible for such barbaric behaviour?'

'Brother and sister Druids?' Malchedoc repeated incredulously. 'My brethren, my sisters, my whole family live within this forest. I hold no ties with anyone who chooses to dwell in the world beyond these trees.'

'And what of the vows you took as a Druid and

a poet? What of the precedents and practices of Brehon law?'

'The Brehon laws do not have any place in this woodland,' Malchedoc answered. 'My vows as a Druid must take second place to a promise that I made to a Danaan queen.'

'Where is this queen?' Mawn asked. 'Can we not appeal to her to judge our case?'

The stranger coughed and turned to the Raven, shrugging his shoulders and showing the palms of his hands. 'They would not ask for her help if they knew what she thought of their kind!' he exclaimed.

'We are innocent,' Sianan insisted. 'We came to the edge of your woods because we were intrigued by the presence of a group of Druids near to where you found us. We had nothing to do with this killing or the folk who committed this crime. Have you considered that perhaps it was those same Druids that did this terrible thing?'

'Maybe it was,' Malchedoc admitted. 'Or maybe you are trying to cover your own involvement in this murder by inventing these other Druids. Whatever the truth is, an example must be made to your folk so that none of them dare return to our domain.'

Around the clearing there was a chorus of approval from all the birds and other forest-dwelling animals gathered to hear the judgment. Only the great Raven was silent, gently preening her feathers as if she were alone in the grove.

'When my wife the Glastig reigned over this forest, none of the field-dwelling folk dared walk here for fear of their lives,' Malchedoc declared. 'The creatures of this place lived in peace then, without the threat of attack. It has been a long while since she took one of the field dwellers and in part I am to blame for that. I convinced her that it was wrong to terrorise the simple people who lived outside. It was I who urged her to cease her sport with those who entered the forest.'

The birds all spoke together, acknowledging his admission and agreeing wholeheartedly.

'But I can see only too well now that I was wrong to interfere in the ways of the Old Ones,' the Druid continued. 'The Gaels hold nothing sacred but their own selfish desires, and they will stop at nothing to get what they want. Today it was the life of a white horse. Tomorrow it will be oak trees for their ships or feathers for their arrows or fox pelts for their coats. If our home is to remain safe from the outsiders we must use every weapon at our disposal to discourage their invasion. If one or two Gaelic folk have to die to keep the rest of them at bay, then I cannot see that it does that much harm.'

All the animals started speaking at once in their own languages, raising a noise that threatened to bring the assembly to a riotous end. There was no doubt that almost every creature present agreed with Malchedoc; after all, he was the best qualified to speak on this subject, being a mortal man himself.

Only the great Raven remained silent, content to wait until the din had died down.

'If you intend to do us harm, I should warn you,' Sianan spoke up, trying to sound more confident than she felt, 'you have no evidence that we have committed this crime and no witnesses who will swear it was by our hands that the white horse perished. If you take this matter into your own hands, the Druid Council will hear of it and it will be you who face the judgment of the Brehon lawmakers.'

'You are on the island of Alba now,' Malchedoc

reminded her. 'The Druid Council of Eirinn is not recognised here as the supreme authority on the law. In this land it is kings and chieftains who make the rulings and the judgments. In this forest it is this assembly that decides what is just. Since I am a chieftain, a Druid judge and the only one of the human kind present, it is my duty to advise my clanspeople on the subject of your sentence.'

'You are not the chieftain,' the Raven spoke up. 'I was elected last summer. Glastig does not rule here anymore.' Then the bird began to repeat the assertion in the Cymru language but had only just begun when she was interrupted.

'You are not the only one here who is a human of the Druid kind, Malchedoc,' a woman's voice boomed from somewhere in among the throng of onlookers.

The animals and birds gasped collectively and then a stunned silence fell over the assembly. Birds were hopping out of the way, clearing a path for the newcomer so that all who were present could see her. The woman marched out into the centre of the grass and took a place at the front of the assembly as if she had as much claim to do so as one of the forest dwellers.

'I challenge your right to sentence these two young people to death,' the woman insisted. 'There is no precedent for it even in this forest, and none but the cruelest tyrants dare to impose it. The Glastig ruled this wood without regard for law for so many generations only because no-one dared stand against her. The truth is that she was as afraid of outsiders as they came to be of her.'

The woman stepped a little closer to the central stone but was still far enough away from Mawn and Sianan that her face was obscured in the shadows.

'You did not come to this forest to wed the Glastig, Malchedoc. You came here to rid the forest of her curse. But when she fell under your spell, you also fell under hers. In time she has turned your distaste for her ways into a belief that they were justified, so that now you do not seem to think that it is such a bad thing to slay intruders.'

The woman paused for a moment to let her words sink in to all the animals and birds at the gathering. Then she took a few steps closer, but Mawn still could not make out the features of her face.

'Even if you had proof that these Druids were involved in this crime, where is the sense in putting one who has committed murder to death? One killing spawns another. That is how wars begin. Once you have the precedent of these two victims being put to death for trespassing, where will the slaying stop? This court has no evidence and consequently no jurisdiction to hand down a sentence on these two Druids. You will release them.'

Malchedoc's face went bright red and for a moment Mawn thought he saw something about the man that was very familiar and very frightening.

'I will not be told what to do in my own forest!' Malchedoc screamed.

'You are not chieftain,' the Raven croaked. 'I am.'

Malchedoc turned to the main assembly, seeking its approval. 'Will you let a clever argument snatch from you the chance to avenge our good friend's death?'

'So that is the heart of the matter, is it? Revenge,' the woman chided.

No bird nor animal stirred in the clearing. Even the trees seemed to cease their gentle sighing and rustling. All was quiet and as still as the corpse of

276

the white horse. Sianan could sense that this last comment had struck a chord with the assembled creatures.

'The best revenge that you can have for the murder of the white one,' the woman continued, 'is that you never let her die in your memory. The killers may have destroyed her physical form but they have not robbed us all of our recollections of her. If we keep her alive in our thoughts, she will be immortal; only then will we have cheated her murderers.'

The Raven cocked her head to one side and clicked her beak in approval, but Malchedoc turned to face the woman as if he were about to explode with rage. When he finally spoke, however, Mawn was surprised at the controlled gentleness of his tone.

'You owe me your life, Druid healer. I plucked you from the very jaws of death. Is this how you repay me? By insulting me in front of all my kinfolk?'

The woman strode forward and struck her staff into the ground. Then she looked up into the sunlight that streamed down into the clearing. The light revealed a face thickly blanketed in ornate dark-blue spirals and fringed with brown hair that was wild and tangled and tied up with scraps of cloth. Sianan thought she recognised this woman; there was something incredibly familiar about her, but the young Druid had never met anyone with so many designs cut into their face.

'I have a duty to these two young ones,' the woman insisted. 'They are in my care and they should be in yours also, Malchedoc. You above all others have a great knowledge to impart to them.'

'They are Gaels and nothing more,' the man retorted.

277

'As you once were.'

'You are not of their people. You are a Cruitne. Their folk slaughter your tribes to clear the land for their cows.'

'It is not their people,' the woman corrected. 'Only some greedy ones among their people.'

'I will not stand here arguing with you all day, Síla!' Malchedoc boomed. 'You have made your point.'

Mawn and Sianan both gasped and stared at the woman in wide-eyed wonder. If this was Síla, she was much thinner than the teacher they had farewelled in Eirinn more than two moons earlier. Her skin had turned an even darker shade of brown since she had been away from them, and the patterns on her body had grown like vines that cover an abandoned wall.

The Raven coughed loudly before either of the young Druids could greet their friend. 'I have decided,' the old bird announced. 'They not killers. We find killers then we find judgment.' With that the Raven broke off into her own language, speaking more quickly and more confidently, her words obviously finding favour with the assembly.

'Very well,' Malchedoc eventually declared when he could see that the majority would accept the Raven's decision. 'We will find the killers and bring them to justice. But it will be our justice and not that of the outsiders.'

All the birds called and shrieked and began to fly off to different parts of the forest, passing the news to every living thing in their homeland. When they had gone Malchedoc turned to face Síla. For a second it looked as though he was going to berate her again, but he withheld his anger with some effort and simply said, 'I release my prisoners into your care.'

Síla sighed heavily, hoping she had not made herself an enemy. 'When the real killers are found, you will be thankful that you did not make a great mistake in harming these two,' she said gently.

Then Síla turned to face Mawn and Sianan. 'How in the name of the goddess Brigid did you come to be in this place?'

'We could well ask you the same question,' Mawn replied with a broad smile.

'Let us go back to the Glastig's cave and on the way I'll tell you,' the healer said as Sianan wrapped her arms around the teacher and hugged her fiercely. 'And when you've heard my tale then you can tell me yours.' She paused for a moment and then added, 'Is Gobann with you?'

'No. We left the main column and lost sight of him the day before yesterday,' Sianan admitted.

'He is very close though,' Síla observed. 'It is almost as if he is listening in on every word.'

Malchedoc turned to leave but as he did so a young Raven of perhaps only three winters came to land on his shoulder. The bird spoke lowly into the woodsman's ear and Malchedoc acknowledged the creature with grunts. When the Raven had passed on its message and flown off again, Malchedoc raised his voice so that every creature still within the clearing would be able to hear him.

'An armed band is marching towards this assembly place with flaming torches. Gather every creature to the defence of our homeland. The enemy will be upon us before midday.'

Immediately there was a flurry of activity as birds flew off and larger ground-dwelling animals stepped out of the underbrush to take up positions around the clearing. A group of seven stags with towering jagged antlers trotted to the track to stand guard. In the distance a howling cry erupted and was answered by a loud low growling on the other side of the woods.

Malchedoc turned to Síla and spoke with great satisfaction. 'They are Gaels,' he hissed. 'The warriors marching here to attack are of the tribes of Eirinn. What more proof do you need that their folk intend to take this forest for their own?'

Síla shook her head, refusing to believe that armed warriors of the Dal Araidhe would venture into the woods to attack the forest dwellers. 'You cannot be sure that they are going to attack us.'

'Then why are they carrying swords and spears and bows?' Malchedoc retorted sharply. 'They have marched across the whole wood and spent one night camped here. If they are only hunters, why would they bother to travel so deeply into the forest?'

The old Raven clicked her beak and screeched. Síla, Mawn and Sianan turned to face her, expecting her to say something, but instead she merely cocked her head to look at them more closely.

'Is this true?' Síla asked the old bird. 'Have these Gaelic warriors come to do the woodland harm?'

'They would not be the first,' the creature cackled. 'And they will not be the last.'

'I have sent word to the Glastig,' Malchedoc announced. 'She and the rest of her folk will be here soon to aid us. No mortal can stand against them.'

'You stood against the Glastig once, did you not?' Síla commented.

'I did not!' the man replied tersely. 'I convinced her to change her ways by offering her something that she lacked.'

'Someone with whom to share her long life?'

'I was in love and believed that forgoing death was a small price to pay for peace in this land. In those days I did not understand things as I do now. If I had seen the world through the eyes of the creatures of the woodland, I might never have come to this forest thinking to persuade the Glastig to change.'

'So you would break the vows that you made as a Druid to keep the laws and traditions of your people? You would turn against your own folk and bring harm to them?'

'I am no longer a Gael!' Malchedoc bellowed, losing his temper again. 'I have made this place my home and call these folk my kin.'

'You best be careful, brother Malchedoc,' Síla warned. 'The Druid Council does not take kindly to poets who choose to do the bidding of the Sidhe-Dubh.'

'I am no servant of the Dark Faeries. Can you not see that because of my sacrifice many Gaelic lives were saved? But times have changed. The evidence of that is lying lifeless under those blankets.' He pointed to the body of the white horse. 'The Gaels have brought their warring ways to this forest and I can no longer answer for the consequences of their brutality.' With that, Malchedoc stormed off towards the track that led to the Glastig's cave so that he would not have to hear any more of Síla's talk.

'That is why he called himself the Wanderer,' Sianan commented. 'He is like us. He has been chosen to walk deathless in the world.'

'He alone made that decision,' Síla pointed out. 'Malchedoc was a famous harper and a poet of the Silver Branch as Gobann is, but in those days the Druid Council would not have considered allowing him to take the steps that he did to placate the Glastig. Malchedoc did not consult with any of his peers or fellow Druids. He did not even inform the

Assembly of the Drúi at Cnoc Pocan of his whereabouts, and they are the highest authority among the Druid kind. To fail in his duty to report to the assembly was considered by some to be an act of arrogance or rebellion.'

'He talks as if the granting of a Wanderer's life has been a great burden on him,' Mawn said, beginning to comprehend all that Gobann had told him and Sianan about the difficulties ahead for them. 'He is a very bitter man.'

'Yes,' Síla agreed. 'He has been given a great gift by the Glastig. He will live with his lover for as long as she draws breath. He does not age, nor does sickness touch him. But that does not guarantee that he is happy. Every day has become a burden to him and he longs for rest.'

'Will Mawn and I become like him?' Sianan began, voicing the fear that they both held. 'Will we be so tired one day that there is no joy left in us, only bitterness and regret?'

Síla put her arm around Sianan and then reached out to hug Mawn to her also. The healer wished that she could tell them their lives would be different because they had been specially trained to manage the challenges of the future. She wished that she could tell them for certain their work would be fulfilling and fruitful. But she knew in her heart that anything could befall them in the future. The Druid Council could only see so far into the mists of time and no further. They could not tell all that would come to pass.

'I do not know,' Síla admitted. 'I simply do not know.'

Caitlin and Gobann had risen when the sentries had judged it to be early morning. The forest was still perfectly dark and so there was no way of knowing whether the sun had come up in the world outside.

The dream that Gobann had experienced was unlike any that he had ever been afflicted with in all his life. Usually when he suffered the Faidh visions he was given a clear indication that he was not merely asleep and imagining the entire experience. But on this occasion there was some doubt still in his mind as to whether the vision was genuine. Ever since his great initiation into the community of the Silver Branch he had longed for the opportunity to take the form of a Raven again. What he could not be sure of was whether he had simply allowed this wish to take hold of his dreams.

One thing was certain—Gobann had suffered none of the usual debilitating after-effects which almost always confined him to bed for several days after a vision. The poet had woken refreshed and eager to get back on the trail. He did not mention the encounter with the five Saxons to Caitlin. Under the circumstances he thought that it would only serve to worry her.

The party packed away the gear after a quick meal washed down this time by water rather than brewed beverages. Then, with the fire well concealed and the torches lit, they set off again down the Avenue of the Seasons, as Gobann now referred to the track that led through the forest.

The poet noticed that the trees were certainly getting younger and younger the further they walked, but within five hundred steps of their camp site the scouts reported another fork in the path up ahead. Once more Caitlin was confronted with a difficult choice.

'Of the footprints that we have been following,' she informed Gobann, 'five sets branch off to take the left fork and one set takes the right.'

'I would think it best that we take the left-hand fork then,' the poet commented.

'If we have been following the tracks of Mawn and Sianan,' the queen muttered, 'then I suppose you're right. But I have a feeling that we have missed them entirely somehow.'

Gobann asked himself whether these tracks could be the footprints of the five foreigners. Had it been Mawn's or Sianan's body he saw lying mauled in the clearing?

'We must press on,' the poet said finally. 'That is all we can do now. Let us take the left-hand path.'

Caitlin nodded her agreement and sent off the scouts. As the party trudged on again Gobann noticed that the trees had changed character. They were no longer arranged according to the calendar, becoming gradually younger. The poet was deeply disappointed for he had been looking forward to coming to the place where no trees yet grew. He had hoped to chance upon the gardener planting the seedling for this month and to ask him some of his secrets.

Here the trees were all old, not ancient as they had been deeper into the forest, but well aged nevertheless. And they seemed to be mostly unremarkable except for the twisted gnarled forms that were common enough where the soil was dry. Gobann let his attention drift to other things. He began to wonder about the tale that had come into his head the previous evening, the one he had told the warriors in front of the fire. The more he considered the possibility, the more convinced he became that this was the forest where Cianan of the Sweet Melody had met the Glastig. If they could only seek out the old Druid and obtain his help in their search, they would certainly stand a better chance of finding the Wanderers.

But Gobann understood that he had as much hope of finding Cianan of the Sweet Melody in this place as he had of coming across his students, especially if Cianan was content not to be found. He caught up to Caitlin to have a word with her.

'Tell the men to keep a lookout for any signs of habitation. Recently cut timber, wheel ruts in the track, wood smoke hanging about in the trees, or even sounds that might indicate someone is living nearby.'

'Are you going to ask the Danaans for their help?' Caitlin asked, a little surprised.

'Perhaps not the Sidhe folk, but one who dwells among them if I come across him,' the poet replied.

'So your story last night was about this forest!' the queen exclaimed. 'I think the men will let us know if they find the Glastig in these woods.'

'I pray that she does not find them first,' Gobann answered sombrely.

A short while later the poet discerned a rumbling sound in the distance and surmised that there must be a river and waterfall nearby. The path, however, veered off in the opposite direction. There was no visible track which might lead them towards the noise, and so the poet had to be content to carry on along the path they were following. Not long afterwards the sound became quite loud again, so he guessed that there was more than one waterfall in this wood.

What the poet did not notice was that apart from the noise of rushing water the forest was strangely silent. It was Caitlin who remarked on it.

'No matter how dark the forest was further back, the calls of birds followed us all along our journey,' she pointed out to Gobann. 'But now it is as if there are no birds or animals at all in this wood.'

The poet agreed that it was indeed very strange but could offer no explanation other than that they had so completely lost track of time that it was now well after sunset in the world outside. Neither he nor Caitlin, however, could entirely convince themselves of that.

They had just finished speaking when a scout returned to the queen's side, keeping his head and body low as if he were avoiding an enemy bowman.

'There are many footprints ahead in the track,' he whispered. 'I fear there may be an enemy force waiting in ambush for us just ahead.'

'How many would you guess?' the queen asked.

'We have no way of knowing,' the warrior replied. 'The footprints of humans are intermingled with the tracks of countless animals. All the tracks are fresh.'

Caitlin passed along the order to proceed with the utmost caution and absolute silence until contact had been made with the enemy. The bowmen in her company placed arrows on the taut strings of their bows in readiness for a fight. The swordsmen drew their blades and the spearmen untied the leather covers that protected the points of their steel spears from the elements.

'If you hear, see or sense anything,' Caitlin told Gobann, 'let me know immediately for I have a very bad feeling about what lies ahead of us.'

'This does not have the characteristics of the work of the Sidhe-Dubh,' the poet reassured her. 'They have no need to lie in wait. They have other more effective and powerful means for our destruction at their disposal. If it were the Dark Faeries who wanted to attack us, they would have done so last night when most of our warriors were asleep.'

Caitlin understood that Gobann was probably right but she was not reassured. Then something happened that convinced her even more of the danger that was upon them. Two piercing calls rang through the forest, chilling the queen to her core.

They were the cries of a fox calling to his mate and she returning his summons, but there was something in the tone that was unusually eerie. Gobann called the entire party to a halt and suggested Caitlin bring the warriors into a defensive formation. She readily agreed, preferring to cease their advance for the moment to ensure that everyone in the party was safe.

The warriors, including the scouts, stood in a tight circle around the queen, none of them making a sound as they waited to see if there were any further noises from the forest. They had not been standing together long when they received confirmation of their worst fears. One of the warriors was lighting a new torch from a rush light that was almost spent when a roar like the growl of a huge dog echoed through the woods. Caitlin jumped and Gobann let his jaw drop in amazement.

'It is the Glastig,' the man standing closest to Caitlin said with resignation. 'She has come to find out why we are wandering in her forest.'

The warriors looked to the poet in awe and terror, but Gobann was as surprised as any of them and could offer no explanation for the strange deep howl. He did not know of any woodland animal that had a call as loud or as wild as the one they had just heard.

Caitlin gripped the blade of her sword and leaned close to the poet. 'What should we do? Should we stand, move on or retreat?'

'Where would we retreat to?' Gobann asked her. 'Back into the forest?' He thought about the situation for a few moments and, unable to offer any better suggestion, said, 'Let us make a stand. If the Sidhe-Dubh are waiting up ahead to ambush us they will tire of waiting soon enough and attack. It is far better that we stand together than spread out in an indefensible line.'

'Very well,' Caitlin replied, 'we will wait.'

The moments dragged on into minutes and still there was no sound from the forest, not even the noise of bees or flies. All the leaves were perfectly still for there was no breeze to stir them. The warriors remained on the alert, watching, waiting, expecting an attack at any moment. But none came. No Faerie host threatened them. No hero of the Sidhe-Dubh stepped out to challenge them.

Eventually Caitlin came to the conclusion that they were wasting precious time.

'It is quite possible that whoever has Mawn and Sianan is trying to keep us at bay by attempting to scare us off,' she commented to Gobann.

'That is a distinct possibility,' the poet agreed.

'We cannot wait here all day,' the queen pressed.

Gobann closed his eyes. He rolled his head back and stretched his arms out wide above his head, pushing two of the warriors out of the way as he did so. Caitlin could see that the poet was trying to focus his senses, so she signalled her men to give him more room.

The warriors did not have to be told twice. They all knew Gobann well enough, but none of them had much experience of Druid ways. To them the poet might just as well have been conjuring up a demon as concentrating his senses. The effect was the same—it frightened them all. Only Caitlin, who had been a Druid initiate herself before she became Queen of Munster, did not flinch.

'There are many creatures gathered nearby,' the poet intoned, reading what he could from the forest. 'Among them are Mawn and Sianan. They are prisoners.' Gobann frowned and breathed hard. It seemed to Caitlin that he was very frustrated about something.

'There is someone else there who is familiar to me,' he said, 'but I cannot quite make out who it is. Perhaps it is Cianan. I sense a great danger unless we tread carefully.'

Caitlin strengthened her resolve. 'We did not march all this way through this forest to stand quivering a few hundred paces away from our goal. Let's go to the Wanderers' rescue. There are twelve of us, armed and battle-tried. At least we will make an impact on the enemy.'

'But the lives of the Wanderers may be placed in peril,' Gobann retorted, opening his eyes and dropping his hands back down to his sides. 'Put your swords away. Our only hope is that we can talk to their captors and perhaps reason with them.'

The poet touched the top of his forehead with the palm of his hand. 'The Glastig certainly is nearby,' he confirmed. 'I can sense her malevolent presence. But I would not think that even a hundred Gaelic warriors, not even all the hosts of Finn Mac Cumhal, would stand much of a chance against her and her clan in a pitched battle. We cannot fight. It is better that we try to talk calmly with the Glastig and her people.'

Caitlin was confused. Only a short while earlier Gobann had counselled her to sit and wait until whoever was waiting for them made the initial contact. Now he was trying to convince her to march into a possible ambush with swords sheathed and spears pointed down. 'I will go and make contact with the Glastig,' she offered eventually. 'I will go alone so that no-one else is placed at risk.'

'If you are injured or captured,' Gobann answered, 'who will command these troops? Not I. I am no warrior. I am a poet. I am a judge. I am a Druid of the Silver Branch. It is my duty to go on ahead and make contact with the Glastig. Besides, you have had experiences with the Sidhe-Dubh that could prejudice your behaviour in such a situation.'

'What makes you think that you stand a better chance of survival than I do?' Caitlin shot back at him. 'At least I would be able to look after myself in a fight.'

'As you did so well against the Cailleach not so long ago,' the poet answered with just a hint of sarcasm which betrayed to all present that he was beginning to lose his patience.

He did not get a chance to finish telling Caitlin that she could not always be at the front of the action. As he opened his mouth to speak, the threatening growl that they had all heard earlier was repeated. This time it was much more ferocious and frightening and even the old veterans were visibly afraid.

'Who spoke the name of my dear sister the Cailleach?' asked a voice both incredibly loud and yet incongruously feminine.

In that instant Gobann realised that he had been extremely foolish to mention the creature that had haunted Caitlin for so many seasons. If the Glastig realised who Caitlin was, it was quite possible that the monster might vent her wrath on the woman who had been partly responsible for the Cailleach's demise. It also crossed his mind that it had really been because of Síla that the Cailleach had finally left Caitlin alone. He was suddenly filled with dread—had his lover fallen prey to the revenge of the Sidhe-Dubh?

'I am Gobann, son of Caillte,' the poet said finally as he stepped out from amongst the warriors, his voice steady even if his palms were sweating and his stomach trembling. He strode forward in the direction of the Cailleach's sister. 'I am a poet of the Silver Branch.'

He had barely finished his introduction when there was a movement on the track not far ahead of him and a woman with long coal-black hair emerged from the forest. She was dressed in elegant forest-green garments which flowed along the ground behind her. Gobann stopped in his tracks and sucked in his breath in alarm.

'Are you acquainted with my sister?' the woman asked sharply, and the poet could see that she had the light grey eyes of the Faerie folk.

'I have never met her, though I know one who was regularly visited by her,' he answered tactfully. He could feel the trembling in his guts spreading to his legs, but he did not allow a flicker of fear to show on his face.

'Do you know who I am?' the woman hissed. Caitlin felt her own stomach turn as memories of the Cailleach flooded her thoughts.

'I would guess that you are the woman known to the Dal Araidhans as the Glastig,' Gobann stated with absolutely no trace of emotion in his voice.

'I am not a woman of the human kind,' the strange woman snapped. 'I am of the Danaan people.'

'In truth the Danaan folk are as beautiful as I

have heard,' Gobann answered, knowing that the Sidhe folk could often be calmed with flattery.

'You are clever, Gobann, son of Caillte. I happen to know that you have met many of my race. You are highly regarded among my people. You are reputed to be a great tale-teller and a competent harper.'

'Thank you, lady,' he replied, caught slightly off guard. The poet had a disconcerting feeling that he was putting himself in great danger and that the Glastig might lose her temper with him at any moment.

'You may approach me, harper,' the Glastig stated. The poet immediately understood that this was not a request. It was a command. Now he broke out into a cold sweat across his lower back and began glancing to left and right making ready in case she struck out at him. He walked slowly forward until he was only a few paces away from the Faerie woman. The skin on her face and hands was really quite a strange colour, like the wax of a candle that has burned down and melted. Her hair was not really black at all but a swirl of many colours, like the underside of a Raven's wing or a film of oil floating on the water. Rainbows seemed to dance among the long locks as she moved her head.

But it was her eyes that caught Gobann's attention. They were very like his own, he noticed; and as he looked closer he saw that they reflected immeasurable sadness. This woman, who was reputed to be a monster that fed on the flesh of Gaels, was in fact a gentle and deeply sensitive soul.

'Will you stay, harper, and play for me?' she asked with a tone that said she might never let him leave if he did so.

'I have left my harp in the Druid hall at Dun Righ,' Gobann explained, realising that the last harper who had agreed to stay in the forest with her was probably somewhere nearby. 'I once knew Cianan of the Sweet Melody,' the poet continued. 'Do you know how he is faring?'

'You should know better than to talk to a queen of her husband when she is seeking to partake of your gifts,' the Glastig chided.

'I am already in the service of a queen,' Gobann stated. 'And I would not think to break my bonds to her and her husband.'

Gobann heard a sound behind him and turned in time to see Caitlin standing with her sword drawn once more. 'I am the Queen of Munster,' she announced.

'Caitlin Ni Uaine,' the Glastig cut in, 'you are the woman who was responsible for my sister's death.'

'Did she die?' Caitlin asked, sincerely hoping that she had.

'Oh yes. The one who was the Cailleach for so long is now dead. It took her many days to pass on for that is the way of our kind, but in the end her spirit fled her body and she found peace. Now there is another Sidhe woman who has been given the name Cailleach.'

'I am sorry,' the Queen of Munster offered. 'I did not intend for her to suffer.'

'Of course you did!' the Glastig snapped, but as quickly as her tone had changed, it became calm and gentle again. 'She did you great harm. But I hope you can find it in your heart to forgive her for what she did.'

Caitlin was a little taken aback at this and suspected immediately that the Glastig's contrition was some sort of a trick to get the queen to take responsibility for the Cailleach's death. She was

293

determined not to show remorse for having fought the creature off but decided that it would be best to make some gesture of reconciliation. 'I forgive her,' Caitlin said.

'Her heart was not always so black. You must try to understand how it is with us. If an apple hangs upon the tree for too long, a day will come when it is no longer sweet to eat. In time the fruit will rot and the seeds that it carries within its body will no longer be fertile. When that happens even the birds will not touch the bitter flesh.'

Suddenly Caitlin was ashamed that she had drawn her sword in the presence of this creature. She hastily put the weapon through her belt again and bowed her head.

'In the ancient days our Druid healers sought to ease the pain of our existence,' the Glastig went on. 'They thought that if they could win the war against the death of the body, they would go some way to enriching the life of the spirit. Over many generations they studied the fruits and herbs of the Earth and the minerals of the sea. They learned to bend the properties of fire and water to their ways and yet they could not conquer death. They cured many ills and discovered countless wonders, but still our people died.'

Gobann could not restrain himself from speaking. 'But in the end they did chance upon a way to remain forever youthful and to banish all pain and sickness, did they not?'

'You have very little understanding for so renowned a poet,' the Glastig answered. 'Of all the marvels that our Druids discovered, this gift of life was the one which all the Danaans dreamed would serve us best. And yet this long dreamt of miracle has ever been the cause of our greatest anguish.'

'How so?' the poet asked. 'A life without pain

or sickness or the prospect of death is the dearest wish of many of my kind.'

'Nevertheless I am sure you do have an idea of just how difficult such a life can be,' the Glastig replied, 'for you have spent some time with the Danaan Druids. I have heard a rumour that you have been preparing two young Wanderers for the path of everlasting life.' Her eyes sparkled as she searched the poet's face for some reaction. 'Our wise ones knew much about the mortal world. They understood the workings of the spirit realms also, but when they cast this curse upon us, they banished all our kind to a place that is neither the realm of the spirits nor the land of mortals.'

Gobann believed then that she was not at all angry about her sister's death. If anything the Glastig was more distressed about the Druid Council's plans for the Wanderers.

'We have come to this forest in search of Mawn and Sianan,' he said. 'They were taken from us and brought here against their will as far as we can tell. Will you let us see them?'

'The Wanderers are my guests,' the Glastig smiled. 'For the time being my husband has them in his charge, though he knows not who they are or what their greater purpose is. But there are some questions that he and the assembly must ask you before they can be released.'

'Very well then,' Gobann replied, relieved that, for the moment at least, Mawn and Sianan were safe and well. 'Take me to your husband and I will answer whatever questions he poses.'

'Your warriors will leave their weapons behind them for you are my guests now and this whole forest can be considered my mead hall. As you would not bring a sword into a chieftain's house, so you must discard your swords and war tools.'

Caitlin would have protested but Gobann grabbed her arm to stop her speaking too rashly. 'We will do whatever you ask if we can be sure that the Wanderers will be well looked after,' he cut in.

'They will not be harmed,' the Glastig answered as she turned to walk back down the track. 'They have already been cleared of all the charges made against them. Now it is your turn to answer for the crimes of your people.'

The Saxons had been very close to forcing their way into the stronghold when Aldor was struck down and the battle horn sounded the retreat. At first many refused to give up the fight. But when the raiders noticed that Aldor's standard had fallen and that the holy man Tyrbrand was giving orders, none of them questioned what they should do.

Without running, each man lifted his shield onto his back to protect himself from Gaelic arrows and then walked calmly away from the breach. The Gaels could not believe what they saw. Without warning the whole Saxon line collapsed and retreated. The warriors of Dun Righ watched stunned as their enemies threw up their arms.

A few of the Dal Araidhans ran out after the raiders and several of the foreigners were struck down, but none of the Saxons or Angles intervened to help any of their comrades who got into trouble. As far as they were concerned the fight was over, for the time being anyway. Their war leader was being carried on a makeshift stretcher consisting of spears and cloaks hastily lashed together.

And Tyrbrand had warned them all beforehand

that if Aldor fell, all would be lost. The holy man had made it clear to them that if their leader was slain, they were all to leave the field quietly and in good order. He had forbidden them to indulge in robbing the dead on their way from the battle.

So the army of Aldor passed by the wounded and dead of both sides and, contrary to long-established tradition, left them unmolested. Tyrbrand was not a warrior; he was a holy mystic. The warriors might have considered disobeying Aldor but the thought of ignoring Tyrbrand's orders did not cross any of their minds. He had the gods on his side.

When Cathal understood what was happening, he gave the order for all his troops to return to within the perimeter of the ramparts. The chieftain did not want to risk the lives of any more of his warriors in chasing the Saxons. It was also possible, he considered, that the foreigners were trying to draw his warriors into the same sort of trap that Cathal had planned for them.

The degree of success that the Saxons had experienced in the short fight had very little to do with the superiority of their forces or the quality of the Saxon and Anglish fighting men. The raiders had only gained the upper hand in the fight because the chieftain of Dun Righ had ordered his own warriors to let them win some ground.

Before the fight Cathal had briefed the guards at the breach to fall back gradually with as few casualties as possible. In this way the chieftain hoped to lure the enemy into pursuing the Dal Araidhans deeper into the fortress at least as far as the inner ramparts. When the Saxons were well within the outer walls Cathal would give a prearranged signal to his warriors, at which they were to fall back to the defensive positions of the inner rampart.

Then archers and spearmen would have the room to close a deadly circle around the foreigners and hem them in. Once he had the Saxons trapped, it was Cathal's intention to slaughter every one of them without showing any mercy whatsoever. This plan was the reason why the previous watch had not gone straight to their beds or to their morning meal. These reinforcements were the warriors who would be responsible for dispatching the surviving raiders.

Cathal had hoped to inflict such a defeat on the enemy that they would no longer pose a threat to the security of Dun Righ. And if his strategy had proceeded as planned, he might have achieved his objective. But two things had happened which he had not counted on.

Firstly Cathal did not know that Tyrbrand had manipulated the Saxon defeat to his own advantage, or in fact that the Saxon holy man had deliberately passed on information about Aldor's plans with that intention. And secondly Cathal had no idea that Murrough's warriors, accompanied by the soldiers under Tatheus, would attempt to make a stand outside the walls in defence of Declan and Isernus if they were threatened.

Cathal had purposefully not told either man of his plans. He had little confidence in the fighting abilities of either Murrough or the Roman. And besides that he did not want anyone stealing his glorious victory away from him. Cathal assumed that the King of Munster would wisely remain safe within the ramparts when he saw the size of the Saxon force and that when the order came to fall back the king would obey it along with everyone else.

But the chieftain did not know Murrough very well. He believed that the king would not risk his

life and the lives of his men for the sake of a couple
of Christian monks and a few Roman mercenaries.

Cathal was wrong.

It only became apparent to Murrough that the
chieftain had a defensive strategy in place after the
enemy was already walking away from the walls.
By that time the king was escorting the wounded
abbot to safety within the inner ramparts. It was
not until then that Murrough noticed all the previous watchmen were gathered at the inner wall
waiting to see action. The king well understood
that if they had been stood down after their watch
it would have been very difficult for the chieftain
to muster them again so quickly. He concluded that
they had been ordered to remain at their posts in
anticipation of an attack.

It was obvious to the king what Cathal's plan
had been. It explained why so few warriors from
Dun Righ had gone to the assistance of Declan and
the wagons. Even when Murrough's own men had
rushed out to their aid, not a single one of the Dal
Araidhans had lifted a finger to help. If at last it
had seemed that the convoy was going to be overrun and everyone slaughtered, Cathal's men still
would have stood at the ramparts and watched.

Murrough understood enough about battle
strategy to realise that the chieftain had laid an
elaborate and what could have proved to be very
effective trap for the Saxons. What really disturbed
the king, however, was that in order to have taken
the action that he had, Cathal must have had certain knowledge of when and where the assault
would take place.

More than this, the chieftain of Dun Righ had
been willing to sacrifice all of Murrough's warriors
and the Roman soldiers in order to gain his objective. The king could not think of one sound

military reason why Cathal should not have informed himself or Tatheus of the plan. Murrough could only surmise that Cathal had considered it necessary that some warriors strike out at the enemy to make his retreat look more genuine. The only way to ensure that would be if the warriors concerned were ignorant of the overall plan.

Ia's contention that the chieftain had been in close contact with the foreigners struck Murrough as very plausible now. The king was furious that his life and the lives of his men had been placed at such risk. It was almost as if Cathal considered them worthless. The king knew that the only reason he was still alive and breathing was that by some chance the Saxon war leader had been struck down and the foreigners had decided not to pursue the engagement.

One of the king's horsemen rode up to report that seventeen men of Munster had been wounded in the fight and eleven warriors killed. The news hit Murrough hard. He stopped in his tracks, saddened by the loss of so many fine warriors and exhausted from the fight. A blow from a Saxon sword had caught his shoulder and, though his armour had prevented it from cutting into his flesh, the muscles were badly bruised. He stood rubbing the arm for a few moments; the pain in his shoulder was dull and the king felt his senses dulling in the same way. He knelt down to rest for a few moments. Not far away, at the inner wall, he could see Cathal, alive and unharmed, giving out orders. Hatred rose in the king's throat, but he swallowed it down.

At Rathowen Murrough had seen many more warriors killed than had fallen in this skirmish. At that battle there had been hundreds of deaths on both sides. More Saxons had fallen at the breach this morning than Gaels, but that did not ease Murrough's heart at all. He recalled the outrage he had felt after Rathowen when Gael had fought against Gael. He remembered the shock that had come upon him when he saw the lines of corpses laid out to be claimed by their families.

'I am a king,' he said aloud to himself. 'I cannot afford to have such feelings. War is the trade of kings. It is our duty to protect our clanspeople and these conflicts are what we must always be prepared for.'

Despite these words Murrough could not help feeling angered. Neither he nor any of his warriors had been ready for this fight. If Cathal had warned them of what was to happen then perhaps some among those eleven dead might have lived.

The king rose wearily from his knees as a group of his men carrying three of the dead warriors headed towards the Druid houses. Murrough called out to them to stop and went over to see if he knew any of the slain.

The king lifted the blanket from one face and saw that it was a woman lying still dressed in her full battle gear. It was the young woman who was the daughter of Omra, Caitlin's serving woman at their home in Cashel. He knew her face well. She had been struck by a Dal Araidhan arrow in the back of the neck and the pain was still etched in her features. The sight of a familiar face was too much for Murrough to bear. Not only had he and his warriors been misled about the battle strategy, they had been cut down by Cathal's archers as indiscriminately as if they had been Saxons.

Murrough could no longer contain his anger. He replaced the blanket carefully, muttered a blessing and then turned on his heel to march over to where Cathal still stood near the inner walls. The king was so distraught that he walked right by Tatheus, who had come to report the condition of his troops, without even noticing him.

The centurion quickly saw where Murrough was headed and, suspecting what was very likely occupying the king's mind, followed after him.

'Cathal!' Murrough bellowed before he had got close enough to the chieftain to be heard without raising his voice. 'Cathal Mac Croneen!' he repeated, his rage already bubbling over.

The chieftain glanced behind him and saw the King of Munster bearing down on him with as much determination as the Saxons had shown when they had first charged at the hill fort. Cathal knew straightaway what had upset the king. Indeed he had expected that there would be words between them after the battle. The chieftain discreetly called four of his warriors to stand close around him so that Murrough would not have any chance of striking at him.

When the king saw the Dal Araidhans moving to put themselves between him and their chieftain, he lost his temper completely. 'You betrayed my trust, you coward!' he shouted, and as he did so he drew the longsword that hung from a leather scabbard by his side. 'Eleven of my warriors lie slain by Gaelic arrows,' the king went on. 'Your arrows!'

Cathal retreated a few steps towards the road where he would easily be able to get out of this man's reach should the need arise. 'What are you talking about, Lord Murrough? If a few of your warriors were struck by my archers, it was purely bad luck. It was not my intention that any harm should come to your people.'

Murrough knew that this was partly true. It was surely an unfortunate blunder that had been responsible for the deaths, but he knew also that it could have been avoided.

'Why did you not tell me all the details of your plan?' the king shouted, still fuming. Murrough was now only ten or twelve paces away from the chieftain and Cathal's guards stepped forward to block his advance. One of the Dal Araidhans reached out to disarm the king, but Murrough dodged out of the fellow's reach. Then he lifted his sword and punched the man out of his way with the hilt of the weapon.

Without another moment's hesitation the other guardsmen leapt on Murrough, grabbing the king's sword and twisting it out of his grip. When the weapon was thrown aside, one of the warriors kicked Murrough behind the knees, and then the rest of them pushed him kicking and fighting to the ground. He struggled against them for a long while, refusing to give up and becoming more enraged by the minute, but it was to no avail.

Suddenly there were more Dal Araidhan warriors running to stand by their chieftain. Before long, word had spread that Murrough and Cathal were locked in a fight and this news brought the warriors of Munster, their swords drawn and their spears readied.

Tatheus tried to break the Dal Araidhan men away from Murrough, but these warriors were taking the task of subduing the king very seriously. One of Cathal's men grabbed the Roman centurion by the throat and pushed him out of the way. Another kicked Tatheus in the ribs as he landed on his back in the dirt. Instinctively the centurion reached for his own sword but thought better of using it under the circumstances. He was clearly heavily outnumbered.

By the time the Roman had managed to get to

his feet again, there were twenty Dal Araidhans gathered in a close impenetrable circle around their chieftain. Four of the largest among them pinned a struggling and swearing Murrough to the ground while Cathal stayed well back out of the way of the fracas. Tatheus could hardly believe his eyes. He had never seen such behaviour from the Gaels before. He thought that convention and strict codes of conduct prevented such scenes.

Unable to stand by and watch the ill treatment of Murrough, the Roman hurried forward to plead with the warriors to let the king rise, but by now it was almost too late to avert a fight. The Munster troops had reacted swiftly. Thirty men and women had formed rank and were marching in formation to come to the king's aid. Tatheus knew he had to act quickly. Deciding it would be best if he tried to placate Murrough's warriors, Tatheus stood between them and Cathal's men.

'Throw down your weapons!' the chieftain of Dun Righ ordered. 'Your king has violated the hospitality of my stronghold. He drew his sword and he threatened me.'

Two of the Munster warriors in Murrough's personal guard stepped towards Cathal's warriors. One struck at the nearest Dal Araidhan with his sword, knocking the man to the ground with an ugly gash to the shoulder. The other pointed his blade directly at one of Cathal's men in a gesture of warning.

Immediately Tatheus took the opportunity to face Cathal. 'Let Murrough stand up and answer for his actions,' he demanded, and all the Munster warriors cheered in chorus. 'If he has wronged you then surely he can make some recompense for his actions without the need for bloodshed.'

'Be quiet, Roman!' Cathal bellowed. 'What

would you know of honour and hospitality? Your people keep slaves in their houses. There is nothing honourable about that.'

'I know enough to question the motives of a chieftain who does not let a king speak in his own defence,' answered Tatheus. 'I have witnessed enough of your customs to understand that even the vilest of all criminals has a right to speak for his alleged crimes and to give an explanation as to why they were committed. Would you deny King Murrough this privilege? For if you do, the result may well be another bitter battle. Only I fear that it will be Gael against Gael.'

Cathal was about to make a defiant rebuke when he was interrupted. Another voice rose from among the Dal Araidhans. It was the Druid woman, Ia. 'By the code of the Brehon law you must let him stand and speak,' she called out. 'You men there,' she commanded, 'let the King of Munster rise to his feet with dignity.'

Cathal's warriors could not help but exhibit confusion at this order and so they did not immediately obey it. Their chieftain did not contradict the command. In fact he was standing silently with his arms folded, looking away from Murrough.

'Let him stand,' Cathal said finally, when he had calmed down a little and realised that Tatheus was right. The chieftain did not really want to risk another fight. 'But do not give him his blade, and keep a good watch over him,' he added.

Before Murrough had got to his feet his voice was already raised once more in anger. 'This is the famous hospitality of Cathal of Dun Righ.'

One of the Dal Araidhans strode towards the king to strike him but thought better of it when he realised that for the moment at least there were more of Murrough's men present than warriors of Dun Righ. Cathal did not flinch at the insult.

'Coward!' Murrough spat at the chieftain. 'You threw my warriors into the thick of the fighting without letting me know any details of your battle strategy or that you had foreknowledge of the attack.'

'It was a hard fight, King Murrough,' Cathal replied, sighing theatrically as he spoke. 'You have lost eleven good warriors and so you are justifiably very distressed. It is honourable to feel grief for the loss of your own folk. But your accusations and your behaviour do not befit your rank as King of Munster.'

The chieftain turned to face his own warriors and held his arms outstretched as if he had nothing to hide. Even though he was not facing the king, he still addressed Murrough directly. 'Be careful of the insinuations that you make, King of the Eoghanacht, for even a monarch can wear out his welcome. No-one asked you to become involved in this fight. No-one expected that your warriors would stand and do battle for the homes of the Dal Araidhan folk. That was why no-one informed you of the battle plan.'

Cathal turned back to face Murrough's warriors again. 'The people of Dun Righ thank you for your help,' the chieftain said. 'But in future, unless your aid is specifically requested, please refrain from becoming involved in our affairs. Your rash behaviour in charging out from the walls to harass the enemy nearly cost us all the victory. It nearly cost my folk their homes.'

'Not one of your warriors came out to help the Christians,' Murrough observed contemptuously. 'None came forward to our assistance when we were in the thick of the affray.'

'We could all see that it was senseless to do so. A child could have understood how dangerous it was to leave the safety of the ramparts,' Cathal retorted. 'Even if my men had left the shelter of the walls, their action would have achieved nothing but to fill a graveyard with futile gestures. That is what the Saxons wanted us to do. I would have thought that you of all men, who have so much experience fighting the Saxons, would have understood that.'

'Your own archers loosed their arrows at us,' Murrough barked. 'Most of the casualties among my warriors came from the Dal Araidhan lines.'

'Then be careful not to let your warriors get in the way in future,' Cathal advised coldly. 'Their deaths are on your head, not mine.'

'Why did you ask me to assemble my force this morning if you did not want us to fight?' the king asked bitterly. 'If it was not your intention to use my warriors to shield your own folk, why did you not call us back to well within the fortress?'

'Once again, Murrough, you forget that you are my guest. I will ignore the insult you aim at my warriors. They are not cowards. We have been fending off the Saxon threat for longer than I care to remember. I requested that your warriors be present because I was unsure of the enemy numbers. I could not be certain whether I would require more troops on the field if the Saxons broke through our line too quickly.'

'You are a liar!' Murrough stormed. 'You are a man who murders those who look to him for protection and profits from their misery. You drive innocent folk from their ancestral lands so that you may people it with your own kind or those who would serve you. You think nothing of using your allies to your own advantage, and when they come to your aid it does not move you to watch them cut down by the enemy. Cathal of the Dal Araidhe is nothing more than a petty tyrant who has filled his stronghold with the riches of his neighbours. He has dishonoured the Gaelic people and I am ashamed to have accepted his hospitality.'

These last words outraged the gathered Dal Araidhans so much that their voices were immediately lifted in anger. As one they denounced Murrough and all that he had had to say. The king's guards had to step in to protect their monarch from the fury of Cathal's people, jostling men aside so that they could not get close to him.

In the blink of an eye the assembled warriors of both sides were shoving violently against one another. Tatheus screamed out at the top of his lungs, reaching out to Murrough to try and calm him, but he could not be heard over the shouts from both groups of grim-faced Gaels.

It was Ia who managed to calm things down before any blood was spilled. After trying unsuccessfully to be heard above the noise, she managed to get hold of a war trumpet. She blew a long loud blast upon the instrument which sounded as close to the signal for alarm as she could approximate. Both sides immediately fell silent, believing that the Saxons had returned to attack the hill fort. Ia took advantage of their silence to speak out.

'Hear me!' she cried in an impatient tone. 'I am chief advisor to Cathal of Dun Righ and I demand your attention.'

There were mumbles of discontent from the Dal Araidhans but they grudgingly gave her the opportunity to speak.

'By order of the Assembly of Druids both parties are to stand down and move to opposite sides of the fort. Any warrior, chieftain or king who

308

disobeys this command will pay a blush fine for the embarrassment they cause to their clanspeople. When you have all calmed down sufficiently that you can behave in a proper manner, I will sit in judgment over this matter.'

'I will not be told what to do by a woman,' Cathal answered immediately. 'No matter that you are of the Druid kind.'

'Then you will pay me a blush fine,' Ia roared. 'And you will suffer to have me compose a satire to your dishonour. You, Cathal, who in front of all his people offers the payment of white horses for the poems I compose about his exploits. But when he is finished boasting about his own generosity, his white horse has turned into a cow. I have heard that the Danaans have the gift of being able to change form into any creature they wish. If this cow you gifted me with is such an animal, tell me then why did she choose to become a cow that gives only insipid watery milk?'

'The white horse was stolen!' Cathal protested. 'I always intended to present it to you.'

'Cathal is a dishonourable man,' Ia intoned as she summoned up her gift for satire. 'He does not give white horses as gifts for poems and praise. He gives an animal that is close to his own nature. A sickly cow.'

'Enough!' bellowed the chieftain. 'I have been wronged by a king and insulted by a Druid this day. Does it not matter to anyone that I have saved my people from the Saxons? Let us take these matters to the judgment of the Druid Assembly and all the folk of Dun Righ. Let us see what they have to say about your slanderous derision.'

'Then move yourself to the far side of the dun,' Ia persisted. 'Let your warriors remain to guard the breach, but you, chieftain, must go and await the summons of the Assembly.'

'How dare you tell me what to do?' Cathal grunted. 'You half-Saxon child of a foreign sorcerer!'

'Very well, since you have decided to speak so,' Ia answered calmly, 'I will not wait for the full Assembly to gather. I am a senior Druid judge and I am the daughter of a great chieftain. Since you do not fear the bite of satire, I will set fines upon you to silence your unwise tongue. Murrough's charges against you are only a few among many that I could bring to your name. And believe me when I say that if I decided to prosecute you for all the dishonour that you have done, you would be impeached and impoverished as a result.'

The crowd was utterly silent, shocked at the tone the Druid was taking with her chieftain.

'Here is my judgment,' she announced. 'You, Cathal of Dun Righ, will pay me twenty cows in recompense for my honour and good name which you have slighted today. And you will yield to King Murrough of the Eoghanacht the cost of two hundred cows for the rough treatment and the begrudging manner in which you have acknowledged his bravery. You will furthermore compensate Declan of Saint Ninian's the cost of all the repairs that must be carried out at his monastery. For it was by your negligence that his home was burned and he came close to losing his life at the gates of this stronghold today.'

The Druid paused to gauge the crowd's reaction to her pronouncement. No-one spoke for, even though Cathal's warriors supported their chieftain, they would not dare speak out against a Druidic judgment and risk being fined themselves.

'You will not speak to Murrough,' the Druid

woman continued, 'nor any of his folk until the full Druid Assembly has sat to consider if any further fines should be laid upon you. If they consider that you are fit to continue ruling this hill fort, there will be an election before Samhain. I am beginning proceedings against you and if you do not begin to show some respect for the rule of law, I will have you impeached and replaced by a person whose honour is unstained. You have brought disgrace on all the folk of Dal Araidhe this day with your behaviour.'

Cathal put a hand to the hilt of his sword and for a moment it seemed certain that he was going to draw the blade. If he had done so, no-one present could doubt that a bloody fight would have been the result and that many lives would have been lost. Murrough's men stood firm a few paces away from the warriors of Dal Araidhe, and they were ready to strike at anyone who dishonoured their lord or threatened his life.

But Cathal knew only too well that any act of violence would have achieved nothing save to weaken the defences of the stronghold. At a time when the Saxons were still a threat, that would be madness. Good sense told him that it was better to back down for the moment and bide his time until the Druid Assembly could sit in judgment.

'I will do as you say,' the chieftain announced. 'I will accept your decision for now. But when the Druid judges meet I will surely be exonerated and it will be you who faces impeachment for your traitorous words.' He pointed directly at Ia and then sheathed his blade loudly so that it rattled in the scabbard. 'And we shall see how they view the behaviour of King Murrough. No honourable warrior lifts a sword to the chieftain of the dun wherein he is a guest.'

He stared at Murrough with no attempt to disguise his malice. 'It will be you, King of Munster, who repays me for your insults. The honour of a chieftain of the Dal Araidhe does not come as cheaply as that of an uninvited meddler from the land of the five kingdoms. If you take my advice, Murrough, you will go crawling back to your high and mighty King Leoghaire of Eirinn before you get yourself killed in the foolish belief that the people of Dun Righ need or even desire your help.'

With that Cathal turned to leave, making his way through his own warriors who parted before him as he walked. He had not gone more than a few steps, though, when he stopped and aimed one last comment at the king.

'But, Murrough, do leave your wife behind with us, won't you. She is a better man than you are and I am sure she would be more use in a fight.' As soon as he had spoken these words he disappeared into the crowd and was gone to his own hall to wait the summons of the Druid Assembly.

Ia went up to Murrough as the soldiers began to disperse and touched his arm to get his attention. 'I am very sorry,' she said, 'that you were subjected to the sharp tongue and the dull wits of that man.'

'You have nothing to be sorry about,' the king assured her. 'Nothing I said was prompted by what you told me yesterday. I was only angry for the sake of my slain warriors.'

'I hope you will not take to heart what he said about Queen Caitlin being a better man than you,' the Druid woman offered.

'I only wish she were here to have heard him,' Murrough confessed with a laugh. 'I have a feeling she might have been inclined to teach him a thing or two about politeness. But then, knowing her, she would probably have taken more insult at being compared to a man than I could at being told that she is superior to me. She is a far better warrior than most of the men in this hill fort.'

Ia laughed. 'I am quite looking forward to getting to know the queen better,' she said thoughtfully. 'If only there were more women like her in the lands of the Dal Araidhe, perhaps the menfolk would not have dared elect that tyrant.'

ThIRTEEN

s Gobann, Caitlin and their warriors
followed the Glastig further into the
forest the poet noticed that the trees
all around them had filled with many
different creatures of all kinds, chat-
tering noisily. He could not be certain why but
guessed that the creatures of these woods had been
reassured when the party had put its weapons
down in the middle of the road.

It was the birds that made the most noise of all,
and among the birds it was the Ravens who cawed
the most. The poet became more and more uneasy
as the party came closer and closer to the clearing
where the forest dwellers had gathered the court.
Had it simply been the appearance of so many
Ravens that disconcerted him, Gobann would have
not been so worried. He suspected that last night's
strange dream had been more than a fantasy of his
sleep.

No, something else was gnawing at his nerves.
A presence pervaded this whole part of the forest.
It was not malevolent or violent, even though
Gobann did not doubt that it could summon such
reactions if necessary. It was intimidating because
it seemed to be so large. Then he realised that he
was feeling the very soul of the woods. There was
a nurturing gentleness here. But it was buried
beneath anger and distrust.

By the time they had come to the grass at the

edge of the clearing Gobann was sweating with anticipation of what he would find there. He could just make out the shape of a large stone in the centre of a great circle of smaller stones, and he could see an old black bird seated upon the top of it. But he was so preoccupied with the overwhelming experience of entangling himself in the spirit of the woods that he did not notice any of those who were gathered at the foot of the stone.

Even when a familiar voice called out to him the poet did not at first respond. This was the clearing that had appeared in last night's dream and that disturbed Gobann greatly. Now he was certain that he had travelled here in the spirit form and for a purpose, though for the present he could not imagine what that purpose might be.

The Raven atop the central standing stone flew down to land in a great flurry of feathers not far from where Gobann had halted.

'Welcome,' the old bird croaked loudly, 'Gobann of the Silver Branch, son of the poet Caillte who was born of the people of Dal Araidhe. I am called Géarintinneach daughter of Branwen Géarchúiseach. I am a queen among the Raven folk.'

Gobann bowed to her and then answered, 'Greetings, Raven Queen. Many seasons ago I witnessed the wisdom of your folk and the sharp-witted judgment of one of your great queens.'

'I remember the time well,' the old Raven replied. 'I too was seated among the branches of the Quicken Tree during the last great assembly that was ever held there.'

Caitlin put her hand on the poet's shoulder. 'What is she talking about? What great assembly?'

'Gobann was a guest among our folk before the cutting of the ancient rowan by the Saxons,' the Raven queen explained. 'I was seated not five

315

wingspans away from the poet when he addressed the Raven clans on behalf of the Gaels. If only we had acted more quickly on your counsel,' she mused, 'the Quicken might have been saved.'

Gobann blushed, embarrassed that the Raven should talk so highly of him in front of the warriors. 'May I introduce you to Queen Caitlin Ni Uaine of Munster,' he stammered.

'You did your best, child,' the Raven admonished her, referring to the attempt Caitlin and Murrough had made to save the Quicken. 'If all the clans of the Raven folk could not rally in time to save the tree of their ancestral assemblies, then what hope had any of the sons or daughters of Míl?'

'We were captured by the Saxons and the Roman called Seginus,' Caitlin explained sadly.

'Yes, I know that, child,' said the Raven gently. 'I was there watching the whole thing. I was among the many who helped finish off the last of the Saxons after they had cut down the tree, and I saw the great foreigner who took you on his horse off to the hills. Those were sad times for all of us.'

'But Gobann was in Teamhair at the time,' Caitlin protested. 'It was the time of his initiation.'

The Raven queen clicked her beak and cocked her head towards Gobann. She saw the blank expression on his face and understood that perhaps she had said too much. 'That is his tale to tell when and if he will. For the while we will speak no more of it. The tribunal has assembled and it is right that we ask you some questions. The accused will approach the speaking stone.'

Gobann nodded acknowledgement and moved forward but had only walked a few steps when he spotted a familiar form among the crowds of creatures that lined the clearing.

'Gobann!' Síla cried. 'You are safe!' She ran

forward to him and the poet, ignoring protocol for perhaps the first time in his life, threw his arms about her and held her for a long moment. As Caitlin made her way towards the stone she passed the couple and touched Síla on the shoulder.

'It gives my heart great joy to see you,' the Queen of Munster whispered to her friend. 'I was beginning to believe that you had been drowned at sea, for we received no word from you.'

'I very nearly was drowned,' Síla admitted. 'If it had not been for the generous actions of Malchedoc, I would have been food for the fishes.'

'Who is this Malchedoc of whom you speak?' Gobann asked her, confused. He had never in all his travels heard the name, though he felt he might know the one who claimed it.

'He is—' Síla began.

'I am Malchedoc,' the stranger interrupted. 'And you must be the great Gobann about whom I have heard so much.'

'I am Gobann of the Silver Branch,' the poet answered humbly. Then he stopped short and looked more closely at the man. 'And you are Cianan of the Sweet Melody.'

'Cianan is dead,' Malchedoc stated coldly. 'He died to his people and to his old loyalties many seasons ago when the Gaels began taking this land from the first inhabitants. I now have a Cymru name and my kinfolk are of the Cymru tribes for all my other clanspeople died long ago.'

Mawn and Sianan stepped forward then to put their arms around their teacher. The expression on Mawn's face revealed to the poet immediately that he still had not realised Malchedoc's true identity. Without greeting the two Wanderers any further, Gobann replied to the stranger's statement.

317

'One of your clansfolk is here among this assembly,' the poet announced. 'He is a young man, yet he and his companion are highly respected by the Druid Council of Teamhair.'

'What are you talking about?' Malchedoc flashed. 'I was the last Druid of my line. There was none after me. They were all blacksmiths.'

'It has indeed been many seasons then since you heard any news from your homeland,' Gobann remarked. 'Ten summers ago I took two students under my wing. One was called Sianan. She is the grand-daughter of Cathach the High-Druid of Eirinn. The other was chosen because of his relationship to you, Cianan. He is called Mawn, son of Midhna the blacksmith who dwelt in the valley of Dobharcú. He is your great-grandson.'

Malchedoc turned around to face the boy, visibly shocked. 'But Mawn,' he began, 'you told Fergus that all your family had been killed by the Saxons.'

'That . . . that is correct,' Mawn answered, equally taken aback. 'Not long after I left the Valley of the Black Otter, raiders came and killed everyone except my elder brother Beoga. They gave him into the hands of the false bishop Palladius who had him tortured and then cruelly murdered.'

Malchedoc stood stunned by this news; shocked at his own inattention to detail in not recognising the Druid as one of his own kin. 'I had news of the birth of Beoga once from a travelling poet who came here long ago.'

'I was that poet,' Gobann asserted. 'I brought you that news.'

'Now I remember you,' Malchedoc said slowly. 'I remember you, Gobann. That was many seasons ago. Your father was of the Dal Araidhan folk, was he not?'

'He was,' the poet agreed. 'But my mother would

318

not live among such lawless people and she returned to Eirinn before I was nine summers old. When she passed away I was given into the care of the Druid Council.'

'You are here to answer a charge of grievous murder,' Malchedoc reminded them all, consciously bringing their attention back to the matter in hand. 'Someone must be brought to account for this terrible death.'

'I can give you an answer,' Gobann said straightaway, 'to the riddle of this murder.'

'Be patient until you have heard the question,' Malchedoc quipped.

'I was here last night,' the poet went on, 'in the spirit form of a Raven.'

'Were you?' Malchedoc asked sceptically. 'And what did you see, Raven Druid?'

'I saw five Saxons dressed in Druid cloaks leaving the forest with blood on their hands. Then I came here and saw that body lying over there.' He pointed in the direction of the corpse.

'So you would be able to identify the victim?' Malchedoc pressed him. 'You could describe the corpse to us?'

'No,' Gobann admitted. 'I did not get close enough to see clearly.'

'And on the strength of that evidence you expect us to believe that it was a band of marauding Saxons who stole into the woods without any of our folk noticing, disguised for good measure in Druid cloaks? Where did they get these cloaks, and why would they choose to wear them anyway? I have never known the foreigners to be anything but proud of their dirty work. They are not known for their attempts to conceal their blood lust from their enemies. Why should they start now?'

'Because I believe that there may be one among

319

them who knows the Druid ways,' Gobann asserted. 'I cannot be sure but I felt a strong bond with one of the Saxons. It was a bond that I cannot explain except to say he seemed to me at first to truly be a brother Druid, though in an inexplicable way.'

'Rubbish!' Malchedoc spat. 'You are trying to cover up for the deeds of your own people at Dun Righ. This is not the first such murder that has taken place in this land. Three other white horses have perished in the same circumstances within the last three moons. They are being killed for a reason, though it is not a reason that any true Druid would subscribe to. Every report of the killings speaks of five men clad in cloaks of the Druid blue. Saxons do not wear the dark Druid colours, nor do they worship in the woods where all the victims have been found. Saxons do not carry the scian-dubh knives of the Druid kind. One of these was discovered near the body of our dear friend here.'

'I am sure that these deaths were not brought about by Druids or Gaels. This is the work of savage Saxons,' Gobann protested.

'And you would have us believe that you had the Raven form last night when you saw all these things?' Malchedoc asked.

'I had taken on the form and the guise of the Raven,' the poet repeated.

'In that case either you were dreaming,' Malchedoc sneered, 'in which case I would suggest that you refrain from eating rich food before bed, or you are lying. Since the lives and liberty of you and your companions are at stake, I would not be surprised at some bending of the truth in order to save yourself.'

'I am a Druid. I am sworn to truth,' Gobann answered indignantly.

'He is not lying,' the Raven queen cut in. 'The poet has the gift of shape-shifting. I told you that I first met him when he had taken the Raven form many seasons ago. But it is his tale to tell if he will, not mine.'

Caitlin's mouth dropped open again in surprise. The poet had never mentioned this to her before. She was eager to hear more about it.

'I was sent to the Raven gathering by the Druid Council as an emissary to the feather folk,' the poet declared. 'At that time the old alliance between the Danaans and the Gaels was uneasy. There were many Ravens who wanted to join with the Saxons and make war on the Gaelic people. I convinced their queen to align with us against the savages and later gained their help in my tuition of the two Wanderers.'

'I am the only Wanderer present here,' Malchedoc snorted.

Gobann understood then that, even though his wife, the Glastig, was clearly aware of the Wanderers and their role, Malchedoc knew nothing about the plans of the Druid Council of Eirinn. He would have to recount the whole tale to this gathering if he was to gain Malchedoc's confidence.

'Long after Cianan of the Sweet Melody became Malchedoc of the Cymru,' Gobann began, 'the Druid Assembly of Cnoc Pocan received strong indications of what was soon to come to pass. Another invasion of Eirinn. But this time it was not the Danaans or the Fir-Bolg or the Fomor who threatened our land.'

The poet went on to describe the warnings that the poet-seers had given about the coming of the Roman Christians and of the increasing threat from the Saxon raiders.

'We were faced with a difficult decision,' Gobann

told them. 'We knew that Eirinn's five kingdoms could not withstand a concerted or prolonged assault by the Saxon hordes. Even the British kings had not been able to stop the foreigners taking large parts of the Cymru homeland for their own, and the Britons had many more warriors at their disposal than the High-King of Eirinn. We could not ally with them either: the British kings tried that and it just made the Saxons more hungry for Cymru gold.'

'What has all this got to do with me?' Malchedoc interrupted.

'I will come to that in a minute,' the poet assured him. 'Please be patient while I tell the whole tale.' Gobann stopped for a moment, checking his thoughts to make sure he had not forgotten anything. 'The other threat to our way of life and to our beliefs was in some ways far more of a concern.' Again, as was his manner, he paused for effect.

'Romans,' he stated. 'And worse still, Roman Christians. These folk have a vowed hatred of the Druid ways. And they have a great military organisation to back them up. Their warriors took Britain from the Cymru peoples when the Saxons were still an unknown clan of no more than a few tribes. The Romans have a reputation for destroying the cultures of their conquered enemies.'

'You have not explained,' Malchedoc insisted, 'why you referred to these two young Druids as Wanderers. That is a title reserved for mortal folk who choose to live among the Danaans and to share their fate. These two do not dwell with the Faerie kind.'

'Yet they are Wanderers in the truest sense of the word,' Gobann insisted. 'The Druid Council chose them from among many for their unique talents.

Sianan has the gifts of music, poetry and a love of the laws of our folk, undoubtedly inherited from her grandfather Cathach. Mawn has the talent for the future-sight, though he has yet to develop his ability fully. But it is certain that he has been touched by the Faidh and that faculty was probably passed down to him from his great-grandfather. You, Cianan or Malchedoc or whatever you prefer to be called now, are the reason Mawn was chosen as a Wanderer.'

'You speak of them as being chosen,' Malchedoc began, 'but who selected them and for what purpose?'

'The Druid Council and the elders of Cnoc Pocan chose them,' Gobann explained, 'because it was considered inevitable that an alliance be struck with one of the two peoples who threatened our homeland. No-one considered the possibility that the Saxons would be worth dealing with. It was to Rome that we turned for help. The Druid Council decided that if the Christians were to be allowed to settle in Eirinn and spread the word of their gospels, then we must do all in our power to preserve the ways of our people. Mawn and Sianan are messengers to the future. They will remember the truth when our clanspeople are overwhelmed by the new doctrines.'

Malchedoc dropped his shoulders in disbelief. It was obvious to him that Gobann was not lying. Such a story was too intricately woven to be false.

'The only way we could be sure that the old ways would survive the onslaught of the black-robed monks,' the poet continued, 'was to ensure that the messengers would outlive the generations to come. Without Mawn and Sianan the history and heritage of our folk might be completely lost within two generations. The Danaans agreed to aid us in our plan, for they also foresaw what would happen if the Christians were to gain total control of Eirinn. In a Christian land the Danaans would have to defend themselves constantly against brutal evangelists who look on the Faerie races as evil.'

'So they have tasted the Water of Life?' Malchedoc asked.

'And eaten of the fruit of the Quicken Tree,' Gobann affirmed. 'We brought them here to Strath-Clóta to be sheltered from the great changes that are taking place in Eirinn. The Roman Pope's emissary to Teamhair, Bishop Patricius Sucatus, is about to launch a great effort to convert all the Druids of Eirinn to the Cross. He may be surprised when they respond willingly and enthusiastically to the call, but I do not think that even he will suspect that this too is part of the great plan. In time these Druids will become priests, monks and nuns, and though they will preach the story of Christ, they will also teach their flock a little about the old traditions. The new religion and the old philosophy will merge in a few generations to become indistinguishable. Then the Wanderers will be able to return to advise and guide the people.'

'And what of myself?' Malchedoc asked. 'Am I required to help in this great effort?'

'That is your decision to make as you think best,' Gobann stated. 'Many of the Danaans are talking about withdrawing completely behind the veil of their enchantments. Their magical arts are beyond the understanding of even the Druid kind but I know that once they withdraw into the hills and wild places beyond the knowledge of mortals, it is very difficult for them to return. Others have already taken the decision to return to the ancient homes in Tir-Nan-Og and the holy isles of the west. You and I may not be able to envisage a world without the Faerie folk, but the sad truth is that the day will come when only a handful of the Danaans are left in the forests and woodlands and under the ancient hills in their palaces. The Druid Council has foreseen a day when the Faerie kind have little contact with our people and common folk scoff at those who claim to have encountered them.'

'If that is so, what is the use of all this planning and strategy?' Malchedoc protested. 'The Danaans are the guardians of Eirinn and Alba. Without the Children of Light to watch over our lands, who will preserve them from the destructive force of the Dark Faeries?'

'The Wanderers will have a duty to teach the common Gaels to respect and protect the soil which gives them life. Our clanspeople will have to take on the duties that the Danaans once performed. You could help in the effort to teach. Your knowledge could be of great benefit to the future generations.'

'I will consider what you have said, Gobann of the Silver Branch,' Malchedoc said finally. 'It is true that the Saxons are a great threat to our people. I have seen their handiwork throughout this land. They delight in murder and pillage. Even their old folk are slaughtered once they reach a certain age so that they will not be a burden on the younger generations. They do not understand that they are snuffing out a great storehouse of knowledge.'

'That is their tradition,' the poet stated. 'Perhaps many generations ago their folk suffered a great famine and this led to the practice of culling their own people in order that there be enough food for the survivors. I do not know their histories. I am told that the Saxons do not keep memories of the deeds of their ancestors. They do not value the wisdom of the aged or the insights of the afflicted and ill. The one focus of all their endeavours seems to be the acquisition of wealth. Gold, fine clothes, new lands and slaves are the measure of their kings. Compassion is a sign of weakness to them. Music, tale-telling, wise words, healing, contemplation and all the things that the Druid way teaches represent the true measure of life, these things take second place to the Saxons.'

'There must be some among them,' Malchedoc reasoned, 'who hold the same values as our folk.'

'I do not know,' the poet admitted. 'I can only say with certainty that last night I saw five Saxons adorned in the blue of the Druid orders at the edge of this forest. There is no doubt in my mind that they are the ones who are responsible for the killing that took place in this clearing. It is no use blaming the Gaels for this tragedy, though I am sure that some among the Danaan kind are grateful for the opportunity to do so. It was the foreigners.'

'I have heard it said,' Malchedoc admitted, 'that the Saxon ways are so different to our own that they are incomprehensible to a Gael or a Cymru, but these murders are so strange that they mirror the evil of the Sidhe-Dubh. Yet I do not truly believe that even the Dark Faeries would indulge themselves in such orgies of blood lust.'

Malchedoc looked towards the body of the slain horse. 'The heart has been torn out of the white steed,' he spluttered. 'Torn out and stolen it was. And it was the same with the others. What purpose could such an act serve? It is worse than barbaric; it is degenerate and inhuman.'

'We cannot hope to understand them,' Gobann agreed, 'but we must work together to defeat them. For until the Saxons are driven from the Strath-Clóta entirely, there can be no safe refuge for Mawn and Sianan. Even this great forest will not be able to provide the Wanderers with a refuge if the foreigners remain in this land. The proof of that is the slain horse that lies in the middle of this clearing.'

'I believe that you are right, Gobann,' Malchedoc sighed. 'We must work together—Danaan, Cymru, Gael and Cruitne—for the sake of the future.'

'Then gather all the Druid kind of the four peoples of Britain for we must pass all these tidings on to them as soon as possible. We must guard against any further murders such as this one. I have a sense that these killings were for a purpose that, though unthinkable to us, may be acceptable to the Saxons. The old tales tell of the Fomor who were led by Balor of the Evil Eye. Those folk were said to indulge in the sacrifice of animals whenever they had some foul magic to work. It is possible that the Saxons have just such a tradition.'

'I fear you may be right,' Malchedoc nodded. 'If they do not respect the lives of their elders, then why should they have any feeling for the animal kind? We must act quickly.'

He strode forward to slap the poet on the shoulder. 'Welcome to this woodland, Gobann of the Silver Branch. I am sorry that I doubted you. I have been alone here separated from my own kind for too long. I have grown suspicious of all the outsiders and forgotten that there are still folk in the world who work hard for the common good.'

At that moment the Glastig stepped forward also and there seemed to be a light that shimmered about her as she spoke. 'Twice welcome, Gobann. And to Queen Caitlin of the Kingdom of Munster. You will lodge in my home this night and while you sleep we will call in the Druids from all the country as far north as Dun Edin. Before the next moon there will be a great calling together of all the wise ones. Then we will talk further of how we will rid the land of the Saxons.'

'Let us sit around the hearth fire and talk this night,' Síla cut in, 'for we have much to discuss. And perhaps Malchedoc might like to spend some time with his great-grandson before we depart for Dun Righ once more.'

'I would like to do that,' Malchedoc sighed, 'for though I know that Midhna, his father, had no respect for me, still I would like to discover what happened at Dobharcú and what became of Midhna.'

'And I have many questions for you, lord Druid,' Mawn said, addressing Malchedoc in a formal tone. 'I am sure that Sianan has as many more again. All our training has been thorough and detailed but for one thing. None among the Druid kind could prepare us for the most daunting part of our task. No-one else but a mortal who has been granted the life of a Danaan can ready us for the adventure that lies ahead.'

'That is true,' Malchedoc admitted. 'Even the Danaans could not speak of it to you because they take their long lives for granted. Let us go away from everyone now and spend some time together. The Druids and the Danaans can plot the future in the cave by the waterfall but they must leave us to live it out.'

'We must send word to Murrough,' Caitlin interrupted. 'Will you send a rider to tell him what has happened here and that we are all safe?'

'I will do better than that,' the Glastig offered. 'I will send one of the Raven folk to let him know the news.'

'That might not be the best method,' Caitlin added quickly. She knew that her husband disliked and distrusted all the great black birds even though he based this judgment on his experience of only a few of their kind. 'Send one of our warriors. A face that Murrough recognises will be worth a hundred words from a stranger.'

'Very well,' the Glastig conceded. 'Choose your man and I will have him guided to the edge of the forest where your horses were left. I will give the messenger one of my own to ride. We let your mounts go home to their stables yesterday for we thought it cruel to leave them tied up without water or food.'

Caitlin bowed her head, shamed that she had been so hasty in her search for Mawn and Sianan that she had neglected her horses.

'It is excusable,' the Glastig continued, 'to forget the care of your animals when there is so much else at stake. It is a different thing entirely to injure them deliberately for one's own selfish ends. That is what we are fighting.'

fOURTEEN

ldor was carried back to his encampment by four of his strongest warriors. It was not a long journey but it was a very uncomfortable one for the eorl. The arrow shaft in his side had been broken as he fell, tearing at his rib cage and leaving a great hole in his side. The wound in his chest was not much better. That arrow point had penetrated between two of his ribs and had twisted as it entered, making its withdrawal almost impossible without breaking one of the ribs.

Most of the raiders in his company had seen injuries such as these at some time in their travels. They all knew that the eorl's chances of survival were slim. Even before their war leader had lost consciousness a few among his bodyguard were talking about releasing Eothain from his bonds and naming him as the new eorl. Aldor squirmed when he heard this, but there was little he could do other than grunt his disapproval.

By the time the warriors carrying Aldor had made it back to the encampment, Tyrbrand had prepared the eorl's tent. The bed was covered with new white linen from Aldor's personal hoard, and a table was laid with knives and saws of all sizes. The fire had been built up outside the tent and there were Cymru oil lamps inside so that even if Tyrbrand was forced to keep working after sundown, he would be able to see clearly. The holy man was determined to save the eorl's life.

Aldor awoke as his men were laying him on the bed. They had already removed his armour after Tyrbrand had trimmed both arrow shafts as close to where they entered the body as was possible. The holy man was burning some sickly smelling incense when the eorl realised what was happening.

'Let me die, you bastard,' Aldor gasped. 'Can't you see I'm finished?'

Tyrbrand approached his patient and pulled the man's eyelids open roughly so that he could see the colour of them better.

'You are not quite dead yet, Eorl Aldor,' the holy man pronounced, 'though I can make no promises about your survival. I have never known a man to live after receiving such a pair of wounds. It may be beyond my skill to help you.'

Tyrbrand called to one of the warriors, 'Bring me the strong tea that has been brewing by the fire. It is time we began this bloody chore. We have not a moment to lose.'

The holy man picked up one of the long thin knives that lay on the table and produced a sharpening stone from his pocket. Slowly, methodically he drew the blade across the surface of the stone, scraping the metal back to a razor-keen edge. Every once in a while he would stop, examine the steel and spit on the stone to lubricate it. Then he would immediately return to the constant, even-handed task.

The sound of the stone scraping against the steel struck dread into Aldor's heart. He knew only too well what the holy man intended for he had assessed his own wounds on the journey back to the camp. To remove the barbed heads it would be

331

necessary to break or cut the ribs around them and then to pull the iron tips out. If the barbs had not become entangled with any internal organs, then Aldor knew he stood a chance—a small chance—of recovery.

But even if he lived after this operation, the eorl knew his fighting days would be well and truly over. He would never be able to lift a heavy blade again, much less a shield to parry a blow. He summoned his strength and attempted to sit up but managed only to grasp at the holy man's sleeve.

'Let me die!' Aldor insisted. 'I do not want to go on living like a cripple.'

'Whether you live or die,' Tyrbrand told him, 'is not in my hands. I am only the instrument of your healing, not the force behind it. Seaxneat has plans for you and, though I may have little respect for you as a leader, I can do no more than follow the bidding of my true master. He has instructed me to serve you and so I shall.'

A man entered the tent carrying a wooden mug full of the tea Tyrbrand had asked for and a red-hot iron. He handed the mug to the holy man and then stood back a little, holding the iron as low to the ground as he could. Aldor saw it, though, and he knew what it meant.

'You will drink this brew,' Tyrbrand commanded. 'It may be some days before you are able to take nourishment and this will help your body to recover.'

'I will not drink,' Aldor answered. 'Let me die.'

'You will do as you are told,' the holy man asserted. 'That is what Seaxneat demands of you.' Tyrbrand took the mug in one hand and held his other down hard over Aldor's nose so that the eorl could not breathe without opening his mouth. As soon as Aldor had gasped in a gulp of air the holy man poured the hot liquid into his mouth and held the war leader's jaws shut until he had swallowed the brew.

'Now you will sleep,' Tyrbrand announced. 'If you do not wake, it is the will of Seaxneat. If you do recover, you will owe me an even greater debt than you did before.'

The man holding the red-hot iron stepped forward and Tyrbrand took the instrument from him. Two more men Aldor had not noticed before came forward and grabbed at the eorl's legs to keep them from thrashing about. The other warrior pulled Aldor's arm above his head so that Tyrbrand could reach the wound in his side without risk of causing further injury.

Then, without speaking another word or even giving the slightest warning, the holy man plunged the hot iron into Aldor's side to burn at the flesh. The eorl screamed in agony as the smell of searing flesh reached his nostrils. The pain was too much for even a battle-hardened fighter like the eorl. Long before the holy man had begun the same treatment on Aldor's chest wound, the war leader had collapsed into a state where he no longer felt any suffering whatsoever.

Murrough went back to his lodgings after the confrontation with Cathal, but he had no mind to stay within the hill fort after the harsh words that had passed between him and the chieftain. So he gathered a dozen of his horse warriors and they rode out towards the spot where Caitlin, Gobann and their party had entered the forest.

Along the way they found several of the mounts Caitlin's warriors had left by the entrance but which had later been released by the Glastig's servants so that they could roam freely in search of food and water. Murrough ordered the horses to be collected wherever one was seen, and by the time they reached the edge of the woods, almost all of the mounts had been recovered. He was careful, though, not to let his men see how crestfallen he felt when the horses were found. This was a sure sign to him that some ill had befallen his queen and he was beginning to believe that the monstrous beings of this forest may have waylaid her party.

The king wandered into the woods for a short distance with a few of his men, but the stifling darkness made them all very nervous and not even Murrough was willing to go beyond where he could plainly see the sunlight at the entrance. He ordered that a fire be lit and a watch kept close to the woods. While this was being done he decided to try and ride around the perimeter of the woods but had not gone far to the north when a fast-flowing stream forced him to turn back.

Then he rode south and west to try and come around the forest from the other side, but the River Cree stopped his progress in this direction. The only way across this waterway was to return to the bridge in the south and that would have meant he would be out alone after dark. The king decided that it was best to wait for Caitlin at the edge of the woods where he had set his sentries.

It was just on dark when he came back to the edge of the woods to find the fire well tended and a messenger waiting for him. The man was one of the warriors of Caitlin's party, sent back by the

Glastig to bring word to Murrough of all that had happened.

Murrough was overjoyed to find that all was well with Caitlin and Gobann and that they had found the two young Druids well and safe. He made sure the messenger had food and drink and as the man ate the king questioned him thoroughly. When Murrough had heard all he could from the messenger, he asked him to return to the home of the Glastig with news of the attack on Dun Righ and of the conflict that had arisen between Cathal and himself. The warrior was reluctant at first to re-enter the woods but soon realised just how urgent the message was.

'The Saxons are on the move,' Murrough insisted. 'Caitlin and all her company must get themselves to safety as soon as possible. And Cathal is not to be trusted either.'

The warrior had sat for a while talking with the king and so, without taking any further rest, he made his way back into the forest with the last rush lights strapped to his belt and one held aloft. Murrough settled down then to wait once more for his wife's return.

Malchedoc the poet, who had once been known among his people as Cianan of the Sweet Melody, led Mawn and Sianan to a house not far from the clearing. In that house a turf fire burned warmly in the central hearth and the ceiling was blackened from the soot of it. Fergus was waiting for his master and brought a jug of mead to him before retreating to sit and listen in a corner of the room. The old man sat the young Druids down and then offered them the cup of welcome. As soon as Mawn and Sianan had each taken a draught he apologised for his ill-treatment of them and begged their forgiveness.

'I had no idea that you were to suffer as I do, or I would have thought more carefully on my words to you both.'

'You speak as though we had been inflicted with a sickness,' Sianan exclaimed. 'But we have been told that the Danaan Druids prepared the Water of Life with the intention of eliminating sickness and old age among their people.'

'Our people,' Malchedoc corrected. 'All those mortals who take the Water of Life are forever after counted among the clans of the Children of the Light. They give us that honour by virtue of the trials we share with them.'

'Trials?' Mawn questioned. 'We were told that the road would not be an easy one, but you make it sound as though there is little else but pain in store for us.'

'How could Gobann or any of the Druid Council know what it is to be given the gift of long life?' Malchedoc scoffed. 'None among their company ever experienced it or even knew any who had. Gobann may have spent a long while among the Danaans but they surely would not have told him all the answers to his questions. Those questions are for you to pose for you are the Wanderers.'

'You have lived here longer than two lifetimes,' Mawn calculated, 'so you can tell us what to expect in the coming seasons. For my part I have not noticed any particular change in myself since I was given the brew and ate the rowan berries.'

'And you will not see any change either,' Malchedoc confirmed. 'You will stay just as you are, unchanged and ageless. Your wisdom will increase and your thoughts will mature but your bodies will never alter.' Malchedoc paused for a second and it seemed he was unsure whether he should say any more. In the end he coughed and continued but Mawn could tell he was not happy to be broaching this subject.

'Have they told you what happened to all the Faerie race when they had taken the brew?' he asked. 'Have they mentioned the curse that falls upon all who take this path?'

'Only that they were freed from age and sickness,' Sianan answered.

'There is more,' Malchedoc went on. 'The Danaans of those days were not as wise as they have grown to be. Their knowledge of the healing arts was limited even though they were able to concoct the Water of Life. The Faerie Druids knew then what all wise folk have known for certain since ancient days—that the body is only a suit of clothes worn by the soul and that when the flesh dies it should be shed with joy, life after life. True immortality lies in the ever-living nature of the spirit. And only those who learn to remember from one life to the next become ever-living in any real sense. For those who can recall their true identity it is as if they only change their cloak in passing from one life to the next.'

Malchedoc picked up a cup and poured some mead into it. 'You both know the story of the Cauldron of Plenty, don't you?'

Sianan and Mawn nodded together.

Malchedoc held up the cup to indicate that it represented the cauldron. 'This great cooking vessel was one of the four treasures which the Danaans brought with them from their homes over the sea when they journeyed to Eirinn. Like the other sacred objects the Cauldron of Plenty had

337

properties which made it extremely helpful to the Faerie people on their travels. For whenever a company sat down to eat of the food cooked within the vessel, no sooner would they finish their meal than the cauldron would be full again to the brim. Thus the Danaans were always supplied with food in abundance.'

'But the cauldron also represents the great cycles of life and death,' Mawn interjected.

Malchedoc looked at the young man before him with a hard gaze that did not betray any of the compassion he truly felt. It was not that he was in any way upset with Mawn or Sianan. It was just that he was beginning to realise they had not been taught enough to prepare them for the life ahead.

'There is no death,' Malchedoc stated succinctly. 'Only the body perishes and is no more than dust. What lives on is much more precious. But you are right to some degree,' he admitted, 'for when the body is worn out it is returned to the great cauldron and will one day become a suit of clothes for a soul once more. But the real significance of the Cauldron of Plenty is that no matter how a life is spent it is always renewed, time after time, forever.'

'Like the new flowers that bloom every springtime,' Sianan added.

'When the Faerie kind realised that they had cheated themselves of that kind of immortality, they shrugged it off as necessary for the survival of their race. Even when they understood that they had committed themselves to unchanging bodies and so had narrowed the experiences that would be open to them throughout their existence, they were able to justify it to themselves. But when they discovered that the very potion that had given them life and health had also stolen from them the ability to procreate, many found it too distressing to bear.'

. Mawn and Sianan both sat in silent shock with eyes glazed and it was immediately apparent to Malchedoc that this last piece of information had not been explained to either of them previously. His heart went out to them and he softened his tone.

'That is why so many of the Danaans take human lovers; in that way they can have children of mixed blood. For the Faeries cannot bear off-spring from among their own bloodlines alone. It was this terrible fact that led the Cailleach into a frenzy of flesh-eating and soul-snatching. She preyed on little children and babies because she yearned so desperately for her own. Before she lost all sense of right and wrong she only stole them away to live with her. My wife, the Glastig, too was once feared for her propensity for consuming human flesh and for stealing away the children of poor farmers.'

'Then why did the Glastig and the Cailleach not take human lovers as other Danaans do?' Sianan asked.

'Because they were stubborn,' Malchedoc explained. 'The Cailleach was among the first of the Sidhe folk to speak out against the treaty be-tween the Gaels and the Danaans which split Eirinn between the two peoples. She and the Glastig were descended of the Fomor on their mother's side and were always reluctant to accept the decisions of the other Danaans. But they got their name as the Children of the Dark from their preference for remaining hidden away from the human kind who associated them with the deep dark places of the Earth and with night. They despised the Gaels and all the Faerie kind who had open relations with them.'

'And in the end their stubbornness led them to acts of senseless brutality?' Mawn asked.

'Yes,' Malchedoc confirmed, 'in many cases that is true. The Glastig changed her ways when I met her, but my harp is a special one. I don't think even Balor of the Evil Eye would have been able to resist the music that comes forth from her strings.'

'The Faerie kind can experience death?' Sianan inquired. 'For the Cailleach was killed after she tried to attack Caitlin and steal her child.'

'The Cailleach died because she had conquered her fear of death,' came Malchedoc's answer. 'She was injured badly and refused to take the herbs of healing. It was her decision to pass on.'

'So we too one day may be allowed to depart this Earth as everyone else does?' Mawn pressed.

'That day may come,' Malchedoc replied. 'But you have been tutored well in the importance of your role to both the Danaan folk and the Gaels. I think that it may be many generations before you can consider that possibility. The most difficult test ahead of you will be when the first of your greatest friends passes away at the end of their natural lives. That was how it was for me. I realised one day that I would always be saying farewell to some dear soul that was free to journey onwards.'

'The *Imramma*,' Sianan mumbled. 'The great voyage of the soul.'

'We and those like us,' Malchedoc went on, 'have stepped on board a boat and, though we are permitted to sail wherever we will, we cannot leave the ship again until perhaps the ocean of life runs dry.'

'But if we were not to undertake this task,' Mawn said, 'then the doctrines of the Romans or the brutal ways of the Saxons would surely overcome our people. We must keep the spirit of our ancestors' wisdom burning bright through the ages.'

'I have heard,' Sianan began, 'and it was Origen of Alexandria who told me this so I have no reason to doubt the truth of it, that the Roman Christians believe that the body and the soul are one. Origen said that they had taken the true teachings of Christ and changed the meanings to suit themselves. Few among the Christians can accept that the soul passes on life after life into new forms.'

'Even Declan of Saint Ninian's,' Mawn agreed, 'has expressed to me that he is shocked by such ideas.'

'And so he would be,' Malchedoc declared. 'By instilling in their followers a fear of death and of eternal punishment, the Romans ensure that their people remain obedient and compliant. In the ancient days before the time of Cormac Mac Airt, the Romans built an empire based on the sweat and the spilled blood of their slaves. And that is what their doctrine of death is accomplishing now. It condemns the believer to a lifetime of slavery.'

'But I don't understand why people would accept such ideas without questioning them,' Sianan said.

'That is because you were awakened to the cycles of the world when you were a child,' Malchedoc explained, 'as is the way with all of our folk. All of our legends speak of the turning of the great wheel of existence. The cycles of birth and death and rebirth are as undeniable to us as the changing seasons which always come again to spring. But the Roman world is driven by another force. A force that most Gaels cannot begin to understand. I will speak to you of it now because very few among the Cruitne or the Gaels have any knowledge of it and I think it unlikely that your teachers would have mentioned it to you.

'I learned about it from the Cymru chieftains of the southern parts of Britain,' Malchedoc went on. 'They were conquered by Rome nine generations ago. Near to this time, I am told, the Christ walked the Earth. There are those who say that Christos came to the Isle of Glass, the great Druid university in the summer sea, though the southern Cymru's bards are not to be trusted entirely for they have taken on Roman ways and do not always refrain from exaggeration. I have been there, however, and seen with my own eyes the staff that the uncle of Christ struck into the ground. Each year it blooms on the day which the Romans count as the sixth day of Janus. This is supposed to be the birthday of Christ.'

'You were speaking about the force that drives the Romans on,' Mawn cut in, realising too late how rude he was to interrupt a storyteller.

Malchedoc shook his head as if to acknowledge that he was straying from the path a little. 'The Romans value gold, silver and precious gems above anything else. With this gold they can barter for things such as slaves, food, fine homes or clothes. Because few people trade the way we do— by simply giving one item in exchange for another—the people who have the most gold are the most able to provide for their clan.'

'But everyone in the clan works for the common good of the tribe, don't they?' Sianan asked, puzzled.

'Some do, but most Romans do not have a responsibility to their clan first and foremost. Usually they hold allegiance to a lord who holds a store of gold and they rely on that lord to provide them with the necessities of life.'

Mawn and Sianan shook their heads to show that they were finding this lesson in Roman ways very difficult to understand.

'Their great kings and chieftains are not elected because of the wise and just treatment of their clanspeople or even for their proven skill,' the teacher continued. 'They are chosen for one of two reasons. The first is usually because this leader has a huge storehouse filled with gold, which enables him to buy vast supplies of food which he then bestows on loyal followers and thus, in time, gains support. But the more usual method employed to be acclaimed a leader is by right of conquest. The chieftain will raise an army, paying the warriors from his personal store of gold, and then he will threaten all the other chieftains until he is elected their overlord. This has happened many times in Rome, though I am told that they had a system of election similar to ours until greed took hold of them.'

'But what is the use of great storehouses of gold in the winter when there are no crops to be brought in?' Sianan asked.

'You are right to pose this question,' Malchedoc congratulated her, 'for one cannot eat gold. The gold is so valued that people will sell their own stores of food for very high prices in order to obtain it. The Romans expanded their empire not for the want of more land or the thrill of conquest. They were driven by the need to find more gold and to find sources of winter food. So many of their folk in the great city were employed in serving the lords that few were involved in actually producing food for the inhabitants.'

Malchedoc took his staff and drew a shape in the fine black soot at the edge of the fire. 'Imagine that this small circle is the hill fort of Dun Righ. Here there live artisans, musicians, healers, warriors and Druids; but everyone, excepting those Druids exempt for various reasons, helps to bring in the harvest. Every person tends the cattle or the goats at some time in their life. Everyone, apart from the Druids who eat no meat, owns at least one pig. In Dun Righ or any settlement like it the survival of each individual relies on the equal contribution of all. Everyone depends on their neighbour and so everyone cares for the wellbeing of their relatives and friends. Children are brought up by the whole tribe so that they consider everyone to be of their own clan. In this way we ensure that the tribe survives the winter and that all are well fed.'

Then Malchedoc lifted his staff high in the air and swung it around his head in a wide circle. 'Now imagine the city of Rome. If Dun Righ is a tiny circle in the soot of the fire, then Rome would take up the space of this whole cottage and more. In that place there are so many people living close together that it is possible to walk only a few hundred steps and be among folk who do not know your name or recognise your face.'

Mawn and Sianan both gasped in disbelief.

'Neighbours do not know one another and may live their whole lives without speaking a single word to each other. When a person falls sick they may die for the want of food or care because no-one knows them well enough to help.'

'And what of the healers?' Sianan exclaimed. 'Do they not help the sick and infirm? Are there no houses of healing in which the afflicted can take refuge?'

'There are houses of healing,' Malchedoc answered. 'And there are healers, of a sort. But they do not give their services freely. They are not granted food and lodging by the chieftain of the clan as we would expect. Nor are the houses of healing open to everyone. Only folk who have storehouses of gold and silver may seek help there.'

'Why do the people allow the chieftains to treat them in such a way?' Mawn asked incredulously. 'Surely they would impeach anyone who behaved so badly.'

'The only impeachment is death,' Malchedoc replied. 'And many of their leaders do die because of their ill-treatment of the common folk. But generally the people who do most of the work bear the burden of their lot in life because they fear what the lords would do to them if they rose up and tried to overthrow their masters.'

'And what of the warriors?' Sianan asked. 'Why do they tolerate such treatment?'

'They are well paid by the lords in gold and so they rarely have any sympathy for the suffering of the ordinary folk. The common people of the Roman lands look on their leaders with envy, and many indulge in thieving from them whenever they get the opportunity. As you can imagine, this drains the resources of the tribe as a whole, but that does not seem to worry the Romans.'

'How did they defeat the clans of the Cymru if they cannot feed all their own people?' Mawn stammered, deeply shocked at all he had heard.

'Sheer weight of numbers,' Malchedoc sighed. 'The Romans paid a reward of gold to each warrior who travelled to Britain to fight. Once they had conquered most of the island, they built garrison forts that were peopled only with warriors. These soldiers came from all over the world, some even from as far away as Alexandria on the Nile or the Straits of the Pillars of Hercules. In time Cymru men signed on as soldiers in the Roman army and were sent to foreign lands to garrison similar forts.

After only a few generations the Roman ways had been adopted by the chieftains and kings of the Cymru. There are still Druids among their people, and the island of Britain still has the great Druid schools of Oak Forest and the Isle of Glass, but the warriors are more powerful now than they are in the Gaelic lands. For they have gold, and gold has become the standard form of barter and trade. Anyone who lacks it can still survive if they can grow their own food, but one who has an abundance of gold can buy the allegiance of many people.'

'And so instead of working together for the common defence of their tribes, the Cymru chieftains argue constantly among themselves,' Sianan commented.

'That is correct,' Malchedoc congratulated her again. 'The British kings are so preoccupied with becoming the most powerful and wealthy of their brethren that they do not trust one another. That is why they could not mount an effective defence against the Saxon invasion. It is a great irony that one of the British kings invited the Saxons to come to Britain to help in the fight against the Cruitne of the north. This king paid the Saxons so well in gold that the foreigners decided to steal whatever he had left and then stay in Britain in defiance.'

'So the Saxons were invited to come here to this land.' Mawn shook his head, finding all this very hard to believe. 'And they came because they were offered gold.'

'Just as the Romans once offered the Saxons and their cousins gold to serve in the Roman army,' Malchedoc affirmed. 'That is where the savages got their taste for plunder and thieving. The quest for gold is what leads them to raiding, to murder and to constant war.'

346

'The White Brother, Origen, who was not a Roman Christian, once told me,' Mawn recalled, 'that Christ had referred to the love of gold as the cause of all the evil in the world. I did not understand exactly what he meant then, but now I am beginning to realise why Origen left his own country and all his kindred to live in Eirinn. He used to say that he needed a place far away from the turmoil and strife of the world. Now I understand that he was seeking to find a life that was free of greed and the misdeeds committed in its name.'

'And I am beginning to realise,' Sianan added, 'that this force which we call greed already exists among our people in much subtler forms. And it will be our greatest enemy in the task we have been allotted.'

'All people are greedy to some degree,' Malchedoc laughed. 'It is not just the Romans who suffer from it. But when greed becomes the overwhelming motivation for a person's actions, even above the welfare of his clan or tribe, then the damage can be very great. Because of greed folk are starved first of all of food and in time of all the other good things in life. Music, stories, healing, knowledge and even love have all become items which can be bought in the markets of Rome.'

'You speak as if you know the city very well,' Mawn commented.

'I do,' Malchedoc admitted. 'When I was your age I went there to that place at the centre of the great empire. My teacher was an emissary for the High-King at the time. Though we were there after all its glory had begun to fade, I will never forget the fear that I felt being among so many countless hungry downtrodden folk. People who would slice open your throat to steal the bread out of it. And people live homeless amid the vast stonework

347

buildings that will likely last for countless generations but are not used to house anyone.'

Malchedoc took the filled cup that represented
the Cauldron of Plenty. 'The Romans fear so many
things,' he said quietly, 'and they inspire so much
fear in others. Fear will be your greatest enemy, not
greed. If you can defeat your own fear and the fear
of others, then you will succeed in your difficult
task.'

He raised the cup in the air and muttered a
blessing over the mead before draining the vessel.
'Now I think we should go to our rest for we have
talked long. We will speak again in time, and
remember that as long as this forest stands it will
be a refuge for you both to return to.'

'We will remember, great-grandfather,' Mawn
replied. 'We will remember.'

'When Malchedoc brought me back to the forest,'
Síla was explaining to the silent figures around the
Glastig's fire, 'I spent a long while resting; nearly
a full moon. The ordeal of the Saxon attack and the
few days at sea had weakened me to the point of
absolute exhaustion.' She stretched her fingers
before the flames and her hands threw shadows
onto the walls of the cave. Gobann shifted in his
seat, realising how close he had come to losing his
dearest friend to the savage brutality of the foreigners.

'Why did you not travel on to Dun Righ to meet
us as arranged?' Sianan asked, confused.

'Malchedoc told me that the hill fort was many
days to the north and that the country in between
was held by the enemy,' Síla explained.

'Why would he lie about such a thing?' Mawn exclaimed.

'To protect his forest,' the healer answered. 'Had I gone to Dun Righ there was a chance that I might tell what I had seen in this forest, and then who knows what may have happened.'

'Cathal's people would not have been so afraid of the Glastig,' Caitlin chimed in. 'That would have meant more visitors to the woods in search of game and timber. But he could not have kept you here forever.'

'I do not know what would have become of me had you not arrived, but I did not waste my time here,' Síla added. 'Once I was well enough I spent my time gathering as many herbs and roots as I could find. Many that I collected are rare in the outside world. I will have enough to last me four or five seasons if I am careful.'

Sianan was about to ask to be shown the collection of herbs when the Glastig returned to the cave. Sianan fell silent, still awed by the water Faerie. It was strange to her that, though the Glastig lived mostly in the pool at the foot of the waterfall, she moved more like an overconfident cat than a water-dwelling creature. Sianan could not help wondering about that black pool, deep and dark and seemingly impenetrable.

'There are other creatures that live in my pool,' the Glastig said and Sianan was jolted from her daydream by the realisation that the Faerie woman had heard her thoughts. 'Do not approach the edge of the pool for there are water horses who dwell near the surface and they will not respect your blue robes. They will drag you to the bottom and, if you are lucky, you will drown before they tear your body to pieces and devour it.'

Sianan shuddered and then the Glastig spoke to

everyone in the room, certain that her warning would be taken seriously. 'The Ravens have brought me news of a Saxon attack on Dun Righ,' she announced. 'The enemy was repulsed but with great loss to the Gaels.'

There was stunned silence. No-one, not even Gobann who knew that such an attack was inevitable, had expected this to happen so soon.

'There is no telling what the foreigners may do next,' the Danaan woman continued. 'Even though their war leader lies severely wounded, they may still have the will to attempt to overrun the stronghold.'

'We must return to Dun Righ,' Caitlin decided. 'Cathal and Murrough will need every able hand to defend the hill fort.'

'Your husband is waiting for you at the place where you entered the forest,' the Glastig informed her. 'And I have been told that he and Cathal of Dun Righ have parted with each other in anger.'

Gobann raised his eyebrows in surprise. 'Are you certain? What could have caused them to argue?'

'Especially at a time when the dun was under threat,' Caitlin said. She knew Murrough better than anyone. He was a man slow to anger, tolerant and forgiving. But when he was pushed too far he could let loose a frightening temper. 'The King of Munster must have had a very good excuse to start a fight with the Chieftain of Dun Righ.'

'I do not know why they fought,' the Glastig said. 'I do know, however, that they nearly came to blows and that it was only the intervention of a Druid woman that prevented bloodshed among the supporters of the two men.'

Caitlin felt a strange sensation when the Danaan mentioned the Druid woman. She asked herself if this was the Druid Ia and could not help feeling that it most certainly was. For some reason that she could not explain, she did not like the thought of that at all.

'You are welcome to stay here with the Wanderers if that is your wish,' the Glastig continued. 'For it seems to me that they might be safer here for the time being.'

'Your offer is very gracious,' Gobann answered, 'but it is better that we all return to Dun Righ together and find out what has taken place there as soon as possible. I have a feeling that my services as a judge and bearer of the Silver Branch may be called upon. The Wanderers will come with us. Síla and I have been named as their guardians and they must accompany us so that they may learn of the ways of the world. This would seem an excellent opportunity for them to gain an understanding of the importance of diplomacy.'

'And what of the Saxons?' the Glastig asked. 'Are you not afraid of what may become of the young ones if they fall into the hands of those savages?'

'The Wanderers will be relatively safe as long as Murrough's guards are close by. As a last resort, however, we may seek to return here for refuge, if you are agreeable to it.'

'Of course,' the Danaan replied. 'There is no question of their welcome, and yours too, whenever you should choose to take our hospitality. If it can be proved that the Saxons have been responsible for the deaths of the white horses, then they will face the wrath of all my clan. Not even those fierce raiders can stand against the fury of Danaan rage. And if it was a Saxon, it will be easy enough to prove. All we need to do now is remain watchful and alert for their next attempt to commit this terrible crime.'

'We should set out for the edge of the forest immediately,' Caitlin suggested, 'for it took us a day and a morning to walk here.'

'But you took the long path,' the Glastig informed her, 'not the secret way that is much shorter and more direct. I will have my servants guide you, and if you walk half a day at a good pace, you will see the daylight shining on the hill fort of Dun Righ. I would come with you myself but I must travel to the north to raise my clanspeople in case there is a need of their numbers to defend this woodland.'

'And what of Malchedoc?' Síla asked. 'Will he come with us?'

'He may do,' the Glastig answered, 'but I would be surprised. He has not ventured far beyond the forest in the last twenty winters. He has no time for the folk who live in the world beyond the green canopy. He only found you on the beach because he was summoned there by one of the Raven kind who had seen you drifting afloat on the ocean.'

'I would like to repay my debt to him,' Síla said. 'He saved my life.'

The Glastig smiled and took the hand of the Druid healer. 'But you gave my sister a gift that you cannot understand. When she passed away from this world as a result of your defence of Caitlin, she was free to travel again as all souls should. You released the Cailleach from an eternity of loneliness and suffering. There is no debt between us that needs repayment. You gave the gift of death and we have given the gift of life.'

With that the Glastig summoned Fergus, the boy that Malchedoc had found half dead in the forest. 'It is time that he went back to his own kind,' she said, 'for it would be wrong for us to deprive him of his clanspeople. Please take him with you back

352

to Dun Righ and see that he is cared for. His wounds have nearly healed and there is nothing more that we can do for him, short of sharing the Water of Life with him to make his body whole once more. I would not do that willingly, even if refraining from the cure means that he will likely be crippled for life. I know what a terrible price must be paid for the healing that the Quicken berries give.'

At that moment Caitlin remembered the bag of rowan berries that she had worn about her neck ever since the Quicken Tree had been cut down. She had found the little bag near the body of a Saxon and had kept the nine berries safe inside ever since.

'I have a gift for you,' the queen announced, 'in gratitude for all that you have done and because I believe that it is better left in your hands.' She untied the cord around her neck, pulled the drawstring undone and held out the little bag to the Glastig. The Danaan woman opened her hands to receive the unexpected gift and Caitlin poured the tiny shrivelled berries into the Glastig's palms.

'These are nine fruit from the Quicken Tree which I picked up just after the bough was cut down. Please take them so that a tree like it will survive in the future.'

The Glastig smiled warmly and Gobann found it hard to imagine how such a beautiful being could have earned such a reputation as a monster.

'I will take three of the berries,' the Danaan said, 'for I already have a tree that was planted from a berry of the Quicken. Three more you should gift to Mawn and Sianan, and the final three should be planted by you, Queen Caitlin. In this way you will be sure that the Quicken lives on somewhere.'

'We did our best to save the tree,' Caitlin repeated.

'There is nothing that you could have done, for all things have their allotted time on Earth, even those things which seem to you to be eternal. Hills are washed away to the sea and the ocean rises to cover some lands or withdraws to expose new ones. The world is ever changing and even the Danaans must come some day to the end and to their peaceful rest.'

'May you find it,' Caitlin answered immediately. 'May you and all your kind find peace.'

FIFTEEN

eginus Gallus, son of a Roman soldier and his Gaulish housekeeper; one-time soldier himself; later a monk, prisoner, penitent and priest; Seginus Gallus with olive skin and shining black hair—the legacy of his father's southern blood—woke in the half-light of early morning and immediately lit a candle by his bedside.

The yellow light filled the space inside his room with a soft homely warmth. Outside, the wind howled, letting the world know that this winter would be a hard one, a season of many deaths, from cold and from hunger, from age and infirmity.

The priest threw back the thick blankets and grabbed at his robes, the cold air stinging his flesh despite the hasty manner in which he dragged the clothes over his head. Even the woollen fabric of his priest's robe was cold, as if the first snow had seeped indifference into everything on Earth that did not live and breathe. Next he found his socks in the covers of the bed and he praised his good sense in keeping them by his body throughout the night for they, at least, were warm.

Then he took his high boots from under the bed and tugged them over his feet until the toes fitted snugly into the rounded ends. There were no fires in the homes of the clergy so the stones on the floor were bitterly cold, like blocks of grey ice. Nevertheless Seginus knelt down by his bed, his bare knees in direct contact with the floor, and began to say the morning prayers of thanksgiving.

As he started mumbling the words he began to worry that perhaps he was not alone. He could not be certain, however, that it was all in his imagination and where he once would have been frightened almost out of his wits by such a presence, he now made a simple gesture into the air behind him to banish any stray spirits that may have wandered into his room. He no longer tolerated the possibility of ghostly intruders as he once had. He took care in every thought, word and deed, aware that his own sharp tongue had often caused him more pain than it had others. Seginus Gallus was a changed man.

The priest turned back to face the wooden cross that hung on his wall and surrendered himself entirely to devotional thoughts and words of praise for his God. Whenever he attained this meditative state of being, Seginus lost all sense of cold or of hunger or of fear or of being in any way alive at all. When he gave himself up totally to the Holy Spirit, Gallus understood that he was only a small insignificant part of the wonder of creation.

In the ecstasy of prayer he found out more about himself than he had ever known before. He saw himself as nothing more than a sinful, wilful and selfish creature that had shunned the discipline of the Christian faith in preference to the satisfaction of the flesh. Here in his room at the start of each day he affirmed his commitment to become a man who could be counted as a true servant of God and the Mother Church.

Only three short months earlier he had been in chains, a prisoner of the Queen of Munster, and a man despised by all who heard his story. Declan was the only person who had seemed to be able to forgive him. Abbot Declan with his compassion and grace had offered Seginus a new life, a new start, a new and noble mission. But on the day that they set out to travel to Saint Ninian's Seginus had given no consideration to the abbot's offer of reconciliation with the faith. Father Gallus had one thought on his mind when the Saxons had attacked the ramparts of Dun Righ. It was not grace or recompense that held his attention, nor fear of what the Saxons might do to him. It was a baser, more primitive and brutal thought that had filled his mind on that day.

Revenge.

Isernus was the object of his hatred; a hatred that Seginus now understood was fed to him through the restless spirit of his brother. As a clear memory of that morning invaded his prayers the priest crossed himself and spoke aloud to his God.

'I was blind,' Seginus began. 'I did not see the Devil, though he announced himself in so many ways. I was weak and I lacked compassion for my fellow human beings. With your help, God of Grace, and your love, I will atone for my sins. I will never again allow myself to sink into the depths of such emotional blackness. That deep pit is where Satan dwells. I thank you, God, that you showed me the Devil's underground realm. The lesson I learned in my despair will stay with me forever.'

Once again he crossed himself. 'I pray for the soul of Brother Isernus who fell at the ramparts and whose life I could have saved. Through my own selfishness I allowed him to die unshriven of his sins. Forgive him his crimes on Earth and forgive me mine, O merciful Lord.'

Seginus then took the cross from around his neck and held it up closely to his face. 'Protect me from all evil, O Christ in Your Majesty. Do not let the servants of the dark one invade my soul again. Guard me in my work, in my sleep and when I am alone. Defend me from the heathen gods and their ways. Amen.'

The priest said the Pater Noster, crossed himself once more and then kissed the crucifix which hung around his neck. Then he rose from his bedside devotion to begin work for the day. Outside his small room one of Caitlin's warriors waited to escort him to the houses of healing where he would spend the daylight hours tending to the sick and those who were still suffering wounds from the Saxon attack.

This was Sunday, so under the terms of his penance the Roman was allowed to cease his work for one hour at midday to attend a mass said by Declan. When the abbot had been recovering from his own wounds, no mass had been held in the stronghold of Dun Righ at all because Gallus was the only other Christian who was ordained to speak the words. As it was considered necessary to guard Seginus closely for a long time after the battle, until it became clear his repentance was genuine, he was not permitted to officiate.

However, among Caitlin's company there was still no-one who trusted him, though none could deny the change that had come over the man. One warrior followed him these days, where once three would have guarded him in chains. There were other changes also. The priest had a room of his own and he had clean clothes in which to dress. He ate regularly, though frugally for that was a part of his penance, but was not yet permitted to attend all the prayer vigils and services that the monks and nuns performed.

On days other than Sundays Seginus worked in

the fields. Now that it was winter he helped to feed the cattle and ensure that they would have enough fodder to keep them through the cold months. The men and women of Dun Righ accepted his aid but few ever spoke to him for they had heard that he was a man haunted by ghosts, a man who had committed many crimes. They left the filthiest tasks to him, such as cleaning out the cattle enclosures and collecting the dung into heaps ready to be spread out for the next spring's planting.

The work that Seginus loved most was when he was sent to repair the dry stone walls that marked the various enclosures around the dun. He was usually left alone to this task. The work was very hard and taxing so he was invariably exhausted at the end of the day. Whenever he worked at the walls he slept soundly afterwards without any disturbances to his rest. He was glad of hard labour for whenever he could not sleep his night hours were spent in painful remorse for all the terrible sins he had committed.

Shadowed by his guard, Seginus Gallus walked up to the houses of healing near to where the Druids of the stronghold lived. From out of the doorway of one of the houses a young boy poked his head, half asleep and yawning widely. The Roman had seen this lad in the company of the Druids ever since Caitlin and Gobann had returned from their search in the forest. Seginus had only heard sketchy accounts of their journey, but his guards had told him that this boy had been rescued from a hideous monster that dwelt in the green woods.

The priest tried not to stare at the lad's scarred face, but as the boy turned to call to someone within the house Seginus saw that his left ear had been almost entirely burned away. The wound had healed but the skin had grown back a bright scarlet colour, blotched and ugly.

'What sort of a demon did that to him?' the Roman muttered, but his guard did not acknowledge the question. As the priest got closer the boy called out again and then stepped outside to sit on the stone seat which lay to the left of all the houses. The lad was closely followed by a young woman whom Seginus immediately recognised, though he had never spoken to her. She was a Druid.

The woman's shining short hair was the same colour as charcoal. The Roman noticed that the locks had begun to grow back very quickly but were still no longer than a boy from Gaul might wear in his late teens. Before the party had left Eirinn this young woman had cut all her beautiful hair off for some reason. Seginus guessed that it was part of some Druidic ritual similar perhaps to the shaving of the head which all novitiate brothers submitted to, but he did not know for certain. He had seen many of the Druid kind with their shaved foreheads and assumed that this too was a tonsure to mark the woman as one of the holy ones of the Gaels.

As the young woman stretched her arms in the cold air Seginus drew level with her and noticed her shivering a little. He did not know why but he suddenly felt a great kinship with her. In the next moment, before his guard could stop him, he had diverted slightly from his path to approach her. The warrior following him made no move to stop the priest, merely grunting when Seginus slowed down a little.

'Good morning, sister Druid,' the Roman said in his best Gaelic. 'May God bless you this day.'

Sianan did not immediately realise who was addressing her so she replied without a thought,

'And may the gods of your people bless you also.'
But when she saw that it was Seginus who had
spoken, she jumped a little in surprise and drew
in her breath sharply.

'There is but one true God, sister,' the priest
replied. 'And if you would wish his blessings upon
me then I would be truly grateful to you for that
mercy.'

'May your God bless you, then,' Sianan stuttered,
unsure whether she should even be speaking to
this man.

Seginus Gallus smiled broadly, obviously
delighted by the friendly response he had received.
The Roman walked briskly on towards the houses
of healing, a new spring in his step. It was rare
that anyone spoke to Seginus and he suddenly
realised how much he missed simple conversation.

Seginus stopped before he entered the building
where the sick and aged were housed and looked
back in Sianan's direction. Surprised to find that
she was still watching him, he offered her a wave,
which she politely returned.

That was the first of many such early morning
meetings and the very beginning of an unlikely
and very guarded friendship.

Aldor's wounds took a long while to mend. Three
moons came and went before he took his first steps,
and even then he could not make them without a
stout stick to support him. His legs had not been
damaged in the battle, but he had spent so long
lying in his bed that they had become weakened
and he had to learn to use them all over again. The
injury to his chest healed very quickly even though

361

it was a deep wound, but the damage to his side took much longer to improve.

Tyrbrand had fed the eorl each day during his convalescence and had been a constant presence in the war leader's tent. Now that Aldor was well enough to walk again, he looked forward to being able to escape the holy man for a while. At times the eorl wished that he had been killed or had died of his wounds; anything to have avoided the great debt that he now owed Tyrbrand.

As for the holy man, he had concluded a peace with the Dal Araidhans on Aldor's behalf. Under the terms of the treaty the Saxons had promised to cease their attacks on the Gaels and withdraw to a place at least a full day's march from Dun Righ. In return the Gaels had granted Aldor's people some land and an old Roman fort to the southeast of their stronghold.

Tyrbrand had surveyed the fort and declared it unfit for their purposes. Then he had commenced the building of a hall and settlement on the edge of the bay formed by the outpouring of the River Cree. The spot had excellent moorings and was relatively sheltered. Most importantly many ships would be able to tie up there without any trouble. Tyrbrand had been thinking and planning far ahead into the future when he chose the place.

The hall was finished in six weeks, but long before that Aldor was moved to the new settlement from the old temporary camp that he and his warriors had inhabited. Upon the eorl's arrival the holy man named the new home Ravenshall and presented the war leader with the gift of a new banner of a black Raven on a bright red background. Aldor wondered where the fine cloth had come from for this gesture, but he never asked. The eorl preferred not to speak to Tyrbrand unless it was absolutely necessary. His hatred and distrust of the holy man had not diminished since Tyrbrand had saved his life. Rather, it had grown now that Aldor was so dependent on him.

The winter was going to be a bitter one, Aldor could see that from the grey skies and the thick frosts which lingered until late morning. The snow had not yet begun to fall, but the air was full of the scent of it and had a bite that gave clear indication of hard weather ahead. On this first day out of his hall and away from his hearth fire he drank in the fresh air untainted by the black smoke of the house. He limped slowly down to the water's edge and stood on the sand, watching the calm sea.

'It looks like a great sheet of ice,' he said aloud to himself. 'As still as death.'

Even the several ships which the Angles had brought with them, tied at their moorings, hardly moved on the tide and the seagulls swam around the boats looking for scraps of food. The beach was only ten paces wide but the sand was fine and golden with shells scattered here and there and black stones which shone like jewels. Aldor stared at the place where the tiny waves struck the beach. The sound of the sea was always soothing to him and he realised that in the three months during his recovery it was probably the sound he had missed most.

The eorl grasped his walking stick tightly and moved to sit down among the tufts of grass which grew where the sand gave way to soil. He was so unsteady on his legs and so exhausted from his short walk from the hall that he decided to take his time in lowering himself to the ground. In the end, however, his left foot slipped and he landed heavily on his back. He lay there after the fall, grateful that he had not injured himself.

Aldor leaned back, stretching his neck so that his head rested on a large tuft of soft grass. He looked at the sky and ignored the chill air. The only sounds were the calls of the gulls and the gentle lapping of the waves. The eorl watched the moving clouds for a while—swirling masses of grey and white—and slowly he began to allow his eyes to close.

Though he was no longer looking directly at the sky, the image of the clouds remained imprinted on his mind, and he imagined that he was still watching their spiralling patterns shift across the heavens. As he watched, flocks of birds soared by in precise formations. Three birds broke ranks to glide down to where Aldor lay. In this half-dreaming state the eorl could not see the birds clearly but he knew from the moment that they had left their flock that they were Ravens. The great black birds came to rest only a few paces away from the war leader and he had to roll over onto one side to get a clear look at them. Then the eorl heard voices and for a moment his attention was taken away from the birds as he tried to discover who was speaking. None of his warriors were anywhere nearby, though, and Aldor could still hear people talking.

This puzzled him greatly until he turned his attention to the Ravens once more and realised that they were moving their beaks in time with the speech. Aldor shook his head to clear his thoughts, aware that he was experiencing something strange but uncertain exactly what. Then he did his best to concentrate on what was being said.

'Where shall we go,' the first bird screeched, 'and dine today?'

'In behind that long green grass,' the second

answered. 'I see there lies a dying war leader. And nobody knows that he lies there but us three.'

'If we feast on him now while he is sleeping,' the third spoke up, 'he will not be able to put up much of a fight and nobody will know he is missing.'

'His warriors will not notice,' the first said, 'for they are busy at the hunt.'

'And he has no lady who would come looking for him,' the second observed.

'Nor anyone to watch over him,' the third enthused. 'So we may go to our meat without being disturbed.'

'And sweet our dinner will be,' the first Raven hissed.

Aldor felt himself go numb with fear. Suddenly he found that he had no control whatsoever over his limbs. He could not even coax his eyelids open. The eorl was incapable of making any attempt to escape. Still he could hear the birds cackling nearby, but he was paralysed, his legs and arms heavier than gold, his body a dead weight.

'You sit on his chest and split it open,' the second instructed the first, 'and I'll bite out his beautiful blue eyes.'

'And I will stand at his head,' the third Raven said, 'and tear out his fine greying hair for to line our nest with in winter.'

'And no-one will notice he is gone,' the first Raven cackled. 'No-one will know where he went to. And his white bones when they are stripped bare will be open to the wind and weather forever.'

The Ravens laughed again in their high-pitched cracking voices. Aldor made a great effort to move his body, summoning all his willpower in a desperate attempt to escape this horrible fate.

'In behind the long green grass,' the first Raven

repeated, 'there lies a newly slain warrior. And nobody knows that he lies there, so we can eat our meal in peace. You may be victorious for a time, Aldor, but in the end we will have you.'

Aldor called on every last measure of his self-control, mustering his strength to battle for his life with these creatures. In a burst of outrage and indignation he managed to cause his arms and legs to tremble slightly. Then unexpectedly every muscle in his body jolted into life at once and the eorl jerked into a waking state. His eyes flew open and, as if the built-up tension had spurred him on, sat bolt upright where he had been lying down only moments before.

The war leader looked nervously over his shoulder. The birds were gone. He searched the beach for them and then scanned the sky in case they were hovering above, ready to swoop down and take him. But there was no sign of the three Ravens; no trace of their cackling mocking speech, and no vestige of their presence. Aldor was alone.

Almost.

A movement far down the beach caught the eorl's attention. A dark figure was walking along the sand and over the mudflats which choked the mouth of a stream to the south. The Ravens had been unearthly and dreamlike but this figure was very real. It sparked another rush of fear. Here, he sensed, was a real threat to his safety, not a half-imagined apparition. His heart froze and his breathing slowed.

As the black-robed form got closer, however, the eorl could plainly see that this man, if man it was, was leaning heavily on a staff and walking in much the same manner as Aldor himself was forced to do with his weakened legs. The man's head was covered entirely by a great hood which drooped over his face and covered his shoulders.

Aldor resolved to be patient. If the figure continued to approach him, the eorl knew he would have time to rise and escape because the stranger was having such difficulty in walking. He lifted himself up a little in readiness and to get a clearer sight of the figure.

As he did so, Aldor noticed another man, dressed in a red cloak, rush out from among the grass and jump onto the beach near the figure. The two men were more than four or five bow shots away, but the eorl could plainly see that they exchanged greetings in a very polite and respectful manner.

The red-cloaked man got down on his bended knee before the black-robed one who in turn touched a hand to the other's forehead. In that instant Aldor knew who the man in the red garment must be. No-one else that the eorl knew ever wore such an outlandish colour.

It was Tyrbrand.

The two men, black and red, continued to walk along the sea strand deep in conversation. Aldor could not think who the black-clad fellow could possibly be, but once again he sensed danger on the wind. The eorl was rarely mistaken in such matters. Fear began to take hold of the war leader again. Some sense told him that he should not let these men get too close to him for if he did, he would live to regret it.

The eorl dug his walking stick into the sand and hauled himself to his feet. Although it was still a struggle, he found that his legs were already feeling much stronger than they had earlier. The short exercise had done him good. Once he was on his feet and feeling confident, Aldor turned to make his way between the large tufts of grass onto the more even ground, but as he was taking his first steps he heard his name on the breeze.

'Aldor!' Tyrbrand was yelling. 'Is that you?'

The eorl resolved to ignore the call, moving as quickly as he could back to the safety of his warm hall and his crackling fire. His throat was dry from the cold air, and for the first time in months Aldor had a thirst for ale, a positive yearning for the brew. He resolved to get himself some as soon as he was back in his seat in the hall.

'Eorl Aldor!' the holy man bellowed at the top of his lungs. 'Wait! I have a visitor for you.'

But Aldor did not pause even for a moment. The eorl was not as fit as the holy man, though, and had not travelled more than twenty steps when he heard a pounding footfall behind him. A few more paces and he heard his name called again, but still he ignored it. Then a hand came down on Aldor's shoulder and spun him around.

'Are you deaf?' Tyrbrand gasped, out of breath from the chase. 'I have been calling to you.'

'I heard you,' Aldor replied. 'I was going back to the hall to get warm.'

'You have a distinguished visitor,' the holy man went on. 'He has travelled far from his home in the southern mountains to speak with you.'

'I will not see anyone today,' the eorl barked. 'Can you not see that I am ill?'

'This man may be of much help to you,' Tyrbrand insisted.

'If indeed he is a man of the flesh,' Aldor muttered.

'What are you talking about?' the holy man asked. 'Of course he is a mortal man. This fellow is no god, though his followers respect him as one.'

'Who is he?'

'It is best that I let him tell his story himself,' Tyrbrand explained, 'for he has much to tell you and an interesting offer to make to you.'

'Tell him to go back to his mountain,' Aldor snarled. 'I will not speak with anyone today.'

'He has word of your brother Guthwine,' the holy man added.

'Guthwine is dead.'

'This man was present when your brother was killed,' Tyrbrand continued provocatively. 'Would you not like to hear what became of your kinsman?'

Aldor looked the holy man in the eye, unable to disguise his exhaustion any longer. 'Send him to the hall,' the eorl relented. 'I'll be waiting by the fire.'

'Very well, my lord. I will do as you command.'

'You will do as you wish,' Aldor pointed out, 'and do your best to make me believe that it is my command.'

Tyrbrand did not say another word but strode off back down the beach towards the visitor. Aldor, meanwhile, limped back to his hall. He was not very far from the outlying buildings when one of his men offered to help him. There had been a time, the eorl recalled bitterly, when such a request would have been deeply insulting to him. It might even have cost this warrior his life. But now Aldor was grateful and leaned on the stronger man all the way back to his fireside.

He had just sat down on a wide bench and stretched his legs out towards the flames of the central hearth when Tyrbrand entered the dimly lit hall. The holy man walked straight up to the fire and spread his hands out before it, flexing his fingers to get the blood moving. Aldor said nothing, waiting for the other man to speak first; but

369

when the silence dragged on, the eorl finally coughed to get Tyrbrand's attention.

'Where is your visitor?' Aldor inquired.

'He is outside making supplications to his god,' the holy man answered.

'Who is he?'

'A man who commands four hundred and fifty able-bodied warriors. A man who is prepared to put his army at your disposal.'

'At my disposal?' the eorl asked incredulously. 'No man offers such a gift without expecting something in return.'

'This man asks for nothing of any value to you,' Tyrbrand answered. 'Nothing that would cost you anything to bestow.'

'Everything has a cost,' Aldor observed. 'Everything. Where is this well-meaning war leader from?'

'His people come from the hills in the south. From the land called Cymbri.'

'And why would a chieftain of the Cymru folk risk the lives of himself and his men in dealing with Saxons?' the eorl asked. 'Has he not heard of our reputation for treachery? Of our fame as brutal slayers of the Britons? Is he such a traitor to his people that he wants to fight alongside the Saxons?'

'He knows our people well,' Tyrbrand began. 'It was he who hired your late brother Guthwine to fight in Eirinn. This man knows something of the Saxon ways and seems to be very tolerant of our customs—if it appears to be to his advantage.'

'You have not answered my question,' Aldor pointed out. 'What does he want?'

'It is his dream to liberate the Strath-Clóta from the Gaels,' the holy man began. 'That makes him as much an enemy of the Dal Araidhans as we are.'

'And what would make me more acceptable an overlord than Cathal of Dun Righ?' Aldor queried sarcastically.

'Cathal has a certain hostility to this man's religion.'

'These Cymru are Christians!' the eorl spat with disgust.

'Yes, my lord,' Tyrbrand admitted. 'But there are four hundred and fifty of them and they are battle-seasoned veterans who fought in the wars against our folk in the south.'

'And they lost!' Aldor barked. 'I do not see the need to barter with a Cymru for the prize that I will take in time anyway.'

'Strath-Clóta will certainly fall to you if you are very patient and prepared to accept many losses among our own folk and perhaps many setbacks also. But imagine the difference four hundred and fifty Cymru could make if they were in the vanguard of the army, taking the brunt of the casualties and softening the Gaels for our final onslaught.'

'What war leader would be foolish enough to put his troops in such a dangerous position?' the eorl scoffed.

'His warriors may be veterans but this man is a religious fanatic with very little understanding of warfare. I believe he could be persuaded to do your bidding if you were prepared to offer him concessions once you held the lordship of this entire peninsula.'

'What concessions would he be likely to ask?' Aldor demanded without any effort to disguise his scepticism. 'I am sure that you have both discussed this.'

'He is seeking the freedom to practise his religion,' Tyrbrand explained, throwing up his arms to indicate the simplicity of the situation. 'I think that you could very safely guarantee him that. Of course once the peninsula is in your hands, you can always choose to see things differently. If his force has suffered high losses they will not be in a position to argue.'

'They will outnumber us on the field,' Aldor murmured.

'We have five hundred and twenty men at arms,' the holy man remarked with relish. 'And one of our warriors is worth two of theirs.'

'What if they strike a deal with the Gaels?' the eorl pointed out. 'What if we let them into our confidence and they turn back to their own folk?'

'The Gaels are not their own folk,' Tyrbrand declared. 'The Cymru and the Dal Araidhans have been enemies ever since the ancestors of the folk of Dun Righ came here from Eirinn to found a new kingdom. They will not turn against us if we offer them a good enough reward for their efforts.'

'I thought you said that all this fellow wants is religious freedom?' Aldor asked with suspicion. 'It sounds to me as if there are other things he might ask from us.'

'He mentioned that he would like to see Dun Righ made into a centre of Christian worship and that he would also rebuild the monastery of Saint Ninian's if he were allowed to remove the current abbot.'

Aldor rested his chin on his hands for a moment and breathed deeply. 'You are right, Tyrbrand. It would be easy for us to promise these things and then when the time comes, who knows what difficulties may arise? There are often misunderstandings when such agreements are reached.'

The eorl found himself admiring Tyrbrand's plotting mind in spite of the fact that he still did not trust him. Aldor realised that there would be many opportunities to rid himself of this interfering holy man in the coming months. In time, he told himself, Tyrbrand would go the way of all other weak traitors.

'Why did you not kill me when you had the chance?' Aldor blurted.

'Seaxneat told me to save your life,' the holy man explained. 'I do his bidding.'

'And Seaxneat has told you to trust this Christian?'

'Yes, lord,' Tyrbrand affirmed. 'The God of Laws has even told me the best time to attack.'

'When would that be?' the eorl asked, surprised that one with such a manipulative mind could be so naive.

'In two weeks' time at the Dal Araidhan festival of Samhain,' the holy man answered. 'On that night their defences will be at their weakest. Everyone takes part in the celebrations and withdraws into their homes for the duration of the dark hours. Once the ramparts are unmanned, we can break through the walls with a minimum of losses.'

'Send this Christian in,' Aldor commanded. 'I will hear what he has to say. This seems too good an opportunity to miss.'

'Yes, lord.'

The holy man left the hall and returned a few moments later leading an old man into the hall. The light was very bad inside the building, which gave Aldor the advantage over his guest. His eyes had already adjusted to the weak light, but it would take his visitor a little while to be able to make out his surroundings. The eorl noted that the man was probably in his late sixties and a strange sound accompanied his every move. Aldor thought it was the noise of a goat bell that had been tied to the man's garments.

The Christian was not, nor ever had been, a warrior. That much was obvious from his physique. He had a long nose that accentuated his thin features, and his bony fingers gripped his staff with remarkable determination and strength. As the Christian shuffled forward Aldor noted that he was shaking slightly and that one leg dragged a little behind the other. But the eorl had enough experience not to mistake physical infirmity for weakness of the spirit.

When the old man stepped into the firelight, Aldor's suspicions were confirmed. This Christian had once been tall and he still carried the pride of one who stands above the heads of others, even though he was now bent with age. The man's eyes shone with a strange fire that the eorl took careful note of for, though they were grey, there was a depth to them that burned like the coals at the bottom of a fire.

Gripping his staff with his left hand, the visitor raised his right in the air and, with two fingers pointed upwards, slowly made a sign in the air. The sign of the Cross. The goat bell around his neck clanked loudly to accompany the gesture.

'My lord Aldor,' Tyrbrand began with a cough, 'this man has travelled far to seek audience with you. He has news and an offer of friendship.'

The holy man paused for a second, watching as the two war leaders sized each other up in silence, then he announced the visitor's name.

'He is a Christian bishop and his name is Palladius.'

SIXTEEN

he last of the autumn sunshine warmed the stones that lay scattered at the bottom of the northern side of the hill fort of Dun Righ. On one rock that was particularly wide and flat, two men were hunched over a gaming board which was spread out between them. The one who was dressed in a long white version of a monk's robe put his hand to his forehead and hissed with frustration. Then he adjusted his position and laid a walking stick down on the ground.

The other man, clad in plain undyed clothes but wrapped in a blue Druid cloak, laughed at his comrade and slapped him on the shoulder.

'You give up too easily, Declan,' the Druid said. 'This is really a very simple game to learn.' The abbot coughed a little, betraying the weakness he had experienced during his convalescence.

'But you have the advantage of having played at it all your life, Mawn,' the abbot replied. 'And you had Gobann to teach you how to play.'

'It was my father who taught me,' the young man corrected. 'He was a champion.'

'You have inherited his skill, my son. I, however, have not got a natural grasp of the finer points as yet.'

'I will show you once more,' Mawn offered. 'Here in the centre is the High-King. Try to think of old Leoghaire sitting in the citadel of Teamhair.

Around him are the four lesser kings: one for Munster, one for Laigin, one for the Ulaid, one for Connachta.' He set the pieces in their places once more, then went on with his explanation.

'At the edge of the board stand the Ravens,' Mawn continued. 'Think of them as the Saxons who threaten the five kingdoms. It is the High-King's duty to escape from the black Ravens and find safety in one of the sanctuaries.' The Druid pointed at each of the four corners one at a time. 'All the pieces move in the same way, including the High-King. They may move along any row of squares as long as there are no other pieces blocking them. They cannot turn corners or jump other pieces.'

'We played a Roman game that is very similar to this when I was first admitted to the monastery,' Declan interrupted. 'In that game the pieces moved along the diagonals.' The abbot shifted position slightly to allay the discomfort he still suffered from the wounds he received at the ramparts.

'There are no such moves in the Brandubh,' Mawn answered, 'only along the rows.' Then the Druid paused for a moment, deciding which rule to mention next.

'Now,' Mawn went on, 'if you were the Raven player, it would be your objective to capture my High-King, and mine to manoeuvre him into the sanctuaries.'

'How do I capture him?' Declan asked, trying to remember every word that was said to him.

'The High-King must be surrounded on all four sides so that he cannot move down any of the rows,' the Druid explained. 'But all the other pieces are captured in a different manner.' Mawn picked up two white pieces and laid them in a row with a Raven in the middle of them. 'If I wanted to capture one of your black pieces, I would have to surround it on only two sides to form a straight of three: one white, one black and one white.' The Druid pointed at each piece to emphasise the strict order.

'In the game at the monastery the pieces jumped each other when being taken,' Declan remembered.

'Pieces do not jump each other in this game,' Mawn asserted. 'Now, only the High-King piece may occupy the central square, though other pieces may pass over it if it is unoccupied. And only the High-King may sit in any of the four corner sanctuaries.'

'It does not seem very fair to me,' the abbot objected. 'The Ravens have twelve pieces and the High-King has only himself and his four lesser kings.'

'Yet they are more than evenly matched,' the Druid pointed out. 'As you will see, it is far easier to win as the white player with only five pieces than it is to be the Raven with twelve. Shall we have a game?'

'Very well,' Declan agreed reluctantly, 'but I don't expect that I will do very well at first. I was never very good at the game we played in the monastery.'

'Then you should take the white pieces,' Mawn suggested. 'A guest always starts the game and the High-King always moves first. You shall be Leoghaire.'

The abbot laughed and picked up one of the pieces to move it. 'Has there been any word from Eirinn?' Declan asked after he had placed the piece down on the board in a new position. Mawn was used to the convention by which the holding of a piece gave the bearer the right to speak. Once the piece was placed down, it was supposed to be the

377

opponent's turn to talk. He decided that it was best not to force Declan to concentrate on too many things at once, so he ignored the break with tradition. He would explain it to him after he had a better grasp of the rules of the game.

'A messenger arrived from Teamhair a few days ago,' the Druid replied, deciding on his own move. 'Did you not hear?'

'I have been busy trying to get Cathal to help with the restoration of Saint Ninian's,' the abbot explained. 'I have hardly had time to eat and drink in the last week. What news is there? How goes Patricius?'

'By all accounts Bishop Patricius Sucatus is doing very well indeed,' Mawn answered. 'Leoghaire has granted him a home on the spot where he first landed less than a day's ride from Teamhair. And because of the constant threat of Saxon attack, the High-King has decreed that the bishop may fortify the house and keep his own warriors in attendance. To that end Tatheus has been recalled. As soon as the Samhain festivities are ended and the seas settle, the Roman soldiers will return to Eirinn.'

'That is unprecedented, is it not?' Declan gasped. 'Foreign warriors garrisoned on the soil of Eirinn within striking distance of Teamhair.'

'Or within half a day's march should there be any threat to the High-Kingship,' Mawn added.

'Is Leoghaire's position in danger?'

'There are many who have taken to the ways of the Cross,' the Druid answered. 'And many who refuse to accept the ways of the black-robed brothers. Most of the Druid orders have converted and accepted the gospels, but a few have steadfastly refused to be a part of this great change.'

'Druids are converting to the Cross?' the abbot asked, surprised.

'Almost every one that I know,' Mawn confirmed. 'Poets, musicians, healers, storytellers, herbalists, genealogists; even the future-seers are being Christianed.'

'And not a drop of blood shed in the effort?' Declan exclaimed. 'No-one among their number has resisted the Word of God?'

'Almost none,' the Druid repeated. 'Save for the few who see the changes as bad for our people. Among their numbers is the King of Laigin, Enda Censelach.'

'I remember him,' the abbot said. 'A hard man he was. Though his daughter was charming and intelligent.'

'Everyone believed that Leoghaire's marriage to Enda's daughter would quieten the King of Laigin,' Mawn went on, 'but alas he has returned from his journey to the British kings with it in his head that he is a man more worthy to be High-King.'

'Has he the support to back up his claim?' Declan cried. 'Surely not!'

'No,' Mawn replied. 'Not for the moment. For now he will have to content himself with travelling throughout the land trying to inspire the chieftains to join his banner against Leoghaire. It will be a long time before he can make any real claim on the throne. But one or two other things have happened while we were away that may aid the King of Laigin by the end of winter.'

'Go on,' the abbot insisted. 'It is so long since we had news from Eirinn.'

'You speak of the land as if it were your home,' the Druid laughed.

'I have often felt that it is more my home than anywhere else on Earth,' the abbot admitted. 'I would dearly love to return there some day and find myself a quiet retreat far from the madness of the world, where I could pray each day and contemplate the beauty of creation.'

'May you have that wish,' Mawn replied. 'If only all your brethren were so inclined. Origen was such a man who valued the peace and quiet of seclusion.'

'Yes, he was,' Declan agreed. 'Origen was a saintly man whom I have come to value as a great teacher. I now wear the white robes of his orders in remembrance of his work and holiness. He once told me that the purity of Christ's message would always be threatened by the selfish motives of imperfect priests and bishops. That was why his monks wore white—to remind them of the true message of our Saviour and to be especially careful never to stain the words that He spoke.'

'Origen was given the blue robe,' Mawn stated. 'The Druid Council granted him the cloak some time before he died.'

'And I believe that he was a Druid,' the abbot confirmed, 'for he had an understanding of the world that went beyond the usual learning of a priest. Tell me, what other news was there?'

'Patricius has appointed Secondinus as the Bishop of the Feni in the south of Eirinn, while Patricius himself has taken the title Bishop of Emain Macha which is in the north.' Mawn paused for a moment. 'Have you heard the tale of Oisin and Niamh?'

'Yes,' Declan replied. 'The first Druid I ever met told me that story. His name was Cieran and he came with me to Saint Ninian's to be a Christian monk.' Declan scratched his head. 'Now, let me see if I remember it correctly. Oisin was the son of Finn Mac Cumhal, a great warrior. Finn and his men were out hunting when a Faerie woman

380

approached them and asked for the hand of Oisin in marriage. Is that right?'

'Yes,' Mawn nodded, 'that's the tale. Niamh of the Golden Hair was her name and she was the daughter of the King of Tir-Nan-Og.'

'The Land of the Ever Young,' the abbot cut in.

'That's right,' said the Druid with a smile. 'He went away with her to that place and broke his father's heart. You see, Finn knew that they would never meet again.'

'That is a lovely story,' Declan agreed. 'Especially when it is told in its entirety.'

'It is more than just a story,' the Druid announced, 'for Oisin returned to Eirinn not long after we left for Dal Araidhe.'

'What? He came back from the Faerie realms?'

'Looking for his father and his clanspeople.'

'But he was supposed to have lived in the time of Cormac Mac Airt?' the abbot protested. 'Three hundred years ago. How could he still be alive?'

'Five generations have passed on since Oisin went to Tir-Nan-Og, and yet he has returned. Those who saw him mounted on his white warhorse say that he was the noblest warrior they ever laid eyes on,' Mawn said. 'But he had a geas laid on him—a prohibition—that he must not touch the soil of Eirinn while he was visiting the five kingdoms lest the Faerie enchantments that bound him to life in the Land of the Ever Young be broken.'

'Where is he now? Did he return to Tir-Nan-Og?'

'No,' the Druid answered. 'He was leaning down from his horse to pick a flower to take back with him to the Faerie Isles when his saddle girths broke and he fell to the ground. Those who saw it say that he instantly became a wizened old man, transforming before their eyes as if three hundred

381

seasons had raced by in less time than it takes to milk a cow.'

'Did he live?' the abbot gasped. 'Is he still alive?'

'He is,' Mawn replied. 'Bishop Patricius has taken him into his care, and the old man Oisin lives within the walls of the church, cared for by Tullia, the abbess of the convent that is being built near the holy shrine of the goddess Brigid.'

'On the plain of Cill Dhaire?' Declan asked. 'They have built a convent alongside the ever-burning flame of the Druid women?'

'Oh yes, my friend, much has changed very quickly in Eirinn since we went away.'

'To think that in the two years that Palladius was in Eirinn all he managed to do was stir up trouble,' Declan hissed, 'then along comes Patricius and within a few short months everything is changed. He is a saint, that is sure.'

'If saints are accounted for in numbers of con-verts,' Mawn said, 'then Patricius is certainly a saint. Though I do not expect that Oisin will be so easily converted to the Cross as were Leoghaire and his wife.'

'And what of yourself?' the abbot pressed. 'Will you leave the ways of your forefathers and take the cloth?'

'One day perhaps,' the Druid conceded. 'For now I am of service to my clanspeople as a Druid, and so I will continue to fulfil my duties until I am no longer needed. But you asked me to accompany you to Saint Ninian's and I would still like to go there and see your book in Greek and to translate the labels on Origen's bottles of spirit.'

'Those lovely bottles!' Declan exclaimed. 'What a pity! It seems almost every one of them was broken by the Saxons. All but a few of those pre-cious remedies was lost.' The abbot reached into his robes and produced a small parcel wrapped in leather. 'This one is almost full and I keep it with me in memory of Origen.'

Declan passed the bottle to Mawn who carefully unwrapped the soft leather covering and held the bottle up to read the inscription on the side.

'"Spirit of the roasted barley",' Mawn began reading the Greek letters aloud, '"for all ailments where pain is great."' Then the Druid stopped, confused by what was written next. 'These letters are Greek but they are not in the Greek language. I don't think I can understand them.'

'I thought they might be something in Gaelic,' Declan offered. 'I could not make anything of them either.'

Mawn mouthed the sounds of the letters aloud. '"Oo-is-kay Ba-ha"' he said and then the answer struck him. 'Uisgce Beatha!' he laughed. 'That's Gaelic written in the Greek letters.'

'What does that mean?' Declan asked.

'The water of life,' Mawn replied, still smiling at the little joke.

Murrough King of Munster stormed across the open field, dodging between the cows and calves that were grazing quietly in the pasture. Behind him his wife walked slower, withholding the full force of her frustration but staring at her husband with fire in her eyes.

The king strode over to a fallen tree trunk and kicked it hard with his riding boot. Splinters of the rotten timber flew in all directions as a large chunk of the soft bark broke off and spun into the air. But Murrough was not content. He drew his broadsword and with a frightening violence hacked into the dead trunk as if it were some Saxon marauder come to do him harm. Blow after blow rained down on the wood until it seemed like nothing could stop the king pulverising the trunk into dust.

Caitlin stood back at a safe distance, shocked at this display of temper and the king's loss of control. She had never in her life seen him act so, not even in the midst of a fight. It was almost as if she was looking on a stranger whom she had never known.

'Murrough!' she called out. 'Murrough!'

The king did not answer her. He did not even acknowledge her. With both hands he gripped the hilt of his sword and lifted it high in the air. It lingered there for a moment before Murrough once more brought the blade down heavily on the battered tree trunk.

'Damn that thieving murderer!' he screamed. 'May the Morrigú feed on his flesh.'

The cattle began to scatter up the hillside in the direction of their pens. The calves went first, shielded from this threatening stranger by the oldest and strongest of the cows. Caitlin turned away to watch them, genuinely understanding how frustrated her husband must be but still confused at the ferocity of his reaction. As she was looking at the cows she noticed Gobann and Síla pushing their way through the herd towards her.

Caitlin wiped the tears away from her eyes. She did not want the Druids to see her so upset. 'I am a queen of Munster and a Druid in my own right,' she said aloud but low enough so that no-one else heard her. 'I must not allow myself to become as distraught as Murrough.'

'Caitlin!' Gobann called out. 'Caitlin! Let him be. Come over here for a moment.'

The queen took another look at her husband, who was still cursing loudly and poking at the tree with his sword, then she turned to walk up the hill to the Druids.

When she got close Síla took the queen's arm to comfort her. 'Do not be disappointed with him, Caitlin,' the Druid healer said in a soothing tone. 'The last three months have been particularly hard on him.'

'He has not been the same since the battle at the ramparts and his quarrel with Cathal,' Caitlin told her.

'The Druid Assembly has not treated him fairly,' Gobann agreed. 'If I were in his position I would be feeling as if I had been unjustly dealt with also. They levelled a fine against him which I find difficult to justify or to understand.'

'Worst of all,' Caitlin added, 'they let that tyrant Cathal get away with almost all his crimes. He was not even reprimanded by the court for his mistreatment of Murrough.'

'Cathal has been removed from office in all but name,' Gobann reminded her gently. 'Not even his own Druid counsellors trust him to hold the power he once had.'

'The king seems to have calmed down considerably,' Síla noted. 'Perhaps we should approach him.'

Gobann waited for Caitlin to agree, and then, with the queen walking between them, he and Síla led Caitlin down to where Murrough was now seated on the hacked trunk. The king had his head in his hands and he had dropped his sword on the grass beside him. As the three came closer he heard their footfall and lifted his head to see who it was. Before he had a chance to tell them to go away, Gobann spoke.

385

'I will convene a special gathering of the Assembly to review this decision after the festival of Samhain,' the poet announced. 'I have that right as a Druid of the Silver Branch. I cannot see any reason why you should have been fined and not Cathal. That will be remedied.'

'I don't give a pig's whisker about the fine they placed on me,' Murrough barked. 'I just can't believe that they would treat Ia in that way. She has evidence that would ensure Cathal's impeachment, yet rather than hear her words they have silenced her and threatened to remove her from her position as chief Druid counsellor.'

'I cannot comment on that decision,' Gobann replied, surprised at the cause of Murrough's anger. 'I could request a full investigation into her allegations,' the poet offered, 'but I must tread very carefully.'

'Another one who treads carefully!' the king bellowed. 'You Druids walk so tenderly that you lose your way on the path.'

'I am considered a foreigner here,' Gobann protested. 'We all are. These people may speak our language but they owe no allegiance to the High-King of Eirinn or to any of the ideals that we hold dear. Their ways are different—a blend of the Roman, the Cymru and the Gael. By convention Síla and I cannot intervene in a matter that is solely a decision for the folk of Dun Righ. Not unless we are invited to give our opinions. Even then we would have to be very careful of what we said. The impeachment of a chieftain is not a matter to be entered into lightly.'

'And what of the impeachment of a fellow Druid?' Murrough shot back. 'Will you do nothing to help her? Do you not agree that Ia has been badly treated in this matter?'

Caitlin closed her eyes, holding in her feelings so that they would not be displayed openly in any way.

'She has not told me of her allegations against Cathal,' Gobann tried to explain. 'But I do agree with you that there is something here that does not seem fair. I promise that I will look into the matter, but I fear that the Dal Araidhans might see this as interference from an outsider. That will not make us any more welcome in the dun.'

'We were not welcome from the first,' Murrough laughed bitterly. 'Cathal did not want us here.'

'His people were under siege from the Saxons,' Caitlin cut in. 'He treated us with nothing but honour from the moment we arrived. How can you say such things about him?'

'His people were besieged by their own chieftain,' Murrough retorted. 'Ask any of the Cruitne folk, ask the Cymru, ask Ia.'

'She is not of these tribes,' the queen answered. 'They say she is half Saxon herself. How can you believe everything she says?'

'I do believe her!' Murrough yelled. 'Just because she had a Saxon mother does not make her one of the savages. A black cow may have a brown calf.'

'Have you thought that she might be taking advantage of you?' Caitlin asked, finding it difficult to stop her voice wavering. 'Have you thought that she might be pitting you against Cathal to sow discord in the ranks of the Gaels and so weaken Cathal's authority?'

'If that is so,' the king replied, 'then why did Cathal let my warriors run into the thick of the fight at the ramparts without a word of warning as to his own plans? Why did the Druid Assembly take three moons to sit in judgment on this matter?

It was summer when the battle took place and now it is nearly Samhain!'

'I agree,' Gobann spoke up. 'Their sitting was postponed for too long after the grievances were made public, and that cannot be easily explained. But it may have been a simple misunderstanding on the part of the chieftain or yourself that led to your warriors being isolated on the field. There may be quite innocent explanations for all of these things.'

'Then explain to me the swift peace that was concluded with the Saxons after the battle. Explain to me why a chieftain would grant a fortified position to a defeated enemy. Explain to me how it is that the Saxons increase their numbers daily without a word of protest from Cathal. Why is it that the Saxons have been allowed to build a settlement on the coast close to good mooring places?'

'The fortified position that you speak of is an abandoned and derelict Roman fort that has not been used by anyone in a long time. It desperately needs repairs if it is to be utilised,' the poet answered as calmly as he could. 'The peace was concluded quickly because both sides saw the need. They both saw that neither could defeat the other. The Saxons had lost their war leader in the battle and were unwilling to fight on as a result. It is as simple as that.'

'Has it not crossed your mind that Cathal may have concluded more than a peace with the foreigners?' Murrough inquired.

'What do you mean?' Caitlin asked, shocked that her husband could accuse another Gaelic chieftain of such treachery.

'Alliance,' the king stated. 'Is it not possible that the Saxons have remained quiet for so long because Cathal has allied with them?'

'Against which enemies?' Caitlin demanded. 'Whom would Cathal want to fight? There are no other tribes on this peninsula apart from the Dal Araidhans and the Saxons.'

'He is planning on making war against the kings of Strath-Clóta,' Murrough revealed. 'Cathal wants to take the whole of this land for himself. He is already calling himself King of the Southern Dal Araidhe, and the Cymru will be his next adversaries.'

'Rubbish!' the queen shouted. 'You have been spending too much time with that half-Saxon sorceress! She has filled your head with these stupid ideas and you are dull-witted enough to believe every word she says. Ia is working with the Saxons to undermine the defences of Dun Righ. It is her plan to set us fighting against each other so that we neglect our posts at the ramparts. While we are busy clutching at one another's throats the foreigners will walk in and take the stronghold and we will not be able to resist them.'

'If that is so,' Murrough countered, 'if the threat of a Saxon attack is imminent, then tell me why the defences have been neglected by Cathal since the battle at the ramparts? Why has he not strengthened the walls?'

'Because there is an officially concluded peace,' Caitlin grunted, showing her frustration. 'You know as well as I do that a chieftain can only call on the warriors of the clan to fight for short periods at a time. It is coming to midwinter and there is hunting to be done to supplement the grain stores from the last harvest. Cathal cannot expect his warriors to stand at the walls waiting for an attack that is unlikely in the cold weather. Not while their families go without fresh meat during snowfall.'

'Cathal is not to be trusted,' the king began. 'Ia says—'

'I do not care what Ia says!' Caitlin shouted. 'You must listen to your counsellors and stop taking any notice of that woman.' With that Caitlin broke away from Gobann and Síla and marched briskly up the hill back towards their lodgings.

The two Druids stood for a moment, both feeling very uncomfortable that they had witnessed such a bitter disagreement between the king and queen.

'I promise that we will look into everything you have said,' Gobann soothed, turning back to Murrough.

'But you must promise to keep an open mind when we present our findings to you,' Síla insisted.

'The truth is never easy to define,' the poet continued. 'It is not black or white or good or bad. The truth usually lies in the middle ground between the two extremes. It is quite possible that you and Caitlin have both based your assessments of the situation on incorrect assumptions. Be prepared to accept that you may have only seen one facet of a wider truth.'

'I will take your advice, Gobann,' Murrough sighed. 'But you must promise me that you will act quickly. Samhain is coming and I have a strong intuition that many events are about to be set in motion which will be difficult to stop once they have begun. I do not trust Cathal.'

'Calm yourself,' Síla said. 'You have spent too long worrying about the affairs of your office. The Saxon threat has been dealt with by Cathal in the best manner available to him. When the winter is past we will be able to judge whether the foreigners can keep to their side of the treaty. If so, you and Caitlin should return to Munster and go on with your lives. Your children are in Eirinn. Unless you make the time for them, they will never have the opportunity to get to know their parents.'

'Our daughter Brigid was rarely ever at home with us even at Cashel,' Murrough sighed. 'Caitlin sent her off to Teamhair every winter to be among the Druid kind. As for the one who was born last Beltinne,' he added bitterly, 'my wife was almost as eager to give him into the care of Leoghaire and Mona as she was to be rid of Brigid. It is almost as if she finds our offspring repulsive.'

'That is not true, Murrough. You know she was haunted by the Cailleach,' Síla argued. 'And you know how hard that was on her. But she has many other troubling memories. The Battle of Rathowen was only the beginning of a long nightmare for her.'

'I have tried to be understanding,' Murrough muttered, 'and there is nothing I want more than to return to our life in the Kingdom of Munster and bring up our family together. But I fear that Caitlin will never be able to stay long in one place. I am afraid that such a life was not meant for her.'

With that Murrough rose from where he had been sitting and walked towards the inner walls of Dun Righ's defences. Gobann and Síla did not try to stop him. They could see that he needed to be alone.

But as Murrough climbed over a low part of the wall a woman in a long blue cloak stepped from the door of one of the nearby buildings and came directly up to him. The king checked quickly that Gobann and Síla could not see him, then he took Ia's hand and let her lead him along the walls to a place where no-one would be able to observe their conversation.

Caitlin, meanwhile, went back to the house that had been allotted to herself and Murrough, and

391

there she sat on the bed for a long long while, hoping that the king would return and regretting every harsh word she had said to him. When he returned she would apologise for upsetting him so. She realised that he had probably been led astray by the Druid woman. Everyone in Dun Righ spoke of Ia's way of twisting the truth to suit her own ends. She was a well-known troublemaker. Caitlin was sure that Murrough would only have to see some evidence of the Druid woman's behaviour to understand that he had been wrong.

Long hours later Caitlin awoke, stirred from a deep sleep by the return of her husband. The room was dark and the queen judged that it was certainly past midnight. Murrough took off his boots and pulled the covers over himself as he turned his back to the fire.

The queen moved a little closer to him, hoping that he might acknowledge her presence, but he did not. And Caitlin did not say anything to him either, not a word, even though she could feel a pain in her soul that was almost unbearable.

SEVENTEEN

he day before Samhain was cold, and heavy rain threatened to restrict the festivities of the following evening to the indoors. So everyone prayed that the clouds would clear and the storms pass. At this festival it was very important to dance. Dance out the old cycles and dance in the new seasons to come. Samhain was a time when even the most bitter enemies among the Gaels put aside their differences for the night.

Nevertheless it would be unusual for two men with the sort of grievances that Murrough and Cathal held against each other to share a common fire on this evening, so the Druids made careful preparations to keep them apart during the celebrations that led up to the feasting, dancing and storytelling.

The Samhain festival was like the time of Beltinne when the doorways to the Otherworld opened wide. And while the doors were open many spirits passed through to visit their loved ones or to create mischief in the world of the human kind. Those of the Danaans who had withdrawn completely from the company of mortals were said to make a royal progression around their former domains.

For the Druid kind this was the time of greatest change in the world; a delicate time when anything could happen, for the natural laws governing the

Earth could be suspended without warning. After Samhain the winter invariably became much colder. Snow and ice encroached on many settlements, isolating many folk in the white prison of cold.

Few dared venture far from their fires after Samhain; indeed on Samhain Eve, after the dancing and the feasting, everyone, including the sentries at the guardposts, returned to their homes and barred the doors. This ritual acknowledgement of the change that was about to come upon their daily routine also ensured that the Faeries could not steal anyone away from the land of mortals.

The older folk sat up in an all-night vigil before the hearth, dispensing with turf and using only timber so that the flames were large and visible. A turf fire was warmer and burned with a greater intensity than wood, for peat was found in the bog lands where, over hundreds of generations, it had transformed from dead plant matter into a blackish brown mass that was similar to raw soil. However, a timber fire was considered to be more cleansing, and the festival of Samhain was above all a ritual purging of all that was no longer considered necessary in one's life. The day of Samhain, after everyone emerged into the morning light, was cherished as the first day of the new year.

Samhain was where the great cycle of the seasons ended and then began turning once again. In secret ceremonies the Druids held their own commemorations, remembering all who had passed away in the last cycle and publicly acclaiming those who would undertake the tests of initiation in readiness for the next Beltinne festival.

Wherever they gathered, the Druids would lock themselves away in a hall for the night in representation of the long confinement that everyone had to endure during the winter. But the Druids did not shun the company of visitors from the spirit world. The poets opened their houses to the Danaans and the wandering souls of their ancestors.

At Dun Righ on this Samhain there would likely be two guests among the holy folk of the Druid order. They were two men who had no other place in the society. They had no clan or family of their own and no rank within the tribe, neither from birthright nor which they had earned. They were both foreigners and they were both Christians. All the other monks and nuns who had taken refuge in the dun were Dal Araidhans or natives of Eirinn and so had clanspeople with which to spend the day. Declan and Seginus were another matter. The simple fact of their lack of relations raised a serious problem for the Druids. Samhain was a time for hospitality to all souls, no matter who they were. It was a festival to welcome spirits into the circle of the holy to commune with them and to learn about the seasons to come. Even folk who had no Druid training hoped for some contact with their dear departed clanspeople or some insight which would comfort them through hardship.

To leave anyone out of the rituals would have been unthinkable, especially strangers. There was always the chance that an unfamiliar person might really be a Danaan in disguise or even one of the great spirits like the goddess Brigid. There were many tales which told of the punishment meted out to an ungenerous host by one of the Great Ones.

New converts to the Cross from Dal Araidhe never forsook the old ways entirely. Declan accepted this, knowing it would not do him any good to do otherwise. But few at Dun Righ trusted the foreign Christians and some openly spoke out against them, saying that the two men should not be welcomed to any hearth on that night. It was well known that most Roman Christians did not believe in the workings of the spirit world but condemned such practices as primitive and savage.

So it was that the Druid Assembly gathered in Cathal's great hall on the day before the festival to discuss a solution to the problem of where to house the Christians for Samhain. This was not Teamhair. Few members of the holy orders ever lodged here for long, so there was no need for a great hall such as the Star of the Poets to accommodate all those who wore the blue. This winter there was a larger gathering than usual but there were still only nine Druids within the walls of Dun Righ.

Though Caitlin was an initiated poet, she no longer attended such meetings because of her marriage to King Murrough. Druids in such positions voluntarily gave themselves over to their duties as chieftains or war leaders and were not permitted to continue their holy vocations as judges and poets. This prevented any conflicts arising from a king's wish to enforce a judgment and the risk to a Druid's impartiality in delivering it.

Gobann, Síla, Mawn and Sianan sat to one side of the central fire in Cathal's hall where they would take up residence for the next few days. The four Druids of Dun Righ sat to the other side with Ia, their chief, who took her place as symbolic head of the hall. She was after all the appointed advisor to Cathal, even though the chieftain rarely, if ever, took any notice of her. She had not been impeached as threatened. Cathal thought it best to wait until after the festival to move against her.

'Is it true that the one called Seginus is under the High-King's banishment?' Ia asked Gobann.

'That is true,' the poet confirmed.

'And what was his crime?' one of the older Druids of Dun Righ cut in.

'His crimes were many,' the poet began. 'Murder was the worst and breaking an order of exile was the least.'

'Then the two foreigners should not be allowed to enter the hall on Samhain Eve,' the old Druid proclaimed. 'Any poet who had committed such crimes would be stripped of office until the debt for his misdemeanours was paid. How much was his eric fine?'

'He was not fined in the usual way,' Gobann tried to explain. 'No eric was laid on him. He was placed under bonds such as the Romans use to punish wrongdoers. In order to pay his debt, Seginus must work and suffer a renunciation of certain privileges until such time as his spiritual mentor is satisfied that he has made recompense.'

'Who is his spiritual mentor?' Ia asked.

'Declan of Saint Ninian's,' the poet answered. 'Though the abbot receives his instructions from Patricius the Bishop of Eirinn.'

'They have a complicated hierarchy, these Christians,' the old Dal Araidhan Druid quipped. 'Are they not permitted to make decisions on their own, or must the Bishop of Eirinn seek permission to say the first observance of the day from his master in Rome?'

'Declan will make the final decision as to whether Seginus is fit to end his penances,' Gobann said slowly, aware now that there was a great deal of hostility towards the Christians from the Dun Righ Druids.

'We have heard that even Leoghaire of Eirinn bows to the will of Patricius,' the old man teased.

397

'Does a High-King have no recognised authority in their world?'

'Leoghaire takes advice from Druid and bishop alike,' the poet replied. 'And I can see the sense in that. Better two opinions to compare than one which may not take into account all the possibilities of a situation.'

'You condone the abolition of the Sacred Groves?' the old Druid barked.

'Of course not, but we cannot deny that a great change is taking place in the world,' Gobann reasoned. 'It would be as foolish to attempt to stop the tide of the ocean from changing as it would be to try and prevent the coming of new ideas and philosophies.'

'You are a young and inexperienced man despite the Silver Branch you bear,' the older Dal Araidhan said, 'and so I can forgive you your impudence. But tell me something if you will. Would the Christian called Palladius need permission from the Bishop of Eirinn to raise an army? And if so, would that mean Leoghaire approved of, say, an invasion of Dal Araidhe?'

'Palladius!' the poet exclaimed. 'My experience of him is that he does as he pleases and ignores the reprimands of his superiors.' Gobann realised that the Dal Araidhans had obviously been keeping some information from him. 'Palladius is under banishment from Eirinn and has certainly fallen from favour with Patricius.' He paused to take a breath and phrase his next question as politely as possible. 'Has the old bishop raised an army?'

'They are marching north at this very moment from the hills in the land of the Cymru,' came the stern answer.

'When did this news arrive?' Síla interrupted. 'And why were we not informed?'

'It was not considered necessary to tell you,' the old Druid drawled, smiling as he did so in a blatantly insincere attempt at politeness. 'You are also foreigners here. Kindly do not forget your place.'

'Mongan, that is enough,' Ia ordered. 'Gobann is a poet of the Silver Branch and a brother of the holy order. You have no right to speak to him or to Síla in such a manner. She is a Cruitne of the north and her folk were in this country long before the Gaels.'

Mongan curled his lip in contempt. 'And you are worse than a foreigner,' the old man said with relish. 'You are a half foreigner.'

'You will apologise to me immediately,' Ia demanded lowly with as much threat in her voice as she could muster. 'Is it not bad enough that the leaders of our communities are at each other's throats? Should we not be setting an example to them?'

'You have set a fine example,' Mongan spat. 'Advisor to the chieftain of Dun Righ spending the night hours in the company of the King of Munster.'

Síla shot a worried glance at Gobann, but neither he nor Mawn nor Sianan made any move to acknowledge that such an accusation should be taken seriously.

'How dare you speak to me in that manner!' Ia erupted. 'You will apologise for that ill-conceived slight against my name.'

'Deny it,' Mongan insisted, 'if you can without perjuring yourself in front of all the Druids in this hall.'

Ia paused for a second, just long enough for Gobann to realise that there must be some truth, however slim, to what Mongan had said.

'I will not give you the satisfaction,' Ia blurted. 'If you do not retract your statement, I will hand this matter over to Gobann, who is the highest ranking judge among us, and I will have you forced to submit to justice.'

'Who told you this story?' Gobann inquired quietly, his disciplined voice cutting through the tension like a cool breeze.

'Cathal himself saw the two of them,' Mongan replied, 'out on the ramparts last night. Ia should be glad that Caitlin Ni Uaine has not yet heard what they were up to. I do not think that the Queen of Munster would hesitate to use her own discretion in dealing with such an infidelity.'

'What two people choose to do or say in the privacy of their friendship is not for any other to judge,' Sianan said softly and respectfully. 'It is not right to speak about such things to anyone. A blush fine is usually the result of such words spoken in haste and not necessarily from the heart.'

'I would not pay it,' the old Druid scoffed, taken aback at such a rebuke from one so young. 'Blush fines are imposed by one's own folk, not by foreigners.'

'Are you aware of the insult that you are offering me?' Gobann asked, incredulous at the old man's lack of respect and good manners.

'You at least may call yourself a Gael,' Mongan answered, 'even if you are not a Dal Araidhan. But in this country we do things differently than is the custom in Eirinn. You see, the people who were here before us were conquered by the Romans, and they learned a few very important things from them. We in turn took on the best of that teaching ourselves when we overran the Cymru. In Dal Araidhe women do as they are told by their menfolk, as is the Roman custom. Females marry and

400

they vow to stay with their man forever. Any hint of interest in any other man is considered shameful.'

'That is a Christian doctrine,' Síla protested.

'It was a Roman one long before the birth of Christ,' Gobann corrected her. 'In the lands of the Gael a woman is free to choose the mate she considers to be the best bloodstock for her children. There is no question of that and no precedent under the Brehon laws for any restrictions on her seeking wherever she will, even among those men already married.'

'Not in Dal Araidhe,' Mongan replied dismissively. 'Here all the women are subject to their men, as it was in the time of the Romans.'

'Are you saying,' Síla asked in shock that a Druid could speak so, 'that on Samhain Eve and at Beltinne the women may not choose a lover for the evening from among the eligible males?'

'Of course not!' the old man gasped. 'Not if it is in contravention of either person's vows to another.'

'And so,' Síla continued, 'if I were to approach a man of this dun tomorrow evening and ask him to spend the night with me by my fireside, he would likely refuse?'

'If he were married, yes,' came the reply.

'The men of Eirinn are not permitted to refuse a woman on Samhain Eve,' the healer said. 'But the men of Dal Araidhe do not prize the happiness and contentment of their women so highly.' Síla laughed and squeezed Gobann's hand under the table. 'The men of Dal Araidhe are very lucky that their womenfolk have not all gone back to Eirinn and left them to their foolish ideas.'

'We have not come to a decision about the Christians,' Gobann cut in, changing the subject before the Dal Araidhan Druids became too agitated. 'Are we going to invite them to join in our ceremonies?'

'They are not initiated,' Mongan snapped, angry at the way he and his kinsmen had been mocked. 'Only the initiated may attend, and that is an end to the matter.'

'Declan lodges among the initiates,' Gobann protested. 'And at the Star of the Poets he was invited to attend many of the rituals.'

'My ancestors did not come to Dal Araidhe,' Mongan hissed, 'in order to remain subservient to the fashions of Teamhair. In this land foreigners are exempt from the rituals.'

'And how do you decide who is a foreigner?' the poet inquired. 'I have lived most of my life in Eirinn though I was born here on this island in the stronghold of Dun Edin. You may not like to admit it but I am a Dal Araidhan myself. So you have no right to address me as foreigner. Besides which, the Brehon laws state clearly the rights and privileges of strangers. Foremost among our duties to them is hospitality. Would you exempt me from the rituals on the basis of your feeble claim that I am not of your clans?'

'You are different,' Mongan grumbled. 'You are a poet of the Silver Branch.'

'He is,' Mawn answered, unable to restrain himself any longer, 'and I think it would be wise of you to remember that, Mongan. He rarely passes judgment but when he is required to do so he can be uncompromising. The decision of a Silver Branch Druid is not something that can easily be argued against or overturned without appeal to the full council at Teamhair. And it cannot be brushed aside like so many thoughtless insults.'

Gobann frowned sensing that this arguing was achieving very little.

'We will vote on the Christians,' Ia announced, as if she had heard the poet's thoughts. 'This discussion has gone on too long. All those who wish the priest and the abbot to be excluded from the rituals raise their hands.'

The four Dal Araidhans shot their arms into the air with flat palms and fingers rigidly outstretched, each of them looking sternly at the Druids who sat on the bench opposite them.

'Four among us would exclude them,' Ia observed.

'And the four from Eirinn will vote to allow the Christians to join the rituals,' Mongan proclaimed. 'That is a tied ballot and in the case of such an equal decision the safest course is always taken. The course of inaction. The foreigners are exempt from the Samhain rituals.' The old man smiled broadly, pleased at the outcome and his own cleverness.

'I have the casting vote,' Ia reminded him.

'But you will vote with the Druids of Dun Righ,' Mongan stated with confidence.

'It is my decision,' Ia said slowly, 'that Father Seginus Gallus and Abbot Declan be invited to attend the ceremonies of Samhain within the Druid hall.'

'You can't be serious,' Mongan protested. 'You have no right to cast such a vote against the advice of your peers.'

'Nevertheless I have done so. And as head of this council I appoint you, Mongan, to issue the invitation.'

'I refuse!' the old man shouted, obviously appalled at the idea.

'Calm yourself, brother,' Gobann soothed, shooting a reproachful glance at Ia. 'You will not have to speak to them if you do not wish. No-one would

403

expect you to perform any duty that was against your conscience.'

'I will ask them,' Sianan volunteered. 'It would be my pleasure.'

'Then, since a decision has been reached,' Ia announced, 'I declare this meeting ended. Go to your duties and we will meet again at sunset tomorrow evening after the dancing.'

All those present rose to leave, eager to escape the atmosphere of tension and distrust that permeated the hall. Síla rushed to the door, however, cornering Mongan on his way out.

'I have a question for you, venerable Druid,' she began. 'One which only you can answer.'

The old man looked at her with some degree of scepticism. 'What is it?' he barked when she smiled at him.

'If I were to come to you tomorrow evening,' she said, moving close enough so that he would not be able to mistake her meaning, and laying a finger delicately on his arm, 'and ask you to help me warm the bedcovers on the last night of the season cycle, would you honestly refuse me?'

Mongan's mouth dropped open, unsure whether or not the healer was serious. For a moment it was clear that the possibility of spending Samhain Eve in the arms of this woman was particularly attractive to the old man. But before he had a chance either to take up her offer or decline it, Síla began to giggle.

Mongan turned bright red as soon as he realised that he was being mocked yet again. 'So this is what passes for respect in the land of Eirinn?' he bellowed. 'How dare you!'

'Has some woman already asked you?' Síla inquired. 'I really don't mind sharing you.'

'I am a married man!' Mongan screeched. 'And

I am more than seventy winters on this Earth. I am not given to such acts of base uncivilised behaviour. And neither are any of the men and women of this country. You had best return to Teamhair if you wish to indulge yourself in such a manner.' With that the old man stormed out of the hall into the lightly falling rain.

The moment he had gone Síla turned to her friends. 'I do pity the women of Dal Araidhe.'

'So you should,' Ia agreed. 'But the ranting of a silly old Druid will not keep any of them from their chosen lovers tomorrow night.' Then she grinned. 'Such a pity that you missed out on your first choice,' she said, taking Síla by the hand and pretending to show sympathy for her plight.

'Yes,' Síla answered reaching out to tug at Gobann's sleeve, 'I suppose I will have to seek out another willing man.' The poet blushed, trying to push towards the door, but Síla held him tightly. 'The question is, where will I find such a one as I seek among so few who are worthy?'

Ia and Síla both collapsed into laughter, but Gobann pulled his cloak around him and broke the hold on his arm. Without another word he strode out of the hall to save himself any further embarrassment. Besides, the poet had not forgotten Mongan's claim that Ia and Murrough had been out alone on the ramparts. It was true that none had the right to judge the king and the Druid woman for their actions, but Gobann had a feeling that Caitlin would not necessarily agree. Indeed he now expected the conflict between the King and Queen of Munster to escalate dramatically.

405

On the outer rampart of Dun Righ a lone warrior stood as the day of Samhain Eve dawned. By tradition he would remain here playing a lament upon the war-pipes until the whole of the settlement was awake and gathered near to where he stood. Then when the man deemed that the time was right, he would strike up a merrier dance tune, the first of many before sunset.

Caitlin woke to the music and immediately rolled over to look for Murrough, but the king was already up and dressed. Each morning since the night he had returned late he had done this: rising without a word to the queen and leaving their lodgings before she had stirred. Caitlin did not know where he had gone but she had a sneaking fear that he had been lured away from her side.

The possibility that another woman had captured his affections was too much pain for her to bear. Through all the seasons that they had been married, through the miscarriages she had suffered and the terrible periods of the worst of the Cailleach's haunting, Murrough had stood by her as a loyal friend and devoted lover. The hag had been destroyed and their lives launched along a new path, but now it seemed that she was losing him to another.

The queen quickly rose and dressed herself, knowing that the piper would not play the slow air for too long before his audience demanded a dance melody from him. Caitlin decided that she must make every effort to find Murrough before some other woman asked him to join her in the dance. It had been so long, she thought, since they had danced together.

Here was the answer to the problem of her relationship with Murrough. At some point she would have to swallow her pride and give some ground to him. Caitlin was well aware that she could be very stubborn at times, and she was beginning to understand that perhaps she had been too harsh on her husband. Now was the time, she resolved, at the turning of the cycles, for them to make amends and join together again.

When she had tied the straps on her riding boots and rolled the tops down, she grabbed her brat-cloak—the one woven with four colours to signify that she had attained the rank of poet—and stepped out into the brisk morning air. The sky was grey and cloudy but Caitlin knew the weather signs well enough to know that there would be no more than a light drizzle today.

Heavy rain had fallen throughout the previous week, soaking the ground all around the dun, but the warriors had laid straw and put timber boards down where the dance was to be held so that no-one would slip and hurt themselves in the mud. The queen looked down from one of the upper walls and saw the area laid out and ready for the first people to tread the boards.

A few other musicians passed Caitlin as she walked towards the ramparts. One man carried a large goatskin drum. Another had a small pipe in his hand with six holes dug into it. These small instruments were played by everyone in the Gaelic-speaking lands. Sometimes the whistles were carved from the thighbones of deer and occasionally from timber that had been left over from the making of a harp. Though every child could perform at least one tune on the small pipes, only a few men and women were recognised as masters of the instrument. However, there was not the prestige attached to the players of these little whistles that there was to an acclaimed specialist of the war-pipes.

Warriors who played the bagpipes spent nearly as long at their craft as harpers did before they were allowed to perform publicly at the great ceremonies and gatherings. But unlike Druids the pipers also had to train as fighters for they were often in the thick of the battle. Their instruments were used to stir up the pride of the warriors on the field. Every clan had their own war march and every warrior could recognise it above the din of conflict.

Caitlin thought back to Rathowen once again as she had done many times since arriving in Dun Righ. She recalled the sound of the pipes on the battlefield which had announced the arrival of King Leoghaire's army to rescue her tiny garrison from the overwhelming forces which Dichu of Laigin had arrayed before them. She had lost a friend and lover in that battle, and she had vowed never to allow that to happen again.

With a quickened pace Caitlin made her way around the path that circled the topmost parts of the hill, heading towards the space between the inner and outer ramparts. This was where the great celebration of the turning to the new year would take place. This was where the dancing ground was laid out.

The piper on the wall was not about to cease his melody though. It was a tremendous honour to be asked to play for Samhain and musicians made the most of this opportunity to exhibit their skill to the whole of the community. This piper had an instrument with two pipes: one for the melody and one that emitted a low single droning note which hummed an accompaniment to the tune. Such bagpipes could be heard over large distances and Caitlin judged that the Glastig would probably just be able to pick up the strains of the melody if she were standing at the edge of her forest.

If the harp was considered to be an instrument which embodied the spirit of all things feminine, then the pipes epitomised the soul of manhood. Even the shape of the bag and the way the melody pipe was sewn to it represented the secret parts of a male. And the piper who played for the Samhain dances was considered a prize among the women that night when all returned to their homes, for his expertise at the bagpipes was considered a sure sign of prowess in other areas.

Caitlin followed the path down past the house that was home to the champion warrior of the hill fort, the man responsible for the changing of sentries and patrolling of the walls. Next to that house were several other buildings which were used by the watchmen in cold or inclement weather as a place to warm up and eat. As she turned a corner the queen came to the inner wall and passed through the gate, which had been left wide open.

In the field beyond, a crowd of Dal Araidhans had gathered and was waiting patiently for the first dance to begin. Most were dressed in long cloaks of varying colours depending on the individual's rank within the society. A woman with dark brown hair and wearing a cloak of five bright colours woven into a pattern of many squares brushed past Caitlin. The queen did not see her face but she knew that it must have been Cathal's wife Aoife.

Caitlin followed after Aoife, pushing through the crowd behind her in the hope of getting herself as close to the place where the piper was standing as possible. The queen felt certain this was where she would find Murrough. So many folk were crowded around the dancing place that Caitlin could not believe that everyone would have an opportunity to share the boards. Then she realised that there were other pipers waiting their turn to play. The dancing was likely to go on all day.

Abruptly the queen came to the edge of the dancing boards and from here she could see all the most influential people who lived in the dun. The old Druid Mongan and his wife were at the front of the crowd and Cathal's chamberlain was standing with them. He did not seem to be paired up with anyone. Then Caitlin noticed a man with red hair facing away from her and standing on the opposite side of the dancing square from Mongan.

It was Murrough, of that there was no doubt, and he was leaning in perilously close to a fair-haired woman dressed in a long blue cloak.

A Druid cloak.

In the next instant the queen had stepped out onto the boards and was marching across towards her husband. She knew that it would be wrong of her to make a scene, but she could barely manage to control her temper. Something within her was bubbling up, threatening to overwhelm her sense of right and wrong. The queen had to force herself to calm down as she strode across the timber floor, slowing her pace so that Murrough would not be too startled by her arrival.

Not wishing to embarrass her husband and thus give them both yet another excuse to fall out of favour with each other, she slowed herself even further and took the last five steps in time with the lament that the piper was playing.

As if sensing her, Murrough turned around suddenly and faced her. There was no sign, the queen noted, that he was feeling at all guilty about being found with Ia at the first dance of Samhain, but then the king was not showing very much emotion at all.

The Druid woman, on the other hand, blushed so that her face turned bright red and pulled her cloak up around her throat in an attempt to hide her surprise at the Queen of Munster's unannounced arrival. Caitlin nodded at Ia and then turned her attention to her husband again.

At that very moment the piper finished the last note of the lament. The man with the goatskin drum struck up a lively series of beats in groups of three, and the piper filled the bag once more in readiness to perform a lively jig. Suddenly people were pouring onto the boards. Without a word Caitlin grabbed Murrough's hand, dragging him out onto the floor and leaving Ia standing alone among the throng.

With screams of delight and shouts of joy the folk of Dun Righ launched into the hearty dance. Even those for whom there was no room on the boards spun their partners around at the edge of the grass or on the road or even ankle deep in the mud. The king was stiff and unwilling at first, but Caitlin was determined not to let him spoil this experience. This Samhain celebration was nothing like those in Eirinn. Free from the constraints of the courts of Teamhair or Cashel, everyone was doing their best to dance their troubles away.

Caitlin called to mind the dances of her youth in the stronghold of Rathowen. The queen remembered a story that her mother had told her about how in long ago times all women had been taught to dance by Faerie men. The queen gripped Murrough to her, hugging his body close so that he would not be able to ignore her; but she need not have done so for the floor was so crowded there was barely room to dance anyway. Most of the people were merely shuffling up against each other or moving their feet in time to the music.

411

A sudden change now took place among all this revelry. The crowd pulled back, creating a circle on the floor, and Cathal and his wife came out into the middle to begin a display for their clanspeople. In a flash of inspiration Caitlin forced her way back through the crowd towards the cleared space, dragging Murrough behind her.

'This dance is for the chieftain and his wife,' the king protested when he saw that she meant for them to join in.

'Are we not the chieftains of our folk?' Caitlin answered. 'And are there not many of our clanspeople here today?'

'We are chieftains but I dare not risk offending Cathal any further,' Murrough retorted.

'I know that you could not better him on the battlefield or in the court,' the queen shot back, 'but would you really let him better you on the dance floor?'

The king looked at his wife, unsure for a moment whether he had understood her correctly. When Caitlin smiled back at him challengingly and pulled him by the arm again, he did not resist but instead led her onto the floor, all the people of the stronghold and of their own company watching.

Cathal saw them immediately and would have left the floor insulted had his wife not had the same idea as Caitlin and refused to let him go. The chieftain danced on, and in a few seconds Murrough and Caitlin were alongside, moving around the dancing boards as if their feet had caught fire. All Murrough's folk pushed forward to see their king and queen dancing against the chieftain of Dun Righ, and a great cheer came up from them.

Cathal was not to be outdone though. He and his wife had danced every day of their lives for the love of it and to keep their friendship alive. The chieftain signalled to his piper and the musician increased the tempo, almost doubling the pace at which he played. Murrough and Caitlin rose to the challenge, and though it had been a long long while since they had danced in such a fashion, they had not forgotten each other and kept a perfect rhythm together.

Suddenly the king swung Caitlin around him, lifting her feet clear off the ground. When she landed again she turned her body around on the balls of her feet so that she faced away from the king. Then Murrough lifted her straight up in the air as high as he could, and all of their clanspeople gave a shout of pride at their lord and lady's style.

When she came to rest on the floor, Caitlin turned around to face the king again and, with her arms fully extended and Murrough gripping her hands to help her balance, launched into a series of perfectly timed footsteps which left some of the Dal Araidhans open-mouthed with shock.

Cathal gave the nod to his piper to speed up the dance once more, though the expression on Aoife's face showed that she was a little concerned at this move. Now Murrough was beginning to sweat and even Caitlin, who rarely ever allowed herself openly to exhibit fatigue, was breathing hard.

The king kept his hands by his side as Caitlin danced in a circle around him, their eyes locked together the whole time. Cathal and Aoife noticed this move and immediately tried to copy it, but they were both so weary that such a series of steps was almost too much for them to imitate. Nevertheless they completed the manoeuvre three times before they saw that Caitlin and Murrough were executing another brilliant sequence of steps.

Facing each other, the king gripped the queen's

right arm with his left and the pair began to spin each other around in a whirling blur as their feet stepped an intricate pattern on the boards. For the briefest moment Cathal was captivated by the movement and that was when disaster struck.

With his eyes on the meticulous footsteps of Murrough and Caitlin, Cathal lost concentration for no more time than it takes to sneeze, and his foot slipped on the damp timber floor. Within seconds he had lost his balance and fallen sideways, pulling his wife down with him as he fell, so that they landed in a heap on the ground, Aoife lying across her husband's chest.

Murrough and Caitlin were so engrossed in their dance that they did not notice the chieftain's fall until the piper abruptly stopped playing. Even so it took a few seconds for them to realise what had happened, and by then the king's guard had pushed forward.

All of a sudden Murrough and Caitlin were lifted up on the shoulders of their jubilant kinsmen and they found themselves looking down on Cathal who was still struggling to his feet. Before the king could offer any sort of apology, his guardsmen had carried himself and his queen off the dance floor, back up towards the houses where they were lodged.

The last glimpse that Caitlin had of the dancing ground was the lone figure of Ia standing apart from the crowd, her Druid eyes fixed on Murrough.

Samhain fires, constructed in the open spaces between the inner and outer ramparts, were lit after midday. There were nine fires all around the hill fort; enough so that everyone would have a chance to dance, feast and wish their friends and relations well in the coming year.

Sianan and Mawn, being of the holy orders, were free to make their way around each of the fires in turn. Mawn carried an old battered harp that had served both Wanderers well as an instrument on which to learn the craft of music. At each fire they would sit themselves down and Sianan would ask which clan tended this particular blaze. Then she would relate the history and genealogy of the family back to earliest times while Mawn strummed the harp.

Then Mawn would tell a tale from the storehouse of legends which related to the clan in some way while Sianan played the harp. Even though their community was very large, it was an uncommon privilege for the people of Dun Righ to have two such Druids among them. Most of their own poets were too old to tell tales or too young to know them well enough.

The Wanderers had visited six of the fires in this manner and were moving on to the seventh when they met Seginus and Declan walking the circuit of fires in the opposite direction. The abbot had granted the priest a day of rest because of the festival and to show acknowledgement of his hard work and determination to pay the penance for his crimes.

It was Sianan who noticed the Christians first. She ran up to Seginus and grabbed his hand, greeting him as if he were a long lost friend. Both Declan and Mawn raised their eyebrows at this, and the abbot was at a loss for words for a moment.

'Greetings to you both,' he said, finally gaining control of his tongue. 'And may God bless you.'

'And also you,' Mawn answered, still surprised at the way Sianan had reached out to Seginus.

'I am to pass a message to you both,' Sianan said excitedly. 'You are invited to attend the Samhain hearth fire of the Druids in the hall of Cathal tonight. You will be required to remain with us throughout the dark hours but are free to engage in your own forms of worship if you feel that it is appropriate.'

Seginus smiled at her broadly but refrained from accepting the invitation. That was Declan's prerogative. The abbot paused to consider the implications and then answered politely.

'It would be our great honour to be present among the learned ones on this night which is so holy to your folk. And I trust that you will always in future share our holy days with us.'

'We will,' Mawn answered. 'And we hope to learn much more about your ways by doing so.'

'Only by learning about one another,' Seginus spoke up, 'can we come to understand and respect our separate traditions.'

Mawn felt his body jolt in shock and hoped that the movement had not been too noticeable. He soon realised, however, that he was not the only one stunned at what the priest had said. Declan was leaning forward on his staff, staring incredulously at Seginus.

'Then come, my friends,' Sianan went on, clearly finding nothing extraordinary in what Seginus had said, 'for tonight above all nights it is best to have the company of those who respect you.'

The abbot forced his gaze away from Seginus for a second but could offer no more than a grunt and a nod to acknowledge Sianan, who continued on as if she had not noticed Declan's shock.

'Have you been dancing?' she asked.

'I beg your pardon?' the abbot replied.

'Have you had an opportunity to dance?' Sianan repeated.

'No,' Declan said, forcing himself to concentrate. 'I have not danced since I was a lad. And since my injury I have had to be careful not to overexert myself. Monks do not engage in such practices; it is considered unseemly.'

'And what about priests?' Sianan asked. 'Do they not dance either?'

Seginus blushed and was about to answer, but Declan spoke before he had opened his mouth. 'Priests are servants of God,' he informed her. 'They give their whole life to God, and though they may take a wife, they rarely do so. And it is unusual for a priest of the Mother Church to have time for such frivolity.'

This time Mawn looked at the abbot with surprise for this did not sound like Declan talking at all, but rather like the old Druid Mongan who had spoken out against women taking Samhain lovers.

'I had no idea that your lives were so ordered,' Mawn said.

Now it was Declan's turn to blush. 'It is not that we may not dance. We are not specifically instructed to refrain from anything that might be enjoyable, it's just that our elders would certainly frown upon us doing so.'

'But your elders are all far away,' Sianan reasoned. 'Who is going to tell them that you danced a single jig at the festival of dances?'

'God will know,' Seginus answered.

'And would your God have you live without joy?' Sianan asked.

'No,' Declan began and then he saw the logic of her argument. 'Perhaps we will have a dance later,' he conceded. 'Origen always said to me that to

417

dance with one's legs and sing with one's voice
was the purest way to worship God. Perhaps he
was right.'

'Then we shall see you this evening after the
Samhain feast?' Sianan pressed.

'You will,' the abbot answered. 'We will come to
the chieftain's hall and share your vigil.'

At that they parted and went their separate
ways, but Mawn could not help looking back in
the direction of Seginus, still incredulous that such
a change had come over the priest. He looked at
Sianan and realised with admiration that somehow
she had affected Seginus; somehow she was
responsible, in part at least, for the change in the
Roman's thinking.

The two young Druids came to the next fire and
settled down on stools to play the harp and to give
their teachings to the common folk. Sianan finished
her part and Mawn passed the harp to her so that
she could strum along to his story.

As he began his tale and she plucked at the harp,
Sianan watched her friend intently. She could see
clearly that he was descended from Malchedoc. He
had the deep-felt compassion that reflected a desire
to teach those around him everything that he had
learned. To her Mawn was the gentlest of all
people; a young man whose fondness for his fellow
beings was such a strong part of his life that she
could not imagine him initiating a violent word or
action. His eyes revealed a soul brimming with
compassion despite the sadness of his youth and
the separation from his family. His spirit shone like
a beacon to all who heard him speak.

Sianan was still staring at her friend when he
finished his story and rose to depart for the last
fire in the circle. But she remained seated with the
harp on her knee, lost in her thoughts. Mawn took

the instrument from her and put it away in its leather bag. Then he slung it over his shoulder ready to move on. But Sianan remained sitting on a low stool with a blank expression on her face.

Mawn decided that it was best not to disturb her, so he put the harp bag down again and squatted on the ground beside her, patiently waiting for her to return from the realm of thoughts to the land of mortals. Several minutes passed and still she had not moved at all. This convinced him that she had probably slipped into a state of profound trance. Careful not to make too much noise, he asked the folk by the fire to move away for a while. When they saw the state of his companion, they did so immediately.

Folk not initiated into the tradition of the Druid path usually had a deep and superstitious respect for those poets who were drawn into trance in this manner. In the days of their ancestors such trance-walkers had been responsible for the very existence of the tribe for it was they who knew where to find game or gather food when all the other supplies had been exhausted. Their ability to travel great distances in spirit form was a thing both feared and admired. Feared because the truth could not be hidden from such folk, and admired because after their experiences such folk could never lie. One of the most prized of all gifts given by the Faeries was a tongue that could only tell the truth. Druids such as Sianan were believed to possess such a gift. But the truth can hurt as well as heal and none of the Dun Righ folk wished to be too close to Sianan when she awoke lest she make some pronouncement about them in front of their neighbours. Everyone has secrets and in such a close-knit community secrets were all the more valuable and guarded simply because they were so rare.

It was not long before Mawn found himself alone by the fire with Sianan. Everyone else had drifted off to other fires and left them in peace. The young man watched her for a long while before he noticed that her eyelids were slowly closing. Carefully he approached her and brushed his hand over her face to shut them for her, knowing from personal experience that she could suffer a lot of pain if she sat with them open for too long.

In the distance Mawn could hear the sound of a piper playing a merry jig and the screams of delight that came from those who danced along to the warrior's tune. As he turned his head and listened deeper, Mawn could also hear many folk talking and yelling to one another; he could hear the noise of plates and cups being gathered up for the feast and of the wind sighing through the trees nearby.

All these things put him in mind of the initiation he and Sianan had undertaken at Teamhair. At some point in that spirit journey they had arrived at a Faerie hall and there had danced with all the great host of the Danaans. They had been offered food and drink but had, of course, refused it. To have accepted any sustenance would have meant that they could have been trapped forever in the Faerie realms.

Mawn turned to face his friend again and noticed that she had a most peaceful expression on her face. He saw that she had the same expression as when she was sleeping—not simply still, but serene. In all the seasons that they had been together, since the time when they had both been chosen to be Wanderers, he had grown to appreciate Sianan in a way that was only just beginning to make itself evident to him.

Here was someone who knew him better than any living soul; better even than Gobann because Mawn did not share all his innermost secrets with his teacher. And here was a person who would always be a part of his life, for so it had been ordained. Mawn could not help but feel a sense of immeasurable joy in her presence, a sense of the eternity that lay before them. And he was grateful to her for all that she had been to him—a friend, a confidant and his only family.

He reached out gently and traced his finger lightly around her face from the top of her brow down her cheek and then across her lips.

'Thank you,' he whispered.

Sianan did not move, but a smile formed on her lips and she opened her eyes slowly.

'I looked down from far above,' she murmured, still seeing the sights of her journey clearly, though the trance had lifted. 'The Earth was a giant ball of blue,' she continued. Then she turned her head to face Mawn and he noticed a fire in her eyes that he had never seen before.

'When I looked carefully at the ball, the sea and land began to move and change shape so that the land looked like two people floating in the ocean, embracing as if they were twins in the womb. And all about them swam the Salmon of Knowledge, weaving between them and nestling into their forms. And their hands were locked in a firm reassuring hold that nothing on Earth could break.'

Mawn could feel the tears welling in his eyes. This had been a vision he had experienced on many occasions, and though he had never mentioned it to her, he knew Sianan must have seen it before also.

'And the two people—' Sianan went on.

'They were us,' Mawn cut in. 'We were those two locked in an eternal embrace.'

'Yes,' Sianan replied, and she reached out to take her friend's hand.

EIGDTEEN

ate into the night the dancing and feasting went on. By the time the midnight hour approached, the piper who had played the first dance of the day had returned to the ramparts to play out the old year and play in the new.

Murrough and Caitlin went together to take their evening meal with the warriors and other folk who had accompanied them from Eirinn. There were few of the folk of Dun Righ at their fire for feelings still ran hot between the chieftain of the hill fort and his guests.

Caitlin noticed with some degree of satisfaction that Ia was nowhere to be seen. Indeed the queen had not spotted the Druid all day long, not since she and her husband had been carried away by their warriors from the first dance of the festival. However, that did not stop Caitlin feeling the other woman's presence for Murrough remained sullen all through the festivities, smiling rarely and not laughing even once, despite the joyous nature of the celebration. He drank only one cup of mead and that was out of duty and politeness rather than a desire to have himself a good time. And worst of all he had not danced again after Cathal and Aoife's fall.

When Gobann and Síla got up to dance a jig, Caitlin's heart sank. These two had always kept their relationship discreet. Not many folk knew that they were lovers. But even they were openly declaring their love for one another, unconcerned about what people might say. On the other hand she and Murrough, who had been together since the time of the Quicken, were so distant from each other that they might as well be strangers. The queen looked over at her husband and hoped that he would notice her staring at him, but he was gazing off into the night sky, watching the clouds swirling around in the heavens.

She watched him for a long while before he finally noticed and looked up at her.

'There was nothing between Ia and myself,' he said low enough so that only his wife could hear.

Caitlin was surprised at this: she had not expected him to answer so directly the question that was in her mind. 'Then what is it that has made you so unhappy?' she asked him.

'I was surprised that my friend and wife was so swift to dismiss my feelings about Cathal,' he began. 'I was not expecting her to take the side of a man who had started a quarrel with me.'

'But there was no quarrel between you both,' Caitlin insisted. 'Just a misunderstanding fuelled by the passion of battle. And I never took Cathal's side in the fight. His Druids made a judgment and we as rulers must abide by the pronouncements of those who know the Brehon law. If we do not, then we set a very bad example for our people.'

'Do you still believe that the judgment was just?' Murrough frowned.

'It does not matter what I think,' Caitlin explained. 'The judgment has been passed and we must respect it to the letter, otherwise our own authority as law keepers will be tarnished. But more than that, if we do not graciously accept it when the Brehon judges pass a ruling, how can we expect our warriors to respect us when we call them to the defence of the kingdom?'

'Even though the judges were all Cathal's men and it was obvious that they had taken his part?' the king asked bitterly. 'Even though every one of our folk knew that they had judged in favour of Cathal because he was their chieftain?'

'That makes you all the more noble for accepting such a corrupt decision,' Caitlin argued, 'for above the letter of the law is respect for the institution of law. If their judgment has wronged you, there are ways to ensure that the matter is brought before a higher authority and judged again. Even if that fails to satisfy your sense of justice, you can take your quarrel to the High-King at Beltinne and he will decide. But you must follow the recognised paths to achieve such considerations. It is of no use to take any other course of action.'

'I am a king,' Murrough began. 'There are some things that a king is not permitted to do that are open to others of lesser rank.'

'What do you mean?' Caitlin asked, confused.

'Kings and queens are not permitted to fast on the doorstep of the one who has wronged them,' he answered.

All of a sudden Caitlin understood why she had not seen Ia all day long. It was obvious that the Druid woman was even now seated in front of Cathal's home and had not taken food all day long. She was fasting in order to draw attention to the injustice that she felt had been done to her.

'That is a rare thing in these times,' the queen began tactfully. 'Few folk have the dedication and belief in themselves to carry such a fast through to its eventual conclusion.'

'That is because few folk have claims which can be so easily substantiated,' Murrough shot back.

425

'It is Ia we are talking about, isn't it?' Caitlin inquired.

'She has spent the whole day at Cathal's door in an attempt to shame him into changing his ways.'

'Ia must believe very strongly that she is right.'

'Her people have been persecuted by Cathal,' Murrough replied. 'They have been moved off the land that their ancestors tilled for generations and they have been replaced with Cathal's cows.'

'How long will she keep up this fast?'

'Until the end,' the king sighed, 'for she says that she can no longer act as chief advisor to such a man or live among his people.'

'We must go and speak with her,' Caitlin said half under her breath. 'If she continues with this fast, the Dal Araidhans will implicate you. They will say that Murrough encouraged her to attempt to shame the chieftain.'

'I tried to talk her out of it,' the king protested, 'but she would not listen to me.'

'Come, let me speak with her,' the queen persisted, taking her husband's arm.

'Very well,' Murrough agreed, getting up from the fire. 'But do not be surprised if she ignores us completely.'

Caitlin led the way back through the inner walls towards the main hall where the chieftain's feasts were held. For the duration of the Samhain feast this hall was the home of the Druids, so it would have been no use to Ia to fast here. She had gone to Cathal's family home where the food was being prepared.

Caitlin had seen immediately that Ia was very clever in choosing this time to begin her fast. Throughout the lands where Druid lore was revered, the feast of Samhain was a time of food and abundance. No-one, not even the sick or the

426

poor, not even criminals or foreign captives, was barred from the ritual sharing of the feast. The Druids especially were served the best of all the food and drink at this festival, so for a Druid of Ia's rank to refuse the communal offering of the dun, there would have to be very serious cause indeed.

Even those among Cathal's folk who had no time for her would very likely sit up and take notice now that she was risking not just her life with the fast but the honour of every living soul who dwelt within the stronghold. Anyone who ignored her pleas for justice would have to contend with the fact that one among them went without while all the others were well provided for.

By the time Caitlin and Murrough arrived at Cathal's house there were many women standing around the stone bench on which Ia sat. They had heaped food on brass platters at her feet, but the Druid had not touched their offerings. She only sat with her eyes fixed on some point in the distance while they begged her not to continue with this course of action.

As Murrough and Caitlin approached, the women hurried back inside Cathal's house, but they only went far enough indoors that they could not be seen. Every one of them wanted to know what would be said between these three people.

'Ia,' the king began when the last of the women had slipped inside. 'Ia!' he repeated, trying to get her attention.

The Druid woman shifted her gaze, turning her face away from Murrough. He shrugged his shoulders and sighed heavily to show that it was no use trying to reach her. But Caitlin was not so easily put off.

'If you do not cease this fast immediately,' the

queen informed the Druid woman, 'there will be consequences that you cannot even begin to imagine.'

Ia did not respond so Caitlin went on. 'First of all,' the queen said calmly, 'there is already a rumour circulating around the hill fort that you and my husband are lovers.'

Ia turned sharply to face Caitlin, her eyes full of rage. But although this information had obviously struck a nerve with the Druid woman, she bit her tongue and did not answer the allegation.

'And folk will say that Murrough put you up to this,' Caitlin went on. 'You may get what you want out of this action, or you may be allowed to starve to death; either way you will achieve what you desired—some form of justice. But those of us who are left behind will have to bear the consequences of your actions. Murrough will be persecuted for his friendship with you.'

'Can you not see that there are other issues at stake here than your own precious honour?' Ia blurted, unable to contain herself any longer. 'My clanspeople are being treated in a dishonourable manner. Murrough, your husband, was denied justice because he was not born in the lands of the Dal Araidhe. You forget, Queen Caitlin, that I was privy to the deliberations of the Druid judges. I was among them. Mongan made a ruling against Murrough simply because he felt that all foreigners should be treated so. It is Cathal's wish that the King and Queen of Muster and all their retinue be on a ship bound for Eirinn and not still billeted in his stronghold. Mongan even suggested that it would not be unprecedented to request that you all camp beyond the outer walls since your king had offered his chieftain such a grave insult. There was never any question of there being a fair and unbiased judgment in the matters between Murrough and Cathal.'

She stopped for a moment to catch her breath and then, at the top of her voice so everyone inside the chieftain's house could hear, she said, 'Cathal is a tyrant who has bought the favour of his judges. He has murdered the innocent and made alliances with the Saxons. He is a greedy man who does not pay his debts but leaves them for his clanspeople to settle. If he had any honour he would come out from hiding behind his wife and face me in person. I will not be moved by the snivelling entreaties of his womenfolk or the threats of his warriors.'

'What do you mean,' Caitlin cut in, 'by the threats of his warriors?'

Ia turned her head to the side, flicking the golden hair away from her head. The queen could see a great bruise along the Druid woman's jawline up to her ear. It was a deep blue and could have only been hours old.

'Cathal sent one of his largest men to beat me into submission,' she yelled, directing her voice at the house again. 'The poor fellow thought he would not face very much resistance from a mere woman. But what woman would lie back and let a warrior compel her to submit to him?'

Caitlin gasped aloud. Straightaway a vision came to her of the massive Saxon who had attempted to force himself on her all those seasons ago. Had it not been for Murrough, the savage might have succeeded for he had been easily twice her size and body weight.

'Are you saying,' the queen interjected, hardly able to believe what she had heard, 'that one of Cathal's men tried to rape you?'

'He dragged me away from the door early this afternoon,' Ia retorted. 'And he surely would have

killed me when he had finished with me if I had
not sliced his leg open with my knife.'

At that instant a woman stepped out from
Cathal's house with her hands on her hips and a
stern look on her face. It was Aoife.

'Is this true?' she demanded of Ia. 'Did one of
the warriors assault you as you claim?'

'Why don't you ask the man whose blood
washed my blade?'

Aoife looked directly at Caitlin, clearly outraged
by what she had heard. 'This stupid quarrel has
gone on long enough!' the chieftain's wife bellowed. She turned and called back into the house,
'Cathal Mac Croneen, there is someone here to see
you.' There was no answer and so Aoife stomped
back inside.

From where they were, Murrough, Caitlin and
Ia could hear Aoife yelling at her husband, order-
ing him to go outside and offer his apologies and
to promise to punish the warrior concerned. The
chieftain was protesting but he kept his voice low
enough so that those outside would not hear
exactly what he had to say.

'Go out there now,' the chieftain's wife stormed,
'or by all that is sacred I will divorce you tonight!
No woman should so much as feel threatened by
the strength of a man in this hill fort, and if you
are content to let that happen, I will find myself a
man for whom such acts are truly repugnant.'

Once again Cathal's voice could be heard as he
tried to put his case to her, but Aoife did not let
him finish.

'And if this man had laid a hand on one of your
daughters or on me,' Aoife screamed, 'would you
be so happy to sit back and say that it was a
misunderstanding? I am shamed by the cowardice
of my husband. Who would have thought that

you would lower yourself to the level of the Saxons? Women can expect harsh treatment from those barbarians, not from their own people.'

'She's a foreigner,' the chieftain bellowed back.

'She is living among us now,' his wife snapped. 'We are not Romans or Saxons who do not value strangers. Everyone has rights under the law in this land, even those who were not born among us, but most especially those who are least able to defend themselves.'

'She was well able to defend herself,' Cathal exploded. 'The man was lucky that she did not aim her weapon any higher or he may have lost his manhood altogether.'

'For a man who could contemplate such an act,' Aoife answered furiously, 'that might not be entirely a bad thing.'

Once again Cathal lowered his voice so that no-one but those nearest to him could hear what he had to say. Then Aoife's voice could be heard in reply, but she was also talking more quietly now. An exchange took place then that lasted a long while before Cathal finally emerged from the house, closely followed by Aoife.

'I have offended you, sister,' the chieftain declared, casting hesitant glances back at his wife. 'Will you accept my apology?' Aoife pushed him hard in the back and he moved forward a step so as not to fall over. It was obvious to all that he was making this speech under duress. 'And also the hospitality of my house.'

'You know the charges that I am making against you,' Ia breathed. 'Will you answer for them all in the presence of a Druid judge?'

'I will,' Cathal replied.

'In front of Gobann of the Silver Branch?' she added.

The chieftain sucked in his cheeks, unwilling to go quite that far in his commitment. If Mongan was to judge the matter, Cathal knew that he would not be found guilty of misconduct; but with Gobann determining the trial it was likely he would be stripped of all his offices.

'Gobann is not one of our people,' the chieftain stated.

'He was born in Dal Araidhe,' Ia shot back.

'He serves the High-King of Eirinn and the King of Munster.'

'He is a Druid poet of the highest degree. There is no-one here more knowledgeable in law.'

Cathal fell silent, bowing his head towards the ground. 'Very well,' he conceded finally, seeing that he would no longer achieve anything by a refusal to do as Ia demanded.

Caitlin wondered what Aoife had said to her husband under her breath that had resulted in such a profound change of heart. Murrough, on the other hand, was more concerned with ensuring that this was not just a trick to make the Druid woman back down from her embarrassing fast on Samhain Eve.

'What assurances will you give,' the king asked, 'that the case will be heard tomorrow?'

'Tomorrow!' Cathal protested. 'I cannot guarantee that any progress will be made so soon.'

'So you will sit on your hands again, as you did with my complaint,' Murrough scoffed. The King of Munster touched Ia on the shoulder. 'Do not trust him. An old fox always leads the longest chase.'

'How dare you?' Cathal snarled. 'I have had enough of your insolent tongue, young king. I am your elder and I am a monarch in my own right. I will not take this from you any longer. You and

432

your people have lived off the fat of this stronghold for too long. We have fed you and clothed you over three months now. We have given you hearth fires and shelter from the rain. And all we have received in return is your rebuke and harsh insults. I don't care that I am breaking with tradition. I don't care what fines the Druid judges impose upon me. I demand that when the sun goes down tomorrow you and all your people be gone from this place. Your welcome here is ended. Do not return!'

With that the chieftain turned around and pushed past his wife and into the house. In moments the rest of the observers in his clan had joined him, all except Aoife who was left alone on the doorstep. The chieftain's wife looked back at the house and for the briefest instant wavered and nearly followed after her husband. Then, with a sigh, she pulled a gold bracelet from her arm and dropped it in the dust at the door. She paused and caught Ia's eye, holding the Druid woman's gaze for a moment before pushing her way past Murrough and Caitlin and into the night. Caitlin could only guess that she was headed to the fires near the ramparts.

'Come along then, Ia,' the queen offered. 'I too have done you an injustice, I am afraid. I would like to take you with us and get you some food if there is any left at this late hour.'

'I do not blame you for believing the rumours that Cathal spread about your Murrough and myself,' Ia replied, 'and I think you should know that if I had ever doubted his love for you even for an instant, I would have gladly taken him from you. He has been a great friend to me when all others would have scorned my company. You are a lucky woman.'

'I know,' Caitlin answered, shamed that she had

ever suspected this woman of doing her ill. 'Will you come with us?'

'If you don't mind, I will go alone,' Ia said proudly. 'It is almost midnight and I have much to do if I am to be a part of the Druid rituals.' The woman stood up and strode off towards the chieftain's hall, leaving Murrough and Caitlin alone at Cathal's door.

'I didn't like this place very much anyway,' the queen said finally as she reached out to take Murrough's hand.

The king smiled. 'Neither did I,' he replied. 'I would much prefer to be at home in Munster with a roaring fire at our hearth and our own people all around us.'

'And our children,' Caitlin added.

'And our children,' Murrough repeated. 'Let's go to the fires again and dance one more jig before we go to bed.'

Caitlin returned his smile and nodded, then she grasped him gently round the waist and kissed him deeply. They held each other tightly for a long time before making their way arm in arm back to the ramparts where the piper was still playing.

Gobann and Síla sat down on the edge of the ramparts to hear the last two dances played. They were both exhausted from a long day of rituals and celebration and they were tired of being surrounded by so many people. Now of all times they wished only to be alone together.

In all the seasons since he had taken the blue mantle, even in the days when he had worn only the four-coloured cloak of a novice, the poet had rarely been by himself. As he sat on the ramparts he wished with all his heart that he and Síla could be away from Dun Righ, if only for a few days, so that they could spend some time enjoying each other's company. Gobann knew that the time of his leave-taking was not far off.

Síla was aware also that the day was fast approaching when they would have to say farewell. Yet both of them concealed their pain at this certainty and determined that they would not speak of that fateful day. They simply sat in the comfortable silence that was the result of their true and deep respect for one another. And as they held each other close Gobann looked out into the sky and searched for his old companion the Evening Star.

'Star of Guidance,' he chanted lowly, 'Keeper of Trysts. As surely as you set me on this path. The road beyond life that leads away from the object of my love and desire. So bring us together again life after life as you have always done.'

Síla wanted to repeat the last few words to reinforce the power of the prayer, but her throat was dry with sorrow and her tongue would not do her bidding. And so she merely sighed.

The ranks of men assembled on the shore in formation. Their numbers stretched down the beach as far as Aldor could see in both directions. The war leader leaned on his walking stick and watched the horsemen galloping between the ranks to pass orders down the line, and he marvelled at the organised manner in which the Cymru troops followed commands.

'With an army like that I could take all of Britain for myself,' the eorl muttered under his breath.

'It was an army like that that first conquered this island,' an old voice crackled and Aldor heard the sound of a goat bell tinkling behind him. The eorl turned to see Palladius standing only a few paces away. The Christian had an unnerving habit of being able to appear without any warning.

'The Cymru learned the art of war from the Romans who were their masters until two generations ago. But the Cymru have also preserved their own ancient style of fighting. I have a little surprise for you, Aldor,' the bishop whispered, stepping closer.

'I have brought a weapon with me from the mountains of Cymbri that is unbeatable in battle. A weapon that no army can resist in the field. A weapon that even the Dal Araidhans will be unprepared for.'

Aldor looked hard into the old man's face. There was a strange light in the Christian's eyes as if he were taking immense pleasure from the thought of the slaughter to come. With effort the eorl dragged his gaze away from Palladius and looked towards the beach again just as the Christian lifted his staff high in the air and swung it around his head.

All the Cymru troops on the beach suddenly dispersed and reformed further down the sand, clearing a large space not forty paces away from where Aldor and Palladius stood. The eorl heard the unmistakable sound of horses neighing wildly and the thundering of hooves. In the next instant his unspoken question was answered.

Across the ground behind the beach a great cloud of dirt and dust rose and a company of horsemen appeared, bounding off the level ground onto the hard sand. They were immediately followed by twenty-two wheeled carts, each drawn by two horses and carrying two standing warriors. Another company of about fifty horsemen followed on after the small carts.

'They are chariots,' Palladius explained. 'Carts such as these were the only thing that held up the Roman advance into Britain for they are light, swift moving and impossible for footmen to catch. When each chariot has an archer mounted on the back you have a rapidly moving detachment of men who can strike at the heart of the enemy line and be gone again before any successful counterattack can be launched against them. After the conquest of Britain the Romans incorporated them into their army and used them very effectively.'

Aldor shook his head. The Saxon way of warfare did not take into account such intricate details as attack and counterattack. The eorl had always employed simple tactics: strike hard, strike fast and force your way to victory. Neither had he ever used mounted troops in battle, and the presence of so many now made him shake his head in confusion.

'We are attacking a stronghold,' the eorl remarked, unsure whether he had misunderstood the whole plan of assault. 'I can see the use of horsemen and chariots in the open field—they would annihilate any enemy footmen—but the Dal Araidhans are not likely to come out and offer us a battle. If they are wise, they are going to stay well within their walls and pick these mounted soldiers off one by one.'

'Unless we can draw them out,' Palladius agreed. 'Ten years ago I led an army against a Gaelic stronghold such as this,' the bishop began. Once again Aldor could see a strange light in the Christian's eyes and it disturbed him to see it. 'At Rathowen in Eirinn my soldiers attempted to storm a dun. We had as many good warriors as you have today and there were only a third the number of defenders that hold Dun Righ. Yet we had no hope of taking that place in a frontal assault. I foolishly believed that the Gaels would merely give up at the sight of our massive army, but I was wrong. They knew that they had the advantage.'

'And how will we wrestle that advantage away from them?' Aldor asked.

Palladius did not answer, he only smiled broadly like a child that has a wonderful secret he is bursting to share with the world. The eorl was about to ask the question again when Tyrbrand approached the two men and bowed to both.

'My lords,' the holy man intoned, 'may you see victory on the field this day.'

'Nothing is more assured,' Palladius replied mirthfully. 'Are the preparations all made?'

'They are,' Tyrbrand answered. 'Though it was not easy to find all the materials you requested and in the quantities required. Nevertheless our raiders have managed to acquire all that you asked for.'

'The oil?' Palladius demanded. 'And the pitch?'

'Yes, lord,' the Saxon holy man answered.

'Then it is time to reveal to you the weapon that will gain us mastery of the stronghold of Dun Righ,' the bishop said. 'Come with me.'

Palladius turned on his heel and strode with remarkable energy for one of his years towards the tent that had been erected for the shelter of his men in a field at the edge of the beach. The little goat bell that hung around the Christian's neck rang out as he walked. Aldor struggled to keep up with the bishop while Tyrbrand respectfully walked along two paces behind his eorl.

At the entrance to the tent Palladius stopped and spoke under his breath to the Cymru guard who was standing watch. As soon as Aldor caught up with the bishop the guardsman hauled on the tent canvas and in moments the interior of the structure was revealed. A great four-wheeled machine constructed of wood, ropes and iron lay there under the cover. It was half the size of any of the houses that Aldor's men had built for themselves and as large as a thirty-man boat. The eorl gasped in surprise and wonder.

'What is it?' he finally muttered.

'It is an old Roman catapult,' Palladius explained. 'It was left here by the Imperial army when they withdrew a hundred years ago. A local chieftain in the land of Cymbri kept it and with his help I had it refurbished.'

'What purpose does it serve?' the eorl inquired, not understanding any of the complicated construction of the device.

'It will throw rocks, fire or even buckets of boiling oil over a vast distance,' the Christian said with relish. 'A wad of burning pitch will travel a distance of three to four bow shots. This means that we can sit far away from the walls of Dun Righ, out of range of the Dal Araidhan archers, and set their stronghold on fire.'

'Eventually they will send troops out to destroy this machine,' Aldor noted.

'And then we will attack their warriors with mounted troops and chariots,' Palladius beamed. 'This is a perfect trap. Once their best troops are wasted on a futile attempt to seize the catapult, we will train it on the breach in the defences and clear all the sentries from that area. As our warriors move forward the catapult will raze everything before them, eliminating all resistance.'

Aldor stood with mouth agape. The advent of this weapon would mean that his army would be difficult to defeat. Combined with cavalry and chariots, his warriors were invincible.

'Aldor will be Eorl of Strath-Clóta,' Tyrbrand announced. 'Soon this whole land will fall to you, my lord.'

With a swift turn of his head Aldor indicated that he appreciated the comment and understood the implications, but he squinted his eyes at the Christian. It was difficult for the eorl to believe that Palladius would not want any share in the spoils other than the possession of Dun Righ for his new monastic community.

'We will need to use the dun as a military stronghold until we have taken the whole peninsula,' Aldor stated, making sure that this was clear to the bishop.

'Naturally,' Palladius agreed. 'How else will we consolidate our position and eliminate all resistance? But in time you will have Dun Breteann to utilise as your main fortification and capital. At that time Dun Righ should revert to me as agreed. I promise not to use it for military purposes. All the buildings will be levelled and a great monastery built there.'

'Dun Breteann is a long way from here,' the eorl stated with some scepticism, 'and on the border of the northern kingdom of Dal Araidhe. It may be more than a year before we manage to bring an assault to that place.'

'With God's help you will be there by the spring,' the bishop enthused. 'And with my catapult your victory even at that large stronghold will be certain.'

'And all you want is that I give you Dun Righ?' Aldor affirmed. 'Nothing else?'

'Take on the mantle of Christ,' Palladius sighed seductively, 'and the Lord will watch over you and protect you. He will march with you to victory and ensure that this whole land is named a Christian domain with Palladius as its bishop.'

The eorl made no reply but glanced at Tyrbrand. 'I will need to consult my advisors,' he hedged.

'There is no better way to ensure victory,' Tyrbrand exclaimed. 'I have seen the power of the Christ god and he is truly great. Take him into our army and we will sweep across the land like a flood of fire.'

Shocked that the man who had so recently expounded the virtues of Seaxneat the god of all the Angles had so dramatically changed his opinion, Aldor paused for a moment to consider the possibilities. The eorl perceived a certain insincerity in Tyrbrand's exhortation which led him to believe that the Saxon holy man was suggesting this alliance out of convenience more than a belief in the power of Christ.

It was also evident that Palladius would probably not join them in the assault on Dun Righ unless he could be assured that in time he would be named Bishop of Strath-Clóta. Aldor decided that it would not hurt him to commit himself to the Christian doctrine. If ever Palladius became too insistent or interfering, Aldor knew that it would be a simple matter to eliminate him.

For the time being the eorl decided to play along with the bishop and give him exactly what he wanted, or at least let him believe that.

'I will do as you ask,' Aldor announced. 'If the Christ gains us victory, I will become a follower and submit to the Christian God.'

'You must submit before the battle,' Palladius explained, 'for my God will not help those who are not of his doctrine.'

Aldor paused again for a second; then, with

another glance at Tyrbrand, he said, 'I will submit now as is your wish, but only if my advisor and holy man Tyrbrand will do so as well.'

Tyrbrand's face drained of its colour and he glared back at the war leader, but it was obvious to him that he had little choice in the matter. What difference would it make, the holy man reasoned to himself, if he attached no meaning to the act of becoming a Christian? In the end they would gain a great victory with a minimum loss of life. That would mean that they could march on to Dun Breteann straightaway. Seaxneat would be victorious in the end.

'I also will submit,' Tyrbrand answered. 'I will take the mantle of the Christ.'

'Then let us Christian you into the faith now,' Palladius announced. 'And all your men who will take the holy chrism that will save their souls. I will meet you at the water's edge as soon as the arrangements have been made. Ready yourself to throw off your heathen ways, renounce your false gods and enter into the Kingdom of Heaven.'

Palladius briefly grasped each man by the hand and then walked briskly off to his own tent to don his vestments for the ceremony. Behind him the two Saxons stood silently looking at the machine which would guarantee them victory.

'I am afraid,' Aldor finally said, 'that I may have bartered my seat in the great Wealhall in exchange for this device. I hope it is worth it.'

'Our seats in the spirit realm of Wealhall are as secure as they ever were,' Tyrbrand retorted, 'for we will be victorious in battle and men will sing of our deeds long after we are gone.'

Aldor coughed a little and then made his way without another word towards the beach where he would be accepted into the Christian faith in front of all his warriors. Tyrbrand remained behind for a little while and then went off to be by himself in preparation for the trial to come.

Despite his bold words, the Saxon holy man was also concerned about what could happen to him after death if he committed to the Christian God. But he decided in the end that Seaxneat would protect him no matter what happened. Bolstered by that thought, he eventually came to the water's edge where Aldor and Palladius were waiting for him.

NINETEEN

hen the piper began the last tune of the evening—a lament—Mawn and Sianan were sitting alone among the tufts of grass where the cows spent their days. They, like their teachers, had sought a degree of solitude on this night, even though it was usual for all Gaelic folk to revel in the company of friends and relatives.

'Gobann has agreed that I am to spend some time with Declan,' Mawn remarked. 'The abbot intends to travel to Saint Ninian's in the next few days to begin rebuilding the monastery.'

Sianan reached out and took her friend's hand. 'I will miss you,' she said gently. 'We have hardly been apart since our initiation at Teamhair. I feel we have still so much to learn together.'

'So do I,' Mawn agreed. 'But we have long lives ahead of us. There is no hurry for ones such as us.'

'I am to go north with Síla,' Sianan added, 'to the lands of the Cruitne where she was born. She tells me that women Druids are highly revered among her people.'

'Do you remember when we were children what we thought about the Cruitne?' Mawn asked.

'I thought they were a wild race of head collectors who stole out at night to thieve little children from their beds and take them home to put in their cooking pots,' Sianan laughed.

Mawn joined in—they had both realised long ago that their parents and guardians had only told them such tales so that they would not wander too far from home at night.

'My father told me,' Mawn confided, 'that the Faeries would take me if I went out singing in the countryside by myself.'

'And did you stop singing?' Sianan asked, horrified.

'I sang all the more and sought out the most deserted places to recite my songs,' Mawn grinned, raising his eyebrows as if to say that all children behave so.

'And did the Faeries take you?' Sianan inquired.

Mawn's expression suddenly changed and he looked skyward at a break in the clouds where the Evening Star was peeking through.

'I have never told anyone, Sianan,' he began, 'but there was one time when I was a boy, shortly before Gobann came to take me to Teamhair, when something strange did happen to me.'

He paused for a moment as if trying to conjure the memory in his mind. Sianan squeezed his hand to let him know she was listening. 'One night I was late coming home with the goats. I had strayed down to a glen where three old standing stones lay on their sides, overgrown with long grass and blackberry bushes. The goats loved that place because the grass was green and sweet. I was so involved in singing my songs that I lost track of the setting of the sun. As soon as I realised that it was dark I herded the goats together and drove them with all speed back up to the road and homeward.'

The Evening Star dimmed as a cloud flew in front of it, and Mawn stopped speaking to watch the sight. When the cloud had completely covered the little light in the sky, he went on.

'Halfway home I met a man standing on the path blocking my way. He was dressed all in black and the goats were afraid of him. They would not even approach him. I had to stop and try to think of an alternate route home for I was far too frightened to speak to him.'

'Who was he?' Sianan asked excitedly.

'I do not know. I never found out,' Mawn explained. 'After a long while he beckoned to me to follow and, for some reason that I have never been able to explain, I did as he bid me. We walked off the path and I let the goats go. Before long we came to a little mound and the man opened a door in the side of it and light streamed out. "Go in," he insisted. "They are waiting for you," and so I did. As soon as I put my head in the door I heard the most beautiful music that I have ever listened to.'

Sianan was squeezing his hand hard and gazing intently into his eyes.

'I do not remember much of what took place there, but I do recall meeting an old Druid who told me a story,' Mawn went on.

'About a boy and a girl who were given a gift by the Faerie folk,' Sianan cut in before Mawn could continue. 'A gift so precious that it took two of them to look after it properly.'

'Yes,' Mawn stuttered. 'How did you know that?'

'I was in a place like that once and an old Druid told me that tale also,' she admitted. 'I thought it was just a dream that I had experienced as a child, but ever since our initiation I have known that it was real.'

'The Faeries in this little mound were not like the ones we met at our initiation. These folk,'

Mawn continued, 'were tall and slender with long white faces and skulls that seemed to be conical near to the crown of their heads.'

'With great dark eyes like those of owls,' Sianan confirmed, 'each shaped like a long leaf.'

'And small mouths they had too,' Mawn recalled. 'Hardly more than slits in their faces. But they never spoke directly to me and never opened their mouths, yet I heard in my mind what they said to each other. The old Druid was the only one who addressed me directly.

'I did not want to leave after the Druid had told me his story. I wanted to stay with them and be like them. They were kinder to me than my own family and they fed me better than I have ever eaten. I remember eating so much that I fell asleep in the lap of a beautiful lady who pillowed me in her long milk-white hair.'

'I ate also of their food,' Sianan confessed, 'even though I knew at the time that it was very dangerous to do so, for those who eat of the Faerie food are never allowed to leave the lands of the Otherworld.'

'And yet they let us return,' Mawn puzzled. 'And if the story is true, they allowed Oisin to come back from Tir-Nan-Og to visit Eirinn once more.'

'A few perhaps are allowed to return,' Sianan decided. 'Or maybe that is just another tale to frighten little children.' Then she laughed again. 'After my visit with them my grandfather found me high in the branches of an old rowan tree that grew on the edge of Lough Sheelin.'

'My father found me sitting in the branches of a tree also,' Mawn recalled with a smile. 'Though I do not remember if it was a rowan or not. He gave me the beating of my life when he found me. I was bruised black all over for a week. Then he locked

447

me in the hay shed for a day and a night. I remember hearing the Faeries come that evening as I lay among the hay and I thought they had come to rescue me. But they had only brought me a little to eat and they played some music to help me sleep. After that I always ate my meals there just in case they came back and I could return the favour.'

'I was never beaten,' Sianan said. 'Grandfather took me back to the dun where we were staying and he asked me to tell him exactly what had happened. He was very protective of me, old Cathach. I told him everything that I could remember and he blessed me. I saw a tear in his eye and wiped it away and he hugged me close to him, but it was not until later that I fully understood why.'

'So it was the Danaans who chose us, do you think?' Mawn asked.

'I believe that they may well have had a hand in the decision.'

'I wished that I could escape my family forever,' Mawn said sadly. 'And shortly afterwards I did. But I did not expect the terrible fate that befell them.'

Sianan leaned over to Mawn and put her head on his chest. 'Do you remember what we said to each other when we were in the Star of the Poets on the night that Cathach died?' she said.

'That we would be each other's family,' Mawn replied. 'I would always be here for you and you for me.'

'That's right,' Sianan sighed and then she lifted her head and kissed Mawn lightly on the lips. Slowly, gently he responded and they drew each other closer as their bodies acknowledged the will of their souls to join together.

Mongan was waiting at the door to Cathal's hall when Gobann and Síla arrived to take part in the midnight ceremonies. The piper's lament still rang through the hill fort and all the other folk of Dun Righ were on their way to their homes or to meet with their lovers before returning to their hearths.

Gobann had stopped by at the lodging he shared with Síla to retrieve his cloak of thick Raven feathers, the symbol of his office as a poet of the Silver Branch. Mongan noticed that the poet had wrapped the great expanse of the black feather garment around himself and his lover. Beneath its sheltering folds the two Druids were hugging each other.

'You are late,' the old Dal Araidhan Druid stated coldly. 'One expects more disciplined behaviour from a poet of the Silver Branch.'

'What are we late for?' Síla asked with a laugh, refusing to take any more of this man's arrogance.

'You are late for the rituals of Samhain,' Mongan replied tersely. 'We have been waiting for you.'

'Is there some ceremony that is practised in Dun Righ that is not observed elsewhere?' Gobann asked as he and Síla separated from their embrace.

'No,' the old Druid replied tersely.

'Then we are here in plenty of time to commence the ritual,' the poet remarked, 'and you should consider very carefully the state of mind in which you enter into this hall. A man of your learning, Mongan, should know full well that whatever thoughts and intentions one takes to the ceremonies are reflected in the near future.'

'I am not a child that you should speak to me so,' the old man snapped.

'I suggest that you spend some time clearing your thoughts outside the hall while we make the final preparations for the Samhain observances. Ill will is not suited to this celebration.'

'We cannot begin in any case,' Mongan spluttered, enraged at being addressed in such a manner. 'Your two students have gone missing again. What shall we do? Raise all the warriors from their beds and send them out to search as we had to last time? Do they not realise that we have better things to do here at Dun Righ than cater for the unruly behaviour of novices?'

'They are not novices, Mongan,' Síla corrected. 'They are fully initiated Druids of exceptional talent and knowledge. One day they will both bear the Silver Branch in their turn.'

'That is always the way, isn't it?' the old man hissed. 'The teacher primes his pupils to walk in his footsteps. My teachers never carried the Branch, though they were well worthy of it. And because my mentors were not good enough for the Great Council of Druids in Teamhair, I will never be considered for that honour either. Indeed I cannot recall one Druid from the Kingdom of Dal Araidhe who has been elevated to the Silver Branch since I was a boy. That seems a little unfair,' he added sarcastically.

'I have told you before,' Gobann chided softly, 'and perhaps it would serve you to listen this time. I was born in these lands. I am a Dal Araidhan and I am the only poet who has been elevated in the last twenty-five winters. Before that there was a Cymru poet called Taleis who, I recall, was a traveller who settled on these shores. If you are implying that the Druid Council selects poets for honour based on the land of their birth or the origin of their mother tongue, then I am surprised at you.'

'The day is coming when all of Dal Araidhe will be free of the domination of Eirinn,' Mongan stated. 'And that means the Druids of this land will be free from the jurisdiction of the Star of the Poets at Teamhair.'

'The Star of the Poets does not control the thoughts and practices of the many Druids who wander the roads,' Gobann informed the old man. 'The Druid Council at Teamhair is no better than the Assembly of Druids on the Isle of Glass in South Britain or the Gathering of Karnac in Armorica. None has more power to make decisions than another. We should stand together in spite of the aspirations of our chieftains or the ambitions of our kings. We all have a responsibility to our clanspeople, but our first duty is to our calling as Druids: truth-tellers, poets, upholders of the law.'

'High and mighty words,' Mongan retorted, 'but such sentiments do not wash with me and my kin. We are Dal Araidhans and we have a right to our own ways, even if that means we must oppose the Great Council at Teamhair in order to retain our independence.'

'Walk a while in the night air, old man,' Síla snapped. 'You are beginning to mistake a stomach full of ale for a head full of wise words.'

Gobann reached out and grabbed Síla's arm, shaking her a little in the hope that she would control her tongue. He could understand her frustration with Mongan but could not excuse her harsh words.

'Very well,' the old Druid replied sharply, 'I will go for a walk. And when I return we will begin the ceremony with or without the two young ones. But remember, Síla of the painted people, once that door is closed there is no force on Earth that will get me to open it again. If your students are late, they will be locked out for the night. That might not worry someone of your savage ancestry, for I hear the Cruitne rarely sleep under the cover of a roof anyway, but I am sure it will give your novices something to think about.'

Before Síla had a chance to reply to Mongan's veiled insults, the old man strode off out of earshot. The healing woman was left to curse him under her breath.

'Be careful what you say,' Gobann soothed. 'Remember, whatever curse you bring on someone returns to you nine times.'

Síla turned to the poet, surprised and hurt that he had reprimanded her. 'And how is it that you are always so right?' she said, betraying how deeply offended she was.

'I am not always right,' Gobann laughed, trying to make light of the situation. 'I simply refuse to allow people like Mongan to ruin my peace of mind. I just accept him for the rude, arrogant, patronising old bull seal that he is and try to ignore the fact that he speaks without knowledge, respect or eloquence.'

Síla sighed heavily. She knew deep down that Gobann was right, though she did not want him to see that. For that reason it was a few moments before she raised her face to meet his eyes again.

'Now,' said the poet, 'let us go inside Cathal's hall and bolt the door so that when the venerable grouch returns he will believe that he has been locked out for the night. That will give him something to think about,' he added in mockery of Mongan's tone.

At this Síla laughed and dragged Gobann by the arm into the hall, glad that she had such a friend

452

and determined to enjoy every moment of their time left together.

'Come to the fire, Gobann of the Silver Branch,' she whispered to him, 'and tell me a tale from the old times.'

TWENTY

ut in the field where the cows gathered after milking, near the fallen tree trunk that had borne the brunt of Murrough's anger only a few days earlier, two figures lay curled up together with their cloaks wrapped around themselves like blankets. Had the sentries been walking their posts instead of closed inside their own houses for the night, they likely would have overlooked Mawn and Sianan sleeping peacefully in the shelter of the dead tree.

In the distance an owl called out a greeting to one of his kindred, and before long the air was full of birdlike voices. Mawn stirred at the sudden noise, but no sooner had he opened his eyes than the sounds abruptly ceased. For a few more moments he tried to rouse himself, but when he heard no further sound, he let his head drop gently down again to rest on Sianan's breast. Then, feeling safe and secure, he closed his eyes once more and continued his peaceful slumber.

As Mawn lay dreaming, unaware that the Samhain celebrations had long since ended, his mind drifted off to a land where there was no hunger, no sickness, no pain and no death. In this country every kind of fruit grew. Herbs and vegetables sprouted from the roadside ready to be eaten. Nuts and berries fell in cone-shaped heaps waiting to be scooped up by passers-by. As his dream went on Mawn traversed a wide field and found himself wandering in an immense apple orchard where all the trees were overburdened with ripe red apples. So heavy were the branches that many were bent down to touch the ground.

As he strolled on Mawn was overcome by hunger and plucked one of the tempting fruit to eat. Immediately the tree from which the apple came gave a loud cry like an animal that has been injured. Mawn touched the bark of the apple tree and thanked it for the fruit; he apologised for hurting it and went on his way, munching on the sweet apple.

He had reached the core of the fruit and his stomach was full when the sky began to grow dark. Ominous black clouds blew in from every edge of the horizon to dance in a great double spiral above his head. Mawn stood with his neck craned back, staring upwards at the spectacle that was presented to him. The clouds changed shape constantly and were lit from within by a silver fire. At one time Mawn was sure that the swirling patterns took the form of two Ravens chasing each other around the spiral until they met in the centre; then he could have sworn that he saw two salmon dancing the same dance, leaping outwards from the middle as they would if they were returning to their spawning grounds.

Finally he discerned the shape of two people—a man and a woman—curled together as if they were twins within the womb. All around them the Salmon of Wisdom coursed and the Ravens wove in an intricate movement that echoed the dances that the folk of Dun Righ had indulged themselves in.

An old poem came into Mawn's head and he spoke it aloud.

'The world is sleeping,
All the fruit of the Earth
Lies buried in the black grave of winter,
Waiting.
The wind whispers a sad lament,
A cold unrelenting cry
That reaches into the depths of the damp soil,
Beckoning buds back to wakefulness.
But the circle will come to summer once again,
Bearing new life in its arms,
Strewing flowers over the greening face of the land,
Lighting a way through
The Maze of the Seasons.
The forest has put on its luscious coat of living
  green.
The King of Summer sits at the high table,
Listening to the sweet strumming of golden harp
  strings.
But the white winter will return
And the harp will hang untouched again
Among the barren branches,
Until the sun sails home.'

As he finished speaking the sky grew very dark
and the clouds lost their luminescence. Mawn
looked back and forth along the lines of trees to
see which one would offer the best shelter against
a storm. Finally he chose a low spreading tree, the
bough of which was bent like an elbow joint with
the weight of its own fruit.

As he crawled beneath the tree Mawn could see
the corpse of a woman laid out underneath it in
the white burial robes of a Druid. All around her
were spread the most colourful and sweetly
scented flowers that he could ever remember
encountering, and they were woven into her hair
so that it looked as if they grew from her body. The

tree hardly moved as the storm descended upon the apple orchard, for this bough was stronger than any gale. Beneath the enfolding branches all was as quiet as if Mawn had crept into a cave for shelter.

The presence of the dead woman intrigued him, though, and before long he found that he could not resist the temptation to take a closer look. As he leaned over her face and slowly lifted the white veil that concealed her features he thought he heard Sianan calling to him.

'Don't look on her!' she cried. 'Don't look at the woman!'

But Mawn's curiosity would not let him be. He hesitated for no more than a second before he took one corner of the veil and raised it high enough that he could make out whether he knew the dead Druid or not. What he saw took his breath away.

Before his eyes was the most beautiful woman he had ever seen. She had hair of dark brown curled in the most delicate of tresses all around her face. Her skin was milk white as if she were not dead at all but merely sleeping soundly. Her lips shone red and enticing, and Mawn began to believe that indeed this woman was only asleep.

With a trembling hand he placed a finger gently on her lips and, to his delight, the flesh was warm. The woman stirred a little and took a deep slumbering breath which poured out in a low-pitched sigh.

'Do not touch the woman!' Sianan was crying somewhere in the distance. 'You must leave her be!'

Mawn heard his friend's warning but was powerless to resist this woman, unable to ignore the radiance that permeated the air around her. He leaned forward and slowly placed his lips upon

those of this sleeping woman with as much anticipation as if he were about to taste the first of the
springtime honey.

The woman's mouth opened to his and her lips
moved gently against his own. Mawn could feel
the passion rise in him, but just as the feeling began
to engulf his senses the woman snapped her eyes
open and placed a hand on his cheek. With the
lightest of touches she pushed Mawn away from
her and stretched her body as she came to wakefulness.

Without taking her eyes off him she raised herself on one elbow and pulled some of the flowers
from her hair.

'Who are you that comes to disturb my slumber?'
she said in a voice that was both ancient and
joyously youthful, at once light-hearted and stern.

'I am known as Mawn,' he answered, marvelling
still at the light of beauty that shone about her.
'How are you called?'

'I am Flidais of the Eternal Hunt,' the woman
replied as if she were surprised that Mawn had not
recognised her. 'I am the Goddess of the Deer
people and my husband is Cerne the Stag God. But
Cerne travels long with the herd and leaves me
here alone to sleep. Now that you have woken me
you must be my consort in his place for a full cycle
of the seasons until the Samhain day next winter.'

'I am a Druid and a Wanderer,' Mawn protested.
'I cannot serve as your consort for my duties lead
me elsewhere.'

Flidais touched her hand against his forehead
and then ran her fingers down his face until they
brushed against his chin. 'You have woken me
from the sleep of winter and now you must keep
me entertained.'

'Run, Mawn!' Sianan cried frantically, but her

words barely reached his ears as Mawn began to succumb to the temptation of staying here in this place with this beautiful woman. 'She will demand your life in return for the pleasures that she offers,' Sianan called out. Mawn started a little when he heard those harsh words.

'But would you not willingly give all that you have for even one night with me?' Flidais asked. 'Am I not the most comely woman you have ever seen?'

Mawn nodded as the goddess placed a hand behind his head and drew him steadily nearer to her lips.

'Run, Mawn!' Sianan cried again, and her warning was followed by an ear-splitting crack of thunder and the unmistakable sound of rain falling in great gushes outside.

Mawn faltered for a moment and tried to push the woman away from him, but her hand was incredibly strong and she was unrelenting in her grip. A sudden panic took hold of Mawn, and with a mighty effort he knocked Flidais over onto her bed of flowers and then crawled as quickly as he could out into the open.

The sky and all the world had turned as black as the darkest charcoal. No star shone in the heavens and nor was there a pale silver moon to light the world. The apple trees all moved together in the wind and the rain pelted down mercilessly, but Mawn tried to make his way as quickly as he could back to the spot where he had entered this Faerie orchard.

Abruptly the rain ceased just as he thought he had glimpsed the last tree in the long line. The clouds cleared and moonlight filled the scene as if someone had lit a great torch in the sky. A few paces ahead of him a figure stepped out from behind one of the apple trees and raised a torch high in the air.

'You must stay here, Mawn,' the voice said teasingly, 'for it is Samhain and I have chosen you to be my lover.' It was Flidais. Somehow she had overtaken him and now blocked his only way out of the orchard.

'I must go now,' Mawn explained. 'I have work to do in the lands of the Gael and you should let me pass back there.'

'You are mine now, Druid,' Flidais answered. 'There is no returning to the land of mortals for you.' And the wind whipped around her, tugging at her clothes and hair as if it would tear them away from her.

'She is lying, Mawn,' Sianan called out. His friend's voice was nearer now and that spurred Mawn on to push past Flidais and make for the edge of the trees.

'You will have to return here one day,' Flidais screamed. 'I have chosen you. Your soul will not rest until you have paid your obligation to me.'

But Mawn did not turn around or slow his pace at all.

'I will curse you for eternity,' the woman cried, 'if you do not come back here this instant.'

Mawn did his best to ignore her and strode on until he reached the edge of the orchard. Beyond the trees he could see Dun Righ spread out before him as if he were standing on some high hill or walking in the clouds.

'Come back,' Flidais pleaded. 'I will give you any gift you desire.'

Mawn hesitated.

'You can live your life out here in peace with me forever,' she offered. 'I will give you the robes of green, ancient symbol of the highest of all Druids.

When you dress yourself in the robes you will instantly have the knowledge that goes along with them. Infinite knowledge, immeasurable wisdom, boundless understanding.'

After a nervous glance at Dun Righ, Mawn turned to face her again, but his expression did not reveal his thoughts.

'I will bestow on you a cloak of silver if you stay with me,' Flidais went on quickly before he had a chance to turn away from her again. 'The cloak that preserves youth forever. When you wear it you will be as you are now, for as long as your days may be, and no woman on Earth will be able to resist your beauty.'

Mawn looked at the ground, ashamed that he was even considering these suggestions. 'I have no need of such gifts,' he said finally.

'If you stay with me I will give you a shawl of gold,' she whispered. 'The golden shawl of plenty. Whatever you wish for will be supplied and in whatever quantity you desire. You and your kinfolk will never want for the finest food again nor the richest clothes nor anything that your heart craves.'

When Mawn placed his hand to his brow at this last offer, Flidais thought for certain that she had ensnared him and she stepped forward to take his hand.

'I cannot stay with you, lady,' he said as he looked into her entrancing eyes for the last time. 'I am sworn to another path. I am sworn to accompany my soul friend on her journey through the seasons that lead to our destiny.'

Flidais let all the tenderness drain from her expression. 'Then I will curse you,' she warned. 'You will never have peace as long as you live. You will never rest in one place more than a full cycle of the seasons. Your life will become an agony of never-ending journeying.'

'Condemn me as you will,' Mawn replied, 'for I am already sworn to another and I would not leave her side if you offered me the lordship of Eirinn for evermore.'

'Very well,' hissed Flidais. 'Since you will not take my gifts, therefore receive my wrath.'

She stepped closer to Mawn so that her face was only a hand span away from his, and then she closed her eyes, taking in a deep breath as she did so. When she let the air out again her eyes opened once more, and where they had earlier had a colour of deepest blue, they were now entirely black. There were no whites to them at all except for an elongated shape in the very middle like the pupils of a cat.

Then Mawn noticed with shock that her mouth was slowly opening to reveal sharp pointed teeth, the longest of which was razor sharp like a talon.

'You have disturbed my slumber and stirred my wrath,' she taunted. 'Since you will not serve me at my Samhain bed, you will suffer for your foolishness.'

High above his head Mawn heard a strange sound like that of a wild forest fire burning out of control. He raised his eyes to the sky and to his horror saw a long yellow-gold flash of light streak across the sky in a flaming arc.

'The dragon will come to devour you and all those closest to you,' she informed him. 'And the one you seek to share your life with will be separated from you for many turnings of the moon. You will not know for certain if she lives or dies, and when you meet again you will barely recognise her. I curse you to spend the rest of your lives seeking for one another in the wild places of the world.

Only once every seven winters may you meet and then for one night only until you agree to be my lover on Samhain night.'

Another fiery streak flew across the sky, roaring like an enormous dragon, splitting the night sky in two on its journey.

'The dragon comes now to sunder your kin forever,' Flidais spat. 'Too late to change your mind this Samhain. The dragons have already been summoned. I cannot send them back again to the realms of the Sidhe-Dubh.'

'Stop this!' Mawn screamed. 'I will do as you say.'

'Too late,' Flidais sang in mockery of him. 'You have brought the curse upon yourself and there is nothing to be done about it. In future you may think twice when a goddess of the Danaan folk offers her bed to you.'

Another flaming dragon passed over, screeching in fury as it flew, and Mawn watched, helpless to stop it flying on towards Dun Righ. In a last desperate effort to persuade Flidais to reconsider her punishment, he reached out to where she had been standing only moments before.

But the goddess was gone, melted into the night air as if she had never been. Mawn looked to the heavens again and yet another dragon was soaring overhead, leaving a trail of fire in its wake. Mawn looked hard at the creature as it passed directly above, and noticed immediately that the dragon seemed to have a body entirely composed of fire.

Blue flames issued forth from its form close to where Mawn imagined its head must be. An infernal orange tail followed after and this scattered sparks across the sky as numerous as the stars. He followed its journey until he could see that the creature was diving towards the ground and would land among the buildings of Dun Righ. Mawn tried to scream a warning to the people of the stronghold, but his throat would not open to let the sound out and his jaw clamped shut against his will.

A split second later Mawn saw the fiery beast crash into a house and there was a sickening crunch as it landed. The ground shook under him and the sparks flew in all directions.

Suddenly Mawn was no longer asleep. He opened his eyes to find himself lying on his back by the fallen tree bough in the cow field. With relief he realised that he and Sianan were still lying in the place where they had fallen asleep together.

'It was only a vision,' he said aloud, expressing his joy to anyone who would hear. 'Thank the gods!'

Then, with a shocking jolt, he realised that he and Sianan had slept too long in the field and were probably late for the Samhain ceremonies. He took his friend's hand and tried to stir her. 'Wake up, Sianan,' he urged. 'We must get back. I am afraid that we may have been locked out of the hall.'

Sianan stretched her legs and arms and slowly began to come back to wakefulness. Her mouth was dry and her back a little bruised from having lain on the uneven ground, so it was a few moments before she noticed that Mawn was staring into the sky and gasping loudly.

'What is it?' she asked, confused.

'Dragons,' Mawn replied. 'There are dragons flying through the air. Flidais, Goddess of the Hunt, sent them to punish me.'

Sianan could make no sense of Mawn's words at all. She sat up, trying to see what it was that had disturbed him. She caught a glimpse of something in the night sky directly above. To her horror it seemed that Mawn was right. An object that resembled every description she had ever heard of a fire-breathing dragon streaked across the night sky, leaving an immense orange track of fire in its wake.

The object passed over them and then began to descend towards the stronghold at an alarming rate as if the creature had decided to make a death dive at the hill fort. As it fell it made an awful sound that was something akin to the noise a stag makes in the rutting season to keep the other males away from his mate. It was at once frightening and fascinating.

Then, with a tremendous force, the dragon crashed to Earth and the ground shook once more under them as the creature seemed to explode in every direction. Nearby, Sianan could hear the cheers of many men, and at that instant she realised that this was no dragon. This was something that had been fashioned by the hand of man.

Sianan grabbed Mawn by the edge of his cloak and dragged him closer to her, directing his gaze down the hill to where the stream flowed past the defences. On the other side of the water there were many fires and countless dark forms moving around in front of the flames.

'What is it?' Mawn gasped. 'Is it the Faerie folk come to bring havoc to Dun Righ?'

'They are not Sidhe-Dubh,' Sianan answered. 'Even though it is Samhain and surely after midnight, I am certain that they are human.'

'Who are they then?'

As Mawn spoke a massive ball of flame rose up from where the small fires were burning and ascended swiftly into the air. It was exactly like the others that Mawn had seen earlier, but he no longer thought these fiery objects were dragons. Something on the ground had forced this missile into the air and these men were responsible.

'I do not know what it is that those men are doing,' Sianan admitted in alarm, 'but I have an awful feeling that Dun Righ is under attack.'

She had no sooner finished speaking when the latest ball of fire landed among the buildings of the stronghold and burst into a rain of countless sparks. It was then that Mawn and Sianan noticed the houses that had caught fire.

'We must go back to the hill fort and warn folk of what is happening,' Sianan decided quickly. 'We must help to put out the fire.'

'Fire . . .' Mawn echoed. 'Fire is one of the favourite weapons of the Saxons. I remember that they rained fire on Rathowen with their burning arrows.'

'Saxons!' Sianan cried. 'If it is an attack then we must make all speed to wake the warriors for there will be no sentries on the walls tonight. If the raiders realise that the ramparts are undefended, the hill fort will be quickly overrun.'

Mawn was on his feet in seconds. 'I'll go and raise the guards,' he exclaimed. 'You rush to Cathal's hall and rouse the Druids. We must run like the wind if we are to have any hope of averting a disaster.'

Another ball of flames shot into the air, but this one was aimed closer to the inner defences.

'They've started a few fires inside the fort to draw warriors away from the walls and now they are beginning to attack the ramparts,' Sianan realised. 'Go!' she yelled. 'We have not a moment to lose.'

Before she had even finished speaking Mawn was running up the steep embankment and skirting around to the right to the place where the watchmen were usually housed. Sianan began climbing the steep hill as fast as her legs could carry her towards the main part of the stronghold where all the houses were clustered together within the central defensive rampart.

When she reached the top of the steep embankment another missile landed down below her near the inner wall, and she found herself suddenly concerned for Mawn's safety. He had headed in that direction. But she forced herself to go on and not to pause to think. The chieftain's hall was not far away, but she had to weave a path between the many houses in order to reach it. In the main part of the settlement one house was already on fire, but only the inhabitants had come out of their building to try and put it out. Their neighbours had remained indoors. Sianan decided that they must be sleeping soundly, having consumed much strong drink, or be too frightened of venturing forth on Samhain Eve to lend a hand.

For a moment she considered stopping to help, but she soon realised that only if the Druids were awakened would there be any chance that all the other folk would come to the defences to keep the invaders at bay.

Cathal's hall seemed to be much further than she remembered. As she turned a corner Sianan came abruptly to a dead end. Where she had expected to see a fine chieftain's hall, there was only a field which led to the embankment.

'I have taken a wrong turn!' she berated herself, beginning to panic. 'I am wasting too much time.'

She could hear the strange noise of another fiery ball being launched into the air and she redoubled her efforts to find her way through the maze of houses that were clustered around the top of the

467

hill. She had almost given up any hope of finding the hall when she stumbled upon it.

The instant that she realised she had found what she was seeking she ran up to the door and threw herself against it with all her force. But the doors would not budge. They were bolted from the inside.

'Gobann!' she screamed. 'Gobann! Síla! Open the door! Let me in!'

There was no response from within. It was almost as if there was no-one at all inside the hall. For a second Sianan thought perhaps the Druids had decided to hold their vigil in some other house, but she carried on banging against the door in a frenzy.

'Gobann!' she called at the top of her voice, straining her throat in anguish and despair. 'The Saxons are upon us! They are attacking the stronghold. We must raise the warriors and bring them to the battlements.'

There was a loud sound of a timber brace sliding away behind the doors and then abruptly they swung inwards. But it was not Gobann who stood on the other side.

It was Mongan.

'You have been excluded from the rituals,' he announced without any attempt to disguise his pleasure. 'Go away and do not return until dawn.'

'The Saxons are at the ramparts and they are raining fire down upon Dun Righ,' Sianan shouted. 'We must bring the guards to the walls.'

'You will have to be much more inventive than that if you wish to trick me, young novice,' Mongan sneered. 'Now, leave us to our holy work.'

Sianan lurched forward and grabbed the old man by the front of his cloak. 'You fool!' she cried. 'Can you not see that we are all in grave danger?'

Mongan gasped, trying to catch his breath, and after a few seconds Sianan noticed that his eyes were bulging out of their sockets. Straightaway she released her grip on him, but the expression on his face did not change. He was looking past her into the sky.

Sianan turned around to see another ball of fire sailing gracefully through the air. 'The Saxons are coming!' she repeated and in the next moment Gobann stepped from within the hall and dragged her through the door.

'What is going on?' the poet demanded.

'Mawn and I fell asleep in the cow field,' Sianan confessed, blushing at the admission. 'When we awoke we saw these great flaming lights in the sky. There is an army of Saxons down at the ramparts making ready to storm the hill fort.'

'Sweet Jesus!' a voice proclaimed from within the hall and Declan stepped forward. 'Are you certain, sister?'

Sianan did not have the chance to answer before the ball of fire that Mongan had seen crashed to the ground with a tremendous noise.

'There are houses on fire and the walls are completely undefended,' Sianan pressed. 'If we do not hurry, the enemy will realise that there is no-one to resist them scaling the defences and overrunning the stronghold.'

The gravity of the situation struck Gobann immediately. There were already many folk running about with buckets of water to douse the flames. There were many others wandering around dazed and confused and looking to the sky in wonder.

The poet turned to Mongan. 'Go to Cathal's home and wake him from his sleep. Let us hope that he has not overindulged himself in fine Dal

Araidhan ale tonight or the hill fort may already be lost.'

Mongan nodded, still in shock, but did not move.

Gobann took the old man by the shoulders and shook him. 'Did you hear me? Go and wake your chieftain.'

Mongan pushed past the poet then and ran out into the night, making for Cathal's house. As soon as he had gone Gobann called Síla to him and Ia emerged at the door, staring up into the sky.

'Síla, you and Sianan must wake all the children, the elderly and as many of the womenfolk who are not warriors, and lead them out of the stronghold and away from the danger of spreading fire.'

Síla opened her mouth to protest, but the poet gently placed his hand on her lips. 'Go now for I do not have time to argue and we do not know how much more fire they are going to send down before their warriors attack. Down by the water will be the safest place to wait, but if you sense any danger, you must take to the forest. Malchedoc and the Glastig will make sure that you are in no danger.'

'I will not leave you,' Síla cried in anguish. 'Not now. I know what all this means. Your dream vision is coming to pass at last.'

'Shush, my friend,' the poet smiled sadly. 'You must do what you can for those who are destined to live after this night. Neither you nor I can prevent the changes that are about to engulf us all.'

Sianan looked first at the poet and then at Síla but could not make any sense of what they were saying. All of a sudden the Druid healer threw herself into Gobann's arms and, sobbing, kissed him. The embrace did not last more than a few short seconds, but Sianan realised that she had

470

never seen them both so publicly exhibit their affection for one another.

'Now go!' the poet insisted, his voice cracking with emotion. 'And may the holy goddess Bridey go with you.'

'And may the blessed Morrigú stand beside you at the last,' Síla answered, staring deep into Gobann's eyes. Then she grabbed Sianan's arm and they ran from the hall to wake as many people as they could on their way to the River Cree.

Gobann turned to the other Druids with tears welling in his eyes and ordered them also to go and wake as many warriors as possible, and all but Ia departed immediately to their task. As soon as they were gone the poet regained his composure.

'How can we help?' Declan pleaded. 'There must be something we can do.'

Gobann looked at the abbot and shook his head. 'This hill fort needs warriors and strong-backed folk to put out the fires. You, brother, are not up to that task. You would be better helping to get the innocent children to safety.'

'And what about me?' Seginus demanded in a stern voice. 'I was a warrior once.'

The poet looked the man directly in the eye. 'You should do as your heart bids, father,' Gobann replied. He had no time to worry about Seginus now. 'No-one will expect you to take any risks for the life of any Gael. Only you know what you are capable of.'

'Then I will go and do what my soul demands and my body allows,' Seginus declared, and before Declan could stop him, the priest had rushed out into the night air without another word to either of them.

The abbot, obviously distressed that Seginus had run off in such a way, muttered a quick prayer before following the priest's footsteps. Then he too set out to wake people from their beds and gather as many of the children together as he could.

Gobann went back outside with Ia following and closed the door to the hall behind him. It was then that he remembered Mawn.

'What has become of him?' he cried aloud. 'I should have asked Sianan.'

'I will find him,' Ia announced, 'and bring him into Síla's keeping.'

The poet realised that he would be too busy uniting the forces of Munster and Dun Righ this night to find his young student. He nodded to Ia and she hurried off. When the doors to Cathal's hall were shut and secure, Gobann raced off to see if Mongan had successfully roused Cathal from his bed and to find himself a war trumpet on which to blow the call to arms.

TWENTY-ONE

hen Mawn reached the watch-houses he found to his dismay that they were completely empty and the doors left wide open. All the warriors had gone to their own homes for the night, leaving the guardhouse deserted and the hearth fire extinguished.

It took Mawn a few moments to decide what to do next. The only course of action open to him, he soon realised, was to run with all speed back to the centre of the hill fort and hope that he would be able to find the houses where the warriors lived.

Without any further hesitation he set out, climbing back up the steep incline he had just bolted down, and though he was out of breath from running, he kept up a good pace. He had only travelled a hundred steps when there was a huge explosion. He turned around to look back at the watch-house where he had been standing only seconds before.

The entire building was engulfed in soaring flames and the walls had collapsed on two sides. Mawn understood immediately that a fireball must have been responsible for this devastation. With a simple sign of banishment he thanked his unseen protectors for sparing him. He did not want to think that it was only pure good fortune that had saved his life.

Then, to his horror, Mawn noticed the outline of

many warriors reflected in the glow of the burning guardhouse. They were still too far away for him to identify their dress and weapons and for a second he prayed that they were not Saxons but the Gaels of Dun Righ come to stand at their posts at the ramparts. The Dal Araidhans, however, would not have been charging headlong through the outer defences back towards the hill fort. These men were beyond doubt the enemy.

His heart pounding in his ears, Mawn turned around again and ran up the path to the stronghold as fast as his legs could carry him. The last time he had seen Saxons at such close quarters was at Rathowen. He recalled the way in which the savage foreigners had called out together in a terrible war cry that was half plaintive melody and half ferocious threat. Leoghaire's troops had almost faltered before that wild chorus. Only the sound of the pipers had spurred the Gaels on to victory that day.

As if his memories had suddenly sprung to life, a call not unlike that one Mawn had heard ten winters ago split the air all around the hill fort. Mawn stopped dead in his tracks, enthralled by the brutish call. He took cover behind a low wall that enclosed a little vegetable garden and peered through the darkness at the approaching warriors.

But the Saxons were no longer charging up the path towards the inner defences. For some reason they were forming into a huge square of men near the burning guardhouse. Their spears shone as if they had been fashioned of pure gold. Mawn knew that this was a trick of the firelight, but he was captivated by the sight nevertheless. Then he noticed that the warriors were edging forward one pace at a time in a strange shuffling motion.

As they did so they periodically thrust their spears points to the sky and every man let out a deep throaty hum that must have been a Saxon word but sounded to Mawn like 'Ah-Hun-Ah'. Another fireball sailed high into the sky and Mawn realised then why the enemy was holding back the warriors from assault. The Saxon plan was to set as many buildings on fire and cause as much havoc as possible before the troops rushed into the stronghold.

Mawn watched the fireball as it reached the zenith of its journey. The massive flaming ball hung in the air for just a second before it began its unstoppable descent. Mawn had a terrible premonition that he was about to die and that if he did not move straightaway he would be directly under the fiery missile when it landed. But though all his senses told him to run, to escape the certain death that was rushing down towards him, he could not move.

Mawn was frozen with fear.

Then, as if a ghost of the Battle of Rathowen had appeared to bolster the morale of all the Dal Araidhans, somewhere close to the top of the fort a piper struck up the skirling noise of his instrument. This was enough to stir Mawn from inaction. He got to his feet and, though he stumbled at first, managed to make for a ditch at the side of the track that wound around the stronghold. No sooner had he crouched low in the ditch than the fireball landed only twenty paces away from him.

The impact of the huge missile was so great that Mawn plainly saw pieces of debris hurled back up into the air as if they were made of feathers. The sound of the fireball hitting the ground was like a lightning strike. Mawn felt his ears ringing from the noise.

Then came something quite unexpected. The sky seemed full of tiny burning fragments which sailed earthward like rain, trailing tiny flames behind them in imitation of the larger fireball. As they began to land Mawn brushed them away from his hair and clothes, but smaller fires started on the ground all around him. Then he smelled a familiar odour.

Pitch.

Instantly he realised that burning pitch was the fuel that fired these missiles. When they landed they spread the resinous liquid over a large area, thus starting other blazes nearby. For that reason the warriors launching the fireballs did not have to be too accurate: if one of these devastating weapons simply landed near a house, it would very likely cause it to begin burning.

Mawn wasted no more time cowering in the ditch. He had to get to the warriors' houses as fast as possible if he did not want to be captured by the Saxons. He stood up to run back up the path but had not made his first step before he noticed a figure outlined against the flames of the burning house.

Mawn had the distinct impression that this person was suffering some kind of shock. He made his way over to where the man was standing staring at the flames. But it was not until he was quite close that Mawn realised the fellow was dressed in the long dark robes of the Christians. A chill flooded through his body.

It was Seginus Gallus.

'What are you doing here?' Mawn asked, ever suspecting the worst of this man.

Gallus turned to face the Druid and replied calmly, 'I came to help extinguish the flames and to tend to the injured.'

'You should go and find Declan and look after

him,' Mawn snapped, barely able to disguise his disbelief. 'These people do not want your help.'

Seginus looked hard at the young man, scanning his face for any clue as to why this Druid in particular should dislike him so much.

'This is the place for me,' the priest insisted. 'It is my vocation to aid the weak and to give my support to the needy. For those who are suffering of the body, I can only do so much; for those who are injured in their spirit, I can bring peace.'

Mawn could contain his feelings no longer. 'You were a murderer and a brigand!' Mawn yelled, his voice carrying above the sound of the roaring flames. 'You killed for sport and out of prejudice. You cut the sacred Quicken Tree down. You lied your way into the confidence of Patricius. I was only a boy when you brought war to Eirinn but I will never forget what horrors came to pass by your design.'

'I was following the orders of my bishop, the one called Palladius. He was my spiritual leader and I was sworn to him. I could not disobey a command and expect to live very long afterwards. If your teacher commanded you to aid him planning a war, would you hesitate?' As if in answer a chorus of battle cries rose to meet their ears.

'I would not do as he said,' Mawn answered heatedly, repelled by the thought and certain that Gobann would never ask such a thing of him. 'I am bound to him by spiritual ties, but they may be severed if I judge that he is acting without a regard for the community. But the poet and the high Druids could not reach their rank if there was ever any hint of such a possibility. They are chosen carefully.' Another missile soared towards the dun with a sound like distant thunder, cutting the night sky in half like a great flaming sword.

'Yet a man may change,' Seginus bellowed back. 'I was led by a corrupt man for many years, but I nevertheless believed in him. I was blinded by my love and respect for him and my own guilt at the death of my brother. Then I was haunted by that guilt in the form of a loathsome ghost which drove me to commit cowardly acts. But I have repented!' he emphasised. The fiery ball landed not far away with an earth-shaking crash and the priest was forced to wait a few moments before continuing. 'I have confessed. I have cleared my conscience and spoken with God. He alone can grant forgiveness. He alone can absolve the sins of mortals.'

At that a shower of sparks descended on the pair and they covered their hair as best they could so that it would not catch fire.

'And what of the countless folk who lost loved ones at Rathowen?' Mawn said in a voice almost inaudible above the noise of all the chaos around them. 'What of all those who were wounded in battle and whose lives have been changed forever? What of those for whom the loss of the Quicken Tree was greater than even the death of their kinfolk? How will you be absolved of the crimes against them? Do you think that those people will forgive you as easily as your God has?'

'I admit my crimes!' Seginus cried. 'And I will repay my debt to all those who were affected by my actions. I am charged with saving their immortal souls. Nothing that I have done on this Earth can compare to that duty. If I have been responsible for many deaths through my misguided actions, then I will save as many souls to the Kingdom of Heaven. That is my debt; that is my penance.'

The rushing din of yet another fireball caught their attention and both men looked up into the sky as it passed over them. The whole of the hill

478

fort was lit by this single man-made star. Mawn looked down toward the guardhouses and could still see the outlines of many warriors gathered around the outer ramparts.

In amongst all these troops a banner was being unfurled. It was made of a beautiful purple cloth which had a sheen that reflected all light so that it seemed to have all the colours of the rainbow woven into its fabric. As the standard fluttered in the breeze Mawn caught sight of the symbol that was central to its design. At first he thought that it must be some strange Saxon device that would be unintelligible to a Gael.

Then it came to him. It was a configuration of Greek letters that Gobann's friend Origen had once shown him.

'That is a Christian sign,' Mawn stated to Seginus. 'Since when have there been Christians among the Saxons?'

Seginus followed the Druid's line of sight and squinted to get a better view of the standard. 'That is one of the old symbols of the Church,' the priest confirmed. 'It is known as the Chi Rho.'

'So your people are behind this,' Mawn snapped, sure that somehow Seginus had betrayed the trust that had been placed in him and arranged for the stronghold to be stormed on Samhain Eve, the only night of the year when the watchmen would not be at their posts.

'I know nothing of this,' the priest protested. 'And I strongly advise that we make our way towards the warriors' marshalling point.'

Mawn turned to Seginus, grabbing the man by the shoulders in an uncharacteristic outpouring of emotion. 'I do not trust you, Seginus Gallus,' he spat. 'You have been responsible for too many deaths and too much sorrow.'

'I have begged forgiveness for my sins and paid the price for my foolishness,' Seginus spluttered, shocked at such behaviour from a Druid. 'I no longer carry the burden of that guilt.'

'But I still carry the burden of loss,' the Druid retorted. 'The burden of my brother's death at your hands.'

'Many died in that war who deserved to live,' Seginus said quickly in an attempt to placate Mawn. 'I myself lost my brother in the service of God.'

'Those who died in armour and with a sword in their hands expected death,' Mawn cried, stifling his tears as best he could. 'At Rathowen there were only two who died as captives and only one of those two was a warrior whose fate was bound up with his cause.'

'I do not know what you are talking about,' Seginus answered nervously. 'What two men are you referring to?'

'Each hung on a tree like the son of your God,' the Druid went on bitterly. 'One was a champion and the friend of Caitlin Ni Uaine. The other was my elder brother Beoga whom you murdered even though he had no part to play in that battle.'

At that very instant the sky lit up once again and Mawn could see clearly the face of the man who stood opposite him. Every feature was outlined in deep shadow and Seginus seemed to have abruptly aged ten winters. The priest's eyes opened wide as the memory of that day flooded back to him. Seginus could hardly remember the boy that had been crucified beside the warrior, but he recalled the man who had humiliated him and then challenged him in battle.

'They were warriors and it was a time of war,' the priest tried to defend himself, though he knew this would not satisfy Mawn. 'I have often wondered why you showed me such contempt,' he finally admitted. 'I did not know that it was my action that took your brother from you.'

As the latest fireball fell to the ground a great cheer rose up from the ranks of the Saxons who had gathered around the Christian banner, and both Mawn and Seginus turned their heads towards the ramparts again. The enemy was advancing at last in a rush of clattering arms and armour.

'We must get to safety,' Seginus insisted. 'We must run for our lives.'

Mawn had not said half the things he wanted to say to this man. There was still so much that he had to tell him about what life had been like without a real family, about what it was like to have held his brother's hand as he died of his wounds.

'We will go, priest,' Mawn agreed eventually, 'but you will not leave my sight, not for a moment, until I have a chance to hand you over to the commander of the guards. I still suspect you of having been involved in this attack in some underhand way.'

With that the two men spun around to make their way to where the Gaels were gathering to defend their hill fort. Seginus went ahead of the Druid, leading the way and never once turning to check whether he was still being followed.

TWENTY-TWO

obann found Cathal organising a response to the attack from outside the front door of his house. There was no sign of Murrough or Caitlin or any of the Munster folk in their retinue. The poet waited for a few moments before approaching the chieftain, not wishing to interrupt the many warriors who were reporting to him. But it was not long before he perceived that Cathal was so swamped with panicked people that he had no hope of sorting out this mess alone.

Gobann pushed through the crowd and took hold of the chieftain's sleeve. 'Cathal!' he cried. 'It is I, Gobann. We must bring some calm to this situation or the enemy will be upon us before we can decide what to do.'

Cathal looked up in dismay. This attack was the last thing he had expected on Samhain Eve. And he was obviously still a little drunk, though Gobann knew there was nothing as effective as the threat of battle in sobering a warrior's senses. At the chieftain's side there was a great war trumpet as long as a man and guarded by a warrior whose task was to blow upon it when Cathal gave him the word.

'Sound the call to arms!' Gobann screamed above the din of the crowd. 'Wake everyone within the hill fort and gather the warriors at the ramparts.'

Cathal looked at him in surprise as if the thought

hadn't crossed his mind that most people were probably still asleep.

'Do as he says,' the chieftain ordered the trumpeter, and the man stepped away from the gathered crowd to perform his duty.

The very moment that the first note rang out all those around Cathal ceased their noise and listened. The only sound was the high-pitched call of the trumpet as it cut through all the other din that had engulfed the fort. It was as if everyone who dwelled within Dun Righ had suddenly held their breath.

Before the call had ceased Cathal and Gobann were organising the commanders responsible for each section of the wall. Within a very short while they had all gone off to see to their tasks and Gobann was left with Cathal and a few of his closest advisors. Mongan, however, was not among them.

'Have Murrough's men and women been roused?' the poet inquired.

'I cannot be sure,' Cathal admitted.

'Then send someone to find out!' Gobann exclaimed, shocked that the chieftain had not done so already.

'I will not fight alongside that man,' Cathal declared. 'He is not fit to aid the noble folk of Dun Righ in this battle.'

Gobann could not believe his ears. 'You would sacrifice the lives of your people and the defence of your stronghold over some petty quarrel that should have been mended months ago?'

'It is more serious than that,' Cathal objected. 'He threatened me and insulted me this very evening and swayed my wife to leave me on Samhain Eve.'

'I do not know what you are talking about,' Gobann retorted, 'but I can plainly see that your stubbornness could cost you everything you have and hold dear. Your children are in danger, your homes are in flames and your cattle may end up no more than a Saxon feast unless you go to Murrough and beg his help.'

'We do not need the aid of the Munster folk,' the chieftain yelled. 'We have held this hill fort against attack before and we will hold it again. There is no army on Earth that can force its way past the inner ramparts.'

'But most of your warriors are busy putting out the fires,' Gobann said slowly, trying to keep his patience. 'Who was standing at the ramparts to stop the Saxons breaking through when these fire-balls first started falling?'

Cathal's face lost all its colour. Since he had been woken from his sleep he had been concerned only with controlling the blazes that had broken out all around the fort. It had not occurred to him that by now the enemy could have already overrun the walls and made it to the inner defences.

'The fireballs have ceased,' the poet said, raising his hand to stop the chieftain from saying anything further. 'That means the Saxons are about to storm the fort in earnest. Not even a Saxon war leader would be ruthless enough to let his own men die in such a fire storm. They have softened us up and now they are closing in for the kill.'

Cathal turned to the nearest warrior. 'Go to the ramparts and find out what the situation is there. Return to me here and report all that you see.'

The warrior sprinted off without even a word of acknowledgement, and the chieftain turned to Gobann. 'I fear that Murrough will take no notice of any plea for help from me. Earlier this evening I ordered him and his people to leave the fort,' he admitted. 'I told them they were no longer welcome.'

'What kind of a fool is it that makes an enemy of the man who holds his destiny in the balance?'

'You must go to him, poet,' Cathal spluttered. 'Murrough will listen to you. Go and convince him to help us.'

'I will do what I can,' Gobann sighed. 'You had best pray that I find him before the Saxons reach your house.' The poet turned around again and walked off down the path that led past the chieftain's hall towards the houses where Murrough and his folk had been lodged.

As he came to the hall where the Druids were to have held their ceremonies he stopped for a moment. He could not decide whether he should pick up his harp and carry her with him or leave the instrument inside the hall. The fireballs had ceased, he reasoned, so she would probably be safe here for the time being. With that decision made he went on down the path.

He had not gone twenty paces when he met Murrough and Caitlin and all their warriors headed back up towards the chieftain's hall.

'The Saxons are within the ramparts,' the king called out to the poet as they met. 'They will soon have all the lower slopes of the hill fort in their hands.'

'And then they will likely begin throwing more fireballs at us,' Gobann cursed loudly, 'until we are weakened enough so that we offer no resistance.'

'The Dal Araidhans are already fleeing,' Caitlin informed him with bitterness in her voice. 'Most of them are not even making an attempt to hold the enemy at the ramparts. The Saxons have broken through in many places.'

'There are many more of them in this army than

there were the last time they attacked Dun Righ,'
Murrough added. 'Many of the folk of Dun Righ
are of the belief that the Sidhe-Dubh have sided
with the foreigners to drive all the Dal Araidhans
out of this land.'

'Nonsense!' Gobann laughed, but it was a laugh
without any mirth in it. 'They are frightened. They
will wish they had not thought so in the morning.
The Saxons have well and truly surprised us all
and we must do something to rally the people of
the stronghold together again. Cathal is still half
drunk and struggling to make any decisions. I fear
that it may already be too late. The defence of this
place could cost us many more lives than we are
willing to sacrifice.'

'Then we must consider withdrawing,' Caitlin
remarked. 'The chieftain of this place has made it
clear that we are not involved in this fight. It would
be better to save as many folk as possible than
make a stand and lose the lives of all our people.'

'I would like to stay,' Murrough asserted. 'If only
to prove to that stubborn old bull that he needed
us after all. It would certainly cheer me to have
him admit that the hill fort would have been lost
without the warriors of Munster.'

'I think that the stronghold may already be lost,'
Gobann admitted. 'It would be best to do as Caitlin
suggests and withdraw. There is also the safety of
the Wanderers to be considered.'

'Of course, you are right and—' Murrough began
but did not get a chance to finish.

Somewhere behind his warriors a great commotion had started up. Then the unwelcome sound of
steel clashing against steel rang through the air.

'They are upon us!' Caitlin cried. 'Now we must
stand and fight for the moment, at least until they
have been driven back a little. Then we will make

our escape.' She drew her sword as she spoke these words and in seconds Murrough had his own blade in his hand.

Before anyone knew what had happened enemy warriors could be seen running up the path towards them. Without a word of command Murrough's warriors formed three tightly packed ranks to block the advance. This was a standard manoeuvre and all these warriors were well trained. The king stood beside his queen in the second rank, surrounded by their guards but still close enough to the fighting to lend a hand and give orders if need be.

Gobann stood behind the formation, wrapping his Raven feather cloak around him so that he would be harder to spot if any of the enemy broke through the defences. Some of the foreigners stopped fifty paces from the Munster lines and loosed arrows at the Gaels. A few passed over the ranks to land in the dirt beside Gobann, and it was then that the poet remembered that the Saxons held no respect for Druids.

If the foreigners managed to break through Murrough's formation, they would not pass by, as any Gael might do, without attacking him. He was unarmed and vulnerable; just the kind of target these savages preferred. The poet turned around then and moved back up towards Cathal's hall, thinking that he should rescue his harp before the Saxons got any closer.

Just as he made that decision the enemy ran into Murrough's men and a great shout went up as the two sides clashed. Gobann swung around to see how things were going and less than a breath later something struck him hard in the chest. For a moment the poet thought that he had been punched and he fell backwards onto the ground in shock. The blow winded him slightly and it was quite a while before he managed to sit up.

When he did he realised what had happened. A Saxon arrow had slammed into his body piercing his left breast close to the heart, but not close enough to kill him outright. This was his vision. This was the moment he had foretold all his life. This was the time of his own passing from the world. But the instinct for survival was still strong. Something told him that he could not give up just yet.

Surprised that he felt no pain at all, the poet grabbed at the shaft of the arrow to see if he could remove it. He had shifted it no more than the breadth of a finger when he felt the most excruciating agony and had to fall back down on his back to relieve the pain. Clearly, he reasoned, the sharp barbs had caught on some internal organ, and if he tried to move the deadly instrument, he could injure himself further.

Gobann knew that he still had to find Mawn and Sianan and see that they were safe. And even though he had said his farewell to Síla he did not, in his heart of hearts, want to leave her yet. Not for the first time he heard the words of his old teacher Lorgan Sorn.

'Nothing is preordained,' the venerable Druid had always said. 'The future-sight gives us only a glimpse of what might be, not what must be. All of us have the power to change the course of events in one way or another. But we must choose our paths wisely and not interfere in the lives of others, or we may entwine ourselves in their existence and forever after be tied to them.'

Deep down Gobann had always known that as a poet of the Silver Branch he would be able to choose the manner and circumstances of his next birth. And if he could do that, he decided, then surely it would not be such a great challenge to change the manner of his death.

'I don't care that I have been witnessing this hour in the dream state throughout my life,' he said aloud, struggling painfully to his feet. 'I have the power in me to alter the course of my life in any direction that I so desire. I am not ready to die.'

His blue undercloak was soaked with blood, so Gobann threw off the Raven cloak and then the blue Druid robe as well. Then he slowly draped the feather garment over his shoulders again. Dragging the blood-soaked Druid robes behind him, he made his way as quickly as he could towards Cathal's hall.

As he reached the doorway, however, he was overcome with a spasm of intense pain which gripped his left arm and shoulders. The agony was so powerful that Gobann slumped on the ground outside the hall, unable to walk another step. He spread his blue cloak out beside him and sat looking back at where Murrough and Caitlin were still holding off the enemy.

As another spasm of pain coursed through his body, the poet decided that it would be best if he laid back for a few minutes and rested to conserve energy. But he kept his eyes wide open, determined not to let himself slip into unconsciousness.

Sianan and Síla endeavoured to make their way through the settlement towards the cow field which led down to the stream, but there were enemy warriors everywhere. More than once they had to turn back in an attempt to find a new way between the houses. It was a long time, though, before they gave up and finally headed back to the top of the hill fort in the hope of meeting with Mawn and Gobann.

Fires had spread to most of the houses in the settlement. The dry thatched roofs of the buildings were always vulnerable to flames, but when the blazes were fuelled by pitch, there was no stopping the spread of sparks and fire. Sianan could see that most of the houses would be destroyed unless the inhabitants made a concerted effort to put out the fires. But the people of Dun Righ were mostly wandering around dazed and confused, unable to lift a finger to help their neighbours or themselves. As the two women reached the path that led to Cathal's hall they saw a row of houses that must have been hit by a fireball quite early in the attack. The flames were spent: there was no more fuel for them to consume. The walls were blackened shells of rammed earth.

'They will be able to rebuild easily enough,' Síla observed. 'Earthen walls become stronger when they are fired. The question is whether enough folk will survive to repair the stronghold.'

As if to reinforce that point, the charred timbers of one house collapsed in a swirling mass of ash, soot and choking smoke. Sianan turned away, unwilling to look on such destruction, and as she did so she saw the Saxons. Countless warriors were pressing together in the middle of the path two hundred paces away up the hill.

Síla quickly pulled Sianan behind one of the wrecked buildings so that if any more of the enemy came up the path the two Druids would not be seen.

'Cathal and Murrough must have them bottled

up at a place where the path narrows,' Síla surmised.

'How are we going to get around?' Sianan asked, seeing that their situation was becoming more desperate by the minute.

'There are Saxons behind us and in front of us,' Síla observed. 'We are caught in between the mortar and the pestle. We can do little else but hide ourselves and hope that the Saxons do not come across us before we have a chance to slip through their lines. With luck Cathal will be able to drive the foreigners back with such force that they do not notice us at all.'

'We should try to find Gobann and Mawn,' Sianan insisted.

'They will likely be behind the Dal Araidhan lines,' Síla answered. Then suddenly the Druid healer stopped short and closed her eyes tightly. Her right hand was suddenly flat against her chest and she was short of breath.

'What's the matter?' Sianan demanded anxiously.

'Gobann is calling to me,' Síla replied almost at the point of tears. 'He needs me at his side. I must go to him.'

Before Sianan had a chance to reason with her teacher, the older woman had run off up the hill directly towards the place where the Saxons and Gaels were desperately fighting for control of the pathway. Sianan sprinted off after her as fast as her legs could carry her, but Síla seemed full of a strange energy that was pushing her on at a great speed.

'Síla!' Sianan cried out urgently. 'Stop! We must find another way around. We must not let the enemy find us.'

But it was already too late.

As Síla reached a house that had so far miraculously escaped destruction two large men stepped out of the low doorway and one of them reached out to grab her. Síla was so focused on her goal that at first she did not realise someone had hold of her, but when she found that she could not move forward, she had to turn and find out the cause.

This man was no Saxon. He wore the clothes of a peasant farmer from the southern lands of the Cymru. The Druid woman recognised the dyed brown fabric and wide brown leather belt that held his trousers in place as typical of those folk, and so she addressed him in his own language as best she could.

'I must go there,' she stammered, trying to remember the words in the Cymru tongue. 'Friend in danger,' she went on, afraid that her limited command of the language was confusing the situation.

The man who held her said something to his companion and the other man laughed and grabbed Síla's other arm. Together they began to drag her back into the house they had just come out of. To begin with Síla did not understand what they were doing and thought that she had likely expressed herself badly and been misunderstood.

Once they were within the house the Druid healer heard the sound of a woman sobbing in the corner of the room and she thought perhaps the warriors wanted her to tend to someone who had been wounded.

'I must go and help Gobann,' she said in Gaelic, abandoning any attempt at using Cymru. 'He is calling to me to come to him.'

She had hardly finished speaking when one of the men grabbed at her cloak and tore it from her shoulders. A cold chill passed through Síla's body as it suddenly dawned on her that these men were not warriors of Dun Righ. These men were the enemy.

What happened next was so unexpected that Síla had no idea exactly what was going on. The door to the house swung violently open and Sianan lurched through to grab one of the warriors from behind. Taken by surprise, the stranger swore at her in Cymru but could not manage to shake her from him.

His comrade laughed as he easily held Síla by the hair with one hand. Somehow Sianan managed to drag the warrior she had hold of outside and the other man, still clutching at Síla's hair, followed after to watch what happened next.

Síla had no chance to resist and just let herself be pulled out after Sianan. No sooner had they got through the door, however, than the grip on her scalp was suddenly and unexpectedly released and she fell back clumsily against the wall of the house.

When she was able to focus on what was happening around her the first thing she heard was the clash of steel against steel. Her head was spinning from the sudden and unprovoked attack and so it took a few seconds for her to realise that a bitter fight was taking place nearby.

'Are you hurt?' a familiar male voice asked her urgently. 'Síla, are you badly injured?'

'No,' she replied without looking at the man who had addressed her. 'I am just a little shaken.'

'Then I will see to Sianan,' the man said. 'She has been wounded, though not badly.'

This statement woke Síla out of her trance as surely as if a bucket of cold water had been thrown over her head. She grabbed the man's arm and looked into his eyes, only then recognising him.

'Mawn!' she cried with relief. 'Thank the Goddess of the Waters that we found you.'

'The fight is not ended yet,' he declared. 'You must make ready to run. If any more enemy warriors come I don't think that Seginus will be able to hold them.'

'Seginus?' Síla repeated, then she focused her attention on the fight that was taking place before her.

The priest had somehow got hold of a sword. One of the warriors—the man Sianan had dragged outside—lay dead in a spreading pool of blood. The other warrior was parrying blow after blow as they were delivered by Seginus.

Mawn hurried over to Sianan and cradled her in his arms, mopping the blood from her face. She was bleeding from a cut on her forehead but Síla knew instinctively that the young Druid woman was otherwise unharmed.

'There is someone else inside the house,' Síla informed Mawn.

Making sure that Sianan was comfortable, Mawn hurried inside, only to return a few moments later with a woman of Sianan's age leaning against him for support. Síla was on her feet in seconds to take the load from him.

'We must get out of here,' Mawn cried, making sure Sianan was still conscious. 'It is too dangerous for us to stay within the stronghold.'

At that very moment Seginus landed a blow on the Cymru warrior that sent the man hurtling backwards against the wall. Síla quickly cast a critical eye over the man and decided that if he was not dead, then he was certainly dead to the world.

Mawn rose to thank Seginus, but the priest had already pushed his sword through his belt and was urging the Druids to get to their feet.

'We must get as far away from here as possible,'

the Roman asserted, 'or else we will surely be slaughtered. We will make for the stream.'

'We have tried that way,' Síla answered. 'It was blocked to us. There are too many enemy warriors about.'

'Then we must try again,' Seginus insisted. 'There is no other way.'

'If we find our way to Cathal's hall—' Síla began.

'Cathal's hall is beyond our reach!' the priest interrupted, his voice loud with urgency. 'There are two hundred or more enemy warriors between us and the chieftain's hall.'

'But I must go to Gobann!' Síla cried. 'He was summoning me. He needs my help.'

'You cannot go to him,' Seginus stated coldly. 'Not without the sacrifice of your own life and the lives of these folk here. They are depending on you to lead them out of this stronghold to safety.'

The Druid woman took a deep breath, fully aware that she was being confronted with a terrible dilemma that would likely affect the rest of her life. If she found her way to Gobann's side, she knew she could save his life and that they would spend many more seasons together. If she took that path, however, Mawn and Sianan might very well perish at the hands of the Saxons and take the hopes of the Druid Council with them to the grave.

Síla knew that she did not really have a choice. Gobann would never forgive her if she failed in her duty to the Wanderers. Their safety had been what he and so many other Druids had been working for through so many seasons.

Mawn's voice cut into her contemplations and distracted her. 'These men are not Saxons,' he declared. 'I never saw any but Cymru dressed in this fashion.'

'They spoke the Cymru language,' Síla confirmed. 'I thought they were warriors of the Strath-Clóta.'

Seginus approached the crumpled form of the warrior who was still propped against the wall of the house. He lifted the fellow's head and looked at his face. Then he pulled out a strip of leather which hung around the warrior's neck. At the end of the strap there was a cross roughly made of black iron. It was not the equal-armed cross of the Druid folk with a circle in its centre. This was a Roman cross, the kind that had a long lower arm; the kind worn only by monks of certain religious orders.

'He was no Saxon,' the Roman observed. 'He was a follower of Christ and I never heard of any Saxon on this island who took the Christian way.'

'Christians!' Síla exclaimed. 'In alliance with the foreigners! I can hardly believe that Cymru folk would fight on the side of the savages.'

'I have a strange feeling these men may have something to do with my old master,' Seginus said ominously.

'Palladius?' Mawn asked. 'Is that likely?'

'I would not be at all surprised at anything that vicious old man got up to,' the priest replied. 'But I cannot be sure of course.'

'We must go,' Síla declared, desperately quelling the anguish that threatened to overwhelm her. 'The poet is beyond our help now.'

'I will go to Gobann,' Mawn cut in. 'He is my teacher and I must see that he is safe.'

'You would not get a hundred paces,' Seginus laughed dryly. 'The Saxon warriors would cut you down because you are defenceless, and the Christians because of the Druid cloak you are dressed in.'

'Then come with me and watch over me,' Mawn

496

demanded. 'I saw the way you handled those two warriors. You can guard me while I make my way to Gobann.'

'There were only two of them!' Seginus gasped. 'And it was no easy task to defeat them. There are many more fighters up on that hill far superior to these two cowards. This pair were looters, rapists. They had no stomach for the fight. I would have not had a chance against them if they had been fanatics.'

'Nevertheless,' Mawn asserted, 'you owe me a debt for the life of my brother. When you have repaid that debt you will be truly absolved of your sins.'

'I do not owe you anything!' the priest spat. 'If you are fool enough to wander up through the ranks of savages, that is your business. But do not involve me.'

'Don't you want my forgiveness?' Mawn countered. 'Is it of no value to you? What will your God say to you when you meet him? After all the crimes you committed in his name, do you not think he will look more kindly on you if you take the responsibility for the absolution of at least one sin?'

'God has already absolved me,' Seginus answered desperately, though he was beginning to see that the Druid was very likely right.

'If you do this I will take on the Christian ways,' Mawn announced unexpectedly. This was the last gambit he had left to play. He knew that he needed Seginus' help if he was to have any hope at all of reaching Gobann. And he also knew that his fate was bound together with the Christian's in a way that was not yet clear. Mawn had known from the very first moment he had heard the name Seginus Gallus that one day they would have to settle their differences.

497

'Mawn, no!' Sianan burst out, though she had always sensed that it would come to this.

'I am not taking this on lightly,' Mawn explained gently. 'I know the implications of my decision. But I will only take the Cross if Seginus aids me in finding Gobann before it is too late.'

'You are trying to manipulate me,' the priest protested. 'How do I know that you will become a good Christian?'

'You only have my word as a Druid,' Mawn replied confidently. 'But try to think of it this way: by saving my soul you stand a chance of truly absolving yourself of your many crimes; in particular the crime that you perpetrated against my brother. In saving me you will save your own soul from eternal damnation.'

Seginus went pale with the realisation that this was something he would have to do. He was overwhelmed by the feeling that God was somehow behind all this. Yet still he hesitated.

'We are going,' Síla announced. 'I know that you have unfinished words to say to Gobann, Mawn. I spent last night speaking with him and so I have less to resolve with the poet than you may. Whether this Christian goes with you or not, take care and promise me that you will not place your life in undue danger. And if you should see the poet again, tell him my thoughts were with him at the last, though my body was elsewhere.' Síla blinked back the hot tears that threatened to betray her calm.

Then she helped the injured woman to her feet, readying to flee. Sianan grabbed Mawn and held him in her arms for a few moments. Neither spoke a word, though they both felt they should have said something.

'Come, Sianan,' Síla insisted. 'We must go. *Now*.'

Sianan pulled away quickly and followed obediently behind her teacher, leaving without a backwards glance. Seginus and Mawn, however, watched the women until they rounded a bend in the path and disappeared behind a row of burning houses.

'I will go with you,' the priest declared. 'But you must do as I say. If I decide that the situation is too dangerous, we will withdraw and save our own lives.'

Mawn looked at the Roman and smiled. 'Thank you,' he said softly. 'Thank you.'

TWENTY-THREE

urrough and Caitlin fought side by side in amongst the incredible crush of warriors who fought for control of the path to the top of the stronghold. The front ranks of their troops were mostly injured or killed soon after the first onslaught. So it was that before long, even though their warriors managed to hold their positions, both the King and Queen of Munster were standing in the thickest part of the fighting.

Murrough looked around and saw that there was nowhere for them to withdraw to. The only way out was to push forward and hope that the Saxons did not set fire to the buildings on either side of the Munster warriors. The king was not sure whether the enemy would find another way around this block and outflank the Gaels from behind.

Though they did not have the chance to talk to each other, Caitlin was of the same opinion. At first she had thought they would easily hold out against this attack, but as more and more of their warriors fell she began to realise that it was only a matter of time before they were swamped.

The Saxons seemed to be attacking in great numbers and the appearance of many Cymru under a Christian banner convinced the queen that the cause was lost. She thought it ironic that she was likely to lose her life fighting to defend a hill fort whose inhabitants really didn't care very much for her and her folk, nor they for them. If she and Murrough fell this day, their sacrifice would be forgotten, valueless.

Both sides had been fighting for a long while before a Cymru chieftain pushed his way to the front of the lines and persuaded his men to fall back a little to rest. He could see that not one footstep worth of ground had been won or lost on this path and he did not want to waste any more of his troops.

Caitlin had no opportunity to take advantage of the respite. Just as the Cymru warriors pulled back, two lines of Saxon archers formed down the road out of range of the Gaels' spear cast. Murrough looked at his wife with an expression of bitter disappointment.

'We cannot hold against them now,' he said, his voice full of defeat. 'Their arrows will cut through the leather shields of our warriors like forged iron through fresh butter.'

Caitlin mirrored his worried expression. 'We must fall back now,' she gasped, trying to catch her breath. 'We must try to escape with our lives.'

She had no sooner finished speaking than they both heard a trumpet blast behind them. Further up the road, past where the chieftain's hall was positioned, there was a mass of Dal Araidhan warriors. At the head of them stood Cathal and he was waving his arms to Murrough's warriors to fall back towards his lines.

'Let us go and make a stand with him,' Murrough declared, 'before these Saxons loose their arrows on us. Most of the Dal Araidhans have iron shields, so they will bear the brunt of the archers' fury without much damage to themselves.'

With that the king pushed his way back through

his warriors, bellowing out the command as he went. The Saxon archers were just about to let loose their first rain of deadly missiles when the Gaels moved. The man in charge of the Saxons called for the archers to slacken the tension on their bows and advance to a point where they could get a clear shot at the defenders.

Murrough's warriors moved as swiftly as they could considering that they had just been fighting a fierce hand-to-hand struggle with their enemies. The Saxon archers shadowed them all the way up the hill until they had almost reached Cathal's lines.

They had just come level with the chieftain's hall when Caitlin heard a mighty shout from behind her and then the sound of steel against steel. She turned around in time to see a hundred or more Dal Araidhan warriors leaping out from the side of the road behind the Saxons and Cymru where they had been lying in wait behind the houses. This manoeuvre effectively hemmed the enemy in on two sides. Caitlin called to Murrough as soon as she realised what had happened, but it was already too late for either of them to stop their warriors reaching Cathal's ranks.

The trumpeter blew a long low blast followed by a high-pitched note in the universal signal to advance at the charge. Cathal's men gave an enormous ear-splitting shout and then careered down the hill, pushing Murrough's warriors aside in their rush.

The Saxons and Cymru did not wait for Cathal's men to reach them. As soon as they saw what was happening they turned around to fight their way out of this situation and retreat. Such was their panic that they managed to break through the lines of Dal Araidhans who had ambushed them and scatter them to each side of the path as they fled in disorder.

When Murrough and Caitlin saw the enemy falling back they rallied their troops again and charged off down the hill to help Cathal chase the Saxons away. In their rush and in all the confusion of the battle no-one noticed Gobann lying in the mud near the chieftain's hall.

The poet woke after the commotion had passed, and sat up a little, leaning on his elbow. The intense heat in his chest told him that the wound was deep and would likely prove fatal after all. This was the way he had always known it would be.

And yet Gobann regretted having to leave just now. He even found himself struggling against his inevitable passing and telling himself there was still hope that he would live to see the dawn.

Although all around there were burning buildings, the chieftain's hall had not yet caught fire. Gobann dragged himself over to it and propped himself against the wall near the door. He spread his blue cloak over his legs and pushed his Raven-feather coat behind him to support his back. His plain undyed tunic was stained a dark red and his brown Dal Araidhan style trousers were torn where he had pulled himself along the ground.

He lay there for a long while imagining that he would soon be able to rise and go inside to find his harp which lay in her otter-skin bag on the far side of the hall. But even after the house opposite him had burned out and was reduced to nothing but smoking ash, the poet still did not have the strength to rise.

'I have not bequeathed her to anyone,' he said aloud, though he knew no-one was present. 'They will bury me with her then.'

A whispered voice carried on the wind and the poet instantly recognised it as Cathach, the old Druid who had helped set Mawn and Sianan's journey in progress.

'Do not fear,' the voice soothed gently, 'Mawn will take her. You must give her into his hands.'

Gobann raised his head to look about him. There was no-one nearby who could help him and he knew he did not have the strength to retrieve the harp himself. He resolved to hang onto life for as long as possible until someone who could fulfil his final instructions chanced along.

The poet closed his eyes and dropped his hands by his sides, knowing that if he did not relax completely he would burn the last of his life force and pass over all the more swiftly. He concentrated his breathing into steady slow deep draughts of air which passed in through his nose and out through his mouth. After several minutes of this he began to feel his heart slowing down and the sweat stopped forming on his brow.

The cool night air kept Gobann awake enough that he did not lose consciousness but instead started to drift into the dream state which the Druid kind termed 'the Aisling'.

The exposed flesh on the poet's arms, legs and face began to tingle as if someone were gliding a feather over his skin. His ears buzzed with the rhythmic pulsing of the blood coursing through his body. The pungent smell of freshly shed blood stung his nostrils, filling the air with a coppery tinge and making him aware of the salty dryness in his mouth.

He imagined that he was standing in the middle

of a tiny flat featureless island that lay in the very centre of a vast lake. The water all around this little island was teaming with otters, salmon and all kinds of fish. Gobann found himself wishing that he could sit here a while and cast a line into the water to catch himself some dinner. As he walked to the water's edge he noticed a long stick of hazelwood floating in the gently lapping lake. He bent down, picked it up and decided that it would be perfect for the purpose. After carefully stripping the bark and twisting it into a long thin twine, he went in search of some bait.

The poet knelt in the water for a long time before he found what he was looking for. A tiny fish, the like of which he had never seen before, jumped into his open hand and in seconds he had it on shore and was threading his line through its gills.

With his bait fish thrashing about, the poet cast the line into the water and almost immediately a fish took hold of his lure. With a nimble twist of the hazel branch he flicked his catch out of the water and up onto the grass that grew close to the water's edge.

Overjoyed at the ease with which he had caught this fish, Gobann dropped his makeshift fishing rod in the lake and made for the shore. There on the grass was a beautiful speckled salmon large enough to feed four men. The great fish did not leap about or squirm but seemed to have accepted its fate and lay staring at the poet with deep dark pool-like eyes.

The poet watched the fish for a while, marvelling at how the sunlight reflected against its scaly skin and showed all the colours of the rainbow. Then he suddenly decided to build a fire. All around the island there were scattered many pieces of dried-out driftwood. Gobann collected armfuls of the precious timber. Once he had stacked it ready to build into a tiny cooking blaze, he searched around in his robes for his fire-making tools.

Gobann produced a leather pouch from which he drew a long thick iron spike and a large piece of flint. Then he brought out a handful of flax threads and some scorched linen with which to start his blaze. He laid the linen on the ground and made a little nest around it out of the flax threads, making sure that he had small kindling timber nearby with which to feed the fire once the sparks had taken.

With a measured blow he struck the flint down hard against the iron spike. The angle at which he hit the iron ensured that any sparks would fall directly onto the scorched fabric, and this was precisely what happened. In moments the linen was glowing red as it began to catch fire. Gobann blew gently onto it and bunched the flax threads close to the smoking linen. Then suddenly and as if by magic a flame appeared. In less time than it takes to draw ten breaths the poet had a tiny fire started.

'Gobann of the Silver Branch,' a sweet feminine voice called enticingly from behind him. The poet spun around in time to see the salmon transforming into a beautiful woman dressed in a long silver-scaled shift that hugged close to her body accentuating her full hips, strong thighs and the curve of her breasts. Her hair was silvery like her clothing and her face was pale as wax.

'Who are you?' Gobann asked, forgetting the fire for the moment.

'I am the Spéirbhan,' she declared. 'I am the guide to the world of the Aisling and to the Otherworld and I have come to take you back to my country where you may rest a while.'

The poet stood up, ready to go with her, but suddenly remembered that he had not yet finished all the work he had to do on Earth.

'I must give my harp into Mawn's keeping,' he informed her. 'Before I go with you I must make sure that the instrument is safe. We have been companions for a long long time.'

The woman looked at him with a questioning stare. 'You have not much time, poet. I must go soon back to my own land and if you are not ready you may not come with me.'

'I must wait until Mawn comes,' Gobann insisted. 'I cannot bear the thought of my harp being left to the mercy of the Saxons.'

'Very well then, I will wait a short while with you,' the Spéirbhan conceded in a gentle voice. With that she went to the water's edge and, cupping her hands, lifted some of the fresh lake water up to the poet's mouth.

'Drink some of this,' she said softly. 'It will ease your passage into the Otherworld.'

Gobann bent his head down and sipped at the water. It was the most refreshing draught he had ever tasted. He closed his eyes to savour the experience and when he opened them again he was suddenly back at Dun Righ, leaning against the chieftain's hall.

In front of him another building was on fire and a strange man carrying a long sword and dressed in long black robes was watching him intensely.

'Master,' a familiar voice said, 'are you awake?'

Gobann struggled to lift his head.

'It is I, Mawn,' the voice went on gently. 'Take another sip of this water and then Seginus and I will try to move you to safety.'

'Seginus?' the poet exclaimed, confused. Then he realised that was who the man dressed in black must be, though Gobann found he was almost unrecognisable as the Roman who had brought so much havoc to Eirinn in earlier times. 'It is too late to move me,' Gobann stammered. 'Where is my harp? Go and fetch her from Cathal's hall.'

'I must tend to you, master,' Mawn soothed. 'The harp can wait.'

'No,' Gobann pressed. 'You will do as I say. Go now and fetch to me my harp.'

Mawn placed the bowl of water that he held in the poet's lap and rushed inside. Moments later he returned with the harp and laid her down in front of Gobann.

'Here she is,' Mawn said. 'Now we must move you to a safe place. There are Saxons all around— they have broken through our lines. It is only by a miracle that we found you without encountering any of them.'

'Her name is Banfa,' the poet whispered so that Seginus could not hear. 'Banfa of the Storms.'

'What are you saying, master?' Mawn cried in dismay. 'You must not tell me such things. The name of your harp is a secret between you and her.'

'A secret no longer,' Gobann sighed. 'She is yours now. You will bear her on your shoulder and you alone will play her from now on. She will teach you much about the world and she will learn much from you in return. Every day you must take the oil and rub it into her body. Afterwards with bees-wax until all the oil is sealed in the timbers. Then you may tune her and begin to play. Every day, mind you!' he coughed, and a droplet of blood formed at each of his nostrils.

'You cannot leave us yet,' Mawn protested. 'You have not finished teaching us.'

'You know already more than most Druids learn

in one lifetime,' Gobann whispered, his voice hoarse with pain. 'Now it is time for you and Sianan to begin collecting knowledge from the four corners of the world wherever Druids and wise folk gather together.'

The poet smiled at his student and coughed. 'Do not forget to rub wool fat into the bag at each fire festival, so that it remains waterproof.'

'How can you think of such things?' Mawn cried. 'You must not go on yet . . . Please, master . . .'

'The Spéirbhan is calling me now,' Gobann said softly, almost inaudibly, 'Tell Síla . . .'

Mawn waited for the poet to finish. Gobann's eyes were still wide open and he gripped Mawn's hand tightly. The poet struggled to go on speaking but an overwhelming feeling of exhaustion engulfed him and he had to concentrate on keeping his breathing steady again. He glanced beyond where Seginus was standing and glimpsed the unmistakable form of the Spéirbhan waiting patiently for him near one of the burning houses.

All of a sudden Gobann felt a surge of energy as if his wound had been miraculously healed. He rolled over onto his side and with very little effort he brought himself to his feet. Cautiously he checked himself from head to foot for any pain, running his hand over his chest as he marvelled at the disappearance of the arrow that had injured him. Try as he might, he could not explain how such a feat of healing could have come about. Jubilant, thinking that the Spéirbhan must have decided to give him another chance at life, Gobann turned to Mawn, sure that his student would be as surprised as he was at this remarkable recovery.

But when the poet looked at Mawn the young Druid was bent over a body on the ground. The poet could not see the face of the man his student

509

was tending, but he assumed that it must be a wounded warrior.

'It is time for us to go on,' the Spéirbhan whispered. 'We cannot tarry here any longer.'

Gobann looked at her in confusion. Had she not just healed him of his terrible chest wound? Was he not standing fit, strong and healthy where he had only moments before been lying in a pool of his own blood?

The poet reached out to touch Mawn, hoping to get his attention and ask him what he made of all of this. As Gobann's hand brushed the younger man's shoulder his body shivered strangely in a way he had never before experienced. Mawn looked up in his direction and the poet saw that his student's eyes were full of tears.

'Goodbye, great teacher,' Mawn said sorrowfully. 'We will all miss you terribly. Do not worry about your harp. I will take good care of her.'

'I am well, Mawn,' the poet protested. 'I am not going anywhere.'

But his student stood up and lifted the harp bag onto his shoulder. 'Perhaps I should play something for you before you leave us forever,' he mused, blinking back his tears.

'We do not have time,' Seginus barked. 'There are too many of the enemy about.'

'I am not leaving,' Gobann repeated. 'I am healed. Can you not see?' he added frantically.

'They cannot see or hear you any more,' the Spéirbhan sighed. 'You have passed over to the other side, Gobann of the Silver Branch.'

'No!' the poet screamed. 'Not yet. I am not ready.'

'It is too late for regret, poet,' she soothed. 'Your time has passed.'

'Perhaps it is better that his harp sing for him. I

will play something for him,' Mawn decided. 'He played so many other folk out of the world, it is only fitting that he be given the same consideration but I am not talented enough to send him on.'

'Are you mad?' Seginus shouted, grabbing the Druid by the arm and shaking him. 'We were lucky to get this far without being killed. If we wait around, the Saxons will surely find us.'

'Until he has heard the Sorrow Strain he cannot be certain that he is dead,' Mawn explained calmly.

'What are you talking about?' the priest exclaimed, 'The poet is dead. He has gone to meet his God in heaven. There is nothing that you can do for him now.'

'We believe that a soul is not aware of its passing from the Earth until the harp plays the Sorrow music for it. Until such time as someone does play for him, Gobann's soul could walk the Earth in confusion. It is my duty to him as his student to ensure that his spirit is freed to continue on its journey.'

In a few seconds Mawn had unwrapped the harp and was pulling the body of the instrument from its case. Before Seginus had a chance to protest further Mawn was tuning the instrument, making it ready to play one last time for the man who had carried it for so long. Then in an unexpected move the Wanderer lifted the harp high above his head. As if in reverence for the passing of the poet, the din of battle died for a second and the wind rose. As it did so the breeze hummed through the harpstrings and the magical instrument sang her own lilting lament for the man she too had loved.

The priest was half enchanted, half frightened by the beautiful sounds that came from the harp. He moved back a few paces and stared in wide-eyed awe at the scene before him.

Gobann was still arguing with the Spéirbhan

511

when he heard the first few notes of that sad song. It was not a tune that the poet had ever heard before, nor was it in a familiar style. The melody was high-pitched and delicate, and the bass notes were correspondingly low and sonorous. Gobann drew closer to his student. He could not understand at first why Mawn was holding the harp above his head or why he could hear the Sorrow Strain at a time of such great danger. He looked a little more closely at the figure slumped against the hall's doorway to see if he could identify the man. A cold shock hit him immediately.

The dead man had a cloak of Raven feathers draped around his shoulders and a blue Druid coat across his knees. He had the shaven forehead of a poet and features that he recognised instantly. Around the man's neck was a silver wheel cross, the same one that Gobann had been given by Lorgan Sorn when he had first agreed to take Mawn and Sianan as his students.

Gobann heard Mawn's gentle voice singing along with the humming harpstrings.

'Cease your weeping,' his young student began,
'you women of the soft wet eye.
All things grow in their time and then must die.
The Silver Branch is withered, dry and old.
Its shrivelled apples no longer shine like gold.
The seeds are there among the rotten flesh,
New life will spring and the bough will bloom afresh.
The Silver Branch will one day live again.
The seeds were scattered by the poet's hand.
Cease your weeping, women of the soft wet eye.
All things grow in their time and then must die.'

'That is *my* body!' Gobann gasped and he felt the Spéirbhan draw nearer to him. Her form was so close now that he could feel the warmth of her. 'I am dead after all,' the poet muttered to himself as he finally accepted the inevitable. 'I must leave.'

'We will go now,' the woman said softly. 'You have other work to do now and there are many folk waiting to speak with you.'

'Yes,' Gobann muttered, 'we must go.'

As he uttered those words the poet heard a tremendous flutter of wings as the Spéirbhan changed form into a beautiful snow-white dove. An instant later Gobann observed that he too was changing. He stretched out his spirit arms for the last time, and when he looked at them they were covered in black feathers.

'I am a Raven,' he declared, and his spirit smiled.

TWENTY-fOUR

urrough and Caitlin fought their way to the bottom of the hill before they realised that most of Cathal's men had been drawn out beyond the walls into the fields surrounding Dun Righ. This was a potentially disastrous situation because, for all they knew, the Saxons could have laid a very clever ambush for them, knowing that they could not resist such a chase.

The king and queen resolved to retreat to the inner defences and hold their positions for as long as possible while they waited to see what had become of Cathal's troops. They knew that there were likely to be Saxons roaming around within the defences, but they decided it was best to stay put and react to any such threats as they arose, rather than leave the ramparts unmanned for the enemy to overrun once more.

It was almost sunrise before the two of them understood that they had severely underestimated the situation, but by then it was too late. The first hint of trouble came when seven men dressed as Dal Araidhans appeared on the path that led to the stronghold. High on their shoulders they carried a long flat shield and laid out upon the shield was the body of a man covered with a chieftain's cloak.

Murrough knew instantly who it was that they carried and, despite the bitter rivalry that had existed between the two men, he felt sorry for the death of Cathal. The guards at the rampart allowed the bearers to pass and the warriors brought their burden straight up to the King of Munster so that he could identify the corpse.

As he stepped forward Murrough took hold of one corner of the cloak and pulled it back to reveal the corpse underneath. But what he saw confused him completely. Instead of Cathal lying face up and pale on the shield, these men were carrying the body of a fully-armed Saxon.

'What is the meaning of this?' the king demanded and less than a breath later he got an answer.

The man lying on the shield opened his eyes and grinned at the king, then lifted the single-bladed sword at his side and pressed it hard into Murrough's throat. The next thing the king knew he was falling back onto the ground, trying to cover the wound with his hands as shouts broke out all around. The clash of steel rang in Murrough's ears as he realised that these men were not Dal Araidhans at all but a small group of Saxons who had set out to assassinate him. Caitlin was at his side in seconds, pressing her hands over the wound to staunch the flow of blood, but she pushed down so hard that Murrough could hardly breathe, let alone speak.

'Lie back,' she ordered him. 'Lie still. You're going to be all right.'

Behind her the eight Saxons were slowly but surely defeated, though they fought bravely against the odds. Each of them was surrounded by at least six of Murrough's warriors, full of vengeance and hatred for this cowardly attack.

Caitlin saw her husband begin to lose consciousness and she knew that it was critical that they get

him to a healer as quickly as possible. Try as she
might she had not been able to stop the gushing
of the precious blood from his body and now
Murrough's eyes were beginning to glaze over. The
queen was certain that he would slip away soon if
they did not do something.

'Four of you take that shield and put the king
upon it,' she commanded. 'We must get him to the
houses of healing before it is too late.'

The warriors did as they were ordered and in
moments they were carrying their lord up the pathway towards the Druid healer's dwellings. All the
way Caitlin held her hands hard over the gash in
Murrough's throat, hoping against hope that this
rough ride did not injure him even further.

As they dodged between the burning buildings
the queen began to lose her resolve. Her body was
incredibly weary and her head throbbed. She had
not slept at all since the night before last. Murrough
tried to speak to her several times on the way to
the houses but she covered his mouth, urging him
to save his strength for the fight ahead. He would
need every measure of energy that he could muster
to survive this ordeal.

The stretcher party soon came to the little crossroads which led to the section of the hill fort which
the Druids and healers inhabited. All the buildings
in this part of the stronghold seemed to have
escaped the fires of the night before, though a thick
pall of smoke lay close to the ground and swirled
about their feet as they rushed towards their goal.

With relief Caitlin and her men rounded the last
bend. Beyond this lay the building set aside as a
hospice for the sick and elderly and used in time
of war to house the wounded. When they turned
the corner, however, every heart sank.

Of all the buildings and houses in this area only

one had been struck by fire and destroyed. The very building they had hoped to reach. The houses of healing. Spread out on the ground all around and spilling out of the nearby houses were hundreds of injured and dying. Warriors, women, children and old folk were laid out in the open, waiting for help.

Caitlin scanned the group of people tending to the injured and to her relief she spotted Mongan the Druid wandering among the many, administering what help he could. With a sharp word to one of her warriors to place the king down gently and take over her position staunching the blood, Caitlin rushed over to where the old Druid was closing the eyes of a recently departed comrade.

'You must come quickly!' the queen shouted. 'It is Murrough, he has been struck by a sword blow to the throat and I cannot stop him bleeding.'

Mongan looked up from his task and sighed, more weary than he could tell. Slowly he got to his feet and made his way over to where the warriors had laid their king. Caitlin grabbed the old man's arm to hurry him along, but Mongan squirmed out of her grip.

'I have been here all night working to save lives and I will probably be here for some days to come. Kindly let me move at my own pace or I may not be able to help at all.'

'Please hurry,' Caitlin begged, close to tears. 'It has been a long while since he was wounded and I am afraid for his life.'

Mongan reached the king's side and pressed his hand into the wound. Then he slowly and methodically brushed the hair away from the man's eyes and looked closely at the pupils. A second later he held a hand over the king's nose and mouth so he could discern whether there was any breath.

'There is nothing I can do for him,' the old man finally said with resignation. 'I must return to my own people.'

'What do you mean there is nothing you can do for him?' Caitlin screamed. 'I will not let you walk away from my husband just because of a petty feud between him and your chieftain. You have a duty to help him.'

Mongan took her hand tenderly. 'He is dying, lady,' the old Druid said in an uncharacteristically gentle tone. 'You were too slow in getting him here. I am sorry. Now please excuse me.'

Caitlin snatched her hand out of Mongan's grasp. Anger welled up in her as it had done many seasons ago when she had discovered her lover Fintan had died at the hands of Dichu's men. This time she did not wail her grief for all to hear. This time she lashed out with her fists.

Before her guards could hold her back Caitlin had launched herself at the old Druid and begun beating him mercilessly around the head and shoulders, raining blow after blow upon him as if somehow he had been responsible for Murrough's injuries. Mongan did not flinch. He merely held his arms up to protect his face and waited until the queen had finished her outpouring of grief.

Caitlin battered him again and again, so tired that her fists missed their mark or fell on the old man's chest or shoulders. The next thing she knew her warriors were dragging her away from the Druid and she was calling at them abusively to let her beat him some more. The old man watched dispassionately as the warriors sat their queen down beside their king.

Murrough's eyes opened then and he gasped for some water. One of the warriors stepped forward with a leather-covered bottle and placed it at the

518

king's lips, but Caitlin snatched it away from the man and he stepped respectfully back.

'Drink slowly, my love,' the queen whispered tenderly. 'All will be well. We are in the houses of healing now.'

Murrough closed his eyes and shook his head slowly for he could hardly speak. The Saxon blow had injured his throat so badly that speech was now almost beyond him.

'You cannot pass away from me now. Do not leave me. Who will dance with me at Samhain?' Caitlin added, trying to smile and lift his spirits.

The king raised himself up a little on his elbows and Caitlin flung her arms around him sobbing. Murrough pressed his lips to her cheek and then he said something in a low whisper. The queen held his shoulders and watched his lips move, trying to discern what it was that he was attempting to say. Her husband's gaze was fixed on the doorway to the house and he repeated the word again. This time Caitlin caught what it was that he was trying to communicate.

'I have not seen Gobann for many hours,' she said. 'Not since last night.'

'Gobann,' Murrough gasped again and then he closed his eyes and Caitlin lowered him down onto his back again. She glanced behind her at the doorway unsure whether the poet might have slipped into the room without her noticing, but she could not see him among all the folk who were crowded around.

When finally she turned her attention back to Murrough, she knew instantly that he was gone and she fell on his chest to weep bitterly.

While the queen was sobbing, one of the senior men sent a runner down to fetch the rest of the troops and then set about trying to convince Caitlin that they would be well advised to find some safer place to camp than in Dun Righ. The queen was inconsolable, however, and sat hugging Murrough's cold form and crying uncontrollably, oblivious to all those around her.

After a long while one of the warriors touched her shoulder and Caitlin shuddered, drawn back into the world of living beings by the warmth of the gesture. She brushed her husband's eyes with her fingertips and thought on all they had been through together in the seasons since they had first met.

'I found you on the battlefield of Rathowen,' she said. 'I fell in love with you among the ruins of the Quicken Tree. It is fitting that we say farewell among the strife of yet another bloody war. You were my strength and my guide. I will always dance with you and no other.'

Finally, choking back the tears, she managed to speak a few words of a Druid blessing which she had heard Gobann utter after the death of his friend Origen. 'May the ever-turning circle of the wheel of life grant that our paths cross again. Go now and await the day when I may join you.' With that she pulled Murrough's cloak over his face and stood up.

Mongan brought her some tea made from the herb they called birthwort which was used as a relaxant and to abate unbearable pain in women who were birthing their first child. It was also used to calm a distressed person, often sending the patient to sleep soon after it was drunk.

The queen relaxed almost as soon as she had

tasted the tea, and she sat down again beside the body of her husband. This was how Tatheus found her when he arrived with two of his surviving soldiers. The Roman sized up the situation quickly, not letting his emotions interfere with his military training for a moment. It was clear to him that there was nothing to be gained for any of them by remaining in Dun Righ. They had a better chance if they attempted to make their way north to the friendly Cymru settlement of Dun Breteann.

The most senior veterans of Caitlin's force agreed and decided that since their queen was unable to give orders, they would take it upon themselves to get her and her husband's body out of the stronghold.

Just before the sun rose the whole of the Munster contingent had made their way around to the northern side of the stronghold where there was a ford over the stream. With their dead king and sleeping queen carried on makeshift stretchers, the warriors from Eirinn slipped into the countryside unobserved by the Saxon scouts, and from there they started their journey to Dun Breteann.

Síla and Sianan stumbled through the burning chaos of the hill fort and out into the cow pasture near where Brother Kilian had been buried. The injured woman who had been with them had begged to be left behind so she could search for members of her family. Síla and Sianan had been unwilling to leave her but could not ignore her desperate entreaties.

Hurrying through the cow pasture, the two Druid women almost fell over the slumped figure

521

of Malchedoc's young companion, Fergus. Huddled in fear, he was shaking uncontrollably and muttering unintelligible phrases to himself. The healer wrapped him in her cloak and carried him down to the stream to bathe his face with water.

When they reached the water's edge Fergus sat on the bank and Sianan splashed a little water on his face to wake him out of his dream state.

'He has seen something which has greatly disturbed him,' Sianan said.

'That is war,' Síla answered, keeping a sharp lookout for any foreigners who might chance upon them. 'I have known battle-hardened warriors who were maddened by the bloody result of such fights. He will recover once we get him to the Glastig's forest.'

The healer searched up and down the stream for a good place to cross, but it seemed that wherever they chose to ford it the water would likely be very deep. There was no question of searching until they found a suitable place, she decided. They must move on immediately if they were to have any chance of escape. Then abruptly Síla turned to look back up the hillside and saw a figure walking serenely down the slope towards them.

Her first instinct was to find a place to hide, but then she thought she recognised something familiar. As the man drew closer she was sure it was the poet. 'Gobann,' she called. 'Is that you?'

The man stopped in his tracks and another form appeared standing close by. It was a warrior dressed in a long flowing cloak and Síla could just make out the colour of his hair in the half light. It was coppery red.

'Murrough,' the healer shouted, 'Is Caitlin with you?'

Neither man moved a muscle but kept their distance and Síla began to feel confused.

'Gobann is dead,' Fergus muttered. 'I saw him lying in the mud and he was cold to the touch.'

Síla shot a glance at the boy and then looked back in the direction of Murrough and Gobann. The poet raised an arm and pointed down towards the stream where there were many small bushes clustered on the bank.

'Gobann!' she called again, unwilling to believe that he was dead. 'Come with us. We will go together to the Glastig's cave.'

The poet shook his head and, taking Murrough by the hand, turned to walk back up the hill. The two figures strolled away as if they were out in the fields for their leisure. Síla coughed to cover the emotions that threatened to burst forth from her. She knew now that the poet had come to show her the best place to ford the stream.

The healer banished all thoughts of her own grief and grabbed Sianan by the arm. She in turn dragged Fergus to his feet.

'We must hurry,' Síla whispered. 'Down there the waters are shallow enough so that we may cross.' She pointed to the bushes Gobann had shown her. 'We must be strong for a little while longer,' Síla told Fergus. 'By morning we will be safe again in the forest where no Saxon will dare come after us.'

Together the three fugitives made their way down to the stream and silently slipped into the water. It was deep enough to soak them through but the current was slow at that point and they made their way across easily, holding hands with one another.

Síla did not notice the cold. She did not even mind that all her clothes were soaked through or that her leather boots were probably ruined beyond repair. In fact she was glad to be able to splash the icy water on her face for it disguised the tears that poured forth from her like the waterfall at the Glastig's pool.

Mawn packed the harp back into its case as soon as he had finished singing for Gobann's spirit. With infinite care, his heart weary with sorrow, he arranged the cloak of Raven feathers around the poet's body so that it covered the corpse completely. As an afterthought Mawn took the silver wheel cross from around his teacher's neck and tied the emblem to the leather straps of the otter-skin harp bag so that he would always have something to remind him of his teacher.

Seginus had run down to some of the nearby houses to check for signs of the enemy. He left soon after Mawn had begun to play, unable to bear the intense emotions that the music brought out in him.

As Mawn finished securing the wheel cross to the harp bag he heard the sound of a fight moving up the hill in his direction. He stood up, shouldered the otter-skin bag and walked down the path a little way to see if he could discern what was going on.

The next thing that Mawn knew, Seginus Gallus was running back up the hill in his direction, a gaping wound in his left shoulder and a deep slash across his neck, both of which were bleeding profusely. This caught the young Druid completely unawares. He had expected that they might encounter a few Saxons, but he had not expected Seginus and himself to meet such a large force.

As the priest reached Mawn's side he let out a scream that frightened the Druid almost as much as the prospect of what might be about to befall them.

'Get yourself hidden!' Seginus cried. 'It is Palladius and his Cymru warriors. He has come to take revenge on the Gaels for all that was done to him.'

'Palladius?' Mawn repeated, unwilling to believe that it was possible.

'Don't just stand there,' the priest insisted. 'Run and hide.'

'I must help you,' the Druid replied and put an arm under the priest to help him make for cover.

'You'll be butchered!' Seginus cried frantically. 'You must leave me.'

'I cannot,' Mawn stated. 'I am a Druid. It would be contrary to all that I have ever been taught to abandon someone in need.'

Mawn manhandled the reluctant Seginus into the nearest house and set him down on the floor to rest. Then the Druid examined the priest's wounds. The cut across the Roman's neck was not serious, though it was deep, for the blood had begun to congeal and would soon stop flowing. The other wound, however, had paralysed the priest's arm from the shoulder down.

Mawn observed with alarm that the fingers of the Roman's left hand did not even twitch when he stuck one of his harper's fingernails into the flesh. Seginus knew that he had lost all feeling in the limb and had already correctly surmised that he might lose his arm to this injury unless it was treated with the utmost care.

'Leave me here,' Seginus advised. 'I will be able to hold them off for a short while and you can get away while Palladius gloats over my capture.'

'You were his favourite,' Mawn said in surprise. 'Why would he be pleased that you have been wounded in this fight?'

'Because I failed in my mission,' the Roman explained. 'Palladius sent me to Ravenna to present the Pope with an entreaty. But I only got as far as the bishop's palace at Nantes before I struck trouble. In the end I returned with Patricius the new Bishop of Eirinn to the court of Teamhair. Doubtless Palladius will have heard how I worked for his successor. I would be very surprised if he treated me leniently.'

'You were following orders,' Mawn remarked. 'And your conscience.'

'My conscience,' Seginus repeated with a wry laugh directed at himself. 'I had no such luxury. I was driven by a desire for vengeance and an ambition to a bishopric of my own. Patricius taught me that my first teacher Palladius was a corrupt and heretic clergyman. I lost all enthusiasm for the cause of either man when I saw that I was simply a piece in their grand games. Neither of them cared if I fell or stood. Neither of them spared a thought for me.'

'Come,' the Druid said, 'we must move or we'll be found here.'

'You go,' the priest demanded again. 'I will stay here.'

Mawn went to the door of the house and peered out, careful not to let himself be seen. Fifty paces away there was a strange procession winding its way through the smoke of the many fires and surrounded on all sides by Cymru warriors dressed in sturdy leather armour.

At the front came two young men dressed in long black robes and each carrying a thick candle. Behind them was another black-robed man carrying a golden box set with many precious stones. The object glittered in the reflected light of the blazing houses, but Mawn had no idea what purpose it could possibly serve. Another man came directly behind, bearing a large piece of folded red cloth over both his outstretched arms.

Then came two more men dressed again in the same black garments as the others, and Mawn recognised one of them immediately. He recalled the first time he had seen this fellow after the Battle of Rathowen. When the High-King of Eirinn had judged him, Palladius had seemed old to Mawn, but now he was ancient. His hair was more white than grey, his skin deeply wrinkled and his eyes deeper sunk than they had been.

But the most obvious difference was that Palladius now walked very very slowly indeed, and his steady pace caused a tiny goat bell that hung around his neck to ring in time with his stride. Mawn had been told the story of how, when Palladius had been set adrift in a tiny boat beyond the ninth wave, one of the High-King's guards had tied a bell about his neck as an affront to the man's honour. This gesture of mockery had reputedly affected the former bishop so deeply that Palladius ever after wore the bell as if it were some kind of holy relic that was imbued with the sacred essence of his God. He was said to have walked throughout the Cymru lands ringing the bell to announce his arrival and telling the tale of his banishment as if it were a hero legend. In time he won many converts to the Cross, through sheer persistence if nothing else.

'It is him,' Mawn whispered. 'Palladius is marching in procession through the stronghold. The defenders must have capitulated to the enemy.'

Seginus opened his eyes widely as he made a

decision on what to do next. For a moment his expression reminded Mawn of the ecstatic trance that the seer Druids fell into just before they embarked on their spirit journeys. Then, before Mawn could do anything to stop him, the priest was on his feet, pressing his sword into the Druid's chest.

'Don't make a move,' the Roman hissed, 'or as God is my witness I'll run this blade through your body and pierce your very heart.'

Mawn was stunned and dismayed. After all that had happened this terrible day, it seemed that Seginus had not changed after all; he had merely done what he knew best: adapted to the situation of his imprisonment and played it out until the role was no longer of any value to him.

'Leoghaire should have had you strangled,' Mawn replied bitterly, 'when the chieftains of Eirinn demanded your life be forfeit for your crimes.'

'Shut up,' Seginus whispered hoarsely, 'or I will surely take your life.' Then the priest peered out into the darkness to see if he could catch a glimpse of what Mawn had described to him.

'You are a treacherous one, Seginus Gallus,' Mawn went on. 'The Gaelic lands have never known one like you. But I am a man of my word. I have promised to convert to the Cross. So if you kill me as you did my elder brother, then by your own customs you will have sent a willing follower of Christ to his death without hope of salvation.'

'Silence!' the Roman repeated. 'I am sorry for your brother,' he went on more gently. 'Truly I am. And I am about to try to make some recompense to you for that awful deed. If you are captured, you will fall under the influence of that old man. It is far better that you seek out Declan and disciple

528

yourself to him. He and I hated the sight of each other for most of our lives, but at the last I saw that his compassion and mercy were far more valuable than the rhetoric of Palladius or even Patricius. Those two have more on their minds than the simple conversion of the Gaels to the Christian faith. They have been sent to pursue political goals set by the College of Cardinals in Rome and Ravenna. Declan may have strayed a little from the path, but his ways are closer to the true message of our Saviour than any I have heard stated in the most beautiful church in Gaul.'

'It is too late to change my brother's fate,' Mawn interrupted. 'He is long dead. What is the use of pretending that you can ever change what happened by some act of penance?'

'It is a holy thing that I am about to do,' Seginus sighed. 'And I do not expect you to understand it, but I want you to witness it and tell the tale of what you see to Declan. Ask him to pray for my soul.'

'I do not understand,' the Druid protested.

'I ask only one thing of you,' the priest continued, ignoring Mawn's question. 'I would like you to absolve me of the murder of your brother. I want you to say the words that will free my spirit from bondage for that crime.'

'How?' Mawn spluttered, utterly confused.

'All you need say is, "Thou art absolved, brother,"' Seginus explained. 'That is all I need you to do. And then I want you to do your best to escape this stronghold with your life.'

The priest did not wait for a reply. He pushed the Druid back against the wall with the point of his sword as he peeped out through the door again. Then in a flash he was out of the door and running directly towards Palladius. Mawn was powerless to stop the foolhardy attack; he could only watch dumbstruck as the Roman lunged headlong at his former master.

Seginus swung the sword around his head as best he could considering the injuries he had suffered, but he never got close enough to the bishop to even scratch him with the blade. Long before Seginus had reached his target he was set upon by the Cymru warriors who guarded Palladius. Mawn saw the priest fall to a frightening barrage of blows from both spears and swords.

When the dust of the fight had cleared and there was a break in the smoke, Mawn looked out again and saw Seginus' crumpled body lying in the centre of a large group of men. He could not make out if Palladius was among them, but he could clearly see that the priest Seginus Gallus was cut to pieces at the orders of the man he had once treated with great respect. The man who had been his teacher and spiritual leader.

Palladius.

That was all that the Druid saw, however. Just then a thick band of smoke wafted over the scene, obscuring the Cymru warriors from view. Mawn realised that if he was going to have any chance of escape he would have to move right away. So, lifting Banfa of the Storms onto his shoulder, he squatted at the doorway in readiness to dash around to the rear of the house.

Before he moved off, Mawn closed his eyes tightly and brought to memory the form of his brother, Beoga, lying on his deathbed after he had been rescued by Leoghaire's men. Somehow it seemed fitting to recall that instance now. Then, with all the concentration that he might have brought to bear at any Samhain or Beltinne ritual,

Mawn spoke the words that Seginus had instructed him to say.

'Thou art absolved, brother,' he whispered. Then, without waiting another second, he rushed through the smoke and out to the rear of the house. From there he made his way to the fields and, after dodging many enemy warriors, crossed the stream just after midday.

A week of walking over high hills in the light snowfalls brought him to the gates of Dun Breteann, hungry, soaked through and exhausted. Here, at this northern Cymru hill fort, Mawn the Wanderer was welcomed as a Druid and a poet and given a place of honour at the chieftain's table as was his right.

epilogue

here was a Road. A Road that led from the end of the valley in which I was born and out into the wide world beyond. This Road has been my constant companion since all the events that shaped my early years. She has led me to places where war rages, or famine denudes. Her path is not easy to follow but she still brings me many new friends. The Road has taken many dear ones away from me too. At first I mourned their passing, as Malchedoc, my great-grandfather, said I would. But I no longer mourn.

The Road also brought many new folk to Eirinn. Even old Cathach and Lorgan Sorn would have marvelled at the changes which have taken place and they had some foreknowledge of events to come. I often wish for their wise counsel and dream of the day when I will see them again.

Most of all I miss my teacher, Gobann, Son of Caillte, Poet of the Silver Branch, who first told me the stories of the ancient days and taught me how to play upon the harp. And when I touch the harpstrings, Banfa of the Storms sings airs that conjure him so clearly in my mind that it is as if he never left my side.

That terrible Samhain night when he departed was only the first of many filled with war and death. The stronghold of Dun Righ was not completely destroyed by the combined force of Saxons and Christian Cymru, but there were few houses that were not touched by the assault. Cathal, the chieftain of the dun, pursued a group of Saxons beyond the ramparts after they had been driven from the summit of the hill. Neither Cathal nor any of the warriors with him were ever seen again.

Less than a week after the disastrous Battle of Dun Righ, Caitlin Ni Uaine sailed from Dun Breteann in the wild winter seas, bound for Eirinn with her husband's body. Few boatmen dared cross the ocean after Samhain and the queen had a hard task convincing any sailors to take the risk. After several days of hard weather, they landed in their homeland near Cushendall, one of King Leoghaire's strongholds. Messages were sent from there to the High-King, and as soon as Leoghaire received word of Caitlin's arrival he sent an escort to bring her in to Teamhair. I arrived in Dun Breteann only two days after her departure and so I missed her.

I have been told that all the citadel of Teamhair mourned the loss of Murrough and a great feast was prepared in his honour. With Caitlin's permission, Patricius Sucatus said a special mass for the soul of the King of Munster, in which he praised Murrough's bravery and good judgment. The bishop had obviously learned that there were certain things that the Gaels liked to hear and he would rather he or his priests were doing the talking than the Druids alone. The balance of power was already shifting into the hands of the new holy order.

King Murrough of Munster was interred within the hill of Teamhair and, as was the custom, his successor was chosen by the southern chieftains as soon as the last sod of earth was placed upon his grave. Caitlin was, as a matter of course, nominated for the position of queen; but Oileel Molt, a distant cousin of Murrough's and the last survivor of the female line of the king's great-grandmother, was elected with a small majority. Oileel had been reigning in Murrough's absence and it made much sense to let the queen grieve while someone else administered the kingdom.

Caitlin went to stay with her children in the convent founded by one of Patricius' followers down on the coast at Cill Dhaire. Tullia of Armorica had gathered a small group of Gaelic women around her and they had a small holding a couple of days' journey from Teamhair. Leoghaire's wife Mona was a regular visitor and patron of the community and that is how Caitlin's children came to be there for they had been left in Mona's care.

Tullia and Caitlin quickly became friends. The Armorican was hungry for all that the former queen knew about herbs and remedies, and in time Caitlin began to regard the community as her home. She rarely ever left that place again.

The poet's body was never recovered from the wreck of the stronghold and, according to tales I have heard, the High-King still held out hope that somehow his friend had survived. It was a vain hope. Some of those who bravely remained behind after the Saxon victory said that all the Gaelic bodies were gathered up and buried under a high cairn of stones.

This cairn was afterwards named Cnoc Glas, meaning the cold desolate hill. None of the kin of anyone buried there was able to farewell their clanspeople in the proper manner because Palladius forbade such heathen practices. So it was said of those who lay there that they had a lonely burial in a deserted place without a tune to cheer them on. A death of this kind was feared by all

Gaelic folk and so the Christians managed to be cruel to their enemies even after they had slaughtered them.

Declan arrived at Dun Breteann after walking the mountain roads with his nuns and monks, living on wild mushrooms, cress and spring water. The abbot took me under his wing soon after he arrived and together we waited at Dun Breteann for three months until the weather improved enough that the voyage south to Armorica would not be hazardous. There the abbot hoped to gather enough willing hands to help him rebuild the chapel and monastery of Saint Ninian's. He also hoped that the northern Cymru who dwelled in Dun Breteann would have by that time had a chance to recapture Saint Ninian's from their southern cousins.

As I promised my strange companion Seginus, I was anointed as a Christian monk when we landed in Armorica. Declan, however, allowed me to retain the tonsure of a Druid. The abbot was wise enough to realise that among the Gaels and Cymru this pattern of shaving the hair commanded great respect, whereas the Christian fashion of shaving the crown of the head was treated with suspicion and derision. The abbot also encouraged me to play the harp during the mass for the music reminded him of happier days.

Síla, Sianan, Fergus, Ia and a few Gaelic women made it safely to the shelter of the woods where the Glastig kept them fed, clothed and concealed from the enemy through the long winter months. When the snow began to melt, Sianan and Síla went to Dun Breteann seeking me, but we missed each other in the same way that I had missed Caitlin. The Danaan woman, Flidais, had warned me this would happen when she laid her curse upon me. Many times my path came close to crossing Sianan's, but I did not meet my beloved friend again until many years later when I had settled my score with Flidais. The years we spent so far apart wearied my heart beyond telling.

Disappointed that they had not found me, Síla and Sianan passed into the high country to take refuge with Síla's people, the Cruitne tribes of the Gorm Tuiscart. Síla's clan still lived in the isolated far north of Alba in among the mountains and valleys that had prevented the Romans from conquering that land. Sianan had only ever met a few of the Cruitne folk and so she went willingly with her teacher to learn from these tribespeople the Romans referred to as the Picti, or the painted people.

Ia remained with Malchedoc and the Glastig and never ventured again beyond the confines of that forest. In time, folk who lived at Dun Righ came to know her as one of the three Danaans who dwelt within the woods. There were those who said she herself married one of the Faerie race and so opted to live out a long life with her Danaan lover, but I cannot say whether that tale is true. Only one thing was certain about her fate: Ia disappeared forever from the sight and knowledge of all folk beyond the woods.

Aldor never took part in the actual assault on Dun Righ; Tyrbrand contrived to keep him in the rearguard. Instead the eorl waited at the outer ramparts with his personal guards around him in case of an enemy counterattack. After the battle Aldor was merciful to those who surrendered to his warriors.

Most of the Dal Araidhans were allowed to return to their homes and carry on with their lives. The eorl's men had strict orders not to take anything that wasn't absolutely necessary to their survival and not to indulge in any further burning of buildings. Palladius, on the other hand, was not impressed by this generous treatment of the Gaels, arguing that they needed a harsh lesson if they were ever going to accept their new overlords. Aldor knew that he would more likely win the support, and perhaps even loyalty, of the Dal Araidhans if he could restrain his warriors from senseless acts of violence.

Aldor's rule was absolute under the terms of his agreement with Palladius, but the old bishop was not happy with the eorl's merciful methods of dealing with the enemy. I have heard tell, though, that Palladius did not have long to wait before that problem was solved for him.

Folk say that just thirty days after the Battle of Dun Righ, Aldor caught a chill while walking the ramparts of his new stronghold. A week later he was dead from a chest infection. Tyrbrand was immediately elected to the position of war leader over all the Saxons and Angles. Palladius anointed him with the title Eorl of Strath-Clóta. At the same ceremony Tyrbrand accepted the Christian faith, thus ensuring the continued support of Palladius and his Cymru warriors from the south.

Their alliance was firm until Palladius became enraged at the way Tyrbrand had organised the rationing of food—giving the best meats to his own warriors and allowing the Cymru to be fed the poorer cuts. It was during an argument regarding this matter one day that the old bishop had a seizure and suddenly dropped dead as if some invisible warrior had struck him silently through the heart with a sword point. Perhaps that is what truly happened.

Tyrbrand took the manner of the old man's death as a sure sign of displeasure from Seaxneat. The new eorl immediately dropped the Christian ways and erected an altar to the Saxon God of War in the chapel that the Christians had used for their worship. The Cymru lost interest in the campaign when the spring came and returned to their homes to plant the next harvest. This left Tyrbrand as overlord of the south of Strath-Clóta in his own right and without troublesome allies to interfere in his future conquests. He ruled for many years unchallenged.

So there is the whole tale and you must forgive me if I have forgotten any part of it, for it is long in the telling. And as the years continue to unfold, my spirit becomes more weary. Memories of the days gone by become steadily less and less reliable.

But whenever I hear the wind wailing down a chimney on the darkest night of winter, or sit by the fire warming my ice-cold limbs, I catch a glimpse of those days long ago when my people, the Feni, lived in the Valley of the Black Otter. Whenever I remember the storytellers and their harps, I call to mind the man who first spoke to me of the Road. I remember our first meeting and our long friendship and the gift he gave me at my initiation. The gift of a name.

I am called Mawn.

NOTES ON PRONUCIATION

Words of Irish Origin

Aenghus Og	ang-us-oge
Airer Gael	arer-gayl
Aisling	ash-ing
Aoife	eff-a
Ardmór	ard-more
Ardrígh	ard-ree
Banba	banva
Beltinne	bell-cheena
Brandubh	bran-doov
Breac	broc
Breas	brash
Brehon	bre-on
Caitlin	kaytlin/kotchlin
Cailleach	kal-yuk
Cathach	kat-ack
Cathal	kat-al
Cerne	kern-ee
Cill Dhaire	kil-derry
Conaire	kon-a-ree
Connachta	kon-oh-ta
Cruitne	krit-nee
Cú Ainé	koo-on-yee
Curragh	koo-rah
Dal Araidhe	dal ree-ah-dah
Desi	dee-siy
Dichu	dee-koo
Dobharcú	doe-bar-koo

Drúi	drew-ee
Dun Righ	dun-ree
Eirinn	air-in
Eoghanacht	yo-an-aakt
Emain Macha	ev-an-ma-ha
Enda Censelach	enda ken-shel-ak
Ethne	un-ya
Eriu	er-roo-oo
Euan	yoo-an
Faidh	fay
Feni	fee-ni
Fianna	fee-an-ah
Fidach	fee-dak
Filidh	feel-ee
Finacre	fin-ak-ah
Fionn	fin
Flidais	flid-aysh
Fodhla	fo-lah
Géarchúiseach	gar-koo-eesh-ak
Géarintinneach	gar-in-chin-ak
Geas	geesh
Glastig	glas-tik
Gobahn	go-bahn
Gorm Tuiscart	gor-um toosh-cart
Ia	ee-ah
Laigin	lah-een
Leoghaire	leer-ree
Lugh	loo-ee
Macha	ma-ha
Magh Tuiread	moy-chu-ra
Malchedoc	mal-ke-dok
Midhna	mee-na
Míl	meel
Morrigán	mor-ri-gan
Morrigú	mor-ri-goo
Muinn	moon
Murrough	morr-uh

Niall	nee-al
Niamh	nee-av
Nuada	noo-ah-dah
Oilleel Molt	ill-eel malt
Oisin	isheen
Ogham	oh-um
Rathowen	raath-oh-wen
Samhain	sah-oon
Scathach	skah-ah/shka-tak
Scian-Dubh	skee-an-doov
Sianan	shee-an-an
Sidhe	shee
Sidhe-Dubh	shee-doov
Síla	shee-la
Spéirbhan	spay-ra-ban
Strath-Clóta	sa-rath-clo-dah
Teamhair	tar-ah
Teighe	teeg/tee
Tir-Nan-Og	cheer-nan-oge
Tuatha-De-Danaan	too-ah-ha-day-dahn-nan
Turnan	choor-nan
Torc	tork
Uisge Beatha	oo-is-kay-ba-ha
Uisnech	ish-nuk
Ulaid	oo-lay

Words of Non-irish Origin

Aelfwine	ulf-wine
Aldor Eikenskald	aldor-ikens-kalt
Centi	kent-ee
Chi Rho	kee-ro
Cumri	koom-ri
Cymru	kim-roo
Eboracum	ebb-or-ahh-coom
Egfrith	ek-frit
Eotenburg	et-en-boorg

Eothain	yo-tin
Isernus	is-er-noos
Origen	oh-ri-gen
Palladius	pall-ahh-dee-oos
Patricius Sucatus	pat-rish-oos soo-kaat-oos
Pretani	bret-ah-nee
Ravenna	rah-ven-ah
Scaramsax	ska-rahm-sax
Seax	sax
Seaxneat	sax-nat
Secondinus	sec-on-deen-oos
Seginus Gallus	seg-een-oos gal-oos
Taleis	tal-eesh
Tatheus Nonus	tat-ay-oos non-oos
Thegn	thayn
Tullia	tool-ee-ah
Tyr	tee-ar
Tyrbrand	tee-ar-brant
Wealhall	val-hal

aiseal mór and the band aisling have worked closely together to compose a collection of music which complements both *the circle and the cross* and *the song of the earth*. the band has blended the haunting melodies that are so much a part of traditional irish music with the exotic tones of indian instruments and the pulse of african rhythms. the result is two compact discs which add a unique dimension to both novels.

the soundtrack for *the circle and the cross* is distributed by polygram australia under the catalogue number ais 2.

the compact discs of music from both *the song of the earth* and *the circle and the cross* are available on the earthworks label (email: ceg@s054.aone.net.au).

Caiseal Mór

The Circle and the Cross
Book One of The Wanderers

A rich historical drama that blends fact and fiction in a sumptuous feast of storytelling.

Imagine that you sit warming yourself by a fire in a tiny settlement lying deep in snow. Sweet peat smoke scents the chill breeze and an old song-maker raises a keening cry for summer's long absence. Here amongst folk who call themselves the Feni was a young lad born and there passed his first years on Earth.

Raised as the son of a blacksmith, Mawn, this very lad, knows little of the world outside his sleepy village.

But Eirinn, his island home, is in turmoil. Black-robed monks have made their way across the tempestuous sea from Rome and have set the people at war with one another.

The High-King and his Druid Council know that they cannot survive the furious might of the Roman Empire so they must find other ways to save their ancient magical traditions from the evils that threaten to engulf them.

For this great task the Council has named a young boy who amongst the Feni was born and there passed his first years on Earth . . .

ISBN 0-671-03728-5

£6.99

Caiseal Mór

The Song of the Earth
Book Two of The Wanderers

'*An immensely satisfying fusion between early Celtic history and fantasy*'

Dr Colleen McCullough

Nine seasons have passed since the Druid Council of Eirinn banished the sadistic Christian, Palladius, from its island shores.

But now an even greater force has arrrived from Rome in the shape of Patricius, a powerful and fearless bishop who is determined to corrupt the ancient traditions of the Druids to his own ends. Aiding him in his task is a monk whose very name inspires fear and hatred in all Eirinn.

It is nine seasons, too, since Mawn and Sianan began their Druid training. Now they face their greatest test: a journey to the Otherworld. Only if they survive can they partake of the Quicken potion brewed by the Faery kind, which will make them Wanderers, keepers of the ancient magical ways.

But as they undergo their testing a fierce confrontation is taking place between Patricius and the High-King of Eirinn. Neither leader wishes for bloodshed but there is one amongst them who is determined to destroy any hope of peace, intent only on violent and bloody revenge.

ISBN 0-671-03729-3

£6.99

EARTHLIGHT

A SELECTED LIST OF FANTASY TITLES
AVAILABLE FROM EARTHLIGHT

THE PRICES SHOWN BELOW WERE CORRECT AT THE TIME OF
GOING TO PRESS. HOWEVER EARTHLIGHT RESERVE THE
RIGHT TO SHOW NEW RETAIL PRICES ON COVERS WHICH MAY
DIFFER FROM THOSE PREVIOUSLY ADVERTISED IN THE TEXT
OR ELSEWHERE.

☐	0 671 03728 5	The Circle and The Cross	*Caiseal Mór*	£6.99
☐	0 671 03729 3	The Song of the Earth	*Caiseal Mór*	£6.99
☐	0 671 02261 X	The Sum Of All Men	*David Farland*	£6.99
☐	0 743 40827 6	Brotherhood of the Wolf	*David Farland*	£6.99
☐	0 671 01787 X	The Lament of Abalone	*Jane Welch*	£5.99
☐	0 671 03391 3	The Bard of Castaguard	*Jane Welch*	£5.99
☐	0 671 01785 3	The Royal Changeling	*John Whitbourn*	£5.99
☐	0 671 03300 X	Downs-Lord Dawn	*John Whitbourn*	£5.99
☐	0 671 02193 1	Sailing to Sarantium	*Guy Gavriel Kay*	£6.99
☐	0 671 02191 5	Beyond the Pale	*Mark Anthony*	£6.99
☐	0 671 02884 7	The Keep of Fire	*Mark Anthony*	£6.99
☐	0 671 02192 3	The Last Dragonlord	*Joanne Bertin*	£6.99
☐	0 671 02939 8	Dragon and Phoenix	*Joanne Bertin*	£6.99
☐	0 671 02208 3	The High House	*James Stoddard*	£5.99
☐	0 671 03749 8	The False House	*James Stoddard*	£5.99
☐	0 671 03303 4	Green Rider	*Kristen Britain*	£6.99
☐	0 671 02190 7	The Amber Citadel	*Freda Warrington*	£5.99
☐	0 671 02282 2	Into The Darkness	*Harry Turtledove*	£6.99

All Earthlight titles are available by post from:

Book Service By Post, P.O. Box 29, Douglas, Isle of Man IM99 1BQ

Credit cards accepted. Please telephone 01624 836000,
fax 01624 670923, Internet http://www.bookpost.co.uk or
e-mail: bookshop@enterprise.net for details.

Free postage and packing in the UK. Overseas customers allow
£1 per book (paperbacks) and £3 per book (hardbacks).